PRAISE FOR
EDGAR & SHAMUS GO GOLDEN

"*Edgar & Shamus Go Golden* is a twenty-four-carat collection of stories by the best in the business, proving that we are in a new Golden Age ourselves, and lucky to be here."

—SJ Rozan, Edgar winner and best-selling author of *Family Business*

"The Golden Age of Mystery will continue for as long as writers produce stories that challenge us to find solutions alongside the detectives. These stories in *Edgar & Shamus Go Golden*—some of the best of the best—offer definitive proof."

—Stephen D. Rogers, Derringer Award-winning author of *Shot to Death*

"*Edgar & Shamus Go Golden* is a must-read. Editors Gay Toltl Kinman and Andrew McAleer assembled a collection of stories that fit together like the songs on a Beatles album, with one story setting up the next. Each piece captures the Golden Age glow the editors promised. I highly recommend it."

—Tom MacDonald, Shamus Award-nominated author of the Dermot Sparhawk P.I. series

LITERARY APPLAUSE FOR
EDGAR & SHAMUS GO GOLDEN AUTHORS

"Martin Edwards is a thoroughly deserved winner of this prized award [Diamond Dagger]. He has contributed so much to the genre, not only through the impressive canon of his own wonderfully written novels, but through his tireless work for crime writing in the UK."

—Peter James

"[Lia Matera's] Willa Jansson is one of the most articulate and surely the wittiest of women sleuths at large in the genre."

—*New York Times Book Review*

"Twice an Edgar Allan Poe Award winner, and the record holder in the *Ellery Queen Mystery Magazine* Readers Award competition, Doug Allyn is one of the best short story writers of his generation—and probably of all time. He is also a novelist with a number of critically-acclaimed books in print."

—*Ellery Queen Mystery Magazine*

"John McAleer's *Coign of Vantage* should please mystery lovers on several levels. This is also a book for lovers of sophisticated dialogue, fanciers of libraries and bookish matters, and those who appreciate their tales laced with romance, satire, and wit."

—*Alfred Hitchcock Mystery Magazine*

"With a gutsy heroine, sharp humor, and strong sense of place, Lori Armstrong has created a winning series (*No Mercy*). The female veteran perspective is particularly fresh...Highly recommended."

—*Library Journal* (starred review)

"Brendan DuBois is a fine novelist and easily, the best short-story writer of his generation."

—Lee Child

"Parrish is my kind of writer—intent on delivering character and plot you just don't see coming. And Kincaid is the detective I would want on the case if it was someone I knew on the slab."

—Michael Connelly

"In 'Molly's Plan,' John M. Floyd maps out a nearly impossible bank robbery with a twist ending that's so ingenious it's tempting to root for the bad guys."

—*Kirkus Reviews*

"[Kristen Lepionka's *The Last Place You Look*] is a remarkably accomplished debut mystery, with sensitive character development and a heart-stopping dénouement."

—*Booklist* (starred review)

"[Art Taylor is] one of the finest short-story writers to come to prominence in the twenty-first century."

—Jon L. Breen, *Ellery Queen Mystery Magazine*

"John McAleer has done more than justice to recording the several stages of Rex Stout's life. He portrays a life every bit as engrossing as a Nero Wolfe mystery."

—*The Washington Post*

"I admire O'Neil De Noux's work tremendously. No one writes New Orleans as well as he does. No one else gets the mix just right, the grime and glory, the shine and shame—as he, to all appearances effortlessly does."

—James Sallis

EDGAR & SHAMUS GO GOLDEN

GAY TOLTL KINMAN
AND ANDREW MCALEER, EDITORS

EDGAR & SHAMUS GO GOLDEN

Twelve Tales of Murder, Mystery,
and Master Detection from the
Golden Age of Mystery and Beyond

DOWN&OUT
BOOKS

Down & Out Books
3959 Van Dyke Road, Suite 265
Lutz, FL 33558
DownAndOutBooks.com

Cover design by Margo Nauert

ISBN: 1-64396-278-7
ISBN-13: 978-1-64396-278-8

TABLE OF CONTENTS

Introduction   1
Gay Toltl Kinman and Andrew McAleer

The Outsider   5
Martin Edwards

The Pearl of the Antilles   35
Carolina Garcia-Aguilera

Scars of Love   57
Brendan DuBois

Saints or Harridans   77
Kristen Lepionka

The Invisible Band   95
Art Taylor

Old Money   129
John M. Floyd

The Party   149
Lia Matera

No Place for a Dame   181
Lori Armstrong

A Jelly of Intrigue   207
O'Neil De Noux

The Dead Snitch   229
Doug Allyn

Remembrance in Deep Red   247
PJ Parrish

The Case of the Illustrious Banker 259
John McAleer

About the Contributors   281

INTRODUCTION

Dear Reader:

Edgar & Shamus welcomes mystery connoisseurs back to the Golden Age of Mystery…

Have we ever really left? Has the Golden Age ever really slipped over the falls? The puzzle, the who-dun-it, the why-dun-it, the how-dun-it, and the unshakable alibi are as much afoot today as they were when, under the glow of gaslight, Dr. Watson documented Holmes's exploits.

More than a century later we still imitate and enjoy these inventors of the modern mystery story. Golden Age writers such as Agatha Christie, Freeman Wills Crofts, Dorothy Sayers, Anthony Berkeley, G. K. Chesterton, Helen Simpson, S. S. Van Dine, R. Austin Freeman, and John Dickson Carr are still big players in the puzzle game today. Considering that Golden Age authors could themselves be as complicated and interesting as their plots, their literary endurance oughtn't be a mystery.

As Diamond Dagger winner Martin Edwards tells us in his Edgar Allan Poe Award-winning book the *Golden Age of Murder*, Golden Age authors were anything but the stuffed shirts they tend to get labeled. These literary pioneers of the poisoned pen consisted of World War I combat veterans, brilliant publicists, tough-minded contract negotiators, and sometimes bickering artists.

Some had less-than-perfect marriages, imbibed in alcohol

after midnight, survived the Blitz, suffered from psychoses, and at least one may have had a secret desire to commit murder. Some enjoyed reciting limericks unsuitable for garden parties. While their works appeared structured around delicate teacups, clipped sod, silk toppers, and faithful servants, Golden Age authors dared to question the justice system, recognized the complexities of the human psyche, battled fascism, meted out their own forms of justice, scorned greedy capitalists, occasionally let the bad guy walk, and even acknowledged the existence of s—x. Additionally, the Golden Age wasn't limited to the confines of Great Britain.

As three-time Edgar winner and tireless devotee of the genre William L. DeAndrea reminds us about the Golden Age in his epic work *Encyclopedia Mysteriosa*, "[I]t should not be forgotten that this was the era that also saw the creation of the hard-boiled detective by Carroll John Daly and the era in which Dashiell Hammett published all his fiction." While the plots, poisons, and punishments could vary on either side of the pond, the crime fiction rules honed to a finer edge in the Golden Age remained sacred. They still do.

Playing fair with the reader never goes out of style. Other rules with no expiration date include: mention the villain early in the story, the detective is bound to declare any discovered clues, and unaccountable intuition is an open-and-shut case of compounded jiggery-pokery. Authors who deviate from "detective sportsmanship" do so at their own peril. Authors who cheat readers run the risk of losing them forever.

Edgar & Shamus is a tour-de-force tribute to this classic era of crime detection. The *Edgar & Shamus* contributors are the best rule followers in the business—while at the same time the cleverest at convincing readers that they aren't. In *Edgar & Shamus*, technology takes a back seat to unique analytic methods of crime detection. Computers and "smart" phones need not apply. The master detectives in *Edgar & Shamus* dig up clues and suspects the old-fashioned way via sweat, shoe leather, and logical deduction. But fear not dear reader: it's not all going to be hard work.

Martin Edwards promises a few relaxing days at a quiet and respectable English resort with criminologist Darius Fortune—or does he? John Floyd's private detective Luke Walker reserves a 1940s seat for you in the New Orleans Quarter—paid for with old money. To save a friend from a murder rap, PJ Parrish's "Salvage Consultant" Mavis Magritte must untangle an unshakable alibi and the only help she's getting is from a set of risqué bunny ears. Brendan DuBois rebuilds Boston's historic and famed Scollay Square without pulling a single building permit. In post-World War II Havana, "vices are annuities" for Carolina Garcia-Aguilera's veteran P.I. Sophie Stevenson. Thanks to Tennessee Williams, O'Neil De Noux's private dick Lucien Caye is up to his hip-pocket in extortion. Doug Allyn's major crimes detective and World War II combat veteran Dolph LaCrosse returns home only to be called the "new guy" by fellow cops.

The war to end all wars may be over, but political skullduggery is still afoot in Lia Matera's "The Party." When a "riverboat" gambler washes up dead, Kristen Lepionka's LA homicide dicks Hewitt and Carmichael are neck deep in suspects—all capable of dealing from the bottom of the deck. Lori Armstrong gins up trouble with a capital "T" when a Tyrone Power look-a-like saunters into the Marlow Detective Agency. In Art Taylor's "The Invisible Band," it's anybody's guess which master detective might solve the big caper—Nero Wolfe, Miss Marple, Charlie Chan, Lord Peter Wimsey, Father Brown, and even Mr. Holmes are among the all-star sleuths assembled to solve the baffling mystery.

In John McAleer's "The Case of the Illustrious Banker," 1920s London-based detective Henry von Stray and his able collaborator in the detection of crime Professor John W. Dilpate are up against a "nippy bit of work" at the behest of Scotland Yard. Discovered more than eight decades after first penned, "Illustrious Banker" makes its debut in *Edgar & Shamus*.

McAleer—forty years before he would win the Edgar Award unanimously beating out Christie's autobiography—created von Stray and Dilpate in 1937 during the Golden Age of Mystery.

It is generally accepted that the Golden Age of Mystery existed between the two world wars. Its postal date stamp, however, isn't as simple as A, B, C...E.C. Bentley published *Trent's Last Case* prior to World War I, and Christie, along with many of her contemporaries, kept the electric torch burning long after World War II. In the *Oxford Companion to Crime & Mystery Writing*, H. R. F. Keating had this to say about Golden Age stamina: "Nor should it be thought that with the advent of World War II the genre disappeared...The glow from the Golden Age reaches far down the years."

During the height of the Blitz in World War II, Martin Edwards shares how Christie (eerily reminiscent of a dying clue) inscribed a copy of *Sad Cypress*: "Wars may come and wars may go, but MURDER, goes on forever!"

Thanks to Christie and company, all the *Edgar & Shamus* contributors, and especially mystery fans throughout the world who continue to insist on a good puzzle, perhaps we are at liberty to paraphrase Dame Agatha: "Technology may come and technology may go, but the Golden Age of Mystery, goes on forever!"

So, dear reader, switch on your electric light, boil up a pot of Earl Grey tea, and enjoy your jaunt through time with *Edgar & Shamus*. Perhaps in the near future we'll catch you on the Orient Express...or is it the 12.30 from Croydon...?

Gay Toltl Kinman and Andrew McAleer

The Outsider
Martin Edwards

'I am *not* a detective,' Darius Fortune said.

I bit my tongue, something that my poor mother, God rest her soul, said I should do more often. Darius Fortune was an enigma, and although I'd only known him for a short time following his arrival from America, already I'd discovered that I got nowhere by arguing with him. Yet I knew I was right. The tireless efforts and sleepless nights that Darius had devoted to solving the puzzle of the Beresford cipher, going through the details of the case he kept so meticulously in bulky scrapbooks, had drained him of energy. Fresh lines had crept across his craggy forehead. I'd noticed a touch of grey in his hair. He needed to recuperate, to relax. Preferably in my company.

'Very well.' I treated myself to another sip of Amontillado. Prior to breaking his neck during a foxhunt, my father laid down a first-class cellar. 'You're a scholar on sabbatical. A dabbler in criminology. The fact remains, you're exhausted and you deserve a break.'

'You believe you know what is best for me.'

Did a faint smile play on his lips as he settled deeper into the leather armchair? His expression was so difficult to read that perhaps I was mistaken. Certainly I didn't interpret his remark as a rebuke. At least he acknowledged my concern for his welfare.

'I just said…'

'That I should get away from it all. Blow away the cobwebs.'

He released a long sigh. 'Well, milady, perhaps you're right to prescribe sea air and summer breezes.'

For a moment I was lost for words, not a familiar experience. Darius Fortune usually spent his time pointing out where I'd gone wrong, especially when I questioned his deductions. Ah well, he was learning. Even if he did persist in calling me *milady* after I'd begged him a hundred times to address me as Guinevere, or preferably Gwyn. Especially when we were tête-à-tête.

I leaned forward, determined to avoid any hint of triumphalism. 'You really can't beat the English seaside.'

'It will be a new experience.' He shook his head. 'Very different from Florida.'

'Absolutely. Palm Beach is hardly Paignton.'

'I'm sure that's true.' He sounded wistful.

'There are endless possibilities.' I couldn't restrain my enthusiasm. 'I've always had a soft spot for Hastings.'

'Hastings?'

'For example,' I said, 'how about Brighton, the queen of watering holes?'

He frowned. 'I'm not sure.'

'Torquay, then? St Loo? Danemouth?'

A dismissive shrug. 'Didn't I read about a place called Easterhead Bay?'

'Easterhead Bay?' I was taken aback. 'I thought you might like something a little more...traditional. The hotels in these new resorts don't have so much character.'

'They may have better plumbing,' he said.

At three o'clock the following afternoon we reached the outskirts of Easterhead Bay. I was behind the wheel of the Lagonda. Darius was not a good passenger. He closed his eyes each time I sped around a sharp bend.

We passed a handful of bungalows and a roadside greeting: *Easterhead Bay Welcomes Careful Drivers.* Darius groaned.

'Not bad, though I say it myself,' I enthused. 'We've made excellent time. Once we've settled in, we'll be ready for a drink.'

'I'm not sure I want anything just at the moment,' he murmured.

'Nonsense, you're on holiday!'

As the words left my mouth, I realised I was beginning to sound as dictatorial as Aunt Persephone. Better change the subject. Taking one hand from the wheel, I gestured towards the coastline.

'That's the River Tern, it empties into the bay. On the other side you can see Gull's Point, hanging over the cliff.'

We approached a signpost pointing to a path for the ferry. A wiry young woman with mousy brown hair and a small suitcase under her arm jumped athletically out of our way as we raced by. I pipped my horn by way of apology. As I glanced back, she glared at me before striding down the path.

Darius twitched. His nerves were in a wretched state. 'Shouldn't you keep your eyes on the road?'

'On a fine spring day, the scenery is too delightful for words,' I said. 'That adorable little fishing village is Saltcreek. Do you see Stark Head, by the mouth of the river? I read something about it only the other day.'

'The day before yesterday, to be precise. Stark Head was mentioned in *The Times*.'

'That must be it!' A thought struck me. 'Is that what prompted you to think of Easterhead Bay? You were reading up about holiday destinations?'

'Not at all. An elderly spinster died at Stark Head. She plunged over the cliffs. The authorities seem undecided about whether her death was an accident or suicide.'

I looked at him. 'She wasn't murdered, then?'

His face was impassive. The queasiness of a few minutes earlier had vanished.

'The report suggested that her death was simply an appalling misfortune.'

'So that wasn't why you proposed a visit to Easterhead Bay?'

A vast white building rose up in the distance, a dazzling confection of curves and horizontal lines perched on the headland. Brochures rhapsodised about the hotel as a shrine to sunshine, a masterpiece of modernism. Killjoys might call it a monstrosity.

Darius expelled a theatrical sigh of relief. 'At least we have got here in one piece.'

Only later did I realise that he hadn't answered my question.

An hour later, we were sipping lemonade and lime outside the Rotunda Bar. The terrace was a sun trap commanding a view over the sandy beach. Across the water, the heights of Stark Head frowned at us. Mr Owen, the portly hotel manager, had fussed over me from the moment we entered a lobby dominated by a mural of mermaids with a saucy look in their eyes. Shading his tiny eyes, he waddled out to check we had everything we needed.

'You really do us a great honour, Lady Guinevere.' Owen was thrilled that I'd chosen to stay here rather than at the hopelessly dated Balmoral Court on the other side of the river. As his gaze wandered, I deduced that he was equally thrilled by the immodest neckline of my Jantzen swimming suit.

'You have my friend here to thank for our presence.' I whipped off my sunglasses, irritated that he persisted in ignoring Darius. 'This was his idea.'

The manager mopped his brow. He was about fifty and looked as if he'd consumed too many hotel dinners.

'Much obliged, sir. Easterhead Bay is the coming place, take it from me. We have great ambitions. Dawlish and St Loo will have to look to their laurels. In five years' time...'

Darius said, 'I was sorry to hear about your recent tragedy, Mr Owen.'

A wary look crept across the manager's face. 'The death of that poor woman at Stark Head, you mean? Dreadful business.

An accident, no doubt.'

'She wasn't a guest here?'

'Goodness me, no.' He allowed himself a mordant smile. 'She was staying at the Balmoral Court in Saltcreek.'

His tone implied that her choice of hotel rendered calamity almost inevitable.

'You never saw her here?'

'Good heavens, no!' Owen snapped. For some reason the question had rattled him. 'Here we cater to a...younger and most discerning clientele. Don't we, Travers?'

This question was addressed to a pert young woman in a waitress's uniform who was clearing the next table. She turned bright pink and nodded nervously.

'I'm sure you do,' Darius said in his slow Southern drawl. 'Actually, I wasn't referring to the death of poor Miss Wilson—that was her name, wasn't it? I meant the recent tragedy at this very hotel.'

I blinked. This was the first I'd heard of it.

Owen turned pale. I caught him giving the waitress a quick glance, as if to shoo her out of harm's way. As she scurried off, he collected himself.

'You will appreciate, Mr...'

'Fortune.'

'Mr Fortune, yes.'

'Professor Fortune,' I said sharply.

'My apologies, Professor.' Owen had the grace to blush. 'I was not aware...'

'As a matter of fact,' I said, 'Professor Fortune is a leading expert in...'

Darius raised his hand. 'Thank you, milady, but it doesn't matter. You were saying, Mr Owen?'

'We pride ourselves here on our discretion.' He sneaked another glance at my swimming costume. 'We cater to a discerning clientele and our guests expect nothing less.'

I raised my eyebrows. I guessed that many of the people who

came here were not so much discerning as filthy rich.

'Frankly, I've always believed that discretion is over-rated.' My mischievous smile made Darius shift uneasily in his chair. 'Professor Fortune is a dear friend of mine. You may speak freely in front of him.'

Owen coughed. It was clear that he was discomfited but I was intent on making him spill the beans. Whatever beans there were to be spilled. Darius never wasted either words or time. If something had snared his attention, I wanted to know what it was.

'You see, it's like this.' Owen lowered his voice. 'The husband of the deceased is still in the hotel.'

I was agog. 'What on earth happened?'

Owen looked around. 'I would normally speak about such a distressing matter only to the proper authorities.'

I treated him to a disingenuous smile. 'You can rely on me to respect a confidence.'

'That's kind of you, your ladyship.' He inhaled. 'A week ago, one of our guests was found dead in her bathroom. Drowned.'

'Goodness,' I said. 'How terrible.'

'Indeed. Poor Mrs Poole had only been married for six months and her husband brought her to Easterhead Bay as a spur of the moment treat. As he put it, they were celebrating their half-anniversary.'

'How sweet,' I said dreamily.

Darius was unmoved. I don't believe he has a sentimental bone in his body.

'How did Mrs Poole drown?'

'She was in her bath,' Owen said. 'The doctor believes she had some kind of fit. She mentioned that she suffered from epilepsy.'

'She actually told you that?' Darius asked sharply.

'Yes, she complained she was a martyr to ill health. Whether the hot water...oh, I don't know, it's too awful to contemplate.'

'You say *her* bath? So this didn't happen in one of the...shared facilities?'

'No, she and her husband had their own set of rooms. Mr Poole booked a suite on the top floor. A generous gesture. He is heartbroken, naturally.'

'Naturally,' Darius said. 'He wasn't in the suite when the tragedy occurred?'

'Dear me, no. Had he been present, disaster might have been averted. At the time of her death, he wasn't even in Easterhead Bay.'

'Is that so?'

'Oh yes. He reproaches himself bitterly, poor fellow, but he had the very best of reasons for his absence.'

'Which was?'

'He was in St Loo for an appointment with an artist, a chap with a studio overlooking the sea. He wanted to commission a portrait of his wife.'

'Another marvellously romantic gesture,' I sighed.

'Quite so.'

Alas, Darius is as unromantic as he is unsentimental. 'So the man came back here and discovered his wife, dead in the bath?'

'Not exactly.' Owen's cheeks turned pink. 'The body was discovered by a member of my staff.'

'Oh dear,' I said.

'Yes, an horrific experience for anyone, let alone an inexperienced chambermaid. She'd gone in to clean the Pooles' suite. The outer door was locked and there was no sign of anyone there. Nor any sound. The bathroom door was locked too. When the girl went inside, she saw Mrs Poole lying motionless in the bath. Quite dead.'

'Terrifying,' I breathed.

'She screamed and then dropped down in a dead faint. As it happens, I was coming up the stairs to see how she was getting on.'

'You were?' Darius asked.

'It was only her second week in the job.' Owen coughed. 'I like to make sure every new member of staff is maintaining our high standards.'

'Naturally.'

'As soon as I heard her scream, I rushed to the suite and was greeted by a pitiful sight.' He mopped his brow. 'I managed to lift the chambermaid up and revive her. She's a strong girl but I did my best to comfort her after such a shock.'

'I'm sure you did,' Darius said. 'And the deceased?'

'She was beyond help.'

'Difficult for you.'

'I'll say!' Owen exclaimed. 'This is my first season here and prurient publicity can be damaging for an hotel of distinction...'

I looked around. 'You seem busy enough.'

'Thankfully, no guests have left and no forthcoming reservations have been cancelled.' He bowed his head. 'These things can happen in these best-run establishments. I recall something of the sort occurring in Rhyl two or three years ago. An act of God, so to speak. Tragic, but nobody's fault. I can only hope that the worst is over.'

Except for the dead woman and her grief-stricken husband, I thought.

'When was the inquest?' Darius asked.

'Two mornings ago, in Saltington.'

'That is the nearest town?'

'Seven or eight miles away, yes.'

'You gave evidence?'

'Yes. The proceedings were straightforward, but upsetting. Poole did his best to be stoical, but the whole business must have been an ordeal for him.'

'And for the chambermaid, I expect.'

Owen sighed. 'She was so distraught that when I asked the doctor to examine her, he said she was in no fit state to attend. Because I'd been on the spot, so to speak, I was able to give evidence about our discovery of the body. I did my utmost to console the girl, to no avail.'

'She is still unwell?'

'Her nerves are shattered, I'm afraid, and she handed in her notice. Couldn't bear to work here any longer. I tried to talk her round, but she left earlier this afternoon. Such a shame.' His eyes strayed to my bare legs. 'She had considerable…um, potential. Even though she was only with us for such a short time, I felt she could go far in the hotel trade. But it was not to be. She's gone home to Manchester.'

He made it sound as far distant as Samarkand. Suddenly he stiffened. A man of about thirty came out of the hotel. He was good-looking and trim in a Savile Row suit but his demeanour was sombre and he wore a black tie.

'You must excuse me,' Owen muttered.

Raising his voice, he said. 'Good afternoon, Mr Poole. Is there anything I can do for you?'

'Just came to say I'll be off first thing tomorrow.'

'Of course, of course.' Owen took his arm, as if guiding an invalid, and led him away from us.

'The bereaved husband,' I murmured to Darius.

'A first-rate piece of deduction,' he said softly.

I gave him a sharp look to see if he was laughing at me. As usual his face was a mask.

Darius was by inclination abstemious, despite my best efforts to lure him into more convivial ways, so I was delighted when he agreed to my suggestion of a drink before dinner. Once I'd squeezed into my new Madeleine Vionnet gown, I joined him at the foot of the spiral staircase, and we entered the lavishly decorated Bay Bar. At the far end, standing on his own, was Poole.

We joined him and I introduced myself. A title does work wonders, and even if Poole was irked by our intrusion, his demeanour softened as he ran his eyes over me. Though I say it myself, the backless style suits me; not that Darius ever seems to notice.

'Leonard Poole. Charmed to meet you, Lady Guinevere.' As an afterthought he murmured, 'You too, Professor Fortune.'

'I hope you'll pardon my being direct,' I said. 'But I simply wanted to express my sincere condolences on your recent loss. Such an awful business.'

Poole expelled a long sigh.

'I heard about your plans to have an artist immortalise your wife,' I said. 'A wonderful gesture.'

'She wasn't blessed with good health,' he muttered. 'I wanted a portrait of her...just in case one day the worst happened. As things turned out...'

'Please don't upset yourself.' I found myself patting the hand he'd rested on the counter of the bar.

'You're very kind, Lady Guinevere, but...oh well, what's the use? What's the use of anything?'

He stared moodily into the distance.

'I'm so sorry,' I said. 'I wonder. I don't wish to impose, but would you care to join us for dinner?'

'I don't think...'—he considered me—'Oh well, why not?'

During the meal we studiously avoided all mention of the tragedy. I did most of the talking. I found Poole a man of considerable charm and intelligence. If things had been different I might have relished his company, despite the fact that he was teetotal. As it was, I felt sorry for him.

His home, I learned, was in north Staffordshire. His late wife Emily came from the Potteries and he'd met her while selling encyclopaedias. He was due to return the following day, though he said he didn't know if he could bear to keep the house. It had been in Emily's family for a hundred years, but it was too big for a solitary widower, and besides, it held too many memories of better times.

As we finished our coffees, Darius startled Poole by asking if he had a picture of his wife.

'Why, yes, as it happens. I borrowed an old photograph she kept in a locket to show to the artist. Taken on her twenty-first birthday.'

After a moment's hesitation he reached into his jacket and brought out a pigskin wallet monogrammed with his initials. The small oval photograph he produced showed a woman with gossamer curls and a heart-shaped face. Her features were small and delicate. She looked so fragile that a breath of breeze might blow her away.

'Of course, she is—was—in her mid-forties now. Before our marriage, life hadn't treated her kindly. But I wanted the artist to see the inner woman. Not the weary invalid Emily had become.'

I exhaled. 'How desperately sad.'

Poole bowed his head. 'Yes, if only I'd been in the suite when she had the attack, I might have been able to save her.'

'You mustn't blame yourself.'

'How can I not, Lady Guinevere? At the very moment Emily was dying in her bath, I was chatting to the artist in St Loo. By the time I got back to the hotel, her body had already been taken away. That morning she seemed a little under the weather and I arranged for her to be brought breakfast in bed, but I hadn't the faintest idea I'd never see her alive again. If I had...'

His voice choked with emotion. I felt helpless.

Darius said, 'You don't think the breakfast contributed to her seizure?'

'I did ask the doctor. He couldn't rule anything out, but he thought it unlikely. It was only a light meal. Scrambled egg and smoked salmon, together with some fruit. And she barely touched it.'

Poole got to his feet. 'Now, I must get back to my room. I'm grateful for your company this evening, Lady Guinevere. And yours, Professor.'

As I watched his retreating back, Darius murmured, 'Well?'

'Poor devil.' I mustered a smile. 'Another drink?'

He shook his head. 'I brought my scrapbooks. I need to do

some work on them and I'm rather tired after the journey. Good night, milady.'

Before I could exercise my powers of persuasion, he was striding out of the dining room.

We lingered over breakfast the next morning. There was no sign of Poole and Darius seemed disinclined to discuss either the bathroom tragedy or the death of the woman at Stark Head. I was relieved. The purpose of our trip was to get away from it all and—I very much hoped—for us to get to know one another even better. Owen came over to our table as the room emptied, greeting me with an unctuous smile.

'Good morning, Lady Guinevere. You certainly brought the fine weather with you!' I glanced meaningfully at my companion and the manager coughed. 'Ah, morning to you, Professor Fortune. You slept well, I hope?'

Darius smiled. 'The sleep of the just.'

'Splendid!'

Owen fiddled with his tie. Darius's presence, I sensed, made him feel ill-at-ease.

'Um, you had a pleasant conversation with Mr Poole last night?'

I beamed. 'It was so sad to see him on his own. The least we could do was to keep him company for a little time.'

'I see. Very decent of you, I'm sure.' Owen paused. 'Did he talk about the tragedy?'

'Only in passing.' I gave him a guileless smile. I'm rather proud of my guileless smiles. 'Why do you ask?'

'Oh, no reason.' He seemed flustered. 'It's just that Mrs Poole had breakfast in bed and the chambermaid asked if she'd eaten something that disagreed with her. Old Doctor French dismissed the suggestion out of hand. Given the woman's history, he said, it was obvious that she'd had a fit. Might have happened at any time. Quite right too. You can imagine the harm it might do us if idle gossips and mischief-makers got hold of a silly idea about an adverse reaction to our cuisine. Thank goodness the inquest made clear that she died of natural causes.'

'The coroner was entirely satisfied?' Darius asked.

Owen gave him a sharp glance. 'Absolutely. He is a very experienced lawyer and he's known French for thirty years. Open-and-shut, that was his phrase.'

'When did Mrs Poole have her breakfast?' Darius asked.

'It was brought to her at nine on the dot, as her husband requested.'

'And her husband?'

'Mr Poole breakfasted an hour earlier. He came down to the dining room on his own and I noticed him setting off in his car at half past eight. Poor chap looked as though he didn't have a care in the world.'

'When was the body discovered?'

'At five to ten.'

'Before Mr Poole returned, I gather?'

'Yes, he didn't arrive back until after eleven.'

I scanned the room. We were the last to leave and the waitresses kept glancing in our direction, no doubt wanting to clear our table.

'We haven't seen him today,' I said.

'No, he slipped off not long after seven. Naturally I made sure to speak to him before he left. To reiterate my sincerest condolences.'

'Did he have much to say?' Darius asked.

'Very little.' Owen sniffed. 'Certainly there was no hint of criticism at the way we have...dealt with things, if that's what you mean.'

Darius nodded.

'Very well, I'd better be getting on.' Owen mustered a smile for my benefit. 'What are your plans for today, Lady Guinevere?'

I glanced at Darius.

'Let's catch the ferry and take a look at the other side of the river,' he said.

'You're going to Saltcreek?' Owen wrinkled his little snout. 'Nice old fishing village, if rather behind the times.'

'Saltcreek, yes,' Darius said. 'And Stark Head.'

'I don't understand,' I told Darius as we wound down the path that led to the ferry. 'Did you choose to come to Easterhead Bay because of what happened here?'

'Like young George Washington, milady, I cannot tell a lie.' He smiled. 'When I read about the death of Mabel Wilson, I was intrigued. Only a few days earlier I'd seen a paragraph about Mrs Poole's sad demise.'

'Two sad incidents, but scarcely remarkable.'

'I'm not so sure. A glance at a map revealed how close Stark Head is to Easterhead Bay. The size of the local population is modest, even when swelled by holidaymakers. I speculated idly about a possible connection between the two tragedies.'

'Without a shred of evidence?'

Darius pretended to hang his head in shame. 'You're right. I allowed myself to be guided by instinct rather than science or rigorous deduction.'

I tutted. 'You complain when I let my imagination run away with me. At least by speaking to the widower you've set your mind at rest.'

He avoided my eye. I was puzzled.

'You still think the death of the old woman at Stark Head is…questionable?'

'I keep an open mind,' he said. 'Let's ask around, see what we can find out.'

'Look, there is the ferry.'

His eyebrows shot up. 'That rowing boat?'

'This isn't Staten Island, you know. Don't worry, you won't get seasick on such a narrow stretch of river. We'll reach the other side in no time.'

* * *

Half an hour later, we were strolling past the old fishing cottages on our way up the lane towards Stark Head. On our way, we'd passed the time of day with a number of people, starting with the boatman. I did most of the talking. As Aunt Persephone keeps saying, I'm a natural chatterbox. Besides, people seem more willing to open up to me. It would be different if Darius were quizzing them.

So far, we hadn't learned much. Most of the folk were tourists like ourselves and the boatman had told us that although he knew the locals, he'd only encountered the late Miss Wilson once, when he took her across the river. I calculated that this must have been on the day before the inquest into Emily Poole's death. In a brief exchange of pleasantries, he'd learned nothing about her other than that she was staying in Saltcreek for a fortnight.

'I've had an idea,' I said.

'Oh yes?'

'That hotel manager, Owen. I don't care for him.'

Darius nodded. 'I don't think he likes me, either.'

'That bonhomie is transparently phoney.'

'He's in the hotel business. His job is to be agreeable.'

'I don't find the way he looks at me agreeable.' I shuddered. 'It's as if he's undressing me with his eyes. And when he speaks to you, he is so rude.'

He shrugged. 'You are an elegant young woman with a title. I'm just a crusty old academic.'

'You're barely old enough to be my father. Besides, you know perfectly well, it's not just that. Owen strikes me as suspicious. Isn't it odd that he was on the spot when the chambermaid discovered Emily Poole' body in the bath?'

'The man runs the place. He is entitled to go anywhere he pleases.'

'He didn't like it when you asked if Miss Wilson had ever

been to the hotel.'

'Yes, that was interesting.'

'I'm not sure I believed his denial.'

'He lied,' Darius said. 'He was startled and said the first thing that came into his mind.'

'So she did come to the hotel?'

'That is my guess,' he said. 'But as you will surely point out, I have no evidence.'

We'd reached the track that brought us to Stark Head. A middle-aged woman with a Labrador on a lead was approaching from the opposite direction and I seized the chance to admire the dog. In my experience, dog lovers can never resist a word of appreciation for their pet. Soon the two of us were chatting away merrily while Darius stroked Rusty's head and listened. He'd said more than once that I was a more effective inquisitor than half the detective-inspectors in Scotland Yard. A rare compliment, and one I prized.

'You live in the village?' I asked.

'Yes, a stone's throw from the old hotel.'

'The Balmoral Court?'

She nodded.

'Terrible business,' I said. 'About that poor lady who fell over the cliff.'

'Awful,' she replied. 'Stark Head looks as pretty as a picture, but people don't realise if they aren't familiar with the terrain. If you stumble over the edge, the drop is sheer. You really must take care up there.'

'We will,' I promised. 'We've just come over from Easterhead Bay.'

'Staying at the new hotel, are you? Very fancy.'

'It was a toss-up between that and the Balmoral Court,' I said untruthfully.

'Well, perhaps the older place isn't to the taste of...'—she considered us with undisguised curiosity—'city folk like you. One or two holiday cottages here are rented out, but I suppose it's nicer to be waited on.'

'Didn't the poor lady who died stay at the Balmoral Court?'

'Miss Wilson, yes. Such a nice woman.'

My pulse quickened. 'You knew her?'

'Just a nodding acquaintance. She liked dogs and one day we started chatting, after she got off the ferry. So sad to think that the very next morning…'

'Absolutely,' I breathed. 'She'd been over to Easterhead Bay?'

'Yes.' The woman shook her head. 'She seemed worried. I got the impression that talking to me about Rusty helped to take her mind off her troubles.'

'How sad to think of her being upset, so soon before she died. Do you know what was wrong?'

'As we parted, I actually asked if she was all right. She simply said that a good memory can be a curse. I've no idea what she meant. And then the very next day…'

She glanced over her shoulder towards the summit of the cliff.

'It's a lonely spot,' I said.

'Even in the height of summer, most people prefer to stay down by the shore.'

'You don't think,' Darius said suddenly, 'that if she was upset, she might have jumped?'

The woman was horrified. 'Oh no, I can't believe that. It must have been an accident. According to the last person to see her, she seemed very distracted.'

'There was a witness?'

'Not to…what actually happened. Mrs Sheringham is a widow who is living next door to me. She's rented Yew Cottage for the month. Lovely young woman, keeps herself to herself. Only yesterday she was telling me that she bumped into poor Miss Wilson the previous morning.' She hesitated. 'Mrs Sheringham said she seemed almost, well, ga-ga.'

'Really?'

'That wasn't my impression, I must say. To me, the lady was

simply upset. But I suppose if something was preying on her mind, well, you never know, do you? You need to keep your wits about you as you walk along the top of Stark Head.'

'Did Mrs Sheringham mention this encounter to the police?'

'She told me she didn't want to be mixed up in anything nasty, like an inquest. But she hoped nobody would get the idea that what happened was...deliberate. Much better to put poor Miss Wilson's death down to an accident than to *felo de se*.' She sighed. 'Anyhow, I must be getting along. Mind your step if you go close to the cliff edge.'

At the top of Stark Head, we looked down at the shimmering water. It was a vertiginous drop.

'A long way to fall,' Darius said.

Despite the sun's warmth, I shivered. 'A terrible way to die.'

'Mmmm.' He wasn't listening, but peering around the stony, jagged terrain.

'Searching for something in particular?'

He gave a bleak smile. 'For nooks and crannies that aren't visible from the hotel terrace.'

'There are plenty. Crevices behind and in between boulders, ledges obscured by trees growing out of the rock. And the Head dips slightly towards the open sea.' I took half a dozen paces to illustrate my point. 'If I stand here, nobody on the hotel terrace can see me.'

He gave me a wicked smile. 'What if they were looking out of a window on the top floor of the hotel?'

I frowned. 'Even then...'

'Yes, yes, I was only teasing you.'

I sighed. 'Such a shame that poor Miss Wilson wasn't lucky enough to get caught in one of those trees as she fell.'

He nodded. 'I think we've seen enough.'

'The view is spectacular,' I said.

'And the rocks below are lethal.' He took my arm in his

courteous way, a proper American gentleman. 'Come away from the edge.'

'Where shall we go?'

'I'd like to speak to Mrs Sheringham.'

As we retraced our steps down towards Saltcreek, I asked him about Owen. If Miss Wilson hadn't committed suicide or died by accident, was it possible that he'd had a hand in her death?'

'You really dislike him,' he said.

'He gives me the creeps.'

'That's not enough to make him a murderer.'

'It's a start.'

He lapsed into silence again and I knew better than to interrupt his train of thought. As we walked through the village, he came to a sudden halt and glanced back over his shoulder. I followed his gaze and realised it had settled on a black Rover Meteor. The car was tucked away, almost out of sight from the lane, on cobbles at the side of a terraced cottage. Above the front door was a small blue lamp. This must be where the local bobby lived.

'Recognise the registration number?' Darius asked.

I shook my head in disbelief. 'It's not our old friend Inspector Bradley?'

'I'm sure it is.'

'What on earth is one of Scotland Yard's terriers doing here?'

'The same as you and me, presumably.'

'You mean, the police aren't satisfied about the old lady's death?'

'It looks very much like it.'

I laughed. 'Shall we stop and say hello?'

'I doubt the inspector would greet us with open arms. He seldom does.'

'He ought to be more grateful. Without your help, the Beresford family...'

Darius waved my words away. 'Never mind that. Our paths are sure to cross soon enough. For now, let's get on. I'd rather speak to the witness before the good inspector browbeats her into saying that black is white.'

Five minutes later we were outside a tiny dwelling with a nameplate next to the door. *Yew Cottage.*

Darius rapped twice, but there was no answer.

'You're out of luck,' a skinny grocer's boy said as he wheeled his bicycle along the lane.

'Mrs Sheringham isn't in?'

'That's her name, is it? Nice-looking piece. Gorgeous red hair. I was chatting to her only yesterday.' The young man sniggered. 'Wouldn't have minded getting to know her better. Anyhow, she's not here.'

'Do you have any idea where we might find her?'

''Fraid not, mister. I spotted her this morning, getting into a taxi with a little suitcase. Looked like she was off for a few days. I bet she's had enough of Saltcreek. Not much here for a pretty thing like that.' He sighed. 'Oh well. Easy come, easy go, eh?'

'What now?' I asked, licking an ice cream as we sat on a low wall by the river. 'Shall we stay here or go back to the hotel and sunbathe?'

'Neither,' Darius said. 'There's work to be done.'

'Should we talk to Owen again? If there's been any funny business, I'd say he's at the heart of it.'

'What is your theory?'

I finished my ice cream and took a breath. 'Owen told us this is his first season as manager of the hotel. To my mind, he's a lecher who almost certainly has a discreditable past.'

'Please excuse me, milady.' Darius took a silk handkerchief from his jacket pocket and carefully wiped a smear of ice cream from my chin. His touch was delightfully tender, his absorption in the task endearing. 'That's better.'

'Thank you. Where was I? Oh yes, Owen followed the chambermaid up to the top of the hotel. She was a new girl, inexperienced, as he said. My bet is that he wanted to take advantage of her.'

Darius pursed his lips. 'Plausible.'

Encouraged, I said, 'Owen presumed that the Pooles' suite was empty. Whatever happened between him and the maid, I think they disturbed Mrs Poole. The shock was too much for a woman whose health was fragile and unfortunately she died. Owen was afraid that a scandal would ruin him, so he persuaded the maid to leave. Perhaps he gave her some money to keep quiet.'

'Mrs Poole knew that the rooms were cleaned once breakfast was over. Wouldn't she have made sure there was a *Do Not Disturb* sign hanging on her door while she took a bath?'

'I suppose she forgot.' I smiled. 'Not everyone is as punctilious as you.'

'What about Miss Wilson? Does her death fit into this scenario, or is it merely a coincidence?'

'I think she came to Easterhead Bay and spotted Owen misbehaving with the chambermaid. Whatever she saw, she found deeply disturbing.'

'So much so that she wandered over the edge of Stark Head by mistake?'

'Mrs Sheringham confirmed that the old lady was in a state of distress.'

'You don't think that Owen popped across to Stark Head and gave Miss Wilson a shove?'

I considered. 'As we've seen, it would be possible for him to do so, if he judged his moment, without anyone on the hotel terrace—let alone the beach below—being any the wiser.'

'Except that...,' he prompted.

Light dawned. 'No, it's impossible! She fell from the cliff while the inquest was in progress. Even if Owen left before the proceedings were concluded and came back here rather than the hotel, it would have been very difficult for him to get back here from Saltington unobserved and do the deed. *Probably* impossible.'

'I agree. The same consideration rules out Poole. Neither of them pushed her over.'

'Not that it matters,' I said firmly. 'As I say, I don't believe she was murdered. Owen is morally responsible for her death, but that's as far as it goes.'

'Mmmm.'

I looked at him. 'What do you make of my theory?'

The mask gave nothing away. 'It's quite ingenious.'

'But?'

'But it's wrong in almost every respect.'

I groaned. 'All right, then. What do you think?'

He got to his feet. 'Let's go in search of Inspector Bradley and see what the pair of you make of my ideas.'

The next twenty-four hours passed in a dreamlike whirl. At noon the following day, I found myself ensconced in the Library of the Easterhead Bay Hotel. It was really a sitting room with a sea view. Shelves on one wall were crammed with books available for guests to borrow, everything from Freeman Wills Crofts to Marie Corelli.

Darius and I sat on a capacious sofa, looking out over the sea. One of his scrapbooks lay on an occasional table. In front of us stood Inspector Bradley. He was tugging his moustache furiously, as if to make it droop even more than usual. His expression was invariably mournful, and I'd heard a whisper that his nickname at the Yard was Sadly Bradley. Even though he'd orchestrated the rendezvous that was about to take place, he couldn't resist a gloomy gibe.

'You don't half like the theatrics, Professor.'

Darius shrugged. 'An occasion of this kind can prove enlightening, Inspector. As you and I have found in the past.'

Bradley snorted. 'I indulge you too much. After all, you're an outsider. If it wasn't for the Assistant Commissioner...'

I'd grown tired of his carping. Wearing my sweetest smile, I said, 'And how is Uncle Peregrine?'

My reward was a dirty look. Bradley hated any reminder of my connection to his superior. He contemplated his shiny black shoes.

'Very well, Lady Guinevere, last time I spoke to him.'

'Oh good. When you report back, you will give him my love, won't you?'

The inspector was saved from any need to reply by a knock at the door.

'Come in,' he barked.

Owen entered the room. The sight of Darius and me made him flinch. 'I wasn't expecting...'

'Don't worry, sir,' Bradley said. 'Everything will become clear shortly. Take a seat.'

The hotel manager's voice rose. 'Really, I must protest! Our guests shouldn't be dragged into a...matter of this kind.'

'Don't mind us,' I said in a meek voice. 'Please sit down. This won't take long.'

With a show of reluctance, Owen occupied one of the armchairs. There was another knock on the door.

'How long will this take?' Owen asked. 'I have a hotel to run.'

'Not too long, sir,' Bradley said. 'Come in, Driffield.'

A smart young constable stepped into the room, followed by Leonard Poole. The widower's expression was thunderous.

Bradley began to introduce himself, but Poole interrupted.

'This is an absolute outrage, Inspector. I hold you personally responsible. As for this pair...' He indicated Darius and myself. 'I have no idea what you people are playing at or why you tried to pump me over the dinner table. You're well aware of the heartbreak I've endured, and now I'm dragged back here—the scene of the tragedy, for goodness sake!—with scarcely a by-your-leave and on the thinnest of pretexts. This is an utter...'

I couldn't help interrupting. 'My uncle is the Assistant Commissioner at Scotland Yard. I'll make sure he's fully aware of your complaint.'

'In the meantime, sir,' Bradley said, 'why not take the weight off your feet?'

He indicated an armchair and Poole sat down, his handsome face disfigured by anger.

Owen leaned forward. 'What on earth is the meaning of this charade?'

Darius coughed and got to his feet. 'I am responsible, gentlemen. If you will bear with me, I shall put forward an explanation for two recent tragedies. The deaths of your wife, Mr Poole, and that of a woman called Mabel Wilson.'

Poole glared. 'Preposterous! Have you taken leave of your senses? What in heaven's name caused you to bring me here to listen to some lecture from a...a...'

Darius shot him a sharp look. 'An American?'

'Go back to your own country! What right have you to stand there talking about two women you never knew, one of them the love of my life?'

'I must ask you to listen to the Professor,' Inspector Bradley said. 'He has rendered the police some service, more than once.'

It was the closest I'd ever heard him come to complimenting Darius in public.

Poole turned to Owen. 'And you! Why have you allowed this hotel to be used for some form of inquisition?'

'I'm as much in the dark as you are, sir.'

'Disquisition might be a better term,' Darius said gently. 'I have no *locus standi* here, no legal right to ask you questions.'

'Absolutely!' Poole said.

'I merely invite you to listen to what I have to say.'

Poole folded his arms. 'I'll give you five minutes.'

'This won't take more than ten,' Darius said. 'Very well, let me put my cards on the table.'

'About time,' Owen snapped.

'I have a keen interest in criminology, shared by my friend Lady Guinevere. You've gathered that milady has a family connection with Scotland Yard, and since coming to England, I've taken advantage of opportunities to pursue my avocation. The catalyst for our visit was a strange coincidence. I read about the tragic demise of Mrs Poole in this hotel, and shortly after that I came across a brief report of Miss Wilson's fall from Stark Head. Two unusual deaths, in a very short space of time, in the same quiet corner of the south coast.'

'I don't see what is so unusual,' Owen objected. 'Two accidents. Mr Poole's late wife had a history of ill health, and the other lady was far from young and perhaps unsteady on her feet.'

'Precisely,' Poole said. 'This is poppycock.'

'Please hear me out. I came here entirely prepared to discover that the twin tragedies were simple mishaps, with no question of foul play.'

'Of course there wasn't,' Poole jeered.

'One or two points did strike me. Your devotion to your late wife was noteworthy. You are still a young man and Lady Guinevere cannot be the only woman who finds you attractive.'

I scowled at Darius, but as usual he took no notice.

'Your wife was much older and physically frail. You were a wealthy couple, but the money came from her.'

'Damned impudence!' Poole half-rose in his chair. 'You're implying that I'm some sort of…'

'Sit down, Mr Poole,' Inspector Bradley said. 'Listen to the Professor.'

Darius nodded. 'It is reasonable to assume that you stood to inherit a considerable sum of money if your wife died. It was abundantly clear, however, that you could not possibly have been responsible for what happened to her. You had a perfect alibi. At the time of her death, you were in St Loo.'

Poole glowered, but said nothing.

'I asked myself if there was some means by which you could have engineered her death remotely. For instance, by some form of poison or other method of inducing a fit.'

'This is absolutely absurd,' Poole muttered.

'I found no evidence whatsoever to substantiate such a theory.'

'Surprise, surprise!'

'I wondered, therefore, if you might have engaged the services of an accomplice.'

Owen mopped his brow. 'Disgraceful! Are you suggesting that I colluded with one guest to ensure the death of another?'

'I considered that possibility too,' Darius said. 'But there was a more credible alternative theory. What if someone was in cahoots with the chambermaid?'

Owen stared at him. 'Young Cissie Walmer? Are you barking mad?'

'I was puzzled,' Darius continued relentlessly, 'that Mrs Poole had taken a bath without putting a *Do Not Disturb* sign on the door to the suite. Yes, she might have forgotten, but I doubted it. More likely, the chambermaid removed it before coming in. The bathroom door would be locked, but she'd have a key. What if she went in and grabbed the startled guest by the heels, causing her to lose consciousness before she could put up any resistance? Water rushing down the throat puts pressure on the vagus. The heart slows and the person faints. Drowning someone in this way is remarkably effective, and a feeble, naked invalid such as Mrs Poole would be no match for a strong and determined young woman like Cissie. No doubt she'd studied the method of the late George Joseph Smith. He left no bruising or signs of struggle on his victims' bodies.'

'The Brides in the Bath case,' Bradley interjected, as if to remind us of his presence.

'Yes. George Joseph Smith's mistake, of course, was to omit to establish a cast-iron alibi for his crimes.'

Poole's face was still red, but I detected fear in his eyes. He was about to speak, but checked himself.

'Ridiculous!' Owen said. 'You're suggesting that Mr Poole arranged a conspiracy with a servant he'd only just met?'

'Far from it,' Darius suggested. 'I'm suggesting that his marriage to Emily Poole was bigamous. He was already married to the woman you employed as a chambermaid. An attractive young woman with a fine head of red hair.'

'You're mistaken,' Owen said. 'Cissie Walmer has brown hair.'

'Hair dye and a pair of scissors come in useful when a woman wants to adopt a disguise,' Darius said dryly. 'The murder of Emily Poole was planned with care. Poole here—it's not his real name, of course, we've established that the name on his birth certificate is Herbert Drigg—found a suitable victim, a wealthy spinster in poor health, courted her, married her, and arranged for her death in this hotel, in circumstances where he was beyond suspicion.'

'We receive ten applications for every vacancy here,' Owen objected. 'There was no guarantee that I would decide to employ Cissie Walmer.'

'A good-looking young woman with no ties who is adept at flattery?' Darius asked. 'Accomplishing that part of the plan was easy. Am I right in believing she persuaded you to give her duties that included cleaning the suites on the top floor?'

Owen bit his lip. 'Well...'

'Quite. I suppose the arrangement suited your amorous inclinations. The suites are very comfortable.'

'How dare you!'

Darius shrugged. 'As a result you were conveniently on hand when, having made sure that Emily Poole was dead, Cissie screamed. The crime was committed with clockwork precision. After all, the pair had experience.'

'What do you mean?' Owen demanded.

'You mentioned a death in Rhyl some time ago.' Darius pointed to his scrapbook. 'I found a clipping about the case. A woman with a weak heart died in her bath while staying at a boarding house. Her name was Millicent Morecambe and the corpse was discovered by a maid called Whitby.'

Poole said hoarsely. 'What of it?'

'The pair of you commit your murders at the seaside, where nobody knows you. It amuses you to borrow your aliases from other resorts. Your first killing was a complete success. Nobody suspected a thing. This time you suffered a piece of outrageous bad luck. You were recognised by Mabel Wilson.'

'Recognised?' Owen looked dumbfounded.

'Yes, Miss Wilson had stayed at the same boarding house as the Morecambes. On this occasion she'd run to a room at the Balmoral Court, but I suppose she was curious to see how the other half lives at Easterhead Bay. So she came over by ferry. I think she caught you misbehaving with the chambermaid, hence your denial that she came here. More importantly she bumped into the grieving widower. A chance in a thousand, perhaps.'

He turned to Poole. 'I suppose you knew at once that the game was up?'

The man bent his head and avoided our eyes.

'You faced a sudden crisis,' Darius said. 'Perhaps nothing was said, perhaps Miss Wilson turned on her heel and fled. But the damage was done. If she told anyone that you are not who you claim to be, you were done for. I suppose she wrestled with the dilemma. Perhaps she couldn't believe her own eyes, perhaps she wondered if the resemblance between you and Morecambe was a simple coincidence. But you'd lost your wives in identical circumstances! No doubt she was bewildered by the fact that you couldn't have killed either of your rich wives and her confusion worked to your advantage. You devised an impromptu plan.'

'Which was?' Owen had overcome his temper; now he was on tenterhooks.

Darius turned to Poole. 'When your wife came here, she took a cottage at Saltcreek under yet another assumed name, Sheringham. For the sake of your homicidal conspiracy, she'd sacrificed her distinctive red locks so that she could apply for jobs with short, mousy brown hair, but in the guise of Mrs Sheringham, she wore an auburn wig. She hoped to find work at this hotel, but failing that she would try the Balmoral Court or one of the smaller guest houses here or further along the coast. Thanks to Mr Owen's recruitment priorities, she secured the first job she applied for. You booked in here at once. A suite with its own bathroom suited your purpose admirably.'

Darius sighed. 'Again you ensured you had an alibi for the crime. I imagine that your wife—as Mrs Sheringham—button-holed Miss Wilson. Perhaps the two women walked to Stark Head, discussing the tragic death at this hotel. After shoving the old lady over the edge, your wife told a tissue of lies designed to support the view that her victim had died as a result of accident or possibly suicide. With the murder accomplished, she resumed her identity as Cissie Walmer, having already made clear that she intended to leave the area. As it happens, Lady Guinevere and I actually saw her go on her way.'

'We did?' I was taken aback.

'Don't you remember the poor woman you almost killed on the way here?' Darius said. 'She was heading for the ferry. Why go to Saltcreek, I wondered, if she was returning to Manchester? How much simpler to go directly to the station at Saltington. In fact she was making for Yew Cottage, in order to change her appearance and identity once again.'

'I reckon that about covers it,' Inspector Bradley said impatiently. 'Have you anything to say?'

Poole remained mute.

'It's like that, is it? All right, let's see if you change your tune down at the station.'

He snapped his fingers and the young constable opened the door of the Library. In came another young policeman, with a woman in handcuffs. I'd last seen her pressed against a hedge as I raced past in the Lagonda.

'Dolly!' Poole cried.

'Don't say a word!' she snapped.

'I haven't! I've admitted nothing. I kept my promise to you!'

'Shut up, you fool!'

'Too late,' Darius said lazily.

The woman turned on her accomplice. 'You've always been weak! You stupid...'

'That will do,' Inspector Bradley said. 'Take them away.'

'Upon my word,' Owen said after the police officers had left with their prisoners.

'I never imagined…'

'No,' Darius said.

The hotel manager considered the two of us. I realise that we make an unlikely pairing, but I still didn't care for the particular brand of puzzlement that I detected in his expression.

'You're a remarkable man, Professor,' he said feebly.

The unspoken words hung in the air: *despite the colour of your skin.*

THE PEARL OF THE ANTILLES
Carolina Garcia-Aguilera

Havana, March 1947

I opened our office door and was greeted by the familiar sight of Big Pete, my secretary and assistant, lying on the sofa in the corner of the reception room. He was wearing the same clothes from the day before, with a musty "morning after the night before" odor emanating from him. Whatever Pete had been doing, it must have been a hell of a time; it was close to eleven o'clock—S.O. Stevenson and Brothers, Private Investigators, didn't keep traditional office hours—and he was still passed out.

"Rough night?" I waited a few seconds. "Again?"

"Save it, Sophie. I already feel like hot garbage without you lecturing me." Pete glared at me with bloodshot eyes that reminded me of roadkill. "Especially since it hasn't been more than a couple weeks since you cleaned up your own act."

I let his comment slide, mostly because it was true. Pete was referring to the recent morning when I had woken up on top of my bed in my apartment wearing another woman's clothes. I had no idea how I ended up that way. I recalled having gone on a bar crawl with some of my *amigos* from the Cuban Navy, but that's about all. Nights with them could be counted on to be wild, which wasn't so unusual for Havana, and it must have been a memorable time even if I couldn't account for the last hours. It was probably better not to know, I decided. That

35

morning I swore to live a clean and wholesome life, regardless of the fact that I was living in probably the most debauched and corrupt city in the world.

When I had been asked to supply a quote for my high school yearbook, I came up with, "Lord, lead me not unto temptation, for I'll find the way myself." I had been pretty precocious. In Havana, in 1947, temptation was everywhere. So far, I'd gone two weeks without succumbing to the vices the city had to offer, but my path had never been a straight and narrow one, so who knew how long that was going to last.

My curiosity got the better of me, so I asked, "Where were you, Pete? Sloppy Joe's?"

Sloppy Joe's was one of the most popular watering holes in town, and Pete was a regular there. Founded in 1933, at the corner of Calle Zuleta, it had always been sketchy and decadent. Pete could down a half dozen of the bar's signature drink, which shared a name with the place: a potent concoction of pineapple juice, cognac, port wine, curacao, and grenadine. It was a mix that could send a weaker man to the hospital, but in a guy with Pete's constitution, it just resulted in the massive hangover I was witnessing that morning.

Pete got up slowly, painfully, holding his breath as he straightened his clothes in a halfhearted effort to pull himself together. He still hadn't answered me, and, as I watched him, I hoped he hadn't gone to Las Fritas Nightclub, a shabby but ridiculously popular place known for such a degree of extreme indulgence in sexual pleasures that it employed two nurses round the clock who were supplied with syringes of penicillin for anyone in need of preventative measures, a service that no doubt helped contribute to its success. The whole arrangement was so notorious that a song, "Penicillin," was written there in tribute. Another trademark of the place was an extremely lewd dance called "shoeing the mare." It wasn't a place to take children.

Post-World War II Havana was a place where anything went.

The wartime boom that followed the war made it an environment that caused vices to explode and sins to become a way of life for much of the city's residents, a free-and-easy mentality that was shocking to moral, churchgoing types. For Pete and me, it was behavior that guaranteed us a very comfortable standard of living. We were one of the few private investigator firms working in the city, and we would never run out of work; for us, vices were annuities.

"Sophie, after you left yesterday, we got a call asking for an appointment today. Guy called himself John Smith." I marveled at how quickly Pete had managed to become reasonably functional. The man had the constitution of an ox. "Didn't ask for you by name." He groaned and rubbed his eyes. "Just wanted to meet with an investigator."

"Another John Smith." I chuckled as I walked into my office. "What's that, the third one this year and it's only March? Never makes sense to me. After all, if a dick is any good, they're going to figure out who's hiring them."

"People don't have to make sense." Pete squeezed his temples as though he was wringing out last night's booze. "That's why we are in business, Sophie."

In my office, I paused at the window that had a perfect view of the Malecon, the seawall that stretched five miles along the coast from the mouth of the harbor in Old Havana to the Almendares River. The wall had been built from reinforced concrete at the beginning of the century, to protect Havana from the sea. In the close to three years that our firm had been located in the building, it was a sight I never tired of.

S.O. Stevenson and Brothers, Private Investigators, was on the fifth floor of a six-story office building that had seen better days—it was a couple of hundred years old and would sway when the wind picked up. It was painted vivid green with dozens of columns on each floor whose sole purpose seemed to be to keep the entire place from toppling over. There were several vendors on the ground floor, a fruit stand, a second- or third-hand clothing shop, and a stall that only sold peanuts. Most of these establishments were open twenty-four hours a day and were constantly packed with customers. With our windows open to the breeze, a cacophony of noise rose up from the street at all hours. And at night, the Malecon became a prime pickup spot for both men and women.

I loved this city so much. It wasn't hard for me to understand why the island was called the Pearl of the Antilles. Havana had been founded in 1519 and was filled with a magic and beauty so profound that at times it could break your heart.

I ended up in here by accident, which was no great surprise. I was twenty-five and had already learned that so much of life mostly worked that way. I grew up in a small farming town in southern Vermont with a population of 273. I had never felt like I belonged there, and as long as I could remember had been looking for a way to escape. The winters there were never-ending, getting dark at four in the afternoon; my hair would stick to my head with static electricity; my nose was perpetually red and dripping, and my skin cracked with the cold. I hated having to put on several layers just to trudge out to the mailbox. True, the magical summers there almost made up for it, but not quite.

I was an only child with older, loving parents, and it could have been a wonderful life, but it never really fit my personality; a longing for adventure was always just under the surface. When I heard that President Roosevelt signed a law in 1942 creating the Navy Women's Reserve Program (the WAVES— Women Accepted for Volunteer Emergency Service), I applied right away. I had grown up hearing stories from my father about the years he had served in the Navy during World War I, so it felt like one tradition I could uphold.

It didn't take long to discover that I was a suitable candidate for the WAVES, and I learned that what I really wanted was to be a Code Girl specializing in intelligence. I fit the requirements: I was twenty years old, good at math, a whiz at crosswords, and I wasn't engaged to be married. Language proficiency was needed, and I was fluent in Spanish thanks to a beloved high school teacher.

Before the WAVES, women weren't anything close to equal to the men in the world of the Navy—they were primarily used as nurses. But more and more people were needed to fight in the war, so women began to be accepted with the goal of releasing officers and enlisted men for sea duty. After I was accepted into the service, I was sent to the Female Officer Training School at Hunter College in New York City. The conditions there weren't ideal: I shared a very cramped apartment with three other recruits, sleeping on a tiny top bunk, but I was so happy to be there that I didn't care. In February 1943, I was sworn into the WAVES by the director, Lieutenant Commander Mildred McAfee. It was the proudest moment of my life. There was a large photo of the event hanging there in my office in Havana. I look pretty innocent in it.

At the beginning of the war, no WAVES served outside the U.S., but as time passed, they were sent wherever it was necessary. I ended up in Havana, serving in intelligence first as a cryptologist breaking codes, but then as a liaison working with American and Cuban Naval officers, a position that required knowledge of Spanish. Cuba, which declared war on both Germany and Japan in 1941, had a close relationship with the U.S., and was a vital ally during the war because of its strategic location on the Gulf of Mexico. The Cuban Navy's most important role was in escorting hundreds of American ships and protecting them from German submarines. Everyone was doing their part for the war effort—even Ernest Hemingway armed his boat, the *Pilar*, with machine guns, bazookas, and hand grenades, and was patrolling the Cuban waters for U-boats.

My wish to be assigned as a Code Girl working in intelligence was realized. Because we had been required to take a vow of secrecy regarding our work, it was only after the war had ended that I found out how vital the contribution of us Code Girls (there were ten thousand of us) had been in the success of the United States and its allies in winning it. The work was a bit tedious, mostly having to do with comparing and recognizing patterns in the communications between the enemy, but our ability in breaking secret codes provided invaluable advantages for the Allied powers. As a Code Girl trained in cryptography, I acquired critical skills in seeing different ways of solving problems that would help with my work as a private investigator. And it wasn't just the experience that I had gained as a Code Girl that served me well; it was the relationships I developed that proved invaluable.

After the war ended, I decided I would stay in Havana, but the big question was what came next. Because my expenses had been minimal—the Navy had covered all my needs while I had been stationed in Cuba—I had quite a bit of money saved up, so I had options. I had met Big Pete while a Code Girl—he had been a radio operator in my office—and we became friends—thankfully we were not attracted to each other, so no romance would complicate our relationship. We both hated winter and refused to return to our hometowns after the war (he was from Minneapolis). Pete said that if I was staying in Havana, that was good enough for him. He would do the same.

It didn't take too long to figure out that a private investigator could make money in Havana, and that not only did the work suit me, it fit my personality and skill set. I conducted a bit of research, looking through phone books in the Navy library and making calls to P.I.s in the States. They were mostly helpful in sharing what was needed to get started, but they were also all men. None of them had ever heard of a woman working in the field. So, I ended up calling the firm S.O. (for Sophie and Ophelia—my mom had been reading *Hamlet* for the fifteenth time when she was pregnant with me) Stevenson and Brothers (because it sounded like there were a lot of men involved). I knew that S.O.S. sounded like we needed help, but it was too late. The name stuck.

My office had been open for over two years, and we never lacked for jobs. We took both Cuban and American clients, pretty much evenly divided between the two. The American cases often involved finance, such as checking out business partners or investigating new expats in the city. The Cuban cases mostly entailed providing proof of a spouse's infidelity—primarily husbands. It was basically engrained in Cuban men's DNA to be unfaithful to their wives, and we had a nearly one hundred percent success rate in proving it. Cuba was a Catholic country, and female clients couldn't resort to divorce to deal with their husbands' treachery, but the situation benefited me and Big Pete. We lived in apartments near each other in Old Havana within walking distance of the office. Both were spacious, with nice furniture and, perhaps more important, views of the sea.

Things worked out well with Pete. In spite of his nightly adventures into the seedy side of Havana, he was remarkably well-organized and a meticulous bookkeeper. He was also six-four and easily three hundred pounds, with a chest as thick as a sequoia tree. He had jet black eyes that could melt ice and curly brown hair that always needed a trim. He was hardly effective working undercover, but he got things done.

Pete really enjoyed following errant husbands into hot-sheets hotels to catch them in their extramarital hijinks with young women who turned out to be their children's piano teachers or their wives' hairdressers. One thing these husbands had in common was they did not wander far from home. A notable exception was when they visited the Casa Marina Brothel on Colon Street, a palatial, luxurious, and notorious place that catered to all levels of society.

With my training in intelligence, I was becoming a bit tired of dealing with cases of infidelity, but, as those were the ones that came through our doors, those were the ones that we worked. Still, I would have welcomed a challenge.

I looked as different from Big Pete as I possibly could. I was five feet if I was in heels and there was an updraft. With a body that was a bit too curvy for my taste (but not for men's), delicate looks with blonde hair, blue eyes, and fair skin, I didn't blend into Havana any better than Pete did.

My job was to handle clients (with a lot of handholding),

direct the investigations, interview witnesses, and write the reports. We had good word of mouth because we got results. There was only one other American-run investigative firm in Havana, owned and operated by John Livingston, a retired FBI agent who had been to Havana on his honeymoon and loved it so much that he ended up here. We were friendly, for the most part, and helped each other out from time to time.

I heard loud voices coming from the reception area. One was Pete's; the other belonged to a stranger. "S.O.S. means Sophie? A dame? What's the gag here! I want to meet one of the brothers, not some little girl!"

"Sorry, Mr. Smith." Pete was trying to calm the man down. "None of the brothers are here at the moment. But Miss Stevenson is. She's one of our very best investigators, and she's able to meet with you now."

I strained to hear the man's response. This wasn't the first time a potential client balked at meeting with me or refused to hire us on a case because I was a woman. I didn't get angry about it; it was just the way things were.

After a long pause, the man spoke again. "All right. I'm already here. Might as well meet with her. Let's get on with it."

I heard Pete getting out of his chair and heading toward my office. He knocked on the door, then opened it with an air of formality. "Miss Stevenson. Mr. Smith is here to see you."

"Please show him in," I watched John Smith walk into the room.

"Mr. Smith, so pleased to meet you. I'm Sophie Stevenson." I held out my hand for him to shake, but he was still angry so it was a few seconds before he reluctantly took it. "Please, sit." The man stared at me, openly checking me out before sitting in the chair across from my desk. A tough customer, but not my first.

In fitting with his surely fake name, he was unremarkable looking, small of build, with light brown eyes and hair that was beginning to thin. He wore a dark blue suit, unusual for Cuba's steamy climate where men mostly wore cotton shirts or the traditional guayabera, a loose-fitting pleated top. He was tightly clutching a black leather satchel.

"What can I help you with?" I asked politely. "Just to start, please understand that whatever you tell me will be kept in confidence. It's privileged information."

From his suspicious expression, it was clear that Smith wasn't convinced that he should share with me his reason for needing an investigator. "No one will know?"

I shook my head. "I assure you, Mr. Smith."

All at once, his composure collapsed. "It's about Fifi LaFleur," he blurted out. "She's missing. I don't know what to do!"

"We have a lot of experience with missing persons cases," I explained. "Let's please start with you giving me background information so we can start looking for Miss LaFleur." From the name, I figured that the missing person was an exotic dancer or worked in some other form of adult entertainment. And it wouldn't be her real name.

Mr. Smith carefully opened his satchel and brought out a manila envelope. He unclasped its folded edge and pulled out an eight-by-ten photograph that he placed face down on his lap. After taking a deep breath and eyeing me with sadness, he turned it over. It was a picture of a very large, very black poodle, with little pink bows on her ears and a larger matching one on her pom-pom. The portrait looked professional: nicely lit, with a candle burning in the background and scarlet drapes to one side. The poodle looked very serious and dignified.

"This is Fifi La Fleur. You have to find her. We only have two more days, then my whole world will crumble. I need you to work fast." He ordered.

"Fifi LaFleur is a dog." I couldn't take my eyes off the photograph. She looked more like someone's beloved aunt than just a pooch. "I have to tell you, Mr. Smith, that we really don't do a lot of work with animals. We mostly find lost humans."

Mr. Smith nodded vigorously and jabbed his finger at the picture. "Fifi is my wife's dog, you see. She loves her very much.

We don't have any children, so Fifi is like our daughter. We've had her for more than ten years."

"I see." To be fair, Fifi looked more like a person than something you would walk on a leash.

"Fifi LaFleur is my wife's entire life." Mr. Smith was babbling now, on the verge of tears. "I just don't know what she'll do if Fifi is gone. I don't know if things could go on as before."

I took a deep breath. "Please start at the beginning. How long has Fifi been missing? What were the circumstances of her disappearance?" I figured someone had left a back gate open and the dog had run away. How many ways were there for a poodle to go missing?

Mr. Smith picked up the photo of Fifi and clutched it to his chest. "She's been gone two days. Since Tuesday. That's the last time I saw her."

"Okay," I jotted that down on a pad of paper. "And how did she disappear?"

Mr. Smith gave me a piercing look. "You said everything I tell you is confidential? That no one will have to know what I've done?" That was an interesting way to put it. I nodded again. "Miss Stevenson, Ethel and I have been married for fifteen years. As I told you, we don't have any children. The marriage has been a good one, for the most part. There's love between us but for the last five years, Ethel has been having lady problems." He spoke those last two words very delicately. "So…you see, as a result, the physical aspect of our relationship has not been satisfying." He looked down at the photo of Fifi as though seeking emotional support. "A man has needs. You understand, Miss Stevenson."

"Of course. I understand." I tried to be encouraging, all the while wondering how this man's sexual needs intersected with a big black poodle.

"Ethel has been home in New Jersey for an entire month. She's been visiting her family. But she's returning this weekend, on Saturday, in fact. And Fifi LaFleur absolutely has to be waiting for her when her flight lands. There's no way Fifi can be missing!"

I jotted down some more notes. "Where was Fifi when you last saw her? I need to know exactly when, where, and under what conditions."

Mr. Smith looked down. "I can't give you a straightforward answer to that question without explaining something delicate to you. And I very much don't want you to judge me."

Okay, now I was really curious. "Mr. Smith, trust me when I say that I've seen and heard all kinds of stories in my work as an investigator. Before I opened this firm, I spent three years in the Navy. There's no way I'm going to judge you for anything. But if I'm going to help you, Fifi, and your wife, you're going to have to tell me everything. And now. Saturday is coming up fast."

He was quiet for a moment before speaking again. "For just a little more than two years, I've been seeing a woman named Rosita Mendoza. She's one of the dancers at the Tropicana. I meet with her about once a week, and I help her out with money. Dancers don't make much, at least not enough for her. She has a lot of expenses. I pay for Rosita's apartment in the Vedado. It's not much. Just three rooms, but it's nice."

That added up—explained how his "needs" were being satisfied. Mr. Smith didn't look like a stereotypical sugar daddy, but apparently that's exactly what he was. "And how is all this with Rosita connected to Fifi's disappearance?"

"Fifi doesn't like to be left alone in the house. She howls so loudly that the neighbors always complain and this time Ethel has been gone for a whole month. You have to understand, we have live-in servants—a maid, a cook, and a driver. I don't want them to know when I leave at night to visit Rosita, so I give them those nights off. And since Fifi can't be left alone, I have to take her to Rosita's place."

I was beginning to see where this was headed. "So, the last time you visited Rosita, this was when Fifi went missing?"

Mr. Smith nodded. "But it gets even more complicated, Miss Stevenson." He reached into his satchel again, brought out a torn piece of paper, and handed it to me. "Here. I received this yesterday."

It was written in Spanish, but I translated it as I read it out loud. "If you want to see your dog alive again, you will have to pay two hundred U.S. dollars. Bring the money in a red handkerchief this Friday to Sloppy Joe's at exactly noon. A man will take it from you and give you the address where your dog is being kept safe for now."

"How did you get this?" I flipped the paper over; it was blank on the other side.

"It was dropped on my receptionist's desk when she was out to lunch," Mr. Smith told me. "I'm in the sugar business. I'm a broker. Our office is very busy, lots of activity. We have messengers and delivery people going in and out all day, so it could have been anyone."

I looked up at him. "Do you have any gut feeling about who might have Fifi?"

"I've been thinking about it a lot, as you might imagine. And no. I really have no idea who might have taken her." Mr. Smith replied.

Somehow, I did not fully believe him. "Okay. Then describe for me the circumstances of how you visited Rosita. You said she has a three-bedroom apartment on the Vedado. So, I assume that's one bedroom and one living room. What does she use the other room for?" I needed more details, delicate as they might be.

"That third room is smaller than the other two. It's where Rosita keeps her costumes. Her makeup, too. Not that there's a much material or fabrics, you know, with the kind of dancing she does, but there's lots of lace and feathers and glittery stuff." Mr. Smith got a faraway look in his eyes. "And she has pasties—you know, the things that cover the breasts. The nipples, to be specific. With tassels on them. The pasties, not the nipples. Rosita twirls them around when she dances. Everyone knows her now for how good she is at that—trick.It's made her famous. It's very exciting."

Men! "So, when you and Rosita go into her bedroom, where does Fifi go then?" I was going to assume that the poodle wasn't a witness to Mr. Smith and Rosita's sexual exploits.

"Fifi stays in the room with all the costumes. There's a little couch in there, where she likes to lie down and sleep. Sometimes I've caught her messing around in Rosita's things, but for the most part she's a good girl," Mr. Smith reported.

"So, you bring Fifi every time when you visit Rosita while your wife is away?" It felt important to establish that there was a pattern. "Does your wife travel a lot? Is it a regular thing for her to be out of town?"

Mr. Smith took a deep breath before speaking again. "Yes. I always take Fifi with me. As I explained, she howls when she's alone which is problematic. I don't want the servants to know that I go out at night when Ethel is away. She travels maybe six times a year—every couple of months—to her family in New Jersey. She misses her home in America. And up until now, there's never been a problem for me. Fifi is always...waiting when we're done."

"Tell me everything you remember about the last time you saw Fifi." Now that Mr. Smith had come clean, I hoped that his memory would be clearer.

His face reddened. "Miss Stevenson, I don't know. I really don't know what I have that can help you."

"Try."

Mr. Smith looked down at his hands. "I took her to Rosita's as always. I was tired. When I got there, Rosita gave me a drink. I think it was a mojito, something with rum in it. I shouldn't have had it, because I fell asleep and I was out for hours. When I woke up, I was alone. Rosita wasn't there any longer, and it was almost morning. I panicked when I couldn't find Fifi or Rosita, but I needed to hurry home before the servants woke up and saw me missing. At lunchtime, I went back to the apartment, figuring I would find Rosita and Fifi. But no one was there! And the place was all locked up."

This didn't make sense. Or maybe it did. "Don't you have a key to the apartment? After all, you're paying for it."

"No, I don't have a key." Mr. Smith shook his head. "Rosita never wanted me to have one. She says she needs her privacy."

Privacy? This was a woman who danced almost naked in front of dozens of men every night twirling her pasties. "After you went to the apartment and found it locked up, did you go looking for Rosita at the Tropicana?"

"Yes, of course I did." Mr. Smith seemed vaguely offended, as though I was calling him an idiot. "Rosita was there. She was rehearsing for the show that night. She said she didn't know anything about Fifi being missing. She told me I had too much to drink, and maybe I did, and that when she left early in the morning, I was still asleep, and Fifi was still in the costume room. At least as far as she knew. She said she didn't check."

"Okay, so Rosita was no help at all." I decided to try something else. "What about the servants? How did you explain why Fifi wasn't in the house? They must have noticed she was gone."

"I told them that Fifi ate something that disagreed with her, and that I had to take her to the vet overnight. I said that Fifi is okay, but that the vet needs to keep her for a few days of observation before letting her come home."

"Mr. Smith, I need you to answer me honestly." I looked into his eyes. It was time to get down to business. "Do you suspect that Rosita had anything to do with Fifi's disappearance? It sounds strange to me that you passed out right after Rosita gave you a drink."

He looked away, then back at me, totally miserable. "I don't know, I really don't." He blinked, as though tears might come. "I've given it a lot of thought."

"And what have you come up with?" It was becoming clear that he had someone in mind.

"The only thing I can think is that Rosita's manager has something to do with all of this. He used to be Rosita's boyfriend, but she broke up with him before she and I got together. But he still hangs around. She says she wants to get rid of him, but he's still involved in her business," Mr. Smith mumbled.

We were getting close. "And does this manager know about you? And the fact that you pay for her apartment?"

Mr. Smith shrugged. "I assume so. Rosita probably told him."

"Do you have the manager's name and address?" From what Mr. Smith was telling me, hopefully finding Fifi LaFleur was not going to be all that difficult.

"His name is Ramon Perez, but I don't know his address. I've never actually met him, but I think I've seen him at the Tropicana. He's short, very short, and stocky and bald. I don't understand what Rosita was doing with him in the first place. But I think I remember her saying that Ramon lives in an apartment in El Vedado, so not far from here."

We didn't have a lot of time—it was already Thursday—so I stood up and walked around my desk. I held out my hand, and he shook it properly this time. "I think I have what I need to start looking for Fifi. Please stop by Pete's desk on your way out and give him your details. And we'll need a retainer."

Mr. Smith almost jumped out of his chair. "You can find her? You can do this?"

"I can't promise you that. But I can tell you that S.O. Stevenson and Brothers will do our very best. We'll work your case as though Fifi were our own...family. I'll let you know as soon as there's anything to report." I ushered him out of the office.

Ten minutes later, Pete came in and sat down in the chair that Mr. Smith had occupied. Pete had been busy making himself presentable while I had been talking to Mr. Smith. He had washed up and put on a clean shirt, a definite improvement.

"So, now we're looking for a French poodle?" Pete teased. "Fifi LaFleur? Your training in intelligence with the Code Girls will come in useful in finding Fifi LaFleur."

"For sure." I couldn't help but laugh. "So, who is Mr. Smith really?" Our client had to give his real name and address when he filled out our retainer agreement—and left a check, of course.

Pete started reading from a sheet of paper in his hand. "His name is Emmett Hillsdale. He's the president and owner of a sugar broker outfit called Almendares and Company. Lives in a house in Alturas de Miramar."

"Nice neighborhood," I commented. "His retainer check should clear with no problem."

"Fingers crossed." Pete chuckled.

I looked down at my notes and told Pete the details of the case. "Sounds like this manager, Ramon Perez, has the dog, based on what Emmett says. You'll probably be able to find him hanging around the Tropicana, sounds like he lurks around Rosita a lot of the time. He's very short, stocky, and bald."

Pete stood up. "Got it. I'd better get going. I'll see if Ramon is there, and if he is, I'll follow him home. He'll have to take Fifi outside at some point to do her business."

"Good plan, but there's more." I showed Pete the ransom note. His Spanish was good enough that I didn't have to translate it for him. "If you don't see him with the dog tonight, there's always this meeting at Sloppy Joe's tomorrow."

Pete looked up from the note. "Sophie, you're assuming that Ramon is the one who has Fifi. But what if it's someone else?"

"Like who?" It's true that I had pretty much come to the conclusion that Ramon was the one who had dognapped Fifi.

"I don't know. A former employee with a grudge? A business partner who hates this guy?" Pete suggested. "A jealous former girlfriend?'

"I know I don't usually make a habit of jumping to conclusions, but my gut tells me it's Ramon," I explained my reasoning. "Rosita has a good thing going with Emmett so I don't think she would risk everything for a couple hundred dollars."

Pete looked only partially convinced. "You're the boss, Sophie."

"And we only have until Saturday to get Fifi back." I reminded him.

"Got it." And with that, Pete left.

I spent the rest of the day catching up on other cases, so,

when I hadn't heard from Pete by eight o'clock, I left the office. It had been a long day, and I was tired and hungry. Walking home, I stopped by the restaurant on the corner by my apartment and ordered a huge plate of *arroz con pollo* and *maduros*—chicken with yellow rice and plantains, the unofficial Cuban national dish—to take home with me. I clearly wasn't in Vermont anymore. I also picked up a bottle of red wine to wash it down with. (The hell with my resolution to quit drinking.) Once I got home, I stripped off my clothes and inhaled it all.

At three in the morning, the telephone on my bedside table rang. It was Pete. "You were right, Sophie. Ramon has the dog. I spotted him at the Tropicana. He stayed there until the show ended about two hours ago. He followed Rosita back to the apartment. The creep is stalking her. It's sick."

"How do you mean?" I flipped the light on.

"I was hiding across the street while he looked in her window and let's just say he took care of his own needs," Pete reported.

"*Gross.*"

"Yeah, and he didn't leave until she had turned off all her lights. After that, I followed him back to his apartment building. Our client was right about one thing—Fifi LaFleur doesn't like to be left alone. I could hear that damn dog howling from halfway down the block."

That poor dog, I couldn't help thinking.

"I waited and watched the entrance to the building. He didn't come out to walk the dog at all. I planned to jump him and clean his clock once he took the dog out, but it never happened. I was pissed off about that. I watched from downstairs until I figured out which apartment is his, then I climbed up the fire escape until I was on his balcony. I looked in and saw a big black dog tied to a chair by a leash. I got a pretty good look at the whole place."

I pictured Pete climbing up a fire escape. It was a wonder he didn't bring down the whole building. "Oh, Pete! You could have fallen!"

Pete ignored my outburst. "Sophie, there was no way I could

get the dog. Ramon was right in the room, sleeping next to her. He would have raised hell if I barged in, and who knows how the dog would have reacted. She doesn't seem young—could she run with me if I grabbed her? Too many variables."

"You did great." I sat up and started thinking, my mind going a mile a minute. "We'll have to get into the apartment and take her tomorrow when Ramon does the drop-off with Emmett at Sloppy Joe's. I'll get in touch with Emmett before then and let him know what's going on—and that he isn't going to have to pay the ransom."

"Good thinking. Your background in intelligence has certainly paid off." Pete chuckled on the other end of the line. "This might be the fastest one we've ever solved. We might have to pad the hours a little to make it seem as if it was more difficult than it was to find Fifi. Show we had to work long and hard to do that."

"I don't think that will be necessary. I have a feeling Emmett is going to be happy to pay us," I told him. "Now go have some fun. You earned it." I fell back asleep, but early the next morning I was awakened by a loud banging on my apartment door.

"It's me, Pete," a voice called from the other side of the door.

I quickly walked towards the door. "Pete? What the hell are you doing here?"

"Open up the door, Sophie. I have something important to show you." Pete called out in a loud voice.

I opened up, and there they were: Pete, and a big black dog standing by his side. "Miss Fifi LaFleur, I presume." I held the door open for both of them.

"I know the plan was for me to grab Fifi while Ramon went to the meeting at Sloppy Joe's, but I got even more pissed off that this scumbag dognapped Fifi. After I saw her in person, I couldn't stand the idea of Ramon having her for a moment longer, so I decided to act." Fifi sat down by Pete's side, calm and collected, as she watched us talking. "This guy Ramon is the lowest form of humanity. Stealing a dog and ransoming her. Stalking Rosita and playing peeping Tom when she doesn't know he's there." Pete reached down and stroked the top of Fifi's head; she closed her eyes happily. "He tied this poor girl to a chair! I had to teach him a lesson about how not to treat females—even if one was a dog."

Teach him a lesson? "Oh, Pete." I couldn't think of anything else to say. Pete often used his fists to settle things, especially when he felt he was righting a wrong. He had been a Golden Gloves contender before the Navy, and I had seen more than once the damage he could do. Pete was looking at me as though seeking my approval.

"Yeah, I broke into Ramon's apartment after we got off the phone. I gave him a little tune-up, took Fifi, and here I am!" Pete pointed to dark spots of what looked like blood on his shirt, flaking a couple of them off with his fingernail. "Oops, I got some of Ramon on me."

I didn't figure this was going to lead to trouble. Ramon sounded like a piece of work who wasn't going to run to the police to file a report. Still, I had to know. "How bad was this tune-up?"

"Well, Sophie, I don't think we really need to go into the details. But he's not going to be fulfilling his naughty-boy needs into anybody's window anytime soon. Or stalking any women." Pete announced with a touch of pride.

Fifi seemed to be looking up at Pete with admiration, so I figured it was time to change the subject. "I'll call Emmett and give him the good news. I'll head to the office once I've gotten dressed."

"Okay. I'll make sure this good girl has some nice clean water. Who knows if that jackass gave her anything to drink or to eat. Probably not, right, good girl?" Pete, the tough guy I had known for years, was lapsing into baby talk with Fifi. Tail wagging, she followed him to the kitchen.

Emmett was waiting for me when I arrived with Fifi at the office a couple of hours later. The poodle started jumping up and down the moment she saw him and showered him with kisses. He checked her out to make sure she wasn't hurt. Once the reunion was complete, the two of them quickly left.

I spent that weekend quietly at home, mostly reading the stack of newspapers I'd accumulated during the busy week. The news of what was happening in Cuba was disturbing. There were reports that there had been a meeting of the U.S. Mafia Cosa Nostra at the Hotel Nacional in December, a mob summit the papers were calling The Havana Conference. Frank Sinatra had sung at the gala dinner that kicked things off. The story was that the crime families had assembled there to make decisions about how they were going to operate in the future.

My main concern was how this was going to impact life in Havana. Fulgencio Batista was the president of the country, and word was that he was allied with the American gangsters. I hoped those stories weren't true, because Havana was already saturated with corruption. I didn't want things to get any worse, and I certainly didn't want to have to go back to Vermont.

On Saturday, I had a mental image of the happy reunion of Ethel Hillsdale with her beloved Fifi LaFleur. I hadn't heard from Emmett, so I assumed all had gone well. We had bailed him out of a disastrous situation.

At around noon on Monday, Pete barged into my office without knocking. He closed the door behind him with a bang, his eyes wide. "Sophie. You won't believe who I have out there."

"I don't feel like guessing." I looked up from a file. "Who is it?"

"Mrs. Ethel Hillsdale, aka: Mrs. John Smith." Pete announced somewhat breathlessly. "She's asking for you by name."

"What? Did she say why?" My heart started beating fast. "Is she alone? Is Fifi LaFleur with her?"

"She's alone. No Emmett. No Fifi." Pete looked as though he might have a stroke.

I had no choice. "Send her in, then."

Pete couldn't get out of my office fast enough. In came a small, well-dressed woman who looked to be in her late forties.

Ethel looked very prim and proper, with light skin, watery-colored eyes, brows that urgently needed plucking, and dirty blonde hair worn in a bun at the back of her neck. Her mouth was set in a tight, unsmiling line. One look at her, and I could understand the appeal of Rosita.

"Welcome. Please sit." I motioned to the chair her husband had occupied last week. "I'm Sophie Stevenson. How can I help you?"

"I came to you because you're a woman and because you're an American." Ethel's tone was extremely serious. "I asked around the American community here, and your name came up more than once. I think you might be the right person to help me. I am here because of a delicate situation. Very delicate, in fact. One that I think requires the services of a woman."

Oh God. What now?

Ethel then gave me the same look her husband had, making up her mind whether she could trust me. It became clear that Emmett did not know that his wife had come to see me, otherwise she would not have had to check me out with the American community. I must have passed the test, because she opened up her purse and took out a manila envelope. The same kind that Emmett had brought.

Like a condemned prisoner who couldn't take his eyes off the firing squad facing him, I stared at that envelope. And sure enough, my fears were realized when she showed me the same portrait photograph of Fifi LaFleur that Emmett had shown me less than a week before.

"This is my dog. Fifi LaFleur. I'm here because of her," Mrs. Hillsdale announced.

"She's beautiful," was all I could manage to say.

Mrs. Hillsdale nodded slowly. "Yes, she is. You see, Miss Stevenson, my husband and I never had children. Fifi is like our daughter."

"I see." A feeling of déjà vu was very strong in that moment.

"I went back home to New Jersey for a month recently. In fact, I got back just this last Saturday. Fifi was acting strangely—

hardly moving and passing a lot of gas. I could tell something was wrong, so I took her to an emergency veterinarian." Mrs. Hillsdale took a handkerchief from her purse and dabbed at the tears that were starting to flow down her cheeks.

"What happened at the emergency vet?" Just then, I could barely speak.

"Fifi has recovered, thank God! But it was touch and go for a few hours." Mrs. Hillsdale raised her eyes toward heaven and crossed herself. "The doctor found out that Fifi had swallowed something that caused an intestinal obstruction. He had to cut open her stomach to remove the object."

"And...what was the object?" A feeling of dread washed over me.

Ethel reached into her purse and took out a small brown paper bag. She opened it, and delicately removed a pair of pasties with gold fringe and a matching pair of tiny panties and placed them in the middle of my desk.

"This is what was in Fifi's stomach. This is what almost killed her!" Mrs. Hillsdale declared. She pointed at the offending items on my desk with a look of total disgust.

I just looked down at my desk. "Oh."

"I plan to punish whoever let her swallow these disgusting things. I need to know where she found them, who knew about it, and who was keeping secrets from me." She gave me a cruel little smile and patted her purse. "I have a gun, Miss Stevenson. A big one. And I know how to use it."

Of course, I knew where Fifi had come across these items, which probably looked shiny and delicious to a dog who was bored while her master was committing adultery in the next room. But there was no way I could tell Mrs. Hillsdale that. I'd never been suicidal.

Suddenly, winter in Vermont didn't seem so terrible.

SCARS OF LOVE
Brendan DuBois

I had another late night barhopping in Southie with uncles, cousins, and second cousins, so my head was throbbing some as I went to the three-story brick building in Boston's famed Scollay Square that housed my office, carrying a take-out coffee from my late breakfast.

I opened the wooden door that led to a grimy small foyer, and then upstairs, the stairs creaking under my heavy footsteps. At the first landing a narrow hallway led off, three doors on each side, each door with a half frame of frosted glass. Mine said B. SULLIVAN, INVESTIGATIONS, and two of the windows down the hallway were blank. The other three announced an attorney, a piano teacher, and a press agent. There was some yelling coming from the press agent's office, a high-pitched girl's voice being part of the action.

I shook my head as I unlocked the door leading into my office. Almost a weekly occurrence, when some poor young girl who's taken a bus from Maine, Vermont, or New Hampshire to seek her initial fame in local theater ends up with that piece of sludge down the way. After a week of promises, new dresses, makeup sessions and the like, the girls are in serious debt, and they're forced to pay it off by dancing at one of the local stages wearing panties and pasties.

Most of these girls—while naïve—are tough farm or mill girls, and they don't like being screwed around like that. When I had first moved here, I had heard the screaming and had gone down to the office, slugged the sleaze press agent in his big nose, and let the girl leave. A day later two heavy-set guys in nice suits and speaking with an Irish lilt told me that while the press agent was an asshole, he was their asshole, and would I please not interfere with his business anymore?

Or words to that effect.

In turn, I said, I'd leave him alone if the yelling stayed yelling. If it turned to screaming, I was going back in.

We all agreed that was a fair deal, and I hadn't seen the two guys since.

I flicked open the light and walked in, and there was a sheet of paper on the wooden floor. I bent down and picked it up, and there was a note for me, the handwriting shaky.

Dear Mister Sullivan, I hope to meet you at ten a.m. on Wednesday to discuss hiring you for a matter, thank you very much, Peter Collins.

I checked my watch. It was ten minutes to ten.

I shook my head, put my take-out coffee on an old oak desk that had been left here when the previous tenant—another bookkeeper—had moved out. Rumor had it that he worked for a couple of the mob families in the city and was caught skimming, and his next place of residence was the bottom of Boston Harbor.

I took my coat off, hung it up on a coat stand, and surveyed my office, which consisted of the desk, a chair, a Remington typewriter on a stand, two solid metal filing cabinets with locks, and two wooden chairs in front of the desk. The only illumination came from a single window that hadn't been washed since at least Pearl Harbor, but it still had a good overview of the square.

There was a curtain near the window that hid a small room with a bed, radio, easy chair, table lamp, and icebox. A closed door there led to a small bathroom that most days had plenty of hot water and a nice big bathtub.

I checked the time again.

Ten a.m.

A shadow came by the glazed glass and there was a knock on the door.

"Come on in," I said, and I went around my desk, wishing I had gotten here a few minutes earlier, at least to brush my teeth and comb my hair.

I was hoping Mister Collins didn't care.

The door swung open and a man about my size and age came in, limping a bit. He had on gray flannel slacks, a white shirt with red and blue necktie, and a blue jacket. He also had on light tan gloves, and his eyes were hooded, haunted, and I think his face explained it all.

About half of his face was furrowed and shiny pink with burn tissue, as was most of his neck.

I didn't blink, didn't move away, but held out a hand. The war had been over just a year and the streets still had the veterans who had come back in wheelchairs, crutches, hooks where hands were once, and faces twisted by scar tissue.

He smiled, best as he could, and held up both of his glove-covered hands.

"Sorry," he said. "Hands still aren't there yet in the healing process. Can't risk it."

I took my hand back. "I understand. Pete Collins?"

He nodded. "And you're Mister Sullivan."

I stepped back. "Please, call me Billy. Everybody else does."

I went back to my desk, sat down, and looked at my potential client limp in, and saw how carefully he lowered himself to the chair, like whatever caused his burns had also made him wary of almost everything else.

"Well, Mister Collins, can I get you anything?"

"If you're Billy, then I'm Pete," he said. "And I could go for a cup of coffee."

It would take time to brew something in my little living space, so I passed over my fresh cardboard cup. "Lucky for you, I brought this along in case you wanted it," I said. "Black, two sugars all right? I've got some cream in my icebox."

"Nope, that'd be fine." He took a long look around my small office and apartment, and said, "Pretty small quarters. You got a wife, girlfriend?"

"No, and no," I said.

"Haven't found the right one yet?"

"You could say that."

He carefully took off the cover from the coffee and said, "How did you become a private investigator?"

"I was in the Military Police during the war, in the ETO," I said. "I found I had a skill for investigating things. When I got mustered out, I decided I'd keep on investigating, and work for myself."

"Why not get a job at the Boston police when you came back home?"

Because I didn't want to become another Sullivan boy in the force, I thought, and I didn't want to be under multiple sets of eyes, and I didn't want to get caught into the whole sleazy world of payoffs, kickbacks, and shaking down dope dealers and hookers.

"My choice," I said.

He took a noisy slurp from the coffee cup, and I saw the burn tissue extended up both wrists. I uncapped my Parker fountain pen and said, "So how do you think I can help you, Pete?"

He put the cup back down on my desk. "I want to hire you to find my wife, Jenny."

I started to write on a notepad. "Did she leave you?"

"No," he said.

"Well, when did you last see her?"

"On the evening of November 28, 1942."

I looked up. "That was four years ago. How are you certain of the date?"

"Because we were together that night, at the Cocoanut Grove nightclub."

I slowly put my pen down on my table, feeling queasy.

"The fire," I said. "The two of you were there."

A slow nod. "Nearly five hundred people died that night. I survived, and I know she did, too. But I don't know where she is."

I stared at his haunted eyes. "What happened that night?"

"You don't know?"

"I was in Mississippi at the time, going through basic," I said. "All I knew about it was the newspaper clippings my mother sent me. It started fast, the cause is still up in the air, and most of the exits were blocked. I read the main entrance was a revolving door that got jammed by...well, got jammed."

"Bodies," he said. "Jammed by desperate people trying to escape."

He blinked, sighed. "The nightclub was a mess of rooms and corridors. Dimly lit. It had passed fire inspection only by bribes and because the mob was connected to the joint. I was there with Jenny, my wife. Just a night out on the town because I got promoted. I worked as a welder at the Fore River Shipyard, over in Quincy. Jenny, she was a schoolteacher. If I didn't get drafted—at the time I had a Class II-A deferment because of my city job—we were making enough to get out of the city, maybe buy a small house, start a family."

My mouth was dry. I had heard similar dreams and thoughts from guys I had served with, over in Europe. Get home, marry the girl next door, have a couple of kids, get a good job with steady pay, and never, ever march or sleep outside ever again.

A lot of those guys, though, never left Europe, having been cut down by a hidden German machine gun nest, or sliced into pieces by mortar fire, or having their truck disintegrated by an 88 mm shell.

"I see," I said. "If you can tell me, what happened that night?"

His voice was flat and nearly unemotional. "The place was done up to look like some sort of South Seas paradise. Fake palm trees, bamboo fences, satin canopies on the ceilings. Very lush, very pretty, not like a standard Boston nightclub at all."

The fountain pen felt heavy in my hand. I didn't know what to say.

He said, "The place was jammed. Really, really jammed, but everyone was having so much fun. I mean, the war was less than a year old, and folks were looking to blow off steam. Lots of soldiers and sailors there...and then we smelled smoke. Didn't think much of it, I mean, maybe something was burning in the kitchen. Then...in a couple of minutes, it all went to hell. The smoke got thicker, people started screaming, and I grabbed Jenny's hand and started to get the hell out. But it was hard, very hard. Pushing against the crowds, the place got dark, and I fell...and crawled...and I got burned...and crawled...and yelled..."

Pete picked up the cup of coffee. It was shaking as he took another sip.

"I came to outside. Had a firefighter, a nurse, and a priest hovering over me. I passed out again, woke up at Boston City Hospital. I was in a coma for a few days, and when I woke up...that's when I was told by another priest that Jenny had died."

"But..."

"Please, let me finish, all right?" His scarred hands reached for the coffee cup, then returned to his lap. "I was at Boston City Hospital for a couple of weeks. Even got what looked like a sympathy card from Jenny's brothers, calling me a killer, 'cause I hadn't gotten her out. Then me and a couple of others were taken by train to Washington, to Walter Reed, for some experimental treatments for burn victims. The war was ramping up and the War Department knew a lot of burn victims would be coming here and other hospitals. I stayed there for almost a year, then lived on relief and did some odd jobs, whatever I could do."

I said, "Then you came back to Boston."

"Yeah," he said. "Missed the old dump, I did. The war was over and the Red Cross got me a train ticket back here. Found me a job as a filing clerk over at the State House. Then, one day, ran into a bud of mine from Southie who was a state rep, and we got to talking. And…and…"

Peter swallowed. "He told me that Jenny was alive."

I picked up the fountain pen again. "All right. Was he sure?"

"Hell yes, he was sure. He said he saw her walking out of her brother's house in Charlestown, a couple of months ago, clear as day, but then he shut up when he saw how spooked I was. Jenny's brother, Ricky Malone, why, you don't want to piss him off."

"But why did the priest say she was dead? And you said you got a card that said you were a killer, because you left her behind at the club?"

"It was chaos back then, Mister Sullivan."

"Billy," I repeated.

"Complete chaos," he said. "Bodies piled up. Men without wallets, women without purses. ID made on the fly…"

"But if she had survived, why didn't she try to contact you?"

"I wasn't around. And Ricky, if he was pissed at me, wouldn't have helped her. But…it's a miracle, Billy, that she's alive. I've got to find her. I need your help."

His scarred face was immobile on one side, but the side that wasn't burnt was looking at me with a mixture of emotions, from hope to sadness to fear.

"All right," I said. "I'll find her for you."

A while later my office was empty, save for me, after we did the customary paperwork signing and agreeing on my fee—which I gave a secret discount for his injuries—and he told me he was staying at the Crimson Boarding House over across the river in Cambridge. He was staying on the second floor, and gave me the number of the pay phone there.

I spent a few minutes going through the Boston phone book and city directory, and found four Richard Malones in

Charlestown. I made two calls and got lucky on the third.

"Yeah?" came the charming voice.

"Good morning," I said, in my most cheerful bureaucratic voice. "I'm looking for Jenny Malone, sister of Ricky Malone."

"Why do you want to talk to her?" he asked.

"I'm calling on behalf of the March of Dimes and—"

Click.

Fair enough.

I wrote down the address on a scrap of paper—16 Monument Lane, Charlestown—and got out of the office, locked the door behind me, and went outside to Scollay Square. It took me about a minute to grab a Yellow Cab—there were always plenty of cabs around the square, dropping off would-be sinners and picking up would-be repenters, and I gave the mug behind the steering wheel the Charlestown address.

He swiveled his big head and said, "Why do you wanna head over there? You looking for some fun, some action, I could hook you up."

"I'm sure you can, but I just want a ride."

"Charlestown's kinda out of my area."

I slipped him a fiver. "I'll make it worth your while."

He flipped down the meter flag. "You're speaking the language I like."

It took about twenty minutes heading north and going over the North Washington Street Bridge, spanning the Charles River and getting a good view of the moored *USS Constitution*, we got on Monument Avenue and told the driver to pull up a few houses from the address I was looking for. I gave him another fiver and said, "Stick around, will you? This might be quick."

He snapped the five-dollar bill from my hand like a snapping turtle going after a goldfish.

"You only got me for fifteen minutes, pal, so keep that in mind."

"Got it," I said. I got out of the cab and walked down Monument Avenue. The houses here being the traditional three-deckers also known as Irish Battleships. Number 10 was different, a single house, relatively large and well-maintained.

I opened the gate to the white picket fence, went past a statue of the Virgin Mary on one side and St. Anthony on the other.

Up the concrete steps I rang the bell, and rang it again.

Waited.

I hoped the cabbie was still in place, otherwise I'd have to find a packie somewhere with a pay phone and—

The door swung open. A sour-faced man in his fifties stared at me, wearing a sleeveless white T-shirt, khaki pants held up by suspenders, his thick hair combed back, his arms muscular and also hairy, and most of his knuckles looking swollen.

"Yeah?"

"Mister Ricky Malone?"

"What do you want?"

"Good morning, sir," I said, holding out my wallet. "My name is William Sullivan, and I'm a licensed private investigator in the Commonwealth of—"

He slammed the door in my face.

I waited.

Rang the doorbell again, and again, and again.

The door swung open even faster. I interrupted him and said, "I'm looking for your sister, Jenny Malone, on an important matter and—"

"Bug off," and once again, the door slammed.

I waited. Thought maybe I shouldn't have given my new client a discount.

Rang the doorbell, rang the doorbell, and the door swung open even faster, and Ricky Malone was there again, with a snub-nosed .38 revolver in his right hand.

I tipped my old fedora to him, said, "So sorry to bother you, I won't do it again," and I turned and left.

***

Back in the cab the driver said, "Bet that went well."

"Won't take that bet, thanks."

"Where to now, bud?"

I gave him the address—941 Boylston Street in Boston—and he got me there in good time. He parked near the old brick and stone building, the oldest fire station in the city, and home to Engine 33, Ladder 15, and my Uncle Rocky, a lieutenant in the department.

I got out of the cab and paid him off. The driver said, "You want me to stick around?"

"Nope, I should be safe here."

"Yeah, well lucky you, it's not a police station."

The bay doors were open, and two young firefighters were polishing the prewar Mack fire truck and ladder truck. Along the walls were framed photos of old-time firefighters, with thick mustaches and high collars, along with some framed newspaper front pages from infernos past. I nodded to a couple of the others and went past the brass pole, and took the rear stairs up to my uncle's office. His booted feet were up on his desk when I came in, and he was reading that day's *Boston Traveler* newspaper.

"Hey, Billy," he said. "Good to see you. How's my favorite shamus doing?"

He dropped the newspaper, grinned, and went over to the desk, lit up a cigarette. My Uncle Rocky was beefy, with thick forearms, a fleshy red face, and thick brown hair going gray. He took a long drag of his Camel and tapped some ash in an overflowing metal ashtray.

I dragged over a chair, sat down. There were more old posters in his crowded office, a girlie pinup calendar, and two dusty plaques, along with a filing cabinet and an alarm bell set up on the wall near the door.

"Doing all right," I said.

"Chasing any more cheating broads?

"Not as many as you'd think," I said.

He took another puff of his cigarette. "Yeah, well, I can't blame 'em. Lot of these gals got married when the war started, maybe knew their guy a couple of months, and years later, he's back, he's skinny, maybe some scars on his skin, and at night, wakes up screaming."

"Sounds like you know a lot about that, Uncle Rocky."

He gestured with his burning cigarette. "A couple of the probies here, they got the same problem. Bunking here during the night shift, waking up, screaming. Sometimes hitting the ground when a truck backfires. But hey, enough of my problems. What's going on, nephew?"

"The Cocoanut Grove fire, back in '42."

His face darkened, eyes narrowed, and with his thick fingers, he stubbed out the cigarette.

"Why the devil do you want to talk about that horror show?"

"I'm looking into a client of mine, who survived."

"One lucky client."

"I guess so."

He leaned back in his chair, the wood creaking in protest, folded hands over his belly. "Alarms came in and I was on one of the first responding engines. It was like something out of...Hell, you know? The smoke, the screaming, the men and women staggering out, their clothes burnt off, burnt skin sloughing off. We got water on the building in just a couple of minutes but it didn't make much of a difference. There was a revolving door street-side that led inside and was jammed with the bodies of people trying to get out. Even the strongest of our guys had a bitch of a time, trying to pull them free...Doctors and nurses and priests started showing up, and the smell...burnt hair, burnt clothes, burnt flesh."

Then he looked at me and came back to 1946. "What are you looking for, Billy?"

"An official list of the dead and injured," I said.

He nodded. "That'd be Gracie Burke, over at City Hall.

Official archivist. Tell her I sent you over, we went to St. Elizabeth's together."

He rubbed at his face for a moment. "A couple of our probies, they served overseas. Good kids but at night, they have those loud screams and dreams. Got so bad we moved their bunks down to the equipment bay. You get dreams like that, Billy?"

"You know I was only an MP," I said.

"Didn't answer the question, shamus."

I got up to leave. "Thanks for your help, Uncle Rocky."

Lucky for me the Boston Public Library was only a four-block walk up Boylston Street, and being a familiar place to me, I quickly got to work. If it's a place for the latest novel or work of nonfiction or popular magazine, it can't be beat, but for a guy like me, it has more than just that.

City directories, phone books, and yearbooks from area high schools.

I found both Jenny Malone and Pete Collins in the same yearbook from North Quincy High School, class of 1941, and I saw that Jenny's life ambition was to be a good housewife and support the household. Pete's was different of course, for it said he wanted to join the Army and see the world.

Well, I thought, putting everything back where I found it, he didn't find the Army, but he did find the Fore River Shipyard, which sent its ships around the world.

Maybe he took some solace from that.

About ninety minutes later I was at the Bel-Aire Diner on Route 1 in Saugus, north of Boston. Earlier I used a couple of rolls of nickels and a pay phone and a list of names, and representing myself as an insurance adjuster, a reunion committee member from good ol' North Quincy High School, and an FBI agent doing a background investigation of Jenny Malone, I found her here, at a diner with large windows, silver metal roof, and blue sides.

I parked my prewar Model A in an empty spot, and slipping on my fedora, walked up the steps into the diner. I kept my car at a garage near Scollay Square and tried to drive it as little as possible. Gas rationing had been lifted for a year, but good tires were still hard to find.

Inside the diner it seemed it was mostly truck trade, with bulky guys in leather coats and worn cloth caps with Teamster pins stuck in them. There was loud chatter, the smell of grease and cigarette smoke. It had about a dozen booths and a large wraparound seating place with stools. I took a free stool and instantly saw Jenny Malone Collins, wife of Pete Collins.

Like the other three waitresses, she wore a pink uniform and her name, Sue, was stitched in white thread over the left breast. She joked and chatted with her customers, but she was different, in a lot of ways. As much as she tried to hide it, she limped going from customer to customer, and to the open area leading to the kitchen where orders were passed through.

While the other waitresses' uniforms were short-sleeved, hers were long-sleeved, and even as hot it must be back there, the sleeves were rolled down and buttoned at the cuff. Her hair was a blonde wig, and at the back of her neck and on one cheek, was the shiny flesh of scar tissue.

She didn't serve me but another waitress did, and I ordered a cheeseburger and a Coke, and kept watching Jenny from out of the corner of my eye. She seemed happy, she seemed to be fitting right in, and I wondered what her reaction was going to be when her long-lost husband showed up and begged her to Forgive All.

I paid for my meal and made sure to keep the receipt, for my eventual invoice to Pete Collins.

Not my worry.

I was just doing my job.

That night I tossed and turned in my little room, sleeping and not sleeping, the sheets wrapped around me, feeling so very cold, so very, very cold, remembering and dreaming of January 1945 and the Ardennes and guarding a crossroads, me and a guy named Boone from Kansas, and it was so cold, so very, very cold. We had on our cold weather gear, heavy coats and trousers, knit caps under our dirty helmets, and we stamped our feet as we waited, watched, and waited.

"Friggin' Army," Boone had said. "What are we doin' out here?"

I said, "Maintaining a checkpoint, that's all."

There were the booms of artillery to the east, where the Germans were grinding their way through the collapsing Allied lines, the well-named Battle of the Bulge. Boone saw the flicker of lights and said, "You know what the Krauts like to do, don't you?"

"Kill folks?"

"Yeah...funny guy," Boone had said. "They know where these crossroads are located. Right down to the inch. So it's easy for them to lob an artillery shell or mortar round and hit any crossroads they want, take out the MPs posted there."

I slapped my hands together, stomped my feet. We both had holstered Colt .45 pistols on web belts around our waists, and over our shoulders, we had Thompson submachine guns.

The wind snapped and bit at us.

At my feet was a field telephone, with a line leading a few hundred yards away at a CP. Besides checking the passes for whatever vehicles ground their way to us, we were also to call if there was a breakout here. Rumors were spreading hard and fast, about the Germans shooting prisoners, them using new jet fighters, and even Nazis wearing captured American uniforms and sneaking through the lines, to kill Patton, Montgomery, or Eisenhower.

Boone said, "All I know is that if I see Panzers coming through those woods, I'm hoofing it back to the CP, and screw the orders."

I was thinking of what to say back to him when a whistle/whine screamed out, and explosions thundered up the road, heading straight our way. I dove right and Boone dove left, into shallow frozen drainage ditches that weren't deep enough but were better than nothing. I curled up in a ball, hands over my helmet, trying to shrink in, trying to be as small as possible, forgetting every prayer I ever learned at St. Joseph's High School.

The barrage suddenly stopped. I rolled up and out.

Smoke and dust were drifting across the snowy fields.

Boone started crawling up from his side of the road. He moved slow.

"Boone?" I asked.

No sound.

He moved a few more inches and his head fell off.

I woke up yelling.

In one of the deep corridors and warren of rooms in Boston City Hall on 45 School Street, I met with Gracie Burke, city archivist. She was plump and her black hair was done up in a series of curls. There were no windows, just bookshelves, long rows of drawers, and flickering fluorescent lights overhead.

I took a chair at her crowded desk, and she stubbed out a cigarette in a stone ashtray, and in a soft voice said, "Your Uncle Rocky asked me to help you out. He was nice to me in high school, so here I am, and here are you. What are you looking for?"

I said, "I'd like to see the list of those who were injured at the Cocoanut Grove fire back in 1942."

She frowned. "A nasty business. Why?"

"For a client, that's all."

She shook her head. "A real nasty business. Hold on."

Gracie got up from her chair and went down a row of crowded bookshelves, and I heard drawers being opened and closed. She murmured some to herself and then emerged, blinking, like she was some sort of mole, emerging into the daylight. She had a file folder in her hand and sat down, sighed, and took out a sheaf of onion-skin papers, handed them over to me.

They were carbon copies of what was called GROVE FIRE INJURED and I started running my fingers down the list. Lucky for me, somebody four years back had gone to the trouble of alphabetizing the list, and after a few minutes, I found one of the names I was looking for.

But despite going through the list three more times, another name was absent.

I gave the list back to Gracie. "Thanks."

"Helpful?"

"Very helpful," I said.

She carefully placed the papers back into the file folder. "My boy Tom was a linebacker for the football team at BC. They had a football game that day, against Holy Cross. Everyone thought BC would win, and they had a celebration party scheduled that night at the Grove. But they lost, and the party was canceled, and my Tom and others were spared."

"Lucky son."

A mournful shrug. "Last year his B-17 was shot down over Germany. No parachutes spotted."

"I'm sorry," I said.

A slight smile. "I got him for an extra three years, that's how I like to think about it."

A couple of hours later I was in my old Ford, parked in front of the Crimson Boarding House in Cambridge, and Pete Collins limped out of the house and got into my car.

"Well?"

"Found her," I said.

"Really?" His eyes were bright. "Where?"

"I'll show you."

"But how—"

"Just be quiet," I said.

Where I had found Jenny was northeast of Boston.

I turned around and drove west.

Close to two hours had passed before my client took a break from threatening me, and I drove down an unmarked narrow country road, maybe beyond Concord or thereabouts, and then I stopped the Ford, switching off the engine.

He said, "What the hell is going on here? What are you pulling off?"

I swiveled in my seat. "What's going on here is that I don't like clients who screw around with me, like you."

"I'm not screwing around with you!"

"I've had husbands who wanted to find their missing wives so they could kill them, and the same with wives who here looking for their husbands. I don't know what you're trying to scam here, but I'm done playing."

His face was twisted with anger. "I'm not playing anything."

I said, "I've gone through the city's archives. I've examined lists of those injured at the Cocoanut Grove fire. Your wife is on the list."

I paused. "But you're not."

He took a deep breath.

But didn't talk.

"You tell me what's going on right now, or I'm going to shove you out of my car, and you can hoof it back to Cambridge. How does that sound?"

He remained quiet, but I saw tears form in his right eye.

Not his left.

Then it came to me.

"Where?" I asked. "Navy? Army? Air Corps?"

A slow nod. "Army."

"What happened?"

"Does it matter?"

I said, "Yeah, if you want a ride back home."

Pete turned so he wasn't looking at me. "Truth was, I was at the Cocoanut Grove that night, with my wife Jenny. The fire broke out, it was nearly pitch black, chaos, I grabbed her hand, practically dragged her to go out...and I lost her. I lost her."

He turned and one eye was heavily weeping. "I lost her. I got outside and I looked for her, and looked for...there were people everywhere, laid out on the ground, some men and women so burned, their skin sloughing off...I was her husband. I should have gone back to find her. I should have."

My mouth was getting dry. "The next couple of days were a blur. I found her at Boston City Hospital, and her brothers were outside of her room, and wouldn't let me see her. Coward, they called me. Second time I tried to visit, they beat the crap out of me and dumped me in an alley. Said if I came back again, they'd kill me. And they meant it."

"When did you join up?"

"About a month later. I wanted to prove I was no coward. But she never replied to any of my letters. Then they started coming back stamped with moved, no forwarding address."

"When did you get wounded?"

"March 1945. I was a loader on an M4 Sherman tank, Eighth Tank Battalion, Fourth Armored Division, part of Patton's Third Army. Lots of hard fighting. You know what we called those tanks?"

I knew but I was going to let him tell his story. "Go on."

"Zippos," Pete said. "One good shot and it would burst into flames. With the crew inside. Going against Tiger tanks or 88 mm anti-tank guns was mostly suicide. We were hit outside a small town in Belgium. Some of us got out, some didn't. At the time, I thought those who burned inside and died had it easy..."

He wiped at a weeping eye. "I don't want to talk about it no more."

74

"Okay."

Pete wiped again. "What now?"

"You tell me," I said. "What were you planning when you first hired me?"

A twisted little smile. "Stupid, probably. I was hoping...praying, maybe, that I could meet up with Jenny. That she'd see me, see what happened to me. And she'd know that I was no coward. And maybe...just maybe, she'd take me back. Even with her brothers."

I pushed in the clutch, turned the key. "All right, let's find out."

"But...but suppose she won't take me back?"

I said, "Not my problem, Pete. You hired me to find her, and find her I did. Everything else is up to you."

It was late afternoon and I was parked at the Bel-Aire Diner. Pete wanted me to go in with him and I said, "No, it's yours now. But I'll stick around if you need a ride home."

I parked my Ford in a good place, where I could look through the large plate-glass windows.

Pete appeared from the right, moving slowly, fedora held in both of his hands, going past a few of the booths.

He stood by himself, briefly talked to a waitress.

The waitress stared at Pete and then walked away.

Long seconds slipped away.

Jenny appeared from the left.

She stopped, frozen, hands up to her face.

Pete took three steps to her, hands held out.

Jenny came closer and raised an arm and a hand and—

She dropped her head, hands back to her face.

More seconds passed.

Pete touched her shoulder.

And time passed, until they were both sitting in a booth.

More time went by, and I remembered my promise, to give Pete a ride, wherever he wanted to go. I wondered how long I'd have to wait.

But I kept my promise, remembering what I had earlier said to Pete.

I also remembered my troubled sleep from last night, waking up yelling, and I remembered two women in my past life—Lucille and Beth—who both left me after some months of courtship.

Because of my nightmares.

Not all scars are so visible.

SAINTS OR HARRIDANS
Kristen Lepionka

1938, Los Angeles

Nick's father had a theory about blue-eyed redheads, which was
this: blue-eyed redheads are always either saints or harridans.
No in between. Had to do with the recessive something or other,
he was no geneticist. Nor was he present to elaborate, him being
at Sanibel Island on account of the rheumatism, but had he been
there he might have warned Nick about Annette Wexley or
maybe even thrown her out of the bar. Annette was a blue-eyed
redhead if ever there was one, and she was certainly no saint.
Case in point: there she was at eleven a.m. on a Tuesday, tapping
the pointed toe of one expensive pump on the sticky wooden floor
of the Imperial like the whole world was late for an appointment
with her.

Nick sighed. He was doing bar prep, slicing lemons into pert
little wedges. He didn't know what a harridan was. What he did
know was that Annette Wexley looked better now than she had
when he'd seen her last, some eight years ago, and she had looked
damn good then. Damn good even walking away from him and
back to her husband, again. "We're closed," he said mildly.

"I need to talk to you, Nicky," Annette said. She knew what
a harridan was. "In private, if you don't mind." She used to have
an earnest, Midwestern drawl, but that had long been replaced
with an insincere Hollywood sneer.

Nick could almost see all the ways that this was going to go badly. But he found himself nodding all the same.

He took Annette down the hall, past the card rooms and to the office, which looked more like a storage room than an office. "Have a seat," he said, pointing to a stack of heavy Hammermill boxes that he knew to contain something other than paper.

"On the boxes?" She sounded offended.

Nick leaned against a file cabinet. "Or you can stand," he said.

Annette sat. Perched on the corner of a box, ankles crossed, hands folded at the hem of her slim wool skirt. She practically batted her long eyelashes at him, saying, "Nicky, I need your help."

Of course she did.

Irony amused the hell out of Nick. Especially the irony of Annette's situation: she wanted his help in saving her marriage, a marriage he had tried pretty hard to prevent and then destroy for the better part of his twenties.

"I know how this works. The only way he'll stop is if he loses, big," said Annette. She was clutching a tissue, which she periodically dabbed at nonexistent tears.

"How do you know he's never lost big?"

"He's a good man, but he's weak. He'd fall apart if he ever got into trouble—real trouble. That's how I know this will work."

"Well, send him by. You know we have action here every night."

Annette shook her head. "He won't go to an illegal card room."

"So what are we talking about?"

"He's a regular at one of these new gambling ships, in Santa Monica Bay. The *S.S. Rex.* It stays three miles offshore in international waters so everything is on the up and up. Have you been?"

Nick shook his head. "I prefer to gamble on land, personally."

"It's nice. Very swanky. French restaurant and everything. And great drinks. Too affordable, the drinks."

Nick also preferred to eat French food on land, but the conversation was getting off-topic. "Sounds like paradise."

"For a while, yes. Then it isn't. He wins until he's had too much to drink, then he starts losing what he just won. Mostly he breaks even."

"So he's not even bad at the game?"

"He's clueless. He lets things happen to him and calls it luck."

"For some people, that is luck."

"Luck is wanting something and having the good fortune of knowing how to get it."

Nick thought about that. Annette did know how to get what she wanted. Her particular shortcoming was in figuring out what she wanted in the first place.

She rubbed the tissue across her face again. "He's out playing poker every single night. Some nights he doesn't even come home. I went to his office to meet him for lunch once and he was asleep at his desk. He sold one of the cars because he wanted to have more cash freed up to play with. He's on a downward spiral, Nick. I don't want to watch Alan go the same way as my father."

She blinked those big blues at him, casting a glance around the office. Annette's old man had been a gambler, sure. Used to own the Imperial, in fact, until the day he owed Nick's father so much that the vigorish alone was equal to what the Imperial pulled down in one year. Things changed hands, as things do, and he ate a .22-caliber bullet within the year.

"You love him?" said Nick.

"My father?" said Annette flatly. "Look, I thought you'd welcome the chance to shove something in Alan's face. All I'm asking you to do is play in one of his games and show him how easy it is to lose big to the wrong person. It's bound to happen eventually, and I'd rather it be to you."

At this, she reached into her bag and pulled out a thick bank teller's envelope, held it there on her lap.

"Alan is used to playing with guys who bluff worse than me," she added. "I've seen you play. You could get him deep in the hole in no time flat."

"And then what?"

"And then he'll be scared out of his mind about losing that much in one night," said Annette, "and when he comes to me just sick over it, I'll finally get him to see that he has to quit gambling for good."

"Why would he come to you over a big loss? He hasn't so far."

"I'm the one he counts on to clean up his messes. He will. It's a perfect plan. Nobody gets hurt, Alan gets his act together, and I finally get my happily ever after."

"You've thought of everything, huh?"

"I just can't go through this again," she added. "First my father, now Alan. This is more about my own pride than love, Nick."

He could understand that.

She held out the envelope to him. "That's for you."

Nick took the envelope but didn't open it. "Why do you think I'd even be interested in this?"

"Because you love winning at cards," said Annette, "and you love being right."

And damn good at both, Nick thought.

"And," Annette continued, standing now, stepping so close that Nick could smell her perfume, "because you know me, and because underneath it all you're still a good guy, and I know you want me to get my happily ever after, our differences aside."

Differences. That was one way to put it. But he didn't object to her leaning in and kissing him lightly on the mouth, hers soft and minty-sweet. Didn't object *much*. Didn't object nearly as much as he should have, because Nick knew two things for sure: Annette Wexley was hardly the happily ever after type, and that regardless of what she said, she was a damn good bluff.

* * *

Ten minutes and a thirty-five-cent water taxi from underneath a neon red X on the Santa Monica Pier took Nick out to the *S.S. Rex*. Massive engines rumbling under the faint strains of Duke Ellington from the bandstand, the vessel was some three hundred feet long, an old windjammer spruced up with new paint and a lot of beautiful, windswept women crowding the balcony. It was the place to be for the semi-famous, the almost-fabulous, and anyone who wanted to rub up against the edges of acceptable society—former bootleggers, card sharps, showgirls—without breaking the skin.

Stud was Nick's game of choice, but he found Alan Wexley at a no-limit hold 'em game, one/two-min/max buy-in. Wexley was fortyish and anxious, with thinning sandy hair and close-set eyes behind a pair of small tortoiseshell glasses, which gave him the appearance of someone who was not only nearsighted, but also shrewd. The other players at the table included two Hollywood types and the sulky, disinterested redhead who'd come with them, a prim grandmother type who held a patent leather pocketbook neatly on her lap the entire time, and a young guy in a straw hat who looked like the water taxi had cost him the last thirty-five cents he had to his name. The table was attended to by a series of identical cocktail waitresses with sumptuous blonde curls, or one particularly dedicated cocktail waitress with sumptuous blonde curls, who ensured the drinks never ran dry.

It had all the trappings of a good night, but a wild sort of energy that could go either way.

Wexley was a loose-aggressive player, playing every hand and betting too fierce. He seemed to lack a basic grasp of the game, that the object was to win the cash and not just the hand. He kept throwing good money after bad, like he could ride a losing streak to the bottom and just wait for it to lift him back up again like a rising tide.

"When you're hot, you're hot," said Wexley nonchalantly, draining his umpteenth gimlet and then switching to beer. One of the Hollywood guys folded, followed by the second one a round later. The kid, who had revealed himself to be a truck driver from Sacramento called Perry, flushed blotchily over his thin cheeks and looked miserable as he raised Wexley's bet even though he was in just as deep.

Nick wondered what would have become of him if, as a young man, he'd had access to enough cash to buy into a game like this. That was before he knew doodly-squat about cards, before he learned that gambling lived at the intersection of math and psychology, that it sure as hell wasn't a hobby. This kid, though, clearly hadn't learned that yet and might not ever learn it. Nick wasn't sure how this was supposed to work—Annette had floated him cash to cover Wexley's debt, but he wasn't feeling great about taking money from the kid. This was not nearly as rewarding as he thought it might be. Ten years ago he would've been gleeful about the chance to nail Wexley to his face, all the while nailing the man's wife semi-weekly on the starched sheets of the Galaxy Motel. Nick and Annette went back twenty years, more, since high school, but it never once occurred to him until now that maybe she wasn't worth it. Any of it.

"You know," said Nick, uncharacteristically, "it's time to go home when it stops being fun."

"Who's not having fun?" Wexley said.

The answer appeared to be *all of us*. Perry started to laugh, a frantic, honking sound. Nick felt like a heel. It was just like Annette to disregard the potential for collateral damage. Nick had been nursing the same snifter of Blue Label all night and now he polished it off in one swallow as he folded on a gorgeous straight flush. This was going to hurt. He ordered another drink and, over the course of the next four hours, proceeded to do the opposite of every player's instinct he had until Perry was in the black again.

Things got a little hazy after that, but at some point the three of them became fast friends, drunkenly belting out "Give a Little

Credit to the Navy" on the prow of the *S.S. Rex* in the moonlight and trying to feed a French fry to a seagull that had alit upon the railing and attempting to entice the beautiful, windswept women into a spin on the dance floor.

At two a.m., Wexley was thrusting a torn sheet of blue paper into Nick's hand. "You call me," he was saying. "Churchill 2496. I mean it. Eighteen holes at Riverside. The three of us. The Three Musketeers!"

They took turns scribbling phone numbers on the scraps of paper so that each man had the contact info for the other two. Nick didn't even golf, but the night's energy had morphed into the kind that maybe inspired a man to turn over a new leaf.

At three a.m., Nick and Perry were half asleep on the water taxi back to the pier, Perry trying hard not to puke.

At five a.m., Alan Wexley was dead.

The following week, Nick watched a black-and-white police car idle outside the Imperial for almost twenty minutes, long enough to make him nervous. Then they emerged, two cops in identical beige raincoats, detective shields clipped to their lapels. One raincoat was wrinkled, the owner a wide, slouchy guy with acrylic-looking brown-gray hair. The other cop was blond, younger, fitter, wearing enough drugstore aftershave to perfume a landfill. Nick didn't know either of them, but they walked into the Imperial like they sure as hell knew him.

"Nick Starner."

It wasn't a question.

"Yeah," said Nick.

The blond one slapped a picture down on the filmy surface of the bar. "You know this guy?"

Nick looked. The open, worried face and owlish glasses didn't register at first, but then it did. Alan Wexley. "Uh," he said, thinking *Annette*.

"Is that a yes?"

"I played cards with him last week."

"Here?"

Nick shook his head, quick to dispel any connection between Wexley and the Imperial. "No, at the gambling boat off Santa Monica Pier. The *Rex*."

"What day?"

"Tuesday. Why? What's the story?"

The blond cop and his partner exchanged glances. They were called, respectively, Carmichael and Hewitt, and they worked Homicide, and they already suspected this was a suicide but were taking their sweet time on this case to fit in as many work-sanctioned trips to the *S.S. Rex* as possible.

"So you saw him last on the *S.S. Rex*. What time?"

"Two, three in the morning," said Nick.

"How was he?" said Carmichael.

"At cards?" said Nick. "Lousy."

"In demeanor, smartass," said Hewitt.

"Maybe if you tell me why you're asking."

"Because maybe you were the last person to see him alive," Carmichael said. "Because he never came home after your little sea voyage that night. Then he washed up on the pier yesterday morning."

Nick rubbed the spot between his eyebrows. The stunning hangover from his night on the *Rex* had faded, but something else was now brewing in its place.

"No wallet, no cash on him, but he had a coat check ticket in his pocket," the cop continued. "And the coat in question had your name in it. You, a known degenerate. So what do you have to say?" He was holding a small cellophane envelope, which contained a scrap of blue paper. Nick recognized the haphazard letters written on it as his own drunkenly scrawled phone number.

"He was fine, when I left the boat. There was another man, Perry something. He can tell you. Wexley was fine."

Carmichael slapped the cellophane envelope down on the bar

top. "Sure. Right up until he went over the railing of the *Rex*."

"He fell overboard?"

"Fell, jumped, was pushed. Take your pick. His wife said she was worried that something like this might happen. Seems he was on a real downward spiral as of late. Does that sound familiar?"

So Annette hadn't mentioned him, Nick thought with short-lived relief. Short-lived, because now the ball was in his court—keeping their past in the past would have to be a conscious choice. His eyes dropped to the scrap of paper, which was now face down on the bar.

My dear Annette, the back of it said. *Tonight, I finally found the darkness at the bottom of my soul—*

Carmichael clocked Nick's gaze and put the envelope back in his pocket.

"Is that supposed to be a suicide note?"

"No," said Hewitt, "it's a grocery list. So what do you say—was Wexley despondent enough to jump overboard? Or would you prefer we pursue the *was pushed* angle?"

Nick wouldn't. But he didn't like the weirdness of Alan Wexley pre-penning a suicide note and walking around with it in his coat all day, either.

As soon as they left, he ransacked the office looking for the jacket he'd been wearing on the boat.

—and I've made the decision to end my life rather than bring more shame to our good name. It's not your fault. It's no one's fault but mine. I know what I am doing. It has been a long night and I have lost too much...I love you always. A.W.

Nick stared at the paper for a long time, waiting for it to make sense of itself, which it rudely did not do. The words were in messy, anonymous block letters, but Nick had a terrible feeling he knew who had written them.

Annette, the woman who thought of everything.

Carmichael and Hewitt were eating greasy meatloaf sandwiches for lunch at the Green Door.

"You ever see that Cary Grant picture, *Gambling Ship*?"

"I'd rather stay home with a book than go to see a picture," said Carmichael. It was true. He would. He also made it a point to disagree on principle with everything his partner said, because he thought Hewitt was an idiot. In return Hewitt thought Carmichael was a know-it-all pain in the ass, which was true as well.

"Well," Hewitt continued, "in that one, Cary Grant gets tangled up with the casino owner's girl and everyone double-crosses each other. Then there's a fire. But the hero gets away with the dame, of course."

Carmichael took out the morose photograph of Alan Wexley. "He's no Cary Grant. And there was no fire. And nobody's getting away with anything."

"Pretty good picture, though."

After lunch, Hewitt and Carmichael sat in a glass-walled conference room at Deforney & Yount for the entire afternoon, talking to Wexley's coworkers. The boss was a middle-aged bearded fellow with approximately twelve strands of hair combed delicately across the pink expanse of his scalp. "For the love of god," Glen Dunlap muttered, ruffling the strands with a frustrated head shake, "a gambling problem? This is the last thing I need. I'm going to be buried under complaints for years."

"Complaints?" said Hewitt.

"Just yesterday morning I got a call from one of Alan's clients," explained Dunlap. "This nutty ninety-five-year-old oil widow who wanted to tell me all about how her daughter had looked over her statements and thought some money was missing."

"And?"

"The daughter is seventy-eight," said Dunlap, "and she's even nuttier than the mother. I've met them both. And the amount of money she said was missing, that's just one bad production day for Chevron El Segundo. But I looked into what she said, and confound it if she wasn't right. Alan had her liquidating variable annuities left and right, but the money never showed back up as anything else. And when I pulled a few other clients' files, I saw the same kind of activity. I was up all night, thinking about this. I was planning on talking with him about it this morning, but then I heard the news."

"Sounds like embezzlement." Carmichael and Hewitt exchanged glances.

"Don't say that," said Dunlap. "Gambling allegations are bad enough."

"Gambling," said Hewitt. "How'd you know about that?"

Dunlap looked confused. "You told me, about five minutes ago."

"Oh. Can we get the names of these other clients?"

Dunlap nodded. "His assistant can help you out," he said.

Wexley's assistant was a twentyish blonde named Camille Ford, her hair pulled back tightly into a long braid. "I knew something was going on with him," she said, repeatedly taking off her black-framed glasses to polish them on the edge of her shirt and then putting them back on. Carmichael thought the effect was not unlike a lenticular nudie poster: boring librarian. Sex kitten. Boring librarian. Sex kitten. "He looked like he wasn't sleeping," she added. "And he'd act really secretive when he made phone calls, you know, getting up to close the door all the time." Boring librarian.

"We think he might have had a gambling problem," said Hewitt.

"Oh, my," said Camille. Sex kitten. "That would make a lot of sense, I guess."

"Do you know anything about this missing client money?"

Boring librarian. "Oh, no, sir, I don't get involved with the numbers. I don't have the head for it. But Alan did seem preoccupied with money. He once asked if he could borrow sixty dollars."

"From you?" said Carmichael.

"Right?" said Camille. She gave him a big smile that transcended the lenticular and made her look like a pornographic angel. "The man makes four times what I make. It was absurd."

"Did you loan it to him?" said Hewitt. He didn't know what a lenticular was, but he did know that glasses or not, he'd prefer the pretty blonde was talking to him instead of his partner.

"I didn't have it," she said, pouting slightly. Sex kitten. "Anyway, he said it was to get his wife's car out of the tow pound—there's not exactly love lost between her and me, so even if I did have it..." She shrugged. When she shrugged, delicious little wells opened up above her collarbones.

"Why's that?"

"She's a chilly one, Annette," said Camille.

Carmichael could believe it. Annette Wexley had seemed more concerned with getting Wexley's personal property back from the *S.S. Rex* than she did about his untimely demise.

"She's never been nice to me," Camille added. "I'm not sure why." She smoothed her blouse over her chest. Carmichael was willing to hazard a guess why.

"Jealous, maybe?" he said.

"Of me? Hardly," said Camille.

"They were happy, then?"

"Happily miserable. You know the type—nagging each other endlessly, but basically inseparable." Here, Camille took off her glasses to wipe her eyes. Both detectives simultaneously reached out comforting hands.

"I never thought in a million years this would happen," Annette was saying. "I'm so sorry for getting you involved."

For a grieving widow, she was trying pretty hard for sexy. Sleeveless black shift, black stiletto pumps. It was working. She laid a manicured hand on his arm, ushering him into the apartment and down a hall, away from the sincere mourners in the other room.

"I thought he'd just get scared," Annette added, pushing him through a doorway that led to a guest bedroom. Thin gray light from a window cast a trapezoid on the blue bedspread. "I never thought he'd be so weak." She stepped close to him, backing him up until he had no choice but to sit. "And the police were here this morning? Apparently he was in hot water at the firm—allegations of embezzlement. Meanwhile, my bank account is bone-dry, Nicky," she said. "He lost everything—our money, his clients' money. He was just out of control." She reached for the knot in his tie, slowly sliding it down.

"It's funny," said Nick, "because he didn't lose that much to me."

"What do you mean, he didn't lose that much?"

"Oh, he lost, all right," said Nick. "But I felt bad for this other kid at the table, so I let them win most of it back."

Annette barely missed a beat, moving on to the buttons on his shirt. "That doesn't sound like you," she said, coy. "Sympathy?"

Nick grabbed both of her wrists in one hand and squeezed. "What are you up to?" he said.

"I don't know what you're talking about."

Nick pulled out the scrap of paper. "I found this," he said. "Alan wanted to give me his number so he wrote it down."

Annette snatched the paper away and squinted at it. Her delicate features were caught in a struggle between surprise and inevitability. "So he did leave a note," she said slowly.

"I don't think that's what this is, Annette."

"He killed himself. That's what happened. I knew it. The police need to see this—"

She started to tuck the paper into a pocket, but Nick grabbed it back first. "I think I'll hang onto it."

"The police—"

"The police, nothing. You wrote this note."

Annette scoffed. She had one of the world's great scoffs, even when being accused of murder. "I wrote a suicide note for my husband and then put it in his coat pocket and sent him on his merry way? That's absurd."

"What's absurd is a note written about a long night and losing money. It's almost like someone knew in advance what kind of evening Alan had in store for him. What was the plan, he loses to me, he goes missing, you tell a story about how messed up he's been, and then somehow this note turns up to corroborate the whole thing?"

"*Corroborate*," Annette said then, abruptly climbing off Nick's lap. "You're nothing but a two-bit bookie, and I'm a grieving widow. My husband stole money from his customers. Obviously that has nothing to do with me. I'm left with nothing here, and I'm not up to *anything*."

Nick stood too. With Annette in heels, they were nearly eye-to-eye. He studied hers, sky blue rimmed in navy, flecked with gold. He used to think they had bottomless-ocean depths. Now, though, all the detail seemed to be on the surface. "Were you there, on the boat? Or did you have someone else helping you? Some other dumb puppy dog like me?"

"I think you should go."

"Hey, Annette…what happened to happily ever after?"

"Grow up," said Annette.

Alan Wexley had to be the unluckiest SOB in California. The bank accounts were strafed, bled white by frequent cash withdrawals. Any money embezzled from Deforney & Yount clients was nowhere to be found. The man had a life insurance policy, but he'd borrowed against it the previous fall. That money, too, appeared to be gone, probably vanished into the coffers of the *S.S. Rex*. Carmichael had heard that the gambling ship cleared almost a hundred grand a week. All in all, it made him feel slightly better about being broke the old-fashioned way.

He shuffled the meager contents of the case file, eyes lingering on a photo from some office Christmas party in happier times. Wexley had his arm around his wife, who smiled coolly at the camera like she had a secret. The boss, Dunlap, was there too, leering at the décolletage of the sex-kitten receptionist. Her hair was loose from its braid, long curls skimming her bare shoulders. Carmichael squinted at the photo, trying to make out her ring finger.

"You ever see that picture, *Motive for Revenge*? Irene Hervey as the grieving widow."

"Irene Hervey's my cousin," said Carmichael.

"Really?"

"No."

To their left, a uniformed cop was leading a wild-eyed woman in a feather boa into an interrogation room. "I ain't never been no fink," she yelled. "Never."

"Shut the fink up," Hewitt yelled back, and then laughed and laughed until Coke came out of his nose.

"You got soda on your eyebrow," said Carmichael.

Then Nick Starner walked in.

He needed more attention from the cops like he needed a hole in the head, but the new-leaf energy from that night made it seem possible—that he could walk into a police station, say his piece, and walk back out again. All afternoon, counting last night's take at the Imperial, Nick had mulled it over. After the conversation with Annette earlier, she was probably planning to do the same. She could claim anything, and who would the police believe? The lovely grieving widow or the two-bit criminal? All Nick knew was he kept losing count in a stack of twenties. Few things could kill his concentration but Annette, in one way or another, could do it every time.

Hewitt said, "You got something you want to tell us?"

Nick sat down, the scrap of paper in hand. "This is going to sound crazy. But I think Annette Wexley staged the whole thing. I don't know how, exactly, but I think that's what she did." Then he saw the files open on Carmichael's desk. "Wait, who is *that*?"

* * *

"We don't like to make a habit of letting two-bit bookies solve our cases," said Hewitt over a beer at the Imperial. "But every so often we let you win one."

"Gee, thanks," said Nick.

"The blonde one caved in ten seconds flat," said Hewitt. "She was sleeping with Wexley when she discovered his embezzlement—the dumb SOB was putting all the money into an account in Annette's name, and the statements came to the office. Get this—he had her open all his mail. There was almost half a million in that account."

"Yeah," said Carmichael with a low whistle. "According to Camille, he broke it off with her a few months ago, and because she knew there was no chance that he was going to live happily ever after with Annette, she figured he was going to cut and run, provided he didn't get caught first. So Camille approached Annette with what she knew, and they decided to get him out of the way and split the money."

"Now there's a man who has been *rejected.*"

"Enter me," said Nick. "A convenient corroboration for a made-up gambling addiction."

"It might've been a real addiction, but it was the least of his troubles. Camille posed as a waitress and kept an eye on things. As far as she could tell, all was going according to plan. Then after you left, she just so happened to bump into Wexley, and they had a few more drinks. She checked his coat and put the claim ticket in his pocket to make sure the suicide angle had corroboration, then over the railing he went."

"Every detail worked out to ensure that things would stop right there. And it probably would have worked perfectly, if Wexley hadn't used his own suicide note to give his phone number to his new golf buddies."

"Or if Annette had trusted Camille to put the note in his pocket."

"And give up that control? Not her."

Nick sighed. "I can't believe I fell for it."

Hewitt shrugged. "A beautiful woman, asking for your help in sticking it to the guy she left you for? I'da done it. I'll tell you, cell-block gray is no color for a blue-eyed redhead like her."

Nick hated to admit it, but that made him feel the tiniest bit better about the whole thing. "Good."

THE INVISIBLE BAND
Art Taylor

Lord Peter was scooping another oyster from its shell when I stepped his way. He stood at a bistro table with Harriet Vane, who had popped a round of cucumber toast into her mouth.

Correction: "Gherkin croute." That was the preferred term—salvaged from some '20s-era menu. (The 1920s, just to be clear.)

"Excited for the big weekend?" I asked, notebook in hand, camera around my neck. "Feeling good about your chances?"

Lord Peter adjusted his monocle, squinted at my name tag. I'd checked his out too—one of three monocles in the room so far, already blurring together.

"I say, it's Dr. Watson." He gave a prim nod. "I presume Mr. Holmes won't be far behind? Or is he getting a head start on recovering Miss Paget's jewels?"

His accent was, frankly, atrocious—high-pitched and drawling.

The "Heiress's Hijacked Heirlooms"—that was what the press release had said. Gloria, the sales and marketing manager at the Hotel Clifford, leaned heavily on alliteration. I was surprised she hadn't tried to rename it the Chateau Clifford for the weekend.

The Clifford's small ballroom was all babble and bustle (to add my own alliteration), everyone meeting and greeting, enjoying their own appetizers, tipping back champagne. The champagne was in plastic flutes instead of the "crystal chalices on silver servers" (from the "history" in the press release), and there was no "seven-man band setting a stylishly syncopated tempo"—only smooth jazz piped through the speaker system—but Gloria worked the room like a pro, all smiles, upbeat as always.

I'd already chatted with several contestants—Hercule Poirot (the first monocle), Miss Marple (knitting needles sticking out of her bag), Charlie Chan (white hat, arching mustache, sharp goatee), and a father-and-son team with Richard and Ellery Queen, whom I wouldn't have known at all without those name tags. (I was quickly realizing the limitations of my crash-course Googling "Golden Age Detectives.") On the opposite side of the room from Gloria, a magician was trying to dazzle with card tricks. Hired entertainment, I'd assumed. Turned out he was a contestant too: the Great Merlini. I made a note to Google him again later.

But I hadn't seen any Sherlock, and you'd think he'd stand out in a crowd.

I shook my head at Lord Peter. "Haven't seen my better half—not yet at least. But I'm not one of the players. I thought Gloria had let everyone know."

"We checked in late," Harriet Vane said. "Haven't really talked to anyone yet. The traffic was tough the last hour, and I was starving, so we went straight for the food."

The bones from a couple of lambchops sat on her plate. A scoop of jellied shrimp stood untouched. The menu had called them prawns in aspic, I recalled—more of the theme.

I held up my notebook. "Reporter," I said. "Covering all this for the *Gazette*—the local paper. You're from out of town then? What drew you to enter?"

"My wife is a big fan of *Masterpiece Mystery*," Lord Peter said, picking at another oyster. He'd dropped the British accent—thankfully.

"The books, too." She poked him in the side. "I'm a big reader. He's the one who only watches the shows."

"They help me sleep."

"Sometimes halfway through." Harriet Vane smiled. "I lured him with the prize money."

That had become the constant refrain. Everyone was focused on the five thousand dollars up for grabs as part of the Clifford's hundredth anniversary celebration, even if the hotel was trying to highlight its history of elegance and luxury.

Gloria had come up with the plans—an avid fan herself of classic mystery fiction, she told me, but a good marketing opportunity too. Centennial Celebration had become Golden Age Anniversary, and Gloria's pitch had concocted an elaborate backstory about heiress Virginia Paget's diamonds having been stolen at an elegant 1920s soiree. (Those "silver chalices" and that "stylishly syncopated" band and even a small cast of suspects: "Virginia's ne'er-do-well fiancé, mesmerized by her money, and well-known as a womanizer" or "her younger sister, jealous to have never been in the limelight herself" or "some other sinister sneak.")

The contestants had registered as iconic characters from the Golden Age of Detection, tasked with solving the crime—some elaborate mix of Escape Room adventure and "How to Host a Murder" dinner party. As Gloria had explained it, clues would be sprinkled scavenger-hunt style at a steady pace throughout the weekend. A lavish Sunday brunch at the end, celebrating whoever had presented the solution quickest.

Marketing opportunity and revenue generator too. Each participant had to sign up for a full three-night package—welcome reception, daily breakfast delivered to your room, and that brunch included. Beyond those, everything was extra: more meals, lots of drinks, souvenirs, all of it.

"Do you know when we'll get the first clue?" Lord Peter asked.

"I told him it was probably in the welcome packet," Harriet said.

The welcome packet was right, and I'd already caught a glimpse from some other participants:

Miss Paget's bluebird tweeted
Some first words—they're the clue.

Yesterday they seemed clear
Though today…what a stew!

But Gloria had told me explicitly that I shouldn't help anyone, and I aimed to keep it that way.

"Check with Gloria," I said, scanning the crowd. "There she is." I pointed her out, talking to a man in priest's garb, collar and robe both. Another name tag to check out, another thing to follow up on. Father Dowling, was it? My parents had been fans of the program, but…

"Good show," Lord Peter said, picking up his plate to head over—and picking up that terrible accent again too. It took me a minute to catch that "good show" wasn't echoing my own thoughts about TV.

I started to head to another interview—an overweight man in a three-piece suit who'd settled down on a chair by himself, his hand wrapped around a foaming pint of beer. Monocle number 3 sat beside him.

Then I spotted Sherlock.

He stood in the corner, hiding behind a life-sized cutout of a woman in a yellow dress patterned with rhinestones and bead-work—Virginia Paget, we'd been told, which had disappointed some of the guests. They'd been expecting hired actors, not a cardboard decoration.

Sherlock had nailed the trademark look: deerstalker hat, Inverness cape, even a stylish pipe. But he still wasn't what I'd expected: barely three and a half feet tall, and his pipe was blowing soap bubbles.

"Hello." I leaned down. "I like your hat and your coat."

"It's a cape," he told me. "Like Superman's."

"Superman?" I said. "You're a superhero instead of a detective?"

"The game's afoot," he said, enunciating each word. And then a forlorn mumble: "My parents told me to say that."

* * *

"It'll be a solid feature," my editor had said. "Good community angle."

"Marketing gimmick," I'd told her.

"Have fun with it, and the readers will too," she'd replied. "Local landmark. Centennial celebration."

My editor was prone to alliteration too.

"So a puff piece," I said—more resignation than question.

And later, a hint of desperation in Gloria's eagerness to welcome me aboard. My editor had been right about the hotel's desire for community support, and the Hotel Clifford likely needed it. Celebrating its hundredth year, the Clifford had clearly seen better days.

"You can pick a character too," Gloria had said. "But not one of the big ones maybe?"

"Keep me on the sidelines," I'd said. "My job's to write it all up."

She percolated on that for a minute. "How about Watson then?"

"Wouldn't he be teamed up with Sherlock?"

Gloria had rolled her eyes at that—which I hadn't understood at the time.

At the start of the reception, before Peter & Harriet arrived, she'd introduced me as Watson, emphasizing my "generous celebration of our big weekend!"

She had expectations about my article too—but other details drew my own eye.

Though the lobby and the restaurant and lounge had been spiffed for the anniversary—brass rails smartly polished, the fountain under the atrium gleaming and gurgling happily—the accommodations generally hadn't aged well. The carpet was worn in places, the leather on the club chairs was cracked—*authentic* and *weathered* Gloria might've said, but I'd simply tried to angle my photographs away from sore spots.

And though that restaurant and lounge promised those same luxuries of old—extravagant lunch buffet, elegant afternoon tea, a vibrant happy hour—the place was sadly understaffed. Long waits at meals, haphazard service. The bellman who'd greeted me when I checked in was also passing appetizers at the event—and as it turned out, he'd be back the next morning, delivering that breakfast to my room: a croissant, orange juice, and coffee.

The croissant and the coffee were cold, the orange juice warm, but I tipped him anyway. Frankly, he looked exhausted.

"All hands on deck," Gloria told me when I asked later about staffing for the centennial weekend. "We want to make this an event for the ages—the *Golden* Ages."

Upbeat *and* on brand.

A puff piece on a marketing gimmick? Or was the real story about how an icon had faded, glory days gone, a sad bid to recapture the past? A glass case near the front desk displayed pictures from those better days, a small write-up about the hotel's distinguished history. No one seemed to pay it much attention.

Gloria had told me that participants had been urged to inhabit their own characters fully for over the weekend—speech and mannerisms too—but as with Lord Peter's bad accent and then dropped accent, Thursday night's welcome reception revealed the truth: treasure hunters indulging a kind of upper-crust cosplay, a clichéd phrase trotted out, a stray quote. Several contestants had stopped short of even that low bar, Sherlock's team among them, letting their son dress up instead of them, spoon-feeding him dialogue.

And then another story presented itself—when Miss Marple announced Friday evening that her own jewelry had been stolen.

Friday flurry, I'd written in my notebook at one point—Gloria's alliteration clearly contagious. The detectives puzzled through clues, rushed and hurried to each next one, took breaks between times, especially since some steps had built-in delays.

The "bluebird tweeted" poem led to the Hotel Clifford's twitter feed; the first words of each tweet from the day before needing to be rearranged to form a message pointing toward the next riddle.

The detectives also had to solve a crossword featuring the titles of crime novels available to borrow from the hotel's reading room—*And Then There Were None, The Tiger in Smoke, The Poisoned Chocolates Case, Miss Pym Disposes,* and several more, supposedly Virginia Paget's favorites. Specific letters had been circled throughout, an anagram that spelled out Elevator Two.

The "Suggestions" box near Elevator Two was unlatched, and inside, all the suggestion slips were printed with another poem, supposedly written by Paget herself.

Light you seek and heat I'd furnish
Unused til when? Find something burnished.

That meant the fireplace in the lobby—gas logs lit each afternoon at three for afternoon tea—and a shiny metal box was promptly placed atop the mantle at the same time for the next stage, envelopes inside with the follow-up clue.

It was amusing to watch the contestants trying to casually check out the box, so no one else might catch what they were doing—at least until Miss Marple herself hadn't been tall enough to reach the hidden envelope.

"Can't *someone* help me?"—despair and irritation.

Other participants took a different approach. The overweight man from the night before—Nero Wolfe, I discovered—took up residence in the lobby, reading a book until the lounge opened and he ordered another beer. Meanwhile, he sent out a younger man—the single name "Archie" on his tag—to fetch clues back for him. And the Great Merlini paid no mind to any of it, concentrating instead on pulling items out of a hat, playing out an array of card tricks. He had a regular audience, many of the other players stopping to watch his tricks, and he'd been there nearly nonstop, much of the morning, all afternoon, well into the evening, even continuing the tricks while he took his meals at a small coffee table.

Sherlock, meanwhile, had found his own games—hitching rides on the bellman's cart, the cape fluttering behind him and bubbles flowing from the pipe, no parents in sight. To his credit, that bellman showed an inexhaustible patience—bellman, valet, room service, and now babysitter too: those cart rides, plus coins in the fountain and trips up and down the elevator. Add cleaner to his job duties too, since someone probably had to wipe up the residue from those bubbles. (Sherlock's parents didn't dress up for any parts—and didn't do much actual parenting either. Sherlock was a free-range child.)

I caught people throughout the day for quick interviews, posed photographs—community angles in mind, how everyone was enjoying their visit, their downtime, gathering shout-outs to various shops, the local art gallery, the nearby park.

Dinner was downtime, many of the detectives settling in groups in the lobby lounge and the hotel restaurant, Wolfe stuck in his same spot, Merlini circulating through the crowd—only half walls separating lounge and restaurant and lobby, so everyone was in full view: Ellery Queen and his father, Nick and Nora Charles, Tommy and Tuppence, Perry Mason and Stella with Charlie Chan, several others.

Miss Marple was sitting alone and so kindly faced that I offered to join her, which I immediately regretted.

She picked at her food, a scrap of torn leather on my chair picked at my arm, and our mini-interview turned into a litany of complaints about the hotel and the area. Her room was too small, it faced the wrong way for morning sunlight, and the drapes were insufficient and inferior. The juice at breakfast was warm and the croissants were cold (I didn't point out I could empathize), and real butter would've been better than margarine. This game they were playing wasn't friendly to older people. What was Twitter anyway? And why put that box so high? The nearby park needed *serious* landscaping attention, and then the housekeeping practices at the hotel, the quality of the help. Frankly, if she hadn't been able to lean heavily into a cup of Earl Grey, and speaking of, where *was* our waiter? She needed more water and…a flutter of fingers, waving down "Jerome, Jerome."

Turned out Jerome was not only bellman, valet, room service, and babysitter, but now waiter too—and fortunately prompt with that water. Several tables away, I saw another waitress watching us, glaring really, a stern shake of the head. Pity clearly.

I felt pity too—for myself—and grateful when the Great Merlini stopped at the table to do a card trick. (Miss Marple shooed him off with another complaint: "I've had quite enough of your silliness.") I was grateful again when she finally headed up to her room.

And then surprised when she returned almost immediately.

She burst from the elevator and toward Gloria, ever on duty at the front desk. More complaints, I assumed, until the word "thief" echoed across the lobby, and everyone's attention turned her way. I headed over—followed by many of the detectives and other curious guests too.

"It's probably misplaced," Gloria said. "I'll phone housekeeping."

"No, no, we must call the police," Miss Marple said—and then the word "thief" again, with some pointed glances at the crowd of detectives gathering.

Gathering and offering assistance, doing their detectively duties—questions suddenly piling one after the other. Where did Miss Marple last see the ring? What kind of ring was it? Where had she kept it? When did it go missing? Was it a wedding band?

"Please." Miss Marple sniffed, stiffened. "I am steadfastly *un*married. It had belonged to my mother."

"Spinster is the word, old dear," I heard someone mutter behind me—his voice dripping with disdain—and turned to see that third monocle again. Not Lord Peter, not Poirot—and where was his name tag?

"Your mother," said the priest. Not Father Dowling, I'd clarified since. Father *Brown.* "An heirloom then!" He turned to Gloria, "Is this part of the game?"

Gloria shook her head.

Poirot pushed his way to the front of the small crowd, pulling on the ends of his mustache. "Make way," he said, "for my little gray cells. With method and logic one can accomplish anything!" The phrase rolled oddly off his Southern twang.

"Not logical deduction," said a tall, thin man with horn-rimmed glasses, "any more than the flash of intuition, but the shoddy path between." Albert Campion on that name tag.

"It was likely spies," said a woman already at the front, and her partner nodded. Tommy and Tuppence, another pair of Christie characters.

But the Christie connections didn't broker any good feelings.

"I don't trust any of you," Miss Marple said, bluntly. "In fact, I'll bet one of *you* stole it to distract me from winning this weekend."

"Almost anyone is capable of a crime under certain circumstances," Perry Mason added dryly, with a grim twist to his lips. But the mood had shifted, shutting down camaraderie in most every direction.

I'd stood on the sidelines, listening, and as the crowd dispersed, I grabbed an armchair with a good view, trying to compile a list of who was where.

Near the front desk, Gloria kept reassuring Miss Marple, even as she dutifully called the police.

Some of the detectives who'd crowded with questions now gathered in clusters to chat about what had happened. Others retreated to the lounge or the restaurant to continue drinks or dinner, keeping their distance.

What caught my attention more, however, were the ones

who hadn't shown any interest in the theft but had kept their seats the whole time. I'd been glancing their way during all the hullabaloo, and their reactions—or lack of—interested me the most, Miss Marple's accusations ringing still.

Nero Wolfe hadn't budged an inch, a fresh tankard of beer foaming in front of him. His Archie was nowhere to be seen, but beside him, Charlie Chan had a beer of his own. He wiped a line of froth from the edges of his mustache.

The Great Merlini had kept his table too at the center of the lounge, slowly resuming his tricks as others returned.

Sherlock's parents had watched from a seat they'd claimed near the fountain, leaving their cocktails only briefly to call their son back from the crowd. (Ignored again, Sherlock Jr. dangled his fingers in the water, glancing back and forth from Jerome waiting tables to the unused bellman's cart by the front desk—wistful for mischief, clearly.)

Nearby, Nick and Nora Charles had been diving into their own overfull martinis. They didn't have a child to take care of, but wasn't there something conspiratorial in their whispering? Their glances in Miss Marple's direction didn't seem concerned— or friendly.

Finally, the police arrived, took Miss Marple aside for a conversation, then headed up the elevator—everyone watching but no one approaching this time. I didn't bother to follow either. I knew the officer, Adam Fenwick, from a short stint covering the police beat for the paper.

I caught Adam later in the lobby, standing by a potted plant, writing in his own notebook.

"So, how are things in your world of bumbling incompetence?" I asked.

He lowered his pen. "Excuse me?"

"All these famous detectives," I said. "From the stories I've read, the police usually have no idea what they're doing."

"Hrmph." He waved a hand in the air. "That's what the lady there thinks." Miss Marple had perched herself in a club chair, knitting—or rather, undoing some knitting. No one had offered to join her.

"Maybe you should tell her to solve the crime herself?"

"I was tempted to tell her to do something else to her own self." Adam's face was a deadpan. "She told me she'd known someone very much like me back at St. Mary's, and he was equally worthless apparently."

"St. Mary Mead," I said—proving some info had stuck. "Any progress on finding the ring?"

"Not much to go on—and she's hardly any help. Where did you keep the ring, ma'am? On my finger, she tells me. So you think it might have dropped off your finger? No, because I laid it down in my room. I thought it was on your finger, ma'am? Well I take it off when I'm not wearing it—which…don't get me started on the circular logic there. And was that the last time you saw the ring, ma'am? Well, I can't remember…" He'd been mimicking Miss Marple's voice—high-pitched, bird-like, like a bird pecking really. "All she knows: someone took it."

"Who does she think that someone is?"

"She's convinced one of the other players did it—players? Is that the word? She doesn't want them anywhere near her."

"And pass up on assistance from the best and the brightest detectives in the world?" I smiled.

"They're cutthroat, that's what I heard. Hoarding clues. Every man for himself—woman, too. She hasn't ruled out the hotel staff either. Everyone's a suspect—and best I can determine, everyone would have a motive."

"At least there's no butler in the mix," I said. "But what do you mean about motive?"

"That lady has tangled with everyone, seems like. Nothing but complaints since she arrived." He ran through them, the same things she'd been telling me at dinner. "And she had trouble with the maid this afternoon," Adam went on. "Miss Marple, as you call her—her name's Dolores Banning, by the way—left the hotel for a little sightseeing, walks for her health, fresh air. She comes back to the room, the maid's making up the bed, but *not* changing the sheets. Ticked Banning off."

"Only use your sheets once?"

More of that bird-like pecking. "'I like to be pampered when I'm on vacation'—told me that, told the maid too. Stood over her while she changed those sheets, all aflutter, I'm sure, watching her like…" Bird-like expression now—nose forward, eyes scrunched. "Maid's still here, doing a second shift, waiting tables in the restaurant."

He gestured over toward the restaurant—the waitress I'd seen glaring at our table. What I'd taken for pity now seemed like something else.

"She's really flustered by all this. Said Banning was horrible, said Banning rushed her out before she could finish the rest of her housekeeping."

"Maybe the maid took revenge?"

"Miss Marple had the ring when the maid left, said she remembered taking it off afterward, remembered 'wringing her hands'"—another glance at the notes—"'in consternation.' She took it off then. I swear, you couldn't make these people up."

"Someone broke into the room afterwards?"

"No sign of the door having been jimmied. And no keys, all electronic key cards."

"Which narrows it down to someone with access, right?"

"You would think, but here's the trick: The system keeps track of who uses what keys on what doors. Security measures."

"And?"

"No one in or out of that room except Banning herself." Another sigh. "She dropped the damn thing somewhere, far as I can tell. Spindly fingers. And what are *we* supposed to do with that?"

* * *

Waiting for my breakfast to arrive Saturday morning, I pulled aside the curtains of my room and saw a Rolls Royce backing into a section of street cordoned off at the front of the hotel—a line of other cars already in place.

I remembered the story of Virginia Paget's party from the press release—"sparkling sedans delivering impeccably attired guests: Rolls Royces and Pierce-Arrows and a sunshine-yellow Roamer Roadster."

The press release had promised a car show as part of the weekend fun. "Donated by a local car club," Gloria explained. "They *want* to show them off. It's not costing us a penny!"

Detectives were already beginning to wander between the cars—admiring them? More likely on the hunt for the next clue. Lord Peter and Harriet Vane appeared to be in deep conversation as they leaned over a sleek roadster, and a few feet behind them, Hercule Poirot stood in the middle of the sidewalk—waiting for something? More likely eavesdropping on his rivals. Coincidentally, both Lord Peter and Poirot were polishing their monocles.

My breakfast never arrived, so I canceled room service (voicemail, no one answered) and grabbed to-go from the restaurant. Ahead of me in line, Charlie Chan ordered a cortado and a croissant. I'd gotten my coffee and a Danish when I heard a voice behind me.

"Watson. Mr. Watson, a moment."

It took me a moment to remember who I was.

I turned finally, and Father Dowling panted to a stop behind me.

Father *Brown*, I corrected myself again—that was the character. All my Googling had been like cramming for an exam, scanning through online articles, a couple of anthologies I'd picked up at the library.

"I'm glad I found you," he told me. "I received a clue this morning, and—"

"I'm not playing—ineligible really." I waved my notebook. Gloria's caution not to help.

"Oh, no, I don't mean about the official contest—well, not technically." Father Brown tugged at his collar, snug against his Adam's apple. "Damned nuisance," he said. "No, I'm talking about Miss Marple's ring—whether you think it is indeed part of the show here? Whether it's only *meant* to look like a real crime? I figured you would know for sure."

A crime? Or lost? "They called the police," I said. "Actual police, not playacting."

Father Brown squinted his eyes, shook his head. "That's so...odd. It has to be."

"Why do you say that?"

"A clue was delivered to me this morning, but..." Father Brown held up a piece of paper. "It's not like the other clues. And I didn't earn it—which seems against the rules."

Even at a glance, the paper was clearly different. Other game pieces had been professionally decorated somehow—the embossed invitation, the clue above the fireplace with its edges lightly burnt as if rescued from the fire itself. But this was a simple sheet from a hotel notepad, the message handwritten, smudged and but not like it was smudged on purpose.

"I would've asked someone with the hotel," Father Brown went on, "but the rules say no assistance from the staff. I didn't want to disqualify myself."

The lobby was mostly empty, but people had been passing by us on their way out to the cars—hotel guests, other detectives. Albert Campion gave us a hard glance, curious, prying even, then moved on.

"May I see it?" I said—motioning Father Brown to an empty sofa.

He followed, handed it over.

Forgive me, Father, for I have sinned.
I don't know how to atone and make amends.
It was anger made me do it.
Shouldn't people be treated better?

"It doesn't rhyme," I said. "That's another difference. No

rhyme, no code. How is this a clue?"

Father Brown pointed to *sinned* and *amends*. "That sort of rhymes, doesn't it?"

"Accidental, I think," I said. "How'd you get this?"

"Slipped under my door this morning."

"Who knows which room you're in?"

He shrugged.

"No call to action," I said. "Nothing to figure out, nothing to do." Could it be part of the game?

I glanced toward the desk, wondering if Gloria was there, if I should simply ask her myself—leaving Father Brown out of it. But someone else was on duty, on the phone, and I didn't see her anywhere else in the lobby.

Father Brown tapped the note. "'Shouldn't people be treated better?'" he read. "That's why I thought of Miss Marple and her ring. She hasn't exactly treated anyone well."

"I heard she's been...snippy. With the staff."

"With everyone. She's been trying to play her part—always hearkening back to something she'd seen in St. Mary Mead and what she knows about human nature, but..." He shook his head. "But when she accused Nora Charles of cheating on Nick, and then what she said about Mr. Chan and Mr. Wolfe and obesity as an indication of inferior intellect, and all those side comments about good parenting..."

Suddenly the disinterest of those people from the night before made greater sense. But was it also a hint toward motive?

"So someone could've stolen the ring to spite her? And then...remorse? Those lines about sins and making amends?"

"You still don't think it's part of the game?"

"I don't," I said. But it could well become part of my story. "Okay for me to hang on to it? Check it out?"

"As long as you let me know what you find out."

I promised I would.

* * *

As Father Brown and I crossed the lobby toward the car show, he flipped a coin in the fountain. "Any luck I can get." He laughed.

He'd already shared with me the official next clue, almost definitely pointing to the car show:

Miss Paget's Journeys
Steer your way toward the secret—
Adventure at every turn.
But which the right direction?
Find the page and you will learn.

Various detectives were already traveling from car to car, puzzling out the riddle. I took a few photos and caught sight of Adam Fenwick talking to Perry Mason—follow-up interrogations? My own search was aimed elsewhere—for Miss Marple herself.

As it turned out, I found her in the small gift shop off the lobby—only room for a few people amidst its mix of Hotel Clifford-branded knickknacks, local jewelry, and travel necessities: toothpaste, aspirin, phone chargers.

The clerk stared at her phone. Miss Marple was holding up a book from a small travel section, riffing though the pages, like she expected the next clue to drop out.

Find the page and you will learn? Adventure? Directions? Maybe the cars *were* a distraction, and she was on the right path.

As I walked up, she turned and snapped at a man hovering nearby—the third monocle, as it turned out.

"Mr. Vance, are you spying on me again?"

"Sorry, old thing." He tipped his hat. "Only passing through."

"Old thing!" Miss Marple huffed, but the man was gone. "He needs a kick in the pants."

I moved closer. "He looks a little like...Lord Peter, is it?"

"Philo Vance," she said. "Honestly, I never liked either of them. Affectation. Pompousness. Now Harriet Vane, she's a different story entirely, I'd—"

"I was wondering," I said, "if the police have learned anything more about your missing ring?"

"What they *call* the police." She tsk-tsked, then raised herself up, imperially. "Mr. Watson, you should bring the power of the press to bear on the matter."

"I'll do my best to get them in line." (In my mind, I was already asking Adam's forgiveness.) "Do you have a moment?"

"Oh, yes, I'd appreciate that."

The gift store clerk didn't notice us leave. As we made our way to a couch in the lobby, Miss Marple touched a passing waitress lightly on the arm, and asked for a cup of Earl Grey. "Not too warm, please, but not too cool either."

I thought I heard a sigh as the waitress moved off. The words from the note to Father Brown resonated: *Shouldn't people be treated better?*

"Can you tell me about the ring?"

"It was a silver band, slim and delicate. My mother's ring—small fingers, like mine—with a pavé setting. That's a row of small diamonds embedded along the entire band. The police asked the value, but I haven't had it appraised. It's *sentimental* value more than anything."

"Of course," I said. "And you were wearing it yesterday when…" I let the sentence hang.

"Afternoon, yes. I came back and found the room in complete shambles."

"Shambles? As if someone had broken in?"

"The break-in must have come later. No, I mean the house-keeping—that *attempt* at housekeeping. That woman had sprayed the bathroom counter, letting chemicals dry on its own, as if that was cleaning. Misting my toiletry bag in the process, since she hadn't bothered to move it aside. The room service tray from breakfast had been moved from the dresser to the end of the bed—not only unsanitary but actually in the way, since she was tugging the old sheets into place at the same time and—"

"How did you know they were the old sheets?" I asked.

She lowered her chin and pursed her lips. "I am a *noticing* kind of person, Dr. Watson. Some of my eyeshadow was, unfortunately, still on the pillowcase."

"So you had her do it correctly?"

"I watched her, yes—fresh sheets at least—but she was so sloppy tucking the corners, I finally shooed her out completely, job undone, and did it myself. Had to wipe up the counter too, using a good hand towel, and that meant requesting more linens, which took forever…Speaking of, where is that girl with my tea? Even talking about this, my nerves need calming again and—" She waved her hand in the air. "Jerome!" she said. "Jerome!"

Jerome was pushing an empty cart across the lobby, Sherlock swinging from the top bar like a monkey, the whole thing swaying side to side. They detoured our way.

Miss Marple leaned in, a conspiratorial whisper. "This establishment is in trouble from the front desk to the backstairs. He's one of the few you can count on."

As Jerome pulled closer, Sherlock eyed us warily, as if in danger of losing his playmate.

Miss Marple smiled. "Do be a dear, Jerome, and check on the tea I ordered. You know how I like it."

"Yes, ma'am," Jerome said and steered off in a new direction, Sherlock casting more glances back our way.

"Patience of Job, and tormented like Job, but always a please and a thank you—and that's the exception. You've heard about the hotel's financial difficulties, haven't you? And the reviews? Yelp and Trip Advisor positively *disparage* the place. This whole weekend is a publicity stunt, people playing dress-up, no respect for the books themselves."

Respect for the books themselves? I didn't remember Miss Marple being quite so severe, but mostly, I'd only known the woman on the PBS shows. Had *she* been so mean? Something else seemed out of character. This modern-day Marple—who claimed to know nothing about Twitter—was suddenly hip to Yelp and Trip Advisor. Perhaps she was more technologically savvy than she let on.

"You were talking about the housekeeper. Was that the last time you saw the ring?"

"I had the ring on after she left. It was taken from my room while I was at dinner."

"I understood that no one had entered your room. The hotel keeps track of the key cards?"

She eyed me suspiciously. "I don't know who you've been talking with, but technology can be bypassed."

"So, you do think the housekeeper, then, or someone on staff?"

"Incompetence isn't necessarily evil," she said. "No, one of the detectives was trying to disrupt my attention, and I know which."

"You do?"

"The Great Merlini," she said. "Sleight of hand, tricks of the trade. It was before you joined me for dinner. He showed me a card trick and spirited away my key somehow, used it to steal my ring."

Merlini had been working the crowd, and I'd seen him standing in the restaurant when Miss Marple reported the theft. Had he disappeared in between times? Could he have swiped the key?

"But wait," I said. "You went back to your room after dinner. You must have had a key then."

She waved that off. "He returned it to my bag—when he stopped by the table under the guise of doing another trick. But it must have been him—who else had I been in contact with?"

I remembered him stopping by—how long had he been there? Could she be right?

Miss Marple leaned in. "Of course, you can't print any of this until the police prove it. Libel."

The waitress was coming across the lobby with a cup and saucer and a small pot of tea on a silver tray. Jerome must have worked his magic.

Dutifully, I called Adam and asked about Merlini.

"Impossible," he said. "She told us the same thing, so I

checked it out. Witnesses say Merlini didn't leave the lounge at all, not until long after the old lady reported the ring gone."

When I caught up with Miss Marple later and asked her about that, she had another quick explanation.

"Don't believe any alibis," she said. "They could all be in on it, plotting against me."

"You don't think much of any of them then?" I asked.

"I always believe the worst," she said, a sigh of resignation. "The sad thing is, one is usually justified in doing so."

Miss Marple had been wrong about the "journeys" clue—all those travel books. One of the car collectors had been enlisted to deliver the clue: a map from the glovebox, with another challenge—a lengthy one—requiring coordinates to be plotted and a route to be discovered, and a four-digit code to be found…and where was *that* supposed to lead?

Several participants returned to their rooms to puzzle it out, while others gathered in the lobby. I continued my interviews— How was the hunt going? What will you do with the money if you win?—while slipping in other questions: Where were you when you heard the news about the actual theft? What do you think happened? What do you think of Miss Marple?

"I was joking about the spies, of course," said Tuppence with a dimpled smile. "At the time I thought it was part of the game. But honestly, don't you imagine she lost it somewhere?"

"No," said Tommy. "It was the maid definitely. And don't give me grief like I'm saying the butler did it. She had"— counting out on his fingers—"motive, opportunity, means. Or wait, is *means* the first *m*?"

"My uncle had sent me running down the next clue," Archie Goodwin said. "Wolfe, I mean. But don't tell him, I went to a bar down the street, ordered a burger and fries, watched a basketball game. Honestly, when my uncle invited me for the weekend, I thought this was going to be a vacation. I didn't know he was expecting me to do all the work."

Ellery Queen was in a similar situation with his dad.

"I'm not really playing," he told me. "Not my thing really. More my dad's. But I think he's having fun."

"Isn't it supposed to be the opposite in the books? The son doing all the solving?" I'd mostly watched the old TV show, but still.

"I'm not much of a reader," he said.

"I was having a daiquiri with Della when I heard her outburst in the lobby," said Perry Mason. "Mr. Chan was with us too. Frankly, I wouldn't trust her on the witness stand myself. But it doesn't matter what she says, I *know* what happened to the ring."

"You do?" I asked—startled by the statement, his casualness about the news.

"Of course I do," he said. "But I can't say now. It wouldn't be good drama without a last-minute reveal, would it?"

"Oh, hush," Della said, laughing. "He's playing with you. He doesn't know anything."

Truth was, no one knew much of anything—and no one had much empathy with Miss Marple herself.

"Man never born who can tell what woman will, or will not, do," Charlie Chan told me. "Would not surprise if Miss Marple manufacture theft to distract us all."

Everyone suspected everyone—suspected or worse.

"She's a witch," said Nora Charles.

"And you spell that," Nick slurred, "with a *b*."

"Miss Marple's become a fan favorite," I told Gloria later in her office. "Any progress on finding her ring?"

"Our guests expect quality service," Gloria said, sitting up a little taller behind her desk, like she was stepping to a podium. "The Hotel Clifford is committed to providing for our guests, their comfort, and their safety to—"

"Got it." I waved her off. "PR to the core."

She loosened her stance, leaned forward, cupping her face in her hands.

"Between us, the whole thing's turned out to be a mess. On top of the complaints, Miss Marple is now threatening to sue, which—we can't be held responsible, of course. Terms, conditions, and limits of liability posted everywhere. By statute. Still, it's not a good look, our big celebration weekend—not good press, but who am I talking to, right?" A gesture my way. "And no, I can't let you interview the maid."

"You're trying to keep her quiet?"

"Not at all. She's not here anymore. She was so upset by all this, she quit."

"Not the best weekend for that either."

"This is *not* for publication." She leveled an eye at me— cautionary. I waved a vague hand in the air that she took for agreement. "Not that you haven't already noticed, but we're short-staffed in all directions. Everybody working extra shifts, taking extra duties, everyone overworked, overwhelmed. I'm getting like five hours of sleep, tops. If we get through the weekend without a staff revolt, we'll be lucky. Lucky to have any staff *left* to revolt."

"Does this mean my breakfast delivery will be late again?"

"I'll bring it myself tomorrow," she said. "And pick up the tray afterwards too. But please...go easy on us in your story, okay?"

<u>Miss Paget Prefers</u>
"Which cognac?"
"Only the creme de la creme," said the Tsar, appropriately.
Which (he reflected) gives us two of the three.
Were all of the clues designed to call attention to some aspect of the hotel? Or even to boost revenue? I'd lost track of where we were in the hunt, but that latest clue brought everyone to the

lounge again.

One by one the detectives had come in, the first of them striving to for their same discretion as they ordered their Brandy Alexanders and stole glances at the cocktail napkin beneath. But quickly, as Jerome (was he everywhere?) began making the drinks by the trayful, the mood eased , everyone settling into conversation and relaxation.

Or almost everyone. Miss Marple was her same bristly self.

"A most *unnecessary* ingredient to my taste," I heard her tell Jerome. "You of all people should've known better than to serve me *cream*."

Neither Nero Wolfe nor the Great Merlini seemed to have ordered the necessary cocktail. Merlini was focused on levitating a pie plate in the air, and Nero Wolfe was still wearing fresh spots in the leather as he lifted pint after pint of beer. His Archie had returned to service, but he was having a beer too—clearly done with the clues.

At a corner table, young Sherlock twirled his deerstalker cap aimlessly. His parents were paying more attention to each other and to their own Brandy Alexanders (already half gone) than to their son. At least he was sitting still for a change.

At the next table, Father Brown took the first sips of his own drink. He read his napkin, opened it, closed it, and opened it once more.

I was talking with Lord Peter and Harriet again, and I'd caught a glimpse of the napkin at their table, silver printing on the blue cotton.

The Hotel hides a riddle
Hidden in plain view.
Go back to the beginning middle.
Skip forward: 3, 1, 2.

"Do you think she even had a ring at all?" Harriet said. "I mean, did anyone ever see it?"

"She's in it for the insurance," Lord Peter said. As it turned out, that was his real-life line of work.

Across the room, Miss Marple sat primly, as if nothing was wrong—except for her drink maybe, which she'd hardly touched. Her hand rested on the arm of her chair, her fingers thin, the skin shriveled. A small band of white perhaps where a ring had been? Or would it have been her other hand?

Abruptly, she stood up and left, a furtive glance behind her. Something was up.

"Excuse me," I told Peter and Harriet, rising to follow.

Miss Marple crossed the lobby, heading toward the front desk, best I could tell. She gave an occasional glance to each side as she went, and then caught sight of me behind her. Abruptly, she shifted direction toward the elevators.

Clearly, I wasn't fit for detective work, at least not tailing someone. Had something on the napkin prompted her this way?

Gloria Stinson was manning the desk again, typing on her keyboard.

"Three, one, two?" I said, leaning against the counter. "I'm assuming that wasn't a typo."

Gloria's cheeks dimpled when she smiled. She shook a finger at me. "You're not supposed to help anyone. And I can't give out any hints."

"No one will get anything from me." I pulled my finger across my lips. "But I caught sight of the clue—fun to try to figure out the puzzles."

"It's not a typo," she said. "But that's all I can say."

But her eyes had darted to the side, I'd caught that. Reflex? Or intentional?

The display case about the early days of the Clifford. Back to the beginning? The photographs in the case surrounded the small panel with a history of the hotel—the middle?

Philo Vance stared into the case, adjusting his monocle. Had he been following Miss Marple too?

I turned to investigate further—then caught sight of Gloria's expression. Her eyes tightened, puzzlement in them—her attention elsewhere.

I followed her gaze. Father Brown was standing by the fountain at the center of the lobby, admiring it, gazing into the spray of the water as if he was reflecting on something.

At several tables around the fountain, people were finishing drinks and dinner. Like them, I wouldn't have thought anything of a guest admiring the décor—except for Gloria's reaction, that is, and what she said next.

"He shouldn't be doing that yet," Gloria said. The word *yet* stood out. She started to come around the front desk, but before she did, Father Brown had walked over.

"The lost diamonds," he whispered, trying to keep Philo Vance out of earshot. "What do you do again when you find them? And should I let everyone else know too?"

The answer to the last question was no.

"Let's let everyone play through," Gloria said. She'd lowered her own voice, talking to Father Brown as if he might be asking for more towels or had lost the key to his room.

Philo Vance had cut his eyes our way a couple of times. I quickly walked his way.

"Catching up on some history?"—raising my voice a bit to cover up whatever Gloria was telling Father Brown.

"Passing the time, old boy, a little light reading." He acted like he'd been caught—same as he'd done in the gift shop. I kept up the small talk, admiring the photos, and scanning through the history panel in the case's center.

Go back to the middle, 3, 1, 2.

I found the sentence—awkward at best: *Our history envelops under each room...*—then skipped through the words.

Envelop(e)s under room desk hold keys.

What key would each detective find there? An actual key? Or a code? It didn't matter now.

I clapped Vance lightly on the shoulder, told him to have a good evening, and then stepped toward the fountain as casually as I could, finding a free table and taking a seat.

The base of the fountain was a little over a foot high, tilework in a mosaic of tans and browns. The fountain in the middle had two copper tiers. Water cascaded gently from a spout at the top and trickled down. The pool itself was crystal clear, but that round curtain of falling water kept an even flow, rippling the surface. Coins were scattered throughout the bottom, and I pulled one from my pocket, flipped it in myself, watched it sink. It landed at an angle—but angled against what?

It wouldn't be hard for Victoria Paget's diamonds to be scattered down there—the pretend diamonds, I meant. Hidden in plain sight.

Or a thin band of silver with a row of diamonds. Nealy invisible itself amongst the dimes and nickels.

When he was done with Gloria, Father Brown came over.

"Did you talk with Gloria about your cocktail napkin?" I asked.

He shrugged. "She asked how I'd solved the case, and I told her."

I remembered how he'd folded and unfolded it. "Did you open the napkin and show her?"

"She'd already know the clues, wouldn't she?"

Which meant he hadn't—and I could only imagine how puzzled she must have been by their conversation.

"Okay if I take a look?" I said. "Since you've already won."

He handed it over. I opened it, and inside was a second message, the same handwriting as the note slipped under Father Brown's door.

I wish my conscience was clear—clear as where it's waiting

It. Not them. It.

The truth came together—some of it at least. The ring, the guilt, the atonement, the covering up. I wasn't sure about the ring, exactly how it was stolen, but the rest made sense—the attempt to confess and to cover up at the same time.

I handed the napkin back. "Keep this between us?"

"Like you said, I've already won." He gestured back toward the restaurant. "Another Brandy Alexander? My treat."

We sat and talked about...nothing really, or rather, anything *except* the hunt and the fountain and the diamonds—or any theft. It took a while to get our drinks—the staff already short, and some had already clocked out, apparently. No Jerome in sight to help us out.

Gradually, others began to leave the lounge, many of the detectives still clutching their cocktail napkins. Over the course of the evening, several of them passed by the display case—a sudden interest in history. But no one checked out the fountain. No one appeared to know the case had been solved.

I'd hoped to catch at least one of the people I needed to talk to—but even as I saw him, I wasn't sure how to make my approach, and I let him pass without stopping him.

His parents were with him, after all.

Despite Gloria's promise of a personally delivered breakfast, I hustled down to the restaurant first thing Sunday.

The lobby was quiet that early in the morning—a lonely custodian vacuuming by the elevators, no bellman on duty, and the front desk unmanned too. (I assumed Gloria or someone else was in the back, ready to jump to duty.)

Nick and Nora were the only people in the restaurant, pointedly not speaking to one another, which made me wonder if Miss Marple had known something after all. Or maybe they were hungover and in urgent need of eggs.

After I'd gotten my coffee and bagel, I caught sight of Sherlock Jr. slumped on a bench near the valet stand, his deerstalker cap angled sideways on his head.

"Aren't you a little young to be down here on your own?" I asked, joining him.

"Mom and Dad are still asleep." He was pushing his foot against an empty luggage cart. "I know my way around. My mom keeps forgetting which stairway goes where."

"No Jerome this morning?"

A snort. "This game is taking too long. I want it to be over."

He was a different child this morning from the one who'd been riding that luggage cart with such abandon. I remembered the way he'd run his fingers through the water in the fountain, the looks he'd given Miss Marple and me when she'd called Jerome about his tea—and then too the way he'd hidden behind the Virginia Paget cutout that first night.

"Want to tell me how you stole Miss Marple's ring?"

He cut me a side-eye. Who knew a child his age could master that kind of look?

"I didn't steal anything."

I arched an eyebrow in return—trying to match him expression for expression. "You know it's not nice to lie, right? Of course, I could wait and ask Jerome when he gets here."

Jerome had known, of course, but he didn't want to get the boy in trouble. That was why he'd been piggybacking on the clues, sending messages Father Brown's way—mercy, forgiveness, resolution. A man of the cloth would give that, wouldn't he?

"Jerome didn't take it either!" Sherlock sat up—his eyes wide now. "No one did. She *gave* it to us."

Excuses, I'd expected, but not this. "She *gave* it to you? Why would she do that?"

"Jerome brought her tea. I knocked on the door. She opened it, and she was mad."

"Mad at you?"

"Mad at the tray."

He must have seen the incomprehension in my face. He met my eye, slowed down his speech, trying to make sure I could keep up.

"Jerome gave her the tea," he said. "She gave him the tray. It had a dirty cup and a plate. The ring was on the tray."

The breakfast tray—the one the maid had left on the bed when Miss Marple had rushed her away. Adam had talked about her wringing her hands "in consternation," taking off the ring. And Jerome knew how she liked her tea.

Was it a mistake then? An accident?

"People give him tips," Sherlock went on. His frown told me I was, perhaps, too dumb to live. "That's how he makes money. But it was a penny tip, and those go in the fountain."

"So you didn't steal it at all? Jerome told you all this?"

He rolled his eyes. "He doesn't even know I saw the ring. But I see lots of things. When people give him dollars, he puts them in his pocket. Pennies aren't worth anything. They're just for luck."

"But the ring *was* worth something," I said. "A lot, in fact."

"Uh-uh." He shook his head. "Or he wouldn't throw it in the fountain."

"Excuse me." A man had come in the front entrance, his wife behind him—guests arriving. "May I borrow this?" He tapped the luggage cart in front of Sherlock.

"We're not using it," I told him. He pulled it out the door, while his wife went to the front desk. Gloria was indeed the one who came up from the back—late nights, early mornings, always.

"Miss Marple wasn't very nice. Maybe he didn't like her very much." *Shouldn't people be treated better?*

And where *was* Jerome? Simply his day off? Had he quit like the maid? Or was it a guilty conscience that had kept him away?

Sherlock was still shaking his head.

"Jerome *did* like her. He liked her *because* she wasn't nice. He told me that."

Maybe I *was* dumb.

"*That* doesn't make any sense."

Sherlock sighed, dramatically—sighs and side-eyes all part of his repertoire. "Grown-ups don't make any sense," he said.

"So…Explain it to me."

"Jerome wasn't happy," Sherlock went on, "but he couldn't

say anything. They didn't hear him."

"They?"

He moved his hands around, gesturing to the hotel itself—the faded icon, the marketing gimmick, the shoestring staff, everyone overworked.

"They didn't see him, that's what he said. But they saw the lady. Jerome said when *she* wasn't happy, they *had* to hear her. And maybe things would change."

"So, he liked her complaining," I said, "and you think he threw the ring in there to have her complain more?"

"They'd have to fix things then, wouldn't they?" He slumped back onto the bench. "But it didn't work. If it had, maybe he and I could've played more."

Nick and Nora had left the restaurant, but others had gone in: Tommy and Tuppence, Perry and Della. Philo Vance and Father Brown were each sitting alone. A lone waitress moved slowly from table to table.

"Do you know where the ring is? Exactly, I mean—where it is in the fountain?"

"I've been watching it to make sure it's still there."

"Want to get the coin back? Help Jerome?"

Sherlock sat up, all attention.

I pulled out a coin, explained what I wanted. "How's your aim?"

"Really good." He was beaming.

He took the coin and headed for the fountain.

After that, things went very quickly—and between Sherlock Jr. and Father Brown, the official announcement of the Mystery Weekend's Winner was undercut twice.

Sherlock overdramatized his part in the play. He sauntered toward the fountain. He held up the coin and examined both sides repeatedly. After he flipped it, he peered theatrically into the water.

"What's that?" His voice echoed through the lobby, and already some of the breakfasting detectives were turning his way. "That's not a coin."

Gloria, who'd finished checking in the couple, rushed over from the front desk—echoes of the night before?—but Father Brown beat her to the fountain.

"Did the boy find the diamonds too?" he asked, his whisper loud enough this time to set off its own flurry of confusion and excitement and questions from the other detectives.

"The mystery's been solved?" and "The contest is over?" and "Why didn't someone tell us?"

Gloria hurried through a speech she clearly hadn't fully rehearsed.

"Oh! Yes! Congratulations! Father Brown discovered them first...last night, he proved himself, um, a...master detective of all...a master of deduction...and charting all the clues..." She plunged her hand awkwardly into the fountain, moved her fingers side to side, retrieved a pair of small gems and held them high. They looked like plastic. "The diamonds are submerged in the water—in plain sight but nearly invisible to—"

"No." Sherlock was standing on the fountain now. "I meant the ring. There." He pointed.

I leaned over to examine it myself, casual bystander. "Miss Marple's ring?" I asked, nonchalantly—hoping that no one noticed Sherlock nodding my way, eager for approval.

More questions from the crowd—"Where?" and "How?" and "Who put it there?" They pushed against the edge of the fountain to get a look, even as a larger crowd spilled out of the elevator: Poirot and Charlie Chan, Ellery Queen and his father.

Gloria's fluster doubled again as she shoved her arm deeper into the fountain, toward where Sherlock pointed, and retrieved the ring to cheers from the crowd.

"What on earth?" Miss Marple said, and behind her stood Sherlock's parents—the same kind of question creasing their brows. No one had noticed that they'd joined the fray.

"Your ring." Gloria's hand was dripping as she presented it to Miss Marple. "This young man found it."

"What?" Sherlock's dad said.

"Oh, my word," said his mother, hugging him closer.

"Like the real Sherlock," I said.

Meanwhile, Miss Marple held up the ring, inspecting it as if it might be a fake—still more peeved than pleased, even as she slipped it on her finger.

"How did it get *there*? That's my question. And who is *responsible*?"

Justice needed to be served, that was another point she kept making. Questions needed to be answered, especially when she heard the diamonds were in the fountain too. Had her personal jewelry been conscripted into the game?

She was affronted when Charlie Chan asked whether the ring might not have slipped off her "oh so slender" fingers. And she turned suspicious side-eyes Sherlock's way too, as if he might have stolen it himself—small comments about responsibility and irresponsibility and immaturity and shouldn't someone have been keeping closer watch?

Any other parents might've taken offense. Sherlock's parents— not surprisingly, given what I'd seen of them—simply didn't notice. But in a nice twist, the reason they didn't notice was because they were so focused on Sherlock himself, giving all their smiles and pride and attention his way.

Miss Marple eventually headed back to the elevator, mumbling about improper parenting and the hotel's poor service and promising to follow up with the authorities. I couldn't wait to hear Adam Fenwick's report.

"Brunch will begin at ten thirty," Gloria reminded everyone, raising her voice to be heard, pushing through. "We'll explain more then, and present Father Brown the grand prize."

I'd heard there would be Bloody Marys on the brunch menu. I hoped they'd spike hers with a little extra vodka.

* * *

As the crowd dispersed, Gloria leaned down to Sherlock, still framed by adoring parents.

"I think we'll come up with a special prize for you."

"Will Jerome be coming back now?" Sherlock asked.

Gloria looked at me—puzzled.

"Jerome?" she said. "The bellman?"

I cleared my throat. "Bellman and barman and more," I said. "He and Sherlock have become fast friends."

"Could he come eat with us too?" Sherlock asked. "He's worked awfully hard."

"Oh, honey," Gloria said. "I wish he was here—we could use him—but it's his *one* day off."

Sherlock's eyes lit up. "Maybe he could come play then!"

"Elliott," his mother said—the first I'd heard his real name. "I don't think…"

But really, wouldn't it be a good idea? What Jerome had done with the ring had caused nothing but trouble—a fool's decision, likely spur of the moment—but he'd clearly regretted it. And he had indeed worked hard.

"Maybe you could invite him to brunch," I said. "It might be a good part of my story getting them together—good photo too. Stellar service to even your, um, petite patrons?"

I don't know if Gloria picked up on my alliteration, but her smile told me she approved of the idea.

"I'll give him a call now."

OLD MONEY
John M. Floyd

Luke Walker's flip-calendar—it said Wednesday, June 18, 1947—was the only thing in his office that worked right. His phone was dead, his desk chair wobbled, his ceiling fan rattled, and his brand-new ballpoint pen was writing in invisible ink. Even his Venetian blinds were broken. He finally yanked the cord that raised them to the top so he could see outside—and wished he hadn't. It was a gloomy morning in the Quarter, and already hot. He was staring at a pair of bums stumbling along Chartres Street when he heard a voice behind him.

"Excuse me—your door was open."

Walker turned from the window to see a young blond woman standing on the other side of his desk. She wore a simple blue dress and was holding some kind of gold-colored lamp in both hands. "Are you a genie?" he asked.

She grinned. "Just a Jean. This was on the floor outside your door." She set the gaudy thing down on his desktop. He now recognized it as a light fixture from the hallway. His building was falling apart as fast as his office. "You're Lucas Walker, right? Private investigator?"

"That's me. Have a seat, Miss—"

"Landsworth. Jean Landsworth." She perched on a chair and said, "I know you're probably busy..."

Busy watching drunks, Walker said to himself. "How can I help you, Miss Landsworth?" He sat, took a pack of Chesterfields from a drawer, and offered her one. She declined. He lit up anyway, using a kitchen match that actually worked. Above them, the ceiling fan rattled away.

"Well…" Her cheeks reddened a bit. "I'm here because I have a friend in Natchez who phoned me yesterday morning. She knows a cop there, and she said he told her a rich guy had died and apparently left no heirs. A man named Edgar Landsworth."

To demonstrate his detection skills, Walker said, "A relative?"

"I'm not sure. My parents died when I was small and I was raised by a family friend in Opelousas. But I remember my daddy saying he had a long-lost uncle named Edgar—"

"And you think you might soon be moving up in the world."

Jean Landsworth let out a sad chuckle. "Up's the only direction I could go, Mr. Walker. I'm single and a waitress at a diner in Chalmette."

Walker studied her through his drifting smoke. Attractive but plain, young but world-weary, polite but cautious. No jewelry, no makeup, no perfume. She was a nice kid, he somehow knew that. But he also knew good things don't always happen to good people.

"Anyhow," she said, "I'd like you to help me find out if this man really could be my great-uncle." She paused and added, "I think Edgar was from Texas, if that helps."

Walker shifted in his chair. "It'll help only if I take the case, Miss Landsworth. My rates aren't cheap, in spite of what you see of my office, and—"

"Would you consider getting paid only if we win? The way I've heard some lawyers do?"

He had to think about that. As an ex-cop, he wasn't fond of doing anything the way lawyers do. Even so…

"Ten percent," she said. "If you can prove I'm the rightful heir."

He examined his cigarette a moment, then looked her in the eye. "Let me ask you a question: I'm not the only private investigator in New Orleans. Why'd you come to me first?"

"I didn't," she said. "The others turned me down."

Attractive *and* honest, Walker thought. Outside, he could hear the two boozers shouting. One apparently wanted to stop for a nap, right there in the street, and the other said they should go down to Canal and beg for handouts. The sleepy guy seemed to be winning the argument.

"Two questions," Walker said. "First, what was the cause of Mr. Landsworth's death?" In other words, why were the police involved? If indeed they *were*.

Jean Landsworth shook her head. "My friend didn't know."

"Second," he said, "how much would the inheritance be?"

More head shaking. "No idea. But...the cop told my friend that the deceased lived in one of those big mansions by the river. That's a good sign, right?"

"That's a very good sign."

After a moment she said, "Maybe we could both move up in the world."

This time they both smiled.

It took Walker almost four hours to drive up to Natchez. He knew the roads because he'd visited his sister there a year ago. This time he drove straight to the police department, which he'd also visited a few times on errands as a rookie cop in Jackson, two hours northeast. That was of course before the war and before his stint with the Army and the MPs (Military Police, he'd once told a British friend—not members of Parliament). He knew no one in the Natchez PD now, but even former cops were considered part of the brotherhood, and his client's friend's contact, Sergeant Neil Allen, seemed willing to talk about Edgar Landsworth's passing. The first thing Walker found out was that Landsworth wasn't the victim of an illness, an accident, or suicide. He was the victim of an attempted murder.

"Attempted?" Walker said. "Sounds to me like it must've been successful."

131

Allen chuckled. "Here's the catch: Landsworth was the attempt*er*, not the attempt*ee*. He apparently tried to kill someone and died in the process. Fell off a bluff beside the river."

"When did all this happen?"

"Two days ago. Monday afternoon, around five."

That was all Allen knew, so he passed Walker along to Officer Wesley Rone, who'd been the first to arrive at the scene. Rone said he'd been standing in the street near the bluff when he saw a man hurrying east, away from the river, and called to him. Rone noticed that the man—one Frank Teal, it turned out, a local mechanic—was panting and sweating like a plow horse.

"He told me somebody had tried to kill him," Rone said. "Said he was sitting in the grass on the bluff above the river like he sometimes did, minding his own business and watching the boats and such, when this fella Landsworth snuck up on him and tried to push him over the edge. But Teal said he realized someone was standing behind him and rolled out of the way just in time. Landsworth charged right past him and off the cliff, a fall of probably seventy, eighty feet."

"Into the river?" Walker asked.

"Nope, solid ground, twenty or thirty yards short of the water. Teal told me he turned then and ran off, which was just before I got involved. He and I went back to the cliff, and the damn wind was blowing so hard out there I didn't want to even get close to the edge. I did, though, and saw Landsworth's body layin' down there at the bottom. I climbed down by a roundabout way and confirmed he was dead and later drove Teal back here to the station house."

Walker stayed quiet awhile, thinking. "Did Teal know why Landsworth attacked him?"

"Not really. He said there'd been an argument a few weeks ago, about repairs Teal did on Landsworth's car at the gas station where he worked. They got into a cussing match, he said, and Landsworth threatened him. Teal never thought much about it, till what happened Monday."

"That doesn't seem worth killing a man."

"No, it doesn't," Rone said.

"Anybody see them arguing, at the station?"

"Nope, Teal said his boss was out and it was just the two of 'em." Officer Rone paused, studying his visitor's face. "Any particular reason you're so interested in this?"

"Yeah." Walker told him about Jean Landsworth, and her hope that she might get lucky, inheritance-wise. "Which reminds me: what can you tell me about Edgar Landsworth?"

"Not much. Tall, quiet, older, from the Northeast someplace. Vermont, I think, or Maine. He just showed up in town one day, bought the old Hedgepeth mansion, and kept to himself."

"Any close friends? Any acquaintances that he *didn't* fight with?"

"Not that I know of."

"The mysterious loner," Walker said.

"Miser, too. We found better'n fifty thousand dollars in cash hidden in a bedroom drawer at his house, and no sign of a will anywhere."

"How'd he make his fortune?"

"Nobody knows. Stocks, oil, real estate? Maybe he inherited it, like your client hopes to do. Natchez is full of old money."

"So, has anybody come forward? As an heir, I mean."

For the first time, Rone smiled. "Are you kidding? Half a dozen. Only one sounds legitimate, though: Howard Gatlin, a retired businessman down in Woodville. Divorced, no children. Claims he's a nephew and has old family pictures to prove it. Says he hasn't seen Landsworth in years. His lawyer's sorting it out."

"Hmm." Walker'd been afraid of something like that. "Mind if I talk to this Mr. Gatlin?"

"Don't see why you shouldn't. Maggie out at the front desk can give you his address."

"Thanks." Walker turned to leave, then stopped. "One more thing. If it was so windy up there on the bluff...how'd Teal hear somebody sneaking up behind him?"

"He said he felt his back and shoulders get cool all of a sudden, and realized he was sitting in somebody's shadow. It was sunny and hot as blazes that day." Rone checked his watch. "Anything else?"

"Not now. Thanks for your time, Officer."

"Better'n walking the beat," Rone said.

After leaving the station Walker drove northwest under clearing skies and parked his '41 Buick in a gravel lot near the railroad building at the end of Jefferson. Everything here was built on a bluff high above the river. To his left, he remembered, was the turnoff to Silver Street and Natchez Under-the-Hill; to his right, up Broadway, was the spot where Rone said he'd been when he saw Teal running. Within two minutes Walker was standing on the grassy cliff. It was a pretty place, with a great view of the water and the newly built bridge across it and the Louisiana riverbank in the distance, so far away it looked like an ocean shoreline. The wind was strong again today, flattening the grass and rustling the green leaves of the trees along the bluff.

Carefully Walker moved to the edge of the drop and looked down. It would be a long fall. When he turned and looked in the opposite direction—east, toward town—he could see that this spot was hidden from all except a few buildings along Broadway. He made note of those in his line of sight and stopped in there on his way back to the car. He was told the same thing at each place: the police had visited them yesterday, asking if anyone working here Monday afternoon had seen anything unusual out the west-facing windows. Nobody had.

And then, a break: "You might check with our janitor, Jake Hensley," a bald and bespectacled manager said. "He was here Monday. He's been off since then, though."

Walker convinced the guy to give him Mr. Hensley's home address, and twenty minutes later Walker found him, mowing the grass at his home just past the city limits. As Hensley mopped his neck with a bandana, he said he had indeed noticed someone down at the edge of the bluff around quitting time, as he was emptying the garbage. Somebody just sitting there looking out at the river. All Hensley could remember—it was quite a distance—was the back of the man's shirt. A red shirt, he was sure of that.

Back at the police station, Walker again found and cornered Officer Rone, whose patience seemed to be wearing thin. No, Rone said, Teal had been wearing a *white* shirt that day, short-sleeved and tieless. But come to think of it, Landsworth's shirt had been red—a bright, stark red as he lay on the ground at the foot of the bluff. "Why do you ask?" Rone said.

"I think you might need to have another talk with Frank Teal," Walker told him.

But the police couldn't find Mr. Teal, and neither could Luke Walker. The unmarried mechanic wasn't at his home address, his neighbors hadn't seen him since Monday, and the cops learned that Teal hadn't shown up today at the Gulf station on East Franklin where—according to its owner, Homer Fitzhugh— he worked Tuesday through Thursday of every week. Walker focused on the neighborhood and the police focused on places of business, and by the end of the afternoon it was obvious that both Teal and his car, an old Packard, had seemingly vanished without a trace. The plot, Walker decided, was thickening.

Walker's sister Lavinia—Vinnie to everyone she knew— agreed with him on that, after he arrived unannounced at her farmhouse Wednesday night and she'd hugged him and asked him about his nonexistent love life and he'd told her about the case. The only interruption in his long story came not from Vinnie but from the big grandfather clock standing against the living room wall next to the kitchen door. It must've come from her late husband's family—Walker didn't remember it from his own childhood—and when it struck seven o'clock its deep BONGs startled him so bad he yelped like a little girl. When he saw Vinnie laughing he felt his face heat up. "You ought to get rid of that thing," he growled, which made her laugh even harder.

Ten minutes later he finished his summary and admitted that at this point he had more questions than answers. Vinnie replied that she had no answers either, but she did have beef stew in the fridge, and after a bit more visiting they sat down to a supper that reminded Walker of their mother's cooking, many years ago.

"Tastes great," he said. "And you look good, Vin."

"You're biased," she said, grinning. "But I gotta admit, I'm doing better than I thought I'd be, this time last year." Which was the last time Walker had seen her, at the funeral of her husband Danny O'Brien. This house was Danny's childhood home, the one he and Vinnie had moved into after their wedding ten years ago. Then Danny went off to war. Walker often felt pangs of guilt about what happened next. While Walker spent his military years arresting drunken GIs in off-base bars, his sister's husband had been dodging Japanese bullets in the South Pacific— and then came home only to die in a car crash on a dirt road two miles from his farm. Nothing in life was fair, Walker decided.

"The place looks swell, too," he said. "Is that neighbor, Ethridge, still helping out?"

"Yep, especially with the planting and plowing and picking and such. I won't be taking any Hy-wah-yah vacations anytime soon, but I get along."

He was about to ask more, but the big clock in the living room struck eight and made him jump again. It sounded like a lumberjack was bashing a sledgehammer against a gong. When the racket stopped, Vinnie changed the subject back to the case and said, "I don't see what makes you so suspicious about the story you say this Frank Teal told the policeman. Why'd you automatically think it was a lie, even before you found out about the red-shirt/white-shirt thing?"

"Because the death happened in late afternoon. Think about

it, Vinnie: Teal said he felt someone's shadow on him, from behind. If he was facing west, toward the river, that couldn't have happened. The setting sun would be in *front* of him."

She gave that some thought. "Okay...he was lying. But if Landsworth was really the one sitting on the bluff all along, and Teal's the murderer, why'd he invent a complicated cover story? Why didn't he just sneak up on Landsworth and push him over the edge and leave?"

"I think he did. I think Teal made up the story only because he ran into the cop and had to tell him *something* to explain his presence there." Walker paused. "He just overdid it a bit."

Both of them stayed quiet a minute. Supper was done, and Walker was satisfied but tired. Finally Vinnie said, "So what happens now? Are you going to charge this young client of yours for your time while you run around helping the Natchez PD solve a murder?"

"I'm not charging her for anything at all, remember, unless I can prove she's the dead man's rightful heir. But to do that I might need to find out if he *was* murdered. And why."

"And you think you can find that out?"

"Not only that," he said, grinning, "I think I can do it tomorrow."

"My confident big brother," she said. "Nothing scares him but clocks."

Walker snorted. "You should sell that damn thing."

Thursday morning, June 19. After a late breakfast of the first homemade pancakes he'd eaten in years, Walker left Vinnie's farm and drove south to Woodville, a town about ten miles from the Louisiana state line, and then to the address he'd been given for Howard Gatlin. He found Landsworth's heir sitting in a rocker on the porch of a large house on a shaded street. Parked in the driveway was an iron-gray '46 Lincoln Zephyr. Both the home and the car looked elegant but somehow out of place, like their owner. Gatlin was in his early sixties, with white hair, glasses, and weary eyes, and was decked out in a three-piece suit and tie. Who wears a suit at home? Walker wondered.

He introduced himself, took a seat, and said, "You look too young to retire, Mr. Gatlin."

"I'm sort of semi-retired. I still go in to the office every day. Just not early, anymore."

"Sounds good to me." Walker fell silent for a beat, then got to the point. "I've been hired by an interested party to help investigate the death of Edgar Landsworth, Mr. Gatlin. You've made an official claim that he was your uncle, is that correct?"

"Yes. On my mother's side. He grew up in New England."

"Where, exactly?"

"Southern Maine." Gatlin fished a pack of Luckies from his pocket, offered Walker one, and took one for himself. They lit up using a cardboard book of matches beside the ashtray on the table between their chairs. On the cover of the matchbook were the printed words THE TIRED FARMER TAVERN.

"Did you know him well?" Walked asked.

"Edgar Landsworth? We hadn't seen or spoken to each other in years. I already told the police that." Gatlin frowned. "Is there a problem?"

"Probably not. It's just that...well, some questions have come up."

"What kind of questions?"

"About what happened, this past Monday," Walker said. "Were you told that a man named Frank Teal has accused the late Mr. Landsworth of trying to kill him, there on the bluff? Before Landsworth fell to his death?"

"I heard that, yes. And before you ask, I'm afraid I don't know Mr. Teal."

"The fact is, Mr. Gatlin, I've come to believe it might've been Landsworth, not Teal, who was sitting on the edge of the cliff facing the mighty Mississippi that day. Which would suggest that Teal might've attacked Landsworth, instead of the other way around."

"I see." Gatlin squinted through a fog of smoke. "But even if that's true...what would it have to do with my claim?"

"Nothing. I'm just trying to find out anything I can about the incident."

"I'm afraid I can't help you, then. I honestly have no idea."

Walker held the older man's gaze a moment more, then nodded and crushed his cigarette out in the astray. "Well," he said, and stood. "Thanks for your time."

"Not at all." Gatlin rose also, and followed his visitor down the porch steps. "I hope you find the answers you're looking for, Mr. Walker."

"I will," Walker said. He returned to his car, backed out, and drove away up the tree-lined street. Before turning north at the corner, he checked his mirror and saw Howard Gatlin still standing in his front yard. Looking at him.

Walker's first stop after arriving back in Natchez was a pay phone at the edge of town. He parked beside it, took Gatlin's book of matches from his pocket, and entered the booth. According to the Yellow Pages in the phone book attached to the wall, The Tired Farmer Tavern was on historic Silver Street, beside the river. It took him less than five minutes to get there.

He drove down the steep street to water level and parked in front of the tavern, twenty yards from a boat landing. Years ago Natchez-Under-the-Hill, a cluster of buildings tucked into the base of the bluff, was one of the most notorious and dangerous places in the South. Now it looked tame. Fat white clouds floated past overhead, and a long barge made its way underneath the bridge, headed south. After watching it a minute, Walker pushed through the door and into a narrow, windowless room with a bar that ran the length of the left-hand wall.

"What's buzzin', cousin?" a man asked.

Walker waited a moment for his eyes to adjust. "Is the manager in?"

The same voice said, "Sure is." Walker could make him out, now: tall and bearded and leaning on the bar with his arms folded and a dead cigar between his teeth. He wore a vest and sleeves with garters on them, as if this were a saloon in the Old West. An empty saloon, at the moment.

"So you're the Tired Farmer?" Walker asked.

"You're half right. I'm not a farmer." The manager scratched his beard. "Who are you?"

"My name's Luke Walker. Private investigator, from New Orleans."

"Anderson," the man said, around the cigar. "You don't sound Cajun to me."

"I'm not. I grew up out in the sticks, north of Jackson. Kept the redneck accent, I guess."

"Fine with me." Anderson narrowed his eyes. "You look a little tired your ownself."

"The clock where I'm staying kept me up all night. I'm surprised you didn't hear it here."

"Ticking?"

"Chiming the hour," Walker said.

"Stop winding it." Anderson took the cigar out of his mouth, seemed surprised that it wasn't lit, and put it back. "So what do you want, Mr. Private Eye?"

Walker showed him the matchbook. "I got this from a man named Howard Gatlin. You seen him here recently?" This was a longshot and Walker knew it, but he also knew that bartenders the world over—managers or not, tired or not—remembered their customers.

"Not here at the bar," Anderson said.

"What does that mean?"

"Means I got a poker table in the back room. The game's legal, and the players buy enough drinks to make it worth my while."

"High stakes?" Walker asked.

"Lot higher'n *I* could play for."

Walker paused a long time, and saw that Anderson knew what was coming.

"Mr. Gatlin doesn't win often, does he?" Walker said.

"No. He loses often. And loses big. Finally stopped coming at all."

"You're saying he's in debt?"

"Up to his bloodshot eyeballs," Anderson said.

Walker nodded, thanked him, and left.

Things were beginning to make sense.

Walker didn't have to look up the next address. After stopping for a quick sandwich, he just drove east on Franklin until he saw what he wanted. How many Gulf stations could there be on one street? Walker parked beside the station's office and walked around to the front.

He finally saw an old-timer in an orange Gulf Pride baseball cap sitting in a lawn chair and reading *The Natchez Democrat* on the other side of the building, in a spot that was shady and still offered a view of the two gas pumps. The man put down his newspaper, studied Walker over the top of his glasses, and said, "You must be here to look for Frank Teal."

"And to ask a question. I take it you're the owner. Homer Fitzhugh?"

"Is that your question?"

Walker grinned. "I guess I have two questions."

The old man returned the smile and said, "I'm the owner. Call me Fitz."

Walker identified himself, shook Fitzhugh's hand, and glanced past him. Besides the big-windowed office, he saw an open bay with a grease rack. No one else was here.

Fitz said, after watching him study their surroundings, "As you can see, Teal's still AWOL. By the way, the cops been here already, asking about him."

"They probably also asked you if you could recall any arguments between Teal and one of your customers, Edgar Landsworth."

"Yep. And I told 'em I couldn't. Landsworth had some work done here a while back, on a Plymouth coupe, but I don't 'member no argument."

That's because Teal made it up, Walker thought. He said, "My question is, since Teal's here part-time—he *is* part-time, right?"

"Yep. Tuesdays, Wednesdays, and Thursdays. Until this week, that is."

"Where does he work on Mondays and Fridays?"

"Nobody's asked me that," Fitz said. "I wondered why, but I ain't one to just up and offer information. Even to the cops."

"Well, I'm asking now. Where does he work?"

"Woodville. That's south a here, in Wilkinson County."

"Where exactly, in Woodville?"

"Car dealership," Fitzhugh said. "Gatlin Ford."

Walker felt the little tingle that always comes when a puzzle piece clicks into place. Not only had Teal told the cops multiple lies about what happened on and before the incident Monday afternoon, Howard Gatlin had lied about knowing Teal. Gatlin, the retired but still-involved owner of an auto dealership, had almost certainly hired one of his employees to kill Gatlin's uncle so he could inherit the money to pay his gambling debts, and when Teal had successfully completed his mission and pushed Edgar Landsworth into the next life, he'd then been splatted with a giant turd of bad luck: he had run right into a cop while fleeing the scene and was forced to invent a story. Afterward, Teal had possibly realized, even though the police hadn't, how many holes his fictional account had contained, and decided to skip town. Walker had already suspected that. But since his visit to The Tired Farmer, Walker now thought Teal hadn't left town at all, because he wouldn't have yet been paid. In fact it now seemed likely that in the interests of damage control, Gatlin had murdered Teal himself. Either way, Walker figured Homer Fitzhugh would soon need to find a new part-time mechanic.

"Sonny?" the old man was saying.

Walker blinked. "Sorry. Guess I was daydreaming."

"I do it all the time. What I said was, I sure admire that car a yours."

"What?"

"Your car. I saw you driving past several times, just 'fore you stopped here. Was you lookin' for Teal, or just trying to figure if this was the right place to ask about him?"

Walker shook his head. "Sorry, Mr. Fitzhugh. You lost me. I didn't drive past, before. My car's parked over on the far side of your building. And it's a plain old Buick."

Fitzhugh frowned. "You mean that wasn't you, in that fine automobile I saw?"

"What kind of automobile was it?"

"A gray '46 Lincoln," Fitz said. "A Zephyr, I think."

Walker took a look around before he pulled out of the Gulf station and into traffic. He saw no sign of Gatlin's Lincoln, but he had little doubt Gatlin had seen him arrive and talk to the owner. Now that he thought about it, Walker even remembered noticing a similar car in his rearview mirror several times after leaving Woodville this morning, but had shrugged it off. He wouldn't let that happen again. Anyhow, if Gatlin had seen Walker or his Buick here or at The Tired Farmer, he must now be aware that his world was about to crumble around him. What Gatlin would do next Walker didn't know, but he did know it was time to visit the cops again.

For the next two hours he told them everything he knew, and found that the helpful but impatient policemen he'd met the day before were now hanging goggle-eyed on his every word. For one thing, they now realized how many facts they'd overlooked, and how much they had yet to do. One was to locate Teal—or his body, Walker thought—but their number-one task was to confront, and probably arrest, Howard Gatlin.

When Walker finally left the police station, it was with mixed feelings. On the one hand, he was convinced a murder had been solved and another murder implied; a good day for justice and the law. On the other hand, he would have to report to his attractive young client that his primary mission had failed. It seemed probable that Gatlin—not Jean—was indeed Edgar Landsworth's only heir. First, there were the old photos Gatlin said he had to prove it; second, Edgar was apparently from up north, not Texas. Walker hated to admit defeat, but—as he'd often heard in his days as an MP—sometimes that was just the way the mop flopped.

Walker pulled into his sister's gravel driveway, parked, and checked his watch. 3:50. With a weary sigh he trudged up the steps of the farmhouse and through the front door.

"Vinnie?" he called, tossing his hat onto a chair beside the living room fireplace.

No answer. He was about to call out again—and stopped in his tracks.

Standing in the open doorway to the kitchen was his sister Vinnie, pale and trembling. Behind her, Howard Gatlin shoved her forward into the living room. "Stand beside him," Gatlin said. In his hand was a pistol that he kept pointed at her back as she inched into the room. When she stopped beside Walker and turned to face the gunman, less than fifteen feet separated them from Gatlin. No one said a word.

The older man was still wearing the suit from this morning, but the tie's knot was loose and his hair unkempt. "I parked around back, Mr. Walker. In case you're wondering."

"I'm wondering why you're here at all. If I were you I'd be running."

"I will be, soon, thanks to you," Gatlin said. "You should've stayed in New Orleans."

Walker shook his head. "The police would've figured it out.

You made too many stupid moves."

Gatlin barked a laugh. "Not as many as you, apparently. I'm the one holding the gun."

Good point, Walker thought. The holstered .38 under his suit jacket seemed miles away.

He could feel his heart pounding next to it.

"How'd you get here?" he asked. "How'd you know where I was staying?"

"You told the doll at the police station—Maggie, I think." Holding both the gun and his eyes steady, Gatlin took off his glasses, wiped them one-handed on his lapel, and put them on again. "When I called in and said I needed to reach you, she was kind enough to give me your sister's name and phone number. And once you have a name it's easy to get an address."

Walker cast a worried glance at Vinnie, who was still shaken but seemed to be holding up—and saw her do something strange: she looked at him, calmly held his gaze, widened her eyes as if shocked, then narrowed them again. He was puzzled at first, and then understanding dawned, along with a surge of hope. Facing Gatlin, he said, "How long have you been here?"

"Thirty minutes or so. Why?"

Walker said nothing, his mind racing now.

Without waiting for an answer, Gatlin said, "I was beginning to think you'd left town."

"Like Frank Teal?" Walker asked. "That was your dumbest mistake, you know—hiring one of your own mechanics to get rid of Landsworth. Next dumbest was killing Teal yourself. You did, didn't you?"

"What choice did I have? That cop who saw him there messed everything up. But I'd have still been fine, if you hadn't shown up."

"No, you wouldn't. Murdering people and getting away with it isn't as easy as it seems."

Gatlin smiled, but his eyes had darkened. "I'm sorry to hear that, because I'm about to murder two more."

Keep him talking, Walker thought.

"There's something else you need to know, Gatlin. After I figured out you were following me today and then lost you, I went to the cops and told them everything. They're probably at your house by now, and the Highway Patrol's searching for your car. How do you plan to get out of this?"

The smile widened. "In your car, that's how. I'll cross the river at Baton Rouge by late tonight and be sipping tequilas with senoritas a week from now. I'm a salesman, remember? I'm no stranger to shady deals. I'll do just fine in Mexico."

Not if I can stall long enough. It had now become a matter of seconds, not minutes. Just a little longer...

"One more question," Walker said.

"No. I got things to do and places to go. Goodbye to you both." Gatlin cocked the pistol, raised it to eye level—

And Vinnie's giant clock struck the hour. Four feet from Gatlin's right ear.

He flinched and jerked his head toward the sound, his gun hand following, and Walker was ready, his hand moving too, underneath his coat and out again with his revolver. As he fired he saw from the corner of his eye that Vinnie had dove to the left and grabbed a fireplace poker.

There was no need. Howard Gatlin stood frozen for a moment, his face slack and a red bullet hole in his left temple. Then he dropped the gun and fell slowly backward. On the clock's fourth chime he hit the floor, landing half in the living room and half in the kitchen.

Dazedly, Walker and Vinnie crossed the room and stared down at the body. He folded his sister into a hug. "You okay?" he murmured. He felt her nod. She was still carrying the poker.

Seconds later they separated. Walker skirted around the body and splashed water on his face at the sink while Vinnie phoned the police. Then they sat together on the couch in silence.

Finally he took a deep breath, let it out, and said, "Vinnie?"

She turned to look at him. "What."

146

"Don't sell the clock."

It was eight p.m. before Walker was done. That night he was the most important person in the Natchez police station, or at least the one getting the most attention. Vinnie had come in also, to endure a marathon of questioning, and by the time all parties were satisfied, the two siblings were dead tired. Frank Teal's body had yet to be found and might never be, Walker thought, but most of the other loose ends were tied up. It had been a strange two days for Luke Walker.

But he was not, it appeared, finished with strange things. When he'd driven Vinnie back to the house and was packed up for his trip south tomorrow morning, he'd used her phone to call his client with the bad news: Edgar Landsworth's fortune, however big it might be, would go to the state since there now appeared to be no legal living heirs.

Jean Landsworth answered on the first ring, but before he could say a word, she told him she'd received some news herself earlier that night. She'd been on the phone with Harriet Perkins, the lady who'd raised her, and happened to mention her father's family, and Miss Harriet had told her that one of the things Jean remembered about what her late father had said about Edgar was wrong.

"I didn't know how to get in touch with you, Mr. Walker," Jean said. "I tried your office, but—"

"I know. The phone's out, and so am I. What was it that Harriet Perkins said?"

"She said Daddy's uncle wasn't from Texas like I told you. He just lived there awhile, in the service. He was originally from—"

"Maine?"

There was a long silence on the phone. Finally Jean said, "Yes. Ogunquit, a little town south of Portland. How did you know?"

Walker couldn't help smiling. Sometimes good things do

happen to good people, he thought. "I believe I might have some welcome news for you, Miss Landsworth. For both of us. I'm in Natchez but I'm leaving first thing tomorrow—can you stop in at my office, maybe around noon?" He nodded. "Good. See you then."

He hung up and walked to the kitchen, where Vinnie was making coffee. "What kind of welcome news?" she asked.

He said nothing, waiting for her to look up at him. When she did, he said, "This Mr. Ethridge, who helps you with the work around here...You think he'd be willing to watch the farm full-time for a while, if you go with me someplace?"

"What? When?"

"Don't know yet. Maybe this fall."

Her eyes were wide now. "Go with you where?" she asked.

He smiled and took both her hands in his. "How about Hy-wah-yah?"

THE PARTY
Lia Matera

Killy felt a tap on his arm and turned, trying to wipe vexation from his face. He'd had his fill, and more, of politicians' glib notions and swaggering certitude. The Great War had made generals of them all, determined to crush dissent to "insure the fruits of peace." They saw mild heterodoxy as sedition in the bud, street violence as tendrils of the Bolshevik Revolution. Adding to his chagrin, they kept quoting his oldest friend, once like a brother, as if to please him.

He watched Jeanette Duran take a backward step, her gloved hand flying to the Dutch lace and seed pearls of her bodice. He bowed slightly, redoubling the effort to iron his brow.

His hostess had backed herself into a table that would shame a museum, with samovars from the household of Peter the Great, Favrile punch bowls, cameo glass decanters, Meriden goblets. A vast mirror behind it reflected several men from the shoulders up, the gilt frame angled to reflect a *quadratura* on the high ceiling. Dimpled cherubs, lit by golden rays through clouds in a turquoise sky, seemed to reach for French doors that opened onto a veranda the size of a ballroom. Most of the guests were out there now, fanning themselves in the heat of a summer still clawing the air in mid-autumn. Maids in uniform poured water and champagne, placed and replaced silver trays of appetizers at tables set for an al fresco dinner. Screens from porch rails to roof held back a determined curtain of mosquitoes.

"Forgive me, Jeanette," Killy said, feeling his face grow hotter, something he didn't think possible in this air like boiled molasses.

That morning, he'd left an oven of city streets, glad to flee the stink of auto exhaust and steaming tenements. He'd hoped the countryside would offer respite, but he'd stepped off the train into a miasma of blown flowers and decayed greenery. In what his Irish father used to call St. Martin's summer, rural Virginia, like nearby Washington, remembered it had once been swampland.

"Not at all, Marshal. You have so much on your minds, all you gentlemen." She waved vaguely around the room. A few voices punched through the murmur of diffident aides and assistants: Ohio Governor Cox's staccato, Assistant Secretary of the Navy Roosevelt's booming laugh, former Treasury Secretary McAdoo's description of pogo sticks. "Ever seen them? Infernal devices. Turned my brood into kangaroos." He was the president's son-in-law, so people listened when he talked about his children. Killy's man, Attorney General Alexander Mitchell Palmer— Mitchell to his friends—was sitting outside with his new protégé. That was the reason Killy remained in this sweatbox of a parlor.

Jeanette continued, "Mr. Gray, my dear butler, you know, says there is a telephone call for you. Long distance. I had him tell the operator to keep your party on the line, and I came straight in to fetch you. In case..." She would not expect Killy, an unmarried man without siblings or living parents, to dread news of a death in the family. Her worry, he knew, was about his city, that it might explode into another race riot. It had taken almost two weeks for his marshals, city police, county sheriffs, state militia, and national guard to quell the last. It had left forty dead, six hundred injured, and nearly two thousand homes and businesses torched. And every week since the tumult of the so-called Red Summer, there had been more bombings, more beatings, more shootings.

With worried glances at him over the spray of flowers on her shoulder, Jeanette led him to the telephone. It had a place of honor in her entryway, on a gilded table beside a staircase broad enough for a horse parade. Its white marble caught the colors of a two-story Tiffany window.

The voice in the earpiece was all too familiar to Killy. It was down low, the way it got when the boys were in the gun locker on their way to something big. "Boss, it's Connell. We got a problem."

"Are you at home?" Meaning their offices in the Courts Building.

"Yes." Connell spoke louder now, remembering this was long distance. "Armed fools out in force, breaking windows, setting fires in Russian and Polish neighborhoods. Drunks driving through trying to shoot people on the street, but nobody hit yet. A lot of shouting—down with Reds and Bolshies, you know the kind of thing. Groups piling into cars, on their way to Little Italy, 'deport the Anarchists' and so on. Waving newspapers open to that speech of the attorney general's." There was a pause Killy interpreted as reluctance, which wasn't like Connell. "You're there with the attorney general tonight? Old friend of yours? You think maybe if you ask him to get on the radio? A few of these guys have crystal sets and maybe if he told them to—"

"No," Killy cut in.

"Just that it's been happening all over, Boss, and they say you're like a top advisor, so we thought—"

"No!" Killy fought to modulate his tone. "No. I'll be on the morning train. Meet me."

He put the earpiece on the hook and set the phone back on the table. Old friend of his, Connell had said. A top advisor. That was before the bombing of the attorney general's house, among others. Before a Rasputin of a new advisor had him publicly bless the so-called citizen militias. As if the marshal service wasn't up to the task, after arresting how many enemy aliens, how many foreign troublemakers?

Some of these groups were better armed than the marshals— better armed than the Allied forces. Gird a certain kind of man for battle and he'll go looking for targets. How many times had Killy urged Mitchell to make it clear his office was not lending its imprimatur to attacking any and all so-called hyphenated Americans—Russian-Americans, Italian-Americans, German-Americans, Polish-, Ukrainian-, Lithuanian- and more. That he did not equate ethnicity with philosophy, that few immigrants were Anarchists, Bolsheviks, Socialists, revolutionaries, traitors. But Killy did not have his old friend's ear anymore.

Once, their mothers—inseparable Quakers in a German Protestant backwater of Pennsylvania—had made brothers of them, so neither would have to face adversity alone. And there had been plenty of adversity for two Quaker boys in a Moravian school. But now Mitchell took his advice from a young prig who'd never suffered a moment's hardship, who'd never been pushed into a single moment of unorthodoxy. John Edgar Hoover was out on the veranda with him, luxuriating in his regard, reminding all present that the attorney general had created a special division for him in the Justice Department. And what was the result of the "Red" Division's roundups and mass deportations, its shuttering of magazine and newspaper offices, its long delays of mail so train cars of letters and parcels could be opened and censored? It was daily gunfire on city streets.

He turned to find Jeanette behind him. Even with upswept white hair and a tiara fit for an empress, she barely reached his shoulder.

"Oh, dear. Trouble at home, Marshal? Another riot?"

"Shootings," he said. "It's hot enough to roast a man alive, and that never helps."

"No." For a moment the heat seemed to wilt her, her tiara slipping forward a fraction. Then she pulled herself to her full height, such as it was, and fluffed the wide skirt of her gown, which had probably cost the moon at the turn of the century. Though she was in her seventies or eighties, maquillage caking in the crepe of her cheeks, there was a girlish charm in her plumping of those outmoded petticoats. He didn't suppose she'd ever been a handsome woman, but he understood how Judge Duran—as fine as Francis X. Bushman when young, judging from a nearby portrait—had lost his heart.

Jeanette Perdue, a poor lawyer's daughter, had been known in the District for her quicksilver wit and unshakable affability. She'd been university educated, a rarity for women of her era, and already making herself indispensable to various Democratic candidates. Mister—not yet Judge—Duran had been an indolent fellow of small intellect, but he'd gone to the best schools his family could endow with buildings or arenas, and he'd read law with a well-compensated uncle. He'd been bright in a way that offended no one, and Jeanette had been able to make something of him. She'd prodded him into local and state offices, gotten him elected to Superior Court and appointed to District Court. She launched her increasingly popular political soirees, carefully targeting the judge's campaign contributions to create a king-maker. When her husband was confirmed as a Court of Appeals justice, she'd worn the triumph like a fine sable coat.

Admiration for her warmed Killy's smile. She was, in her way, as regal as a Velázquez queen. But at her age, with no host beside her, she could look forward to few (if any) more of these events. The Westfields, some fifteen miles down the road, were already starting to host them, in anticipation. Killy had attended one a few months ago, adding to his reluctance to join Mitchell here today. But the party owed Jeanette Duran too much, had relied too heavily on her connections and contributions over half a century, to snub her in her widowhood.

She tucked her hand into his arm and drew him back toward the arches framing the parlor. As if wafting out on tumbles of cigarette and cigar smoke, the chatter of guests rose and fell, glittering with laughter and the clink of cut crystal.

"There's a Mr. Lancaster here, Marshal, hired by the judge before he passed." She was quiet for a heartbroken beat, then added, "He would have started working for him a few weeks after...Well, he never got the chance. And my wits were so scattered during the judge's last weeks, with his illness and all the doctors and arrangements...I don't even recall him telling me he'd hired a clerk." She flushed slightly, casting him a guilty look, as if afraid she'd transgressed. "Most years, you know, he didn't bother with one."

"But last year he did?" Killy couldn't keep surprise from his voice. He knew—everyone knew—Jeanette had acted as the judge's clerk. She'd sat in on his trials, researched the law, written up the judge's opinions and (it was rumored) explained them to him.

"So it seems. And as Mr. Lancaster was in the neighborhood today, he came to pay his respects." A frown touched her brow. "I dare say Mr. Gray wouldn't have admitted him, but I was outside at the time, seeing to the carpet being rolled down the steps and walkway. He introduced himself very prettily, and as he'd seen the red carpet, it would have felt rude not to ask him to stay for the soiree." She stopped Killy just shy of the parlor. "I suppose the judge thought we needed younger eyes. I won't tell you how many years ago I started helping him. Oh dear, how old I've gotten. But come!" She waved a lace-gloved hand to indicate a guest. "I particularly want you to meet Belle's new assistant, Ann Heriville. She's over there with Belle and Mr. Lancaster, the boy with the lovely curls. I sent him to Ann because she was a cloud of gloom, not that I blame her. Nothing cheers one up like a pair of broad shoulders and a charming dimple."

Killy saw Belle Moskowitz in a silk dress of emerald green. It wasn't quite modern, its hemline longer than the current mode, as befit a woman over forty. But it was free of the bustles and lace and ruffles still worn by older ladies, and it was cut to flatter, not pad, an ample figure. Beside her, the young man might have looked shabby if his face hadn't been fine enough to chisel in marble. The dimple Jeanette had mentioned was very much in evidence now, as he leaned flirtatiously close to a woman of about thirty.

"Oh my, how conspicuous he looks in that daytime suit." Jeanette whispered so only he could hear. "But he's not the only one, tonight. I suppose with the war, so many dead in the trenches, young men don't stand on ceremony anymore." She glanced with approval at Killy's dinner jacket.

He had not been to the manor born, but he had known better than to come to Jeanette Duran's in a daytime suit.

She patted his arm, leading him through the arches. "How I miss the judge. He took so much pleasure in these soirees, in how good they were for the party, how useful to talk things through without reporters and bureaucrats listening and pestering." A rueful smile. "I hate to think I'm too old to give another, but one never knows. And with the campaigning next year…Well, it was hard enough to fit together all the schedules this year. You must have noticed Homer Cummings isn't here, though there are several others from the national committee. And Ed Edwards had to send an aide in his place, prickly young man—you know how people from New Jersey can be. And we nearly didn't have Bill McAdoo. He said he'd still be in Hollywood, so imagine my surprise when he stepped out of the vice president's car."

She walked Killy past a table with a dozen kinds of alcohol, which he noticed the "dry" politicians eyeing from a disapproving distance. Jeanette paused there, pretending to inspect a tumbler with facets cut to show men in chariots. "Do be attentive to Mrs. Heriville, won't you?" He bent closer to hear her. "Poor thing. Her husband has been conspicuously shaming her all over town, squiring a stage actress to concerts and restaurants, and she, gaudy with new emeralds and gowns. He's some sort of banker, not the kind who works in banks but the kind who gets rich from them. A potato of a man, portly and drab, half bald— flattered, I suppose, to be pursued by a dazzling girl. They say she's straight out of a Rosetti painting, flaming red hair. I knew at once something like that was going on when I saw him in town. He was overdressed in that way of men who want to look dashing, and men never want to look dashing for their wives, do they? I told Belle she absolutely *must* bring Ann with her tonight. I want her flanked by the two handsomest men in the room, and I hope it gets back to that banker of hers."

"You cannot mean me, dear lady."

"Don't tease, Marshal. You're a fine figure indeed, and those eyes, oh my—cobalt around sky. I've never seen any like them. And a good head of hair, and an important job, though I suppose if you had a wife, she'd worry. About your safety, I mean, for you don't strike me as a philanderer."

Killy laughed, then said, because she seemed to expect it, "No, that I am not."

He'd heard about the judge's liaisons, decades ago when Jeanette was repeatedly in the family way. But word was, she'd made short work of that tendency after having her last child. She'd taken over as the judge's secretary and clerk, spending virtually every moment with him. And she'd started this tradition of political gatherings, making herself too popular a hostess, too important to the careers of important men, for her husband to dream of (as she'd said of Mr. Heriville) shaming her.

"I was glad that Belle gave Ann a good living working for Al Smith." Jeanette's chin went up in approval. "Belle ran Al's campaign for governor almost single-handedly, as you know. And she'll make him president one day, mark my words. But he's a handful, isn't he? Always doing doing doing. He needs a great deal of tending, that's why she hired Ann. And a good thing for the girl. She'll have money of her own while that porcine husband makes a fool of himself with his redhead." She flushed and looked away, and Killy wondered if pride had made her disdain the judge's wealth while he played her false.

"I've often wished," Killy said, to shift the subject to less painful ground, "that we could coax Belle over to Mitchell's campaign."

Jeanette fixed him with an intense look that showed her on the verge of saying something pointed. But she checked herself, murmuring instead, "She's far too devoted to Al, you know

that. What he's done in New York for workers and women."
She seemed on the brink of saying more, then shook her head
slightly, as if vowing not to.

In her silence, Killy heard what others must be saying: that
Attorney General A. Mitchell Palmer had been going too far.
Mass raids, arrests, deportations, giving his blessing to rowdy
"militias" who shot up neighborhoods and pretended they were
fighting Reds.

Mr. Gray, Jeanette's elegant butler, approached then, and
she gave Killy a ladylike push. "Go smile at poor Ann," she
whispered, and turned away.

Killy threaded past Franklin Roosevelt and the several men
he was charming. "Mitchell Palmer, poor fellow," Roosevelt
was saying, "covered in dust. I live across the street from him,
we'd both thrown coats over pajamas. He was so overcome that
the Quaker came out in him—*thee*-ing and *thou*-ing us."

Fairly or unfairly, Killy resented that casual mention of
Mitchell's faith. After a war that made Quakers unpopular for
refusing from conscience to carry arms, the reminder would do
Mitchell no good with these men. They would recall that
Mitchell refused, due to his Quaker beliefs, to be Wilson's
minister of war, settling instead for custodian of alien property.
They would forget they later called him "the Fighting Quaker"
for seizing five hundred million dollars in foreign assets.

Belle Moskowitz, clearly excluded from a flirtation between
Lancaster and Ann Heriville, looked relieved to see Killy. She
offered her plump cheeks to be kissed while the younger pair
waxed enthusiastic about *Sunnyside*, the latest Chaplin film.
Killy had seen the silly confection, and as ever, was baffled by
the appeal of slapstick.

He smiled at Belle. She was no beauty, to be sure, but her
broad face had a look of intelligent goodwill, her eyes a brilliance
that promised discernment without malice.

"I saw your husband earlier," he said. "I meant to speak
with him but he moved on before we could cross paths."

"Henry's a good mingler." She smiled her approval. "That's the point of these soirees, talk to as many as one can. Though…" She glanced at the young man laughing with her assistant. "You'd think that would be especially important to someone who, I'm told, is looking for work."

"Sticking close to her, is he? Jeanette sent me over to meet the lady, says she needs cheering up."

"Jeanette is talkative tonight." Belle sounded less than pleased. "I'm afraid this Mr. Lancaster is making a bit of a spectacle of Ann. Hanging on her words with an enthusiasm usually accompanied by cash payment." Though she was speaking quietly, her voice pitched only to him in the general din, she lowered it another notch. "I've been wondering, to be honest, if Jeanette *did* pay him, or at least exhort him, to flirt with Ann."

"A word in his ear? I wouldn't be surprised. I was told to distract her from the sins of a porcine husband. But perhaps the lad is genuinely taken with her." He could see that Belle doubted it, and so did he. Lancaster was a great deal more comely than Ann Heriville, and at a guess, five years younger. She was by no means ugly but certainly plain of face and carrying too much weight. Her mulberry dress, though of fine cloth, made her appear sallow. The style suggested it had gone into aromatic cedar at her last pregnancy, and the fit suggested it had been removed too soon.

Killy heard Jeanette's carrying voice from somewhere behind him. "If he expects to be someone's running mate next year," she was saying, "he'd better learn not to gossip like a shop girl. I don't care if his name *is* Roosevelt."

"Jeanette has no love for Franklin this night." Belle's tone was dry with amusement. "It's not the first time she's caviled over something he's said. Do you know what he's done to annoy her?"

"I do not."

Roosevelt, cousin to the former president, was still discussing the bombing of Mitchell's brownstone. Its façade, he told a rapt audience, had been blown off when the bomber apparently tripped and detonated his bomb before getting it inside. They'd found his torso, natty in a striped vest and bow tie, on the roof of a building across the street.

"Ann?" Belle jumped into a pause in her assistant's chat with Lancaster. "I'd like you to meet Marshal Killy, Mitchell Palmer's advisor and sometime campaign chair."

Ann Heriville said all the right things but she was clearly distracted, her eyes drifting back to Lancaster more often than they should. If that man wanted an easy conquest tonight, Killy thought, he would have one. There was no more powerful aphrodisiac than sauce for the gander.

Killy shook Lancaster's hand, finding him even prettier up close. It was clear he was not a politician. He had none of the pallor or puffiness of long hours indoors. And it appeared from his too-heavy brown wool and the sweat on his brow that he had not dressed for the climate. From a cooler part of the country, or not able to afford a suit for every season?

"Mrs. Duran tells me you're a lawyer, that you meant to clerk for the judge. Did she say you're from California?" Killy picked a more temperate state at random.

"San Francisco. But not since my school days." Lancaster's tone had a certain smugness. It reminded Killy of men he'd questioned, men certain they'd avoided a trap.

"And what school was that?"

"Everett Academy."

On a hunch, Killy said, "It's no longer standing, I believe?"

"No." His tone held no regret. "It collapsed in the earthquake."

"A pity." That was interesting. Con men often claimed matriculation from schools no longer able to offer records and attendance lists. "You weren't still there at the time, I hope?"

"Oh, no, I was in college by then, at McNeese in Lake Charles. Judge Duran's family has roots there. It made my application to clerk for him stand out, or so he wrote to me."

"I wouldn't have thought you old enough to be in college by aught six."

Lancaster bowed slightly. "I'll take that as a compliment."

There was something very smooth about him, Killy thought. It made him wonder if he'd find McNeese College had suffered a calamity, as well. He took a guess. "Big fire there, or am I misremembering?"

"A flood, but just as devastating." Lancaster shrugged. "The judge, I believe, gave generously to help it rebuild."

"Did you stay on to read law with someone in town?"

"That's right. It's a charming place. The flowers are a marvel. If I hadn't meant to go into law, I'd have studied botany." He flashed a smile at Ann Heriville, adding, "It's a particular affection of Mrs. Heriville's, too."

It was a safe guess that any Southern town would have marvelous flowers, Killy thought. The wet heat was kinder to plants than to people. Through the open veranda doors across the room, he could see white blooms tumbling over yellow ones, orange ones, red ones on vines winding around porch support pillars.

"The lawyer you apprenticed with," Killy said. "Anyone known to us here in the party?"

Lancaster mentioned a name Killy had not heard before, adding, "An older gentleman, close to retiring or I'd have gone into practice with him rather than make other arrangements. Like Judge Duran, he died when I was in the war."

"And now you're looking for a post? Perhaps you'll meet someone tonight looking to hire. Mrs. Duran, it seems, has done you a kindness."

He nodded, and Killy caught Belle's eye. Lancaster would meet few potential employers at Ann Heriville's elbow.

Killy turned to her. "I understand you work for Al Smith. He certainly inspires devotion."

"Yes," Ann said, and there was devotion in her eyes, all

right. "He deserves it."

"Mrs. Duran is convinced Belle here will make him president."

"Yes, I will," Belle said. "Perhaps not next year. Just between us, I despair of any Democrat winning in '20. All this discombobulation—the war, the flu, these bombings, the riots, the strikes...The party in power always catches the blame. And now we're rounding up—" She feigned a cough, and Killy knew she'd have said something about mass deportations if he hadn't been beside her.

Another twist of the knife. How had Mitchell let himself be mesmerized by that young bluenose Hoover, who had no sense of proportion and no notion of how to win elections (or how to deserve to win them)?

He thought of Connell on the phone, pleading with him to ask the attorney general to cool things down. But like Ann Heriville, Killy had been pushed aside for a young seducer.

He was glad of the distraction when a stocky man joined them, saying, "Belle, m'dear!" He might have looked the caricature of a businessman but for his kindly squint and slight but winning smile.

He and Belle exchanged kisses on the cheeks. Killy said, "Good to see you, Governor Cox. I've been following the situations in Youngstown and Canton."

"Not another strike, Jimmie?" Jeanette glided up to them as only Southern women could, as if on wheels rather than feet. Her tone was petulant. "Do the steelworkers *want* more Republicans in office? They must know they'll get no help from them."

"True, true, but they're in a spot," Cox said. "They were promised more pay now if they put aside wage and hour demands during the war. They made the sacrifice from patriotism, knowing we couldn't win without their steel. And now the owners renege. It's more than just the pay, it's the betrayal."

"The betrayal," Jeanette repeated. She cast a tactless glance at Ann.

When a florid man clapped Cox on the back, causing him to

turn away, Jeanette whispered to Killy, "Mr. Lancaster seems to be cheering the poor girl."

Praying she hadn't overheard, he too spoke *sotto voce.* "But Jeanette, have you checked his credentials? He seems rather...slippery in his details."

"Oh, no!" But there was little surprise in her tone. "He seemed so fond of the judge, what he knew of him. And he's obviously taken with Ann. You can see it's doing her good."

Killy wasn't so sure about that, but Jeanette had pinned on a bright smile and turned to Governor Cox. "Come and have a drink, sir—reassure us if you're the nominee our cocktails will be safe."

Belle, Killy saw, was still watching Lancaster. She waited till he and Ann resumed conversation, then turned to Killy. "Is he acting on Jeanette's command, do you suppose? I'm glad he shows an interest...if it's sincere. But honestly, have you ever met a man so fascinated by flowers?"

"You think Jeanette coached him?"

"I don't know what to think. Why introduce him into this company at all?"

"Jeanette said he showed up unannounced, and she didn't know what to do but invite him."

"And she's certain the judge hired him? Would he have done that without her knowing? *Could* he have? It's no secret she composed and typed his letters."

"She's getting on in years," he said. "She thinks perhaps it was to spare her a bit of work."

Belle shook her head. "With no discussion or warning? I'd be furious if Henry did that. Wouldn't any wife, in a working partnership?"

"It was a well-chosen lie, if Lancaster came just to coax an invitation. I gather he offered fond details about the judge."

"And no doubt flattered her. He certainly has the knack." Her glance at Lancaster was censorious. "His behavior is more suited to a beer hall. Ann has troubles enough without being made conspicuous."

"Is the husband a jealous man?"

"I doubt he notices anything she does. I telephoned her when Jeanette ordered me to bring her here. I heard her check with him, ask if he had plans for this day. And he said, in the coldest voice, 'None that include you.' He could outspend Croesus, but if he has anything else to recommend him, I've never seen it."

Killy had the impression Lancaster was straining to overhear. His smile had grown fixed, his gaze distracted as he listened (or pretended to listen) to Ann enthuse about the garden at her lakeside cottage.

Perhaps to Lancaster's relief, Franklin Roosevelt came up behind him. He said, in his refined and jovial (but never too jovial) voice, "The judge's clerk, I believe? Mrs. Duran sent me over to meet you." Then, extending a hand to be shaken, "A sad day when we lost the judge. I hear you didn't get a chance to meet him? Only corresponded, as I understand it?" With a nod to Killy, he said to Belle, "Are you and Henry ready to leave Al and come work for me?" And then to Ann, "Glad to make room for you, too, Mrs. Heriville. I hear you're doing great things for the governor."

Belle smiled. "Speaking of governors, Jeanette says Jimmie Cox has been making cow eyes at you all evening. She thinks it's a ticket in the bud."

"Cow eyes!" Roosevelt had a face that wore delight well. "I'll tell Jimmie she said so. I believe he's out on the veranda talking to your man, Marshal. Palmer would be a strong choice, I'll grant you. I'm sure you know he's my neighbor." When Killy nodded, he added, "That was a terrifying business last June, that bombing. Wife and daughter inside with him. I hear he's working on a series of raids now—round up Anarchists and Bolsheviks and so on. What you marshals have been doing since the before the war, but on a massive scale, not one or two here and a few more there. That serious young man of his is with him now, talking about lists he's compiling, Reds in every city.

Thousands of names so far—tens of thousands by year's end, he says."

Killy was spared having to reply by a laconic "How do," as Bill McAdoo stepped into their circle.

Roosevelt grinned. "McAdoo! Glad you made it, old boy. Aren't you supposed to be in Hollywood hobnobbing with film stars? How's Mrs. M?"

"Dandy." A slender man with a serious face atop a comically long neck—one that figured prominently in political cartoons—nodded to Killy and Belle, then cast a curious glance at the couple with them.

Roosevelt said, "Mrs. Heriville, Mr. Lancaster, may I introduce Bill McAdoo. Not content to remain secretary of the treasury, he's now a motion picture studio executive. And the newly wed father of fifteen children. Or is it sixteen now, Bill?"

"Eight, Franklin, only eight." His smile was wry. "And to clarify, before becoming a newlywed, I was a widower with seven."

"Young Lancaster was set to be the judge's clerk," Roosevelt said. Then, in apparent response to McAdoo's puzzled expression, "Hired by the judge before he passed."

"I see." McAdoo raised his brows as doubting it.

Killy knew him to be a sharp man, and it magnified his own disquiet.

"Mrs. Duran was very kind." Beads of sweat stood out on Lancaster's face. "I came today to pay my respects, and she asked me to stay."

"I see," McAdoo said again, tone neutral—studiously so, Killy thought. "Are you a party man?"

"Oh, no. She was just...just being gracious."

"You live in the District?"

"No. I'm just here..." He trailed off as if unsure what purpose to assign himself.

"Are you a California man?" McAdoo persisted. "I've spent a good deal of time there lately. Haven't I seen you at some events, festivities?"

"No," Lancaster said. "I live in Louisiana."

McAdoo stared at Lancaster for another long moment, and Killy and Belle exchanged glances. It would have been natural to mention he'd gone to school in San Francisco, Killy thought. If he *had* to gone to school there.

With a shrug, McAdoo said, "Well, excuse me, gentlemen, Mrs. Moskowitz, Mrs. Heriville. I was on my way out to needle Al. Hearst accuses him again, in seventy-two-point headlines, of killing babies by refusing to fix the price of milk. Care to join me, Franklin?"

Roosevelt fell in beside McAdoo like a fish finding its school. McAdoo inclined his head toward Roosevelt as if sharing a confidence. He cast a glance over his shoulder at Lancaster, who turned away.

Well, well, Killy thought. He'd make a point of chatting with McAdoo later.

There was a clatter on the veranda, and Killy saw servants rolling carts with covered chafing dishes. Small tables along the railing had been cleared of early evening litter. Papers, full ashtrays, half-empty tumblers, the remains of appetizers on salvers of ice were gone. Starched linen cloths and elaborately folded napkins had been laid with (if Killy recalled from last year's supper) antique Veyrat silver, replacing sturdy Paul Revere, and three layers of Louis XVI Limoges—ringed with blue then white then red—succeeding hand-painted Tressemann plates. Mr. Gray, Jeanette's elderly butler, orchestrated the changes with the elegance of a maestro conducting a symphony.

Killy considered asking Ann if she'd take his arm, allow him to convey her out to Al Smith's table (and away from Lancaster). But he couldn't catch her eye. She had no glance to spare for anyone but the Adonis at her side. Her cheeks were so flushed she put Killy in mind of a paper lantern beginning to char.

"It was grand meeting Mr. Roosevelt." Lancaster spoke at higher volume, as if to be heard over the shuffling and salutations of the exodus. "He'd be a grand vice president. I said so to Mrs. Duran when I learned he'd be here. But she didn't suppose Governor Cox or the attorney general would want an adulterer on his ticket. She thinks Warren Harding will be the GOP nominee, and I've heard the same from others. She says if there's a licentious man on our ticket, we won't be able to go after Harding for *his* philandering."

The word "philandering" made Ann jerk as if lashed. Killy wanted to change the subject, but nothing came to his lips.

"Adulterer?" she said, her voice small.

"His wife will leave him, according to Mrs. Duran, if the mother-in-law doesn't bully her out of it. Mrs. Roosevelt would have been here tonight, but she's in anguish over the betrayal."

Belle came to the rescue before Killy managed it. "So Jeanette thinks Harding will be the nominee? He's a puppet." She was a shade too loud, too emphatic, as if to bulldoze over Lancaster's words. "Republicans installed him in the Senate because he leaves everything to them, to his handlers. He brags he's never read a Senate bill. Or a newspaper or a book, if I'm any judge. He'll do whatever they tell him." Her laugh was brittle. "To think the country might settle for him when it could have Al Smith."

"Mrs. Duran says Republicans lend Harding apartments around town for his rendezvous," Lancaster added. "To keep him obedient. That it would be brazen of them to nominate him, when his debauchery is so well-known around the capital. But Democrats won't dare bring it up if there's similar shame on our ticket."

Why, Killy wondered, had Lancaster tossed this explosive bit of hearsay into casual conversation? It sounded rehearsed.

For Ann Heriville's sake, he gave voice to the first subject-changing thought that entered his mind. "I'd love to see Al Smith nominated. And Bill McAdoo is a good man." He realized from Belle's palpable shock that he should have been touting Mitchell Palmer. "If my man isn't the choice, of course."

Belle said, "Bill's father-in-law will block him."

"You think President Wilson will try for a third term?"

"Yes. I think he's counting on a wave of postwar patriotism to sweep him in. But I wouldn't say it was a popular war, even in victory." She turned to Lancaster, apparently waiting for him to weigh in, given that he had (he claimed) fought in it. But he stood silent, looking inattentive, even bored.

Killy said, "He'll have a hard time arguing it brought the nation together."

Belle nodded. "But of course we'll work our hearts out for him if we nominate him." She cast a worried glance at Ann. "All of us who support the governor will do whatever we can for the ticket regardless of who's on it." She seemed about to insist that Ann agree, but Lancaster cut in.

"Harding's debauchery would be a good issue for us," he said. "If our ticket wasn't open to that charge, too. We have to show we respect women."

Why, Killy wondered, did Lancaster refuse to let this drop?

Belle scowled, not hiding her annoyance. "There's no advantage to us in bandying rumors about our own people, Mr. Lancaster."

Lancaster bowed slightly, as if chastened. "I hope I didn't give the impression Mrs. Duran was spreading rumors. She was only telling me who'd be here, and she mentioned she was sorry Mrs. Roosevelt felt too shamed to come." He turned back to Ann, now as stiff as a waxwork. "But you were going to tell me which is your favorite Chaplin film? You've made me revise my opinion of *A Dog's Life*." His smile seemed to envelop her.

It took Ann a moment to compose herself, then Killy watched her plunge back into the man's attentions like a nymph into a pool.

Belle stepped closer to Killy, speaking quietly enough for the general din to keep the words between the two of them. "That was ill done of Mr. Lancaster. I almost wish Jeanette had told him Ann's situation, warned him off the subject of infidelity." She scowled across the room. Through the French doors, Roosevelt could be seen standing under a colored lantern, bent over the seated McAdoo as if paying court. "Mitchell wouldn't use this rumor against Franklin, I don't suppose. I know Al wouldn't."

"But perhaps an aide would?" Killy glanced at Ann Heriville. "A devoted aide with a particular reason to care?"

"I'll fire her if she breathes a word of this," Belle said. "Al wouldn't like it. And I'd better have a chat with Jeanette, too. I don't suppose it matters about Mr. Lancaster. Unless someone here hires him, which would surprise me with his thin credentials, we won't see him again."

"He's made no effort to circulate," Killy noted. As a man would, who had no fear of having his bona fides checked. "I wonder if Jeanette—"

"Go on, go on!" As if summoned by this mention of her, Jeanette was abruptly upon them. "Out to the veranda with you two. Nearly everyone's seated, the candles are lit, the wine's being poured." She flashed a bright smile at Belle. "I do like your Ann. We'll leave her here with that nice young man a few more minutes. He's putting color in her cheeks. You'll save her a seat at Al's table, I'm sure." Before Belle could reply, Jeanette had taken her arm and started them toward the door. She glanced over her shoulder, now covered with a shawl despite humid heat bloating the twilight. "Come along, Marshal."

If Jeanette had joined them five minutes earlier, Belle would not have heard Lancaster spread his noxious gossip. Ann might have passed it on before Belle could stop her.

With a slight bow, he said to Lancaster, "Mrs. Duran has commanded me. Good to meet you, sir, and you, too, Mrs. Heriville."

When he reached the French doors, he saw Mitchell sitting elbow to elbow with Hoover. Mitchell was angled in his seat so Killy mostly saw the back of his broad head, the hair Killy still saw in his mind's eye as brown now nearly all white. He realized with a pang that the last of Mitchell's gray had given way after the bombing attempts on his life.

Hoover was speaking, his voice coming to Killy in snatches.

He heard "with due respect" and "only course." It was a pompous man's voice, the occasional R an *ah*, the occasional syllable drawn out for emphasis.

A wave of pure hatred swept through Killy, as severely physical as vertigo or nausea. He turned, stepping back into the parlor.

An hour ago, Connell had said to him on the telephone, "You're there with the attorney general tonight? Old friend of yours? You think maybe if you ask him to…?" Killy had stopped listening then because Mitchell no longer took the advice of his old friend, whom he'd once called brother.

He needed to sit. His stomach was clenching, blood roared in his ears. He saw Lancaster coming toward him with Ann Heriville, and he realized the man had diagnosed what ailed him. It was shame—shame at being supplanted, at seeing decades of devotion brushed aside for a twenty-four-year-old fanatic. He nodded to Ann as she passed him, Lancaster close behind. The pain in Killy's gut almost had him groping for a chair. Instead, he grabbed Lancaster's arm. "Come with me," he said into the man's ear, jerking him to face the entryway, tugging him toward it so he had no choice.

It wasn't easy keeping hold of Lancaster as he greeted, without pausing, a few friends and acquaintances making their way to the veranda. But he'd arrested many an important man in a crowded place without creating a scene, and experience was on his side.

He knew, once they left the room, that they'd have only a few moments alone. The servants were busy seating guests and pouring drinks and serving chilled soup, but they would come inside soon to tidy things.

He grabbed two fistfuls of Lancaster's jacket, meaning to press him to the wall beside the arch, where they would not be visible from the parlor or veranda. But he pushed Lancaster too hard, heard the man's head crack against the ornate frame of a portrait. The judge smiled down from it, still a young man, no older than Lancaster, his hands on the reins of horse, his lips curled in a roguish smile.

"Who are you, really?" Killy demanded. "You were coached as to schools; I'd be shocked to find you attended either."

Lancaster shook off a dazed look, meeting Killy's eye. He didn't reply.

"Are you even a lawyer? Is your name really Lancaster?"

"What's it to you?" Lancaster tried to break Killy's grip, but there too, Killy's experience came in handy. "You're not my host."

"We'll have this conversation before Mrs. Duran, before the whole party, if that's how you want it. Or you can answer my questions here, and I might let you slip away without setting the law on you."

Lancaster stopped struggling.

"What sort of fraud is this?" Killy demanded. "You knew exactly what to say to bamboozle Mrs. Duran. You knew how to wheedle gossip out of her. Unless you invented all that about Roosevelt, putting the words into her mouth? Is that it? Did one of the other campaigns hire you to come here today and ingratiate yourself, pass along the gossip as if it came from her?" He was practically nose-to-nose with Lancaster now. He could smell the sour wool of his suit, the musk of his sweat. "I could let that pass. I don't like it, but politics is a dirty business, and I'm no tender maiden. It's the way you used Mrs. Heriville." He wasn't aware of pulling Lancaster forward then slamming him back again, not till he heard his head thud again against the picture frame. "It's the way you poured honey all over a wronged wife to be sure she'd mark your words. I suppose Mrs. Duran told you the lady's troubles, as she told me, and you saw her as easy fruit." He wanted to slap Lancaster, barely restrained himself. "I would shrug off all the rest. What do I care about Franklin Roosevelt? Or for that matter, the party, now it's—well, never mind that. But to torment that poor woman?" Slam. "Did it make you feel a big man to make her admire you? Lead her on step by step so you could remind her of her shame, twist the knife in her bosom?" Slam. "Just to make your point?"

But Killy knew his rage wasn't really about this paltry fellow. It wasn't Lancaster making a hell of Killy's streets, shooting out store windows, beating immigrants, setting fires. And it wasn't Lancaster making a cat's paw of the attorney general of the United States.

He was already stepping back when a voice behind him quavered, "Oh, no! Stop, Marshal."

When he let go of Lancaster's suit, one of the buttons skipped across the marble floor. Killy took a deep breath and turned to see Jeanette, both hands over her heart, her mouth in an O of horror.

"Please," she pleaded. "He's my guest."

"He is that, yes," Killy said, "but he's no lawyer, dear lady." He was still standing close enough to Lancaster to wheel around and bloody his nose, break his jaw. He took another stride forward, away from that temptation. To his chagrin, Jeanette backed up.

"He's an actor," she said, hands raised as if to ward him off. "That's what Bill McAdoo just told me. He recognized him from some motion picture studio party in California. And oh dear, I suppose I should have known, but...Why would I think a young man would...Please, Marshal, I can't bear a scene here tonight. Not tonight of all nights, my first time hosting this supper without the judge." A tear leaked down her cheek. "I couldn't bear it if everyone knew I'd let in a...I don't know how I'll ever look Bill in the face again."

With the concentration of someone making her way along a tightrope, she crossed to the settee by the telephone. She gripped the back with a shaking hand, eased herself into it as if from a great height.

Killy turned to Lancaster, a dozen more questions on his lips (and worse, on his knuckles), but his hostess had begged him. What could he do but step aside, let Lancaster walk away?

"Do you truly not wish to know his purpose here, Jeanette?"

Killy asked, when Lancaster was halfway to the door. "Say the word and I'll—"

"No!" Her voice was shrill, a half note from hysteria. "Whoever he is, I invited him. I won't have this party ruined because I was foolish."

Lancaster was out the front door by then. He'd slipped out quickly, not shutting it behind him. A dozen mosquitoes left the dusk of the front portico and buzzed into the room.

Killy waved one away as he stared down at Jeanette. She was worrying the fingers of one lace glove, staring down at her lap.

"Did you think I meant to beat the truth from him?" He forced some calm into his voice. "I'm sorry, Jeanette. But I could have questioned him without anyone seeing, if you'd ushered us to the judge's library, or down into the kitchen, or..." He waited for her to speak. When she didn't, he sighed, dropping onto the seat beside her. "If you'd wanted to know."

But it was clear to him she hadn't.

Her head was bowed. A scent of lilacs and powder rose from her, with a tiny hint of camphor from her gown.

"I suppose you told Bill McAdoo that you didn't know the man was an actor, that you're getting old and addled and believed his story?" He felt exhausted. Deflated. "You can count on McAdoo to say nothing about it to your other guests." His voice was harder than it should have been to a woman Jeanette's age. He tried to soften it. "He's too much the gentleman to do that." He patted Jeanette's hand, the lace of her glove slightly rough under his palm. "As am I."

But neither was he a fool. He had too much respect for Jeanette to believe she could learn an actor had insinuated himself into a gathering like this and not want to know why. Not even want to ask to him, with no other ears listening.

She didn't look at him. Her, "Oh, Marshal," was barely audible.

He'd never seen a lady of her generation and class slump before. Like his mother, like Mitchell's mother, Jeanette Duran

172

had always seemed to have a ramrod for a spine.

She'd had spine enough to decide she didn't want Franklin Roosevelt on the ticket. Spine enough to do what she could to cut out a man who'd betrayed his wife the way the judge had betrayed her. There would be other voters of her mind and so, for the sake of the party, she'd put words into an actor's mouth. She'd asked him to flatter Ann Heriville, to feign interest in her passions. A wronged wife would be more likely to credit gossip coming from a man who charmed her. She would be more likely to carry it to her employer.

Jeanette had sent Killy to Ann, and thus to Lancaster, because Killy had been conspicuously cast aside, too. Killy might take the rumor to Mitchell to prove he was still of value to him.

It was ugly, it was beneath her. Did it matter that it might help the party and through the party, the nation?

He ran a hand over his hair, damp with the sweat of this interminable day.

Jeanette's maquillage was melting like hardpan, showing every furrow in her cheeks and jowls. She had been a plain woman without money or power, and perhaps she'd put up with much from her handsome husband. But she'd squared her shoulders and made a judge of him, a power broker. She'd poured his wealth into the party that stood for fair treatment of workers, women's right to vote, an end to child labor. Could he fault her for caring so much? The party did not always pursue its aims with vigor. And with men like John Edgar Hoover on the ascendant, it abandoned some ideals altogether. But who else was there? Harding and his puppeteers?

Killy could not find it in himself to take Jeanette Duran to task, but neither could he find it in himself to continue to support Mitchell Palmer. He would always love his one-time brother; he would be here if ever Mitchell ever came to his senses. He would spread no rumors to help him, but neither would he make phone calls or raise funds or speak to police groups on his behalf. He would offer no advice to his candidate nor censure to his hostess.

That was as much as he could do for the party at the moment.

Jeanette was staring at him now, expecting him to speak.

He patted her hand. "Tell Mitchell I was called away, that I'm catching the train tonight. I've things to manage back home." It was the truth. He needed to deal with the violence Mitchell helped create. It was all he could do for his old friend.

A thousand memories rushed back. Mitchell at the dinner table, explaining Killy's choice of career to his mother, who could barely look upon a gun without weeping. There was no better service to community, to equality, Mitchell had told her, than to keep the peace with integrity.

And he remembered Mitchell planning his run for a House seat, their schemes for what he'd accomplish when elected— workplace safety rules, anti-lynching laws, universal suffrage. Killy had taken the train to be with Mitchell when the House passed his bill to end child labor, and he'd stayed to share Mitchell's woe when the president told the Senate to kill it.

"But, Marshal," Jeanette said, "weren't you meant to ride back to the District with the attorney general tonight, stay with him, and take the train in the—"

"My two legs will get me to the village fast enough." It would be a relief not to share a car with Mitchell and Hoover. "If there's no train from there tonight, I'll hire someone at the inn to drive me to town."

"Oh, no. I've ruined the evening, haven't I, with this Lancaster business?"

"No, no." He pitied her, so dispirited at what might be the last of her beloved soirees. "Lancaster is just a worm in the apple. Think of the good men dining with you—Al and Jimmie and Bill and Franklin." He added Roosevelt so she wouldn't know he'd guessed her purpose. "And think how many others you've you blessed with your hospitality over the years. Lancaster doesn't matter."

He crossed to the door, was outside on her red carpet before she could speak again.

The last glow of sunset was fading. The veranda's colored lanterns painted parked cars with neon streaks. He could hear the music of conversation, the tinkle of forks on porcelain, the clink of glasses meeting in toasts. He even fancied he could hear the fizz of champagne, but it may have been mosquitoes.

Jacket over his shoulder, shirt drenched in sweat, he passed dark fields that smelled of hay and horse manure, that ticked with grasshoppers. This would be his last time here. He was through with Washington, through with the meetings and soirees.

He was right, he thought, to have spared Jeanette his vitriol. Her half century of good works—or at least, of support for a party that sometimes did good—demanded it. But the words she'd put into Lancaster's mouth disgusted Killy. Her motives disgusted him. Politics disgusted him.

When he was within sight of the small village inn, he saw a man in its car park. He stood directly beneath a gas lamp, and there was no mistaking those bright curls. It was Lancaster, one foot on the running board of a Pierce-Arrow roadster, a gorgeous machine, deep crimson with a white ragtop. He was speaking to someone through the driver's open window.

Killy picked up his pace as Lancaster made a sweeping gesture in his direction, toward the Duran manor. Killy was too far away to hear more than timbre and tone, and as he got closer, Lancaster leaned in so the conversation was inaudible. Then, with a letter-sized packet in his hand, Lancaster turned and crossed the street. As he climbed into an old Ford, the Pierce-Arrow's engine engaged. Killy was equidistant from both cars.

He cursed his luck. If he went to Lancaster, the roadster would likely drive away. Lancaster might tell him who was in it—the person who had, Killy supposed, just paid him for his day's work. But he might not.

He made for the car park, though his fists itched to finish what he'd started in Jeanette's entryway. But he was no "militia" man, to mistake brutality for justice.

Lancaster drove away as Killy reached the roadster, a jewel

that likely cost more than the inn beside it.

He stepped up to the window, panting, conscious of looking a sight, his face contorted with frustration, his damp shirt caked with road dust. He startled the driver, a deep-voiced woman who swore like a sailor rolling snake eyes. He reached in and grabbed the steering wheel to tell her she wouldn't be driving away just yet.

"Let go! I'll honk. Someone at the inn will come out and—"

"I'll have a moment of your time." He looked her over, adjusting his presumptions. He'd expected to see a man, a rich man. An enemy of Roosevelt's, perhaps. Or of Ann Heriville's banker husband.

This was a Greek myth come to life. This was Athena, strong-jawed and tall, with full lips and flashing eyes. This was Aphrodite, luxuriant hair slipping from a silk scarf to cover one shoulder. The tumble of curls was so red against her driving coat that it seemed to glow. It was not an Irish girl's orange but a dark auburn with ruby undertones.

"Ah." A sigh escaped him as the knowledge sank in: Mr. Heriville's red-haired actress, the one with whom he shamed his wife.

"What do you want?" she demanded. Her tone was insolent, pitched to reach the cheap seats.

"It's what *you* want that interests me," he said. "Grounds for divorce, I suppose. A stage actress must live hand to mouth compared to a banker's wife. I assume Mr. Heriville is very rich, to give his fancy woman such a car." He looked at the fine leather seat, the elegant fittings on the dash, the polished wood panel in the door. "Does he know what you're up to?"

She shook her head in a gesture that seemed less a *no* than a preparation for a close-up. "Take your hand off the wheel. I'll scream if you don't."

"You'll hear me out or Heriville will. It's your choice."

He'd been so distracted by the rumor of Roosevelt's troubles that he hadn't considered Heriville's. It would not be easy for a respectable banker to divorce a wife who'd done him no wrong, who'd dutifully raised his children and caused no scandal. A wife who, moreover, worked for a popular governor looking to become president. And if it could be managed without taint to reputation, which was doubtful, it might cost more than even a tycoon could comfortably afford. A banker would consider the finances. He would know that without justification in the eyes of his peers and the courts, he'd be mad to consider making a wife of his mistress.

It would be different, of course, if his wife strayed. A man in his position would not be expected to forgive a wife for behavior his wife would be expected to forgive in him.

"That?" Killy nodded to a foot-square box of nobbled leather beside the passenger door. It had polished brass fittings and an embossed handle. "High-priced new camera, is it? Would your hired actor have taken Mrs. Heriville to a room at the inn? Or would he have abandoned her once you took photos of them going in together?"

She smiled slightly, as if she just couldn't help it. And why not, Killy thought. It had been a grand scheme, a sound gamble, with Lancaster on track to succeed before Killy pulled him away.

Pulled him away, it seemed, for the wrong reasons. Roosevelt had been a mere conversational gambit, a rumor Lancaster (whatever his real name) could exploit to salt Ann Heriville's wounds, to draw her into his consoling embrace.

How many ways had Killy been wrong tonight? He'd suspected Lancaster of trying to defraud Jeanette, of wanting to wring money or a post or introductions from her. Then he'd suspected the man of simple lechery, of seeing a betrayed wife as an easy mark. Then he'd decided Jeanette had paid Lancaster to offer Ann and Killy gossip to take to their candidates. He'd even wondered, for a moment with Belle, if Heriville might be a target for blackmail.

He'd never considered how far a rich man's mistress might

go to make herself a rich man's wife.

"I've a deal for you," Killy said. A hint of perfume, light and delicious, rose from her pale skin. Gardenia? "I won't tell anyone about this. Not Heriville, if he had no part in it. Nor his wife. Nor the hostess your friend bamboozled tonight. No one."

"If?" Her tone was wry, world-weary. Not outraged, not worried.

"If you make sure, in whatever way you can, that Ann Heriville never learns you hired that man."

She laughed. "So I'll have bought her an evening's fine flirtation? The fancy woman pays for the dowdy wife to feel desired?"

"That's my deal. I'll say nothing if you guarantee me that. I won't have Mrs. Heriville feel even more shamed. I won't have her know she was made a fool of tonight."

"But she *was* a fool—a fool to think a man like that would fawn over her. You've seen the cow."

"The cow, as you call her, is likely to get a good man elected president and be at his side while he changes the world. And you? Who will be beside you? A philanderer looking for his next bonny gold-digger?"

She made an impatient clicking sound. She was too young, perhaps, too lovely and admired, to believe she'd ever taste that medicine.

"You don't expect me to stop seeing him?" She made a gesture indicating the car and camera, then turned her hand to show an emerald ring.

"That's your business." He released the steering wheel. "But it's clear you can afford whatever you paid that man tonight. You'll bear the cost of it and say nothing, or I'll tell Mr. Heriville what you've done. He's a banker, is he not? Cautious about scandal, I'd suppose. And no man wants his wife to betray him, however publicly he betrays her."

She shrugged. "Tell him what you want. I'll deny it."

Killy drew out his star, a constant reassuring weight in his pocket. For a long moment, he held it steady a foot from her face. "He'll believe me, not you."

She stared at the words *U.S. Marshal* stamped into the thick nickel between six points. There was, he thought, a grudging respect in her eyes. He knew it was for his threat, not his profession.

"Make sure Mrs. Heriville never sees your actor again," Killy said. "Make sure she never learns he was hired to feign interest. You'll spare her that, on top of all else."

She watched him put the star away. "Maybe you're a little sweet on the missus yourself?"

"That, I am not. But your scheme upset her hostess, a lady I admire. Right now, only a bit of this is known, and only to one of her guests. He won't speak of it, and neither will I."

Her brows, dark and beautifully arched, went up. "So this deal's for her sake, not the wife's?"

"Let's just say it's for the party."

NO PLACE FOR A DAME
Lori Armstrong

September 1942
Minneapolis, Minnesota

When he sauntered into the Marlow Detective Agency, I knew
he'd be trouble.

Trouble with a capital *T*—T for Tyrone Power. This guy,
sporting slicked-back hair, a tight-lipped smile, and haunted
eyes, was a dead ringer for my cinematic crush.

God, but I'd mooned over that man. I'd seen *The Mark of
Zorro* and *Jesse James* so many times my friends had teasingly
called me Mrs. Power.

When I became Mrs. Marlow, my Power crush remained,
even after my weekly Saturday matinees ended. I still resented
my husband for taking that simple joy from me.

Trouble pointedly cleared his throat.

My gaze caught his as I lifted a stack of papers, realigning
the edges with a *snap snap* on the wooden desktop. "You lost?
The Barton Talent Agency is on the second floor."

"If only I had some talent besides being mistaken for a famous
Hollywood film star."

Add charmingly self-deprecating to his list of attributes? Oh
he was trouble, all right.

He ambled closer; his gait smooth enough I barely noticed
the cane gripped in his right hand. "But I believe I'm in the right

place. I'm looking for Dennis Marlow."

You're not the only one, pal. I hadn't seen my husband for two weeks.

While Dennis regularly skipped out on me for some big "job," he'd never been gone this long. Since he had a habit of making enemies more often than friends, I had good reason to be wary of this guy, not knowing which category he fit into. I opened the side drawer on my desk to file the papers in my hand, double-checking that my H&R top break revolver was within grabbing distance. Someone had broken into the office two nights ago. Nothing had been taken, but all the files had been tossed around like confetti.

"What does your business with him pertain to?"

"I'd like to hire him."

"I'm sorry, Mr. Marlow is unavailable. He's already on a case."

His gaze flicked to the closed door behind me. The opaque glass revealed a silhouette of a desk and an empty coat rack. "Do you know when he'll return? I need to speak with him. Quite urgently." Then he glanced at me again.

Good Lord. Even his eyes held the same smolder as his famous doppelganger. "Mr. Marlow's schedule is unpredictable. I don't know when he'll be back."

"Blast it, that doesn't help me at all." He gestured to the chair in front of my desk. "Mind if I sit? Hoofing it up six flights of stairs with this cane was a chore."

"Be my guest."

He lowered himself into the chair, taking a moment to prop his ornately carved cane against the desk and adjust the cuffs of his shirt, the cufflinks glimmering gold against his wrist. Then he straightened his silk tie, drawing my focus to his long fingers, pale and smooth. Definitely not the rough mitts of a working man. The diamond inset into the gold band encircling his fourth finger flashed when he rested his left hand on an upholstered armchair.

His fashionable attire screamed money. The subtle stripe in his charcoal-hued trousers matched the dove gray suit coat. The crispness of his white shirt was set off against his maroon tie and pocket square. I couldn't see his shoes, but I'd bet my last nickel they were Italian leather polished to a fine sheen.

"I might've gone with my second choice for an investigator if I'd known the elevator was out," he grumbled.

"It's been broken for almost a year. With the war, parts are hard to come by, as well as men who know how to fix things."

"And now I feel like an ingrate, complaining about my small pain when soldiers and their families are sacrificing so much." He sighed. "I'll take my leave if you'll grant me a moment to catch my breath, Miss...?"

"Mrs.," I automatically corrected. "Mrs. Marlow."

"Ah. Well, I'm almost sorry to hear that you're Mrs. Marlow." My stomach fluttered. "Why?"

"If you were merely a secretary, I could believe you weren't privy to your boss's current location. But as Mr. Marlow's spouse, you must know exactly where he is and what he's doing."

"Why would you assume that?"

He lifted a dark brow. "What wife doesn't know her husband's whereabouts?"

Many of them; that's why we stay in business. "Like I said, Mr....?"

"Evans," he supplied. "First name is Evan. And yes, my parents inflicted me with the name Evan Evans. Feel free to mock me. Everyone else does." He smiled.

I found myself smiling back. "As I've spent most my life Vivian Vifquain, I'll refrain from mockery."

"Vivian is a lovely name. You're a lovely woman and I've taken up far too much of your time. Since Mr. Marlow is unavailable, I'll be on my way."

"Do you mind telling me who recommended our agency?" I asked as he shifted forward to stand.

"My pal Jimbo Wentz. He said Dennis did some work for

him a while back and he was pleased with Dennis's discretion."
He paused. "Do you know Jimbo? You'd likely recognize him
by his lawyerly name, James Wentz."

"Never heard of him. But I don't know half of the clients
Dennis takes on. He claims it keeps the client's confidentiality."

"Even from you?"

Especially from me. Then I'd know exactly what sleazy
scheme Dennis had cooking. "Yes."

His gaze turned shrewd. "Does he afford you the same
courtesy?"

"Meaning what?"

"Your clients. Does Mr. Marlow involve himself in your client
dealings or does he let you handle them without his input?"

I managed to bank my surprise. He was the first man to
suggest I was Dennis's business partner, not merely his wifely
lackey. And make no mistake: I run this business. If anyone is
the lackey, it's my husband.

"Am I wrong?" Evans asked cautiously.

I refocused on him. "You're not wrong, Mr. Evans. Dennis
and I each have our own...specialties." I allowed my lips to
curve into a smile.

"Beauty *and* brains," he murmured.

"Which means I'm as qualified as my husband to consider
taking on your case."

"I don't doubt that, Mrs. Marlow." Evans fiddled with the
head of his cane. "But this is a...delicate matter. I'm not sure
that it's a suitable—"

"Job for a dame?" I inserted dryly. How many times had I
heard that? Leaning across the desk put my assets on full display.
"Three guesses as to the nature of that delicate matter, Mr. Evans.
One, you want proof your business partner is cheating you.
Two, you want proof your *wife* is cheating on you. Three, you
want us to search for a missing person the cops don't give a
damn about."

His focus moved from my eye-catching cleavage to my eyes.

"Is my situation that obvious?"

"No. This is what we do. Deal with the ugly stuff."

Several long beats passed before he spoke. "You were correct with the second guess. Sunny—that's my wife—and I...we've been having issues since my accident. Intimate issues. During my recovery I understood why she gave me space and time to heal. Although we've always had separate bedrooms, we frequently shared a bed. That intimacy had been the mainstay of our relationship. I miss it. Apparently, Sunny doesn't."

"The lack of intimacy leads you to suspect she's been stepping out on you?"

He nodded glumly.

"For how long?"

"A month. Maybe more." His cheeks flushed. "I've been in denial because I didn't want to believe Sunny is that type of person."

"What type is that?" What kind of woman went out for chopped liver when she had beefsteak at home?

"The type that's embarrassed to be seen in public with a man she considers a cripple."

That statement hung between us like a bloated calf, daring me to poke at it. Thankfully in my years away from the farm, I'd learned to curb such impulsiveness. I focused on something he'd said earlier. "You mentioned this being an urgent matter?"

"Only in that I know she'll be at a rubber and paper drive tonight." He scratched his cleanly shaven chin. "Or maybe it's a scrap metal drive. Sunny is involved in so many war-support organizations it's hard to keep track. I suspect whoever she's cheating on me with is a fellow volunteer."

"Why's that?"

"Why else would she devote every waking minute to helping with the war effort? She never gave a second thought to charity work before."

I cocked my head. "If you've got this figured out, what do you need me for?"

"All I have are suspicions. I need confirmation. I need a name. That's where you'd come in." He placed a crisp fifty-dollar bill in front of me. "I'll hire you to watch her for one night and tell me who you see her with. Don't talk to her. Don't engage with her and do not let her find out you're an investigator. I need the upper hand in this...situation."

"You think I parade around surveillance ops with a giant magnifying glass like Sherlock Holmes?"

"No. But I need you to be clear there's no interaction with her of any kind."

That wasn't the weirdest request I'd agreed to for a case, so I said, "Sure. Just as long as you tell me about the accident that's caused this rift in your marriage."

Annoyance flashed in his eyes. "I never talk about it."

"That's the deal. Take it or leave it."

A put-upon sigh followed. "Late January my buddy and I headed to his place in the North Woods. After we'd downed a bottle of his god-awful moonshine, we figured it'd be a swell idea to go hunting. We left the cabin loaded for bear. I had limited experience with guns, but Beebo swore he'd turn me into an expert marksman by the end of our weekend. And for some reason, I trusted him."

He'd trusted a guy named *Beebo*? Who owned a remote cabin in the wilderness and had access to moonshine and firearms? Maybe Evans wasn't as bright as I first thought if that scenario hadn't raised some red flags with him.

"We shot at a few fenceposts. Drank some more. The next part is a blur. We were walking in the woods and I don't know if Beebo lost his footing in the snow or what, but his gun went off and I was in the line of fire. The bullet ripped through my galoshes and blasted away half of my right foot. I remember pain and blood and screams. Mine or his, I don't know. Beebo left me there to get help.

"The next thing I remember was flying down the road, strapped onto the back of some rickety snow machine. I thought I was hallucinating. Or dead and on my way to hell." He offered a sheepish smile. "Beebo got me to the local country doctor and he called an ambulance from the next town. Not that I remember anything because I'd passed out. I woke up the next day in a hospital room, with a teary-eyed Sunny at my bedside. I thought she'd be angry, but she seemed grateful the accident hadn't been worse. After surgery to remove the remaining bone fragments, I spent a month at the University of Minnesota's medical center. Then I spent another couple of weeks at the Mayo Clinic doing rehabilitation. Sunny was so loving and attentive during that time..." He shook his head as if confused by the memories. "That's it."

"Good enough for me. Do you have a picture of her?"

From his inner pocket, he pulled out a newspaper clipping and laid it in front of me. "This is the most recent one."

I leaned over, eager to check out the image. The woman wasn't movie star gorgeous, but she was attractive, reminding me of the actress Ruby Keeler. Her short curls peeped out from beneath a chic cloche as she received a service award, smiling at someone off camera. My eyes scanned the page and came to a dead stop at seeing the woman's full name. Susanna "Sunny" Washburn.

My expression must've indicated my surprise because Evans said, "Do you recognize her?"

"Her personally? No. But I recognize the Washburn name. Mill owners and flour magnates. Movers and shakers in the right circles."

"Yes. So you understand the need for discretion."

I nodded. With that sigh-worthy face of his I shouldn't have been surprised that he'd married into one of the richest families not only in Minnesota, but in America. The Washburn family estate in the Lake Minnetonka area—the priciest address in the Twin Cities—rivaled castles in England for size and housed several generations of Washburns. No wonder Evans and Sunny had separate bedrooms; they likely had an entire wing of the house to themselves.

"How long have you been married?"

"Three years."

My finger tapped the caption beneath the photo. "She didn't take your last name?"

Evans shook his head. "She likes the cache the Washburn name affords her, even when she prefers to stay out of the public eye."

Rich people. I didn't understand the pseudo-humble games they played just because they had the time and money to do so.

I refolded the clipping and handed it back. "Where's this drive taking place?"

"A warehouse off Hennepin. There's a dance afterward with a live band."

A dance? So the upper crust were dancing and eating cake during a war, while the rest of us listened to the radio beneath blackout curtains and scrounged for sugar for our coffee. I shoved down my disgust.

But not quick enough; Evans saw it. "It's not a high society shindig," he said testily. "It's for soldiers' families." He picked up a pencil wrote on the bottom of the clipping, then he tore off the strip and handed it to me.

My eyebrows rose when I read the address. Off Hennepin and close to Washington Avenue, which was not a good part of town.

"Something wrong?"

"Just trying to remember if there's a trolley stop near there." Or if I should pack a weapon in my pocketbook.

Evans pushed to his feet, and I followed him to the door. I said, "We should be able to wrap this up tomorrow."

He turned. "No offense, but my foot can't take another dozen flights of stairs. How about we meet at the Rainbow Café down the street, say around ten?"

I chirped, "It's a date," and immediately wished I could retract my awkward phrasing.

Then Evans entered my space, smelling of clean cotton and man. "I hope you don't mind me saying so, Vivian, but I'm glad your husband wasn't here."

I blushed.

"Dennis Marlow is one lucky fella." He gifted me with a roguish smile. "Wear that dress tonight. The color red suits you."

I ended up wearing the red dress—not at Evans's suggestion—but I didn't have time to go home and change before I had to leave for the job.

With the warm September evening, I wouldn't need a coat. But after double-checking myself in the mirror, I decided the top half of my dress revealed too much skin for undercover work. I snagged a long scarf and artfully tied it around my neck, the triangle shape camouflaging my double Ds. With trolley fare, lipstick, and the slip of paper in my purse, I locked up the office. As I made my way downstairs, I silently cursed the pointy-toed black heels I'd slipped on this morning. My dogs would be barking by night's end for sure.

The trolley was jam-packed with workers heading home. Used to be the after-work crowd was comprised mainly of men. But with the war in full swing, most males of enlistment age were a scarce commodity. Now tired women, rowdy kids, and older folk filled the car.

The trolley lurched past my usual stop and I watched the city fly by through the window. Chatter around me focused on the war. The general consensus was fear; fear more men would be drafted, fear more items would be rationed, fear of bombings and invasions. Like most Americans, I soaked up every bit of news from over there. It felt so far away, yet everyone I knew had a loved one in military training or already stationed overseas or somehow involved in our defense. Some folks called me lucky because my husband was too old to be conscripted and could stay home. Which was ironic, given he'd been absent from home *more* often since the U.S. had joined the war.

I'd begun to think something bad *had* happened to him. After the office break-in two days ago, I wondered if the person who'd tossed the office hadn't found what they were looking for, maybe they'd show up at our home. Last night I went over our apartment with a fine-toothed comb. I hadn't expected to find anything. To my utter disbelief, I'd discovered more than two thousand dollars squirreled away between the pages of books, taped beneath dresser drawers, and stuffed into a cereal box. I'd never seen that much money in my life, and I doubted Dennis had earned that dough honestly. After gathering the fifty-dollar bills, I secreted them beneath a loose floorboard under the radiator. At least if Dennis didn't return, I had enough cash to live on for the next year.

The trolley reached my stop and I exited the car. Three blocks and two sketchy alleys later, I'd reached the address.

I hung back, watching the lines of people bisecting the warehouse. One entrance was for scrap drive donations, so I strode toward line number two.

Upon reaching the head of the queue, I saw the woman holding the clipboard and writing down attendees was none other than Sunny Washburn herself.

Although she carried an air of authority, seeing her dressed plainly in a tweed skirt, rust-colored blouse, and penny loafers, I wouldn't peg her as a million-heiress. Her brown eyes were genuinely kind when she asked, "Name and company, please."

I should've known I'd need a military connection to get into the event. When I didn't immediately respond, she looked up sharply. "Is there a problem?"

"Umm, no. I was just distracted by your hat. It's lovely." I smiled, hoping my lie wouldn't get me kicked out before I'd even begun my mission. "Last name is Powell. He's with the forty-fifth." I held my breath; I had no idea if there was a forty-fifth company in any branch of the armed forces. Dennis was forty-five and that'd been the first number to come to mind.

"Thank you, Mrs. Powell, for your husband's service."

And just like that, I was in. I wished I'd slipped a flask into my purse to calm my nerves. Instead I walked off my nervous energy by completing a full circuit of the inside space.

Sunny manned the door for another hour. Then she made rounds, chatting with groups of people, checking on the band, and restocking the refreshment table. No one joined her on her walkabout. Right after the band began to play, a gaggle of ladies tried to drag her onto the dance floor, but she refused.

When Sunny relocated to another table, I snagged a glass of punch and stood at a community table behind her. I wanted desperately to sit down, but Sunny didn't stay in one place for long.

As I watched her, that niggling sensation of wrongness tightened my gut. Something was off about this situation. Sunny wasn't here to socialize; she was here to work. I could tell she was an old pro at this type of event, which did not jibe with Evans's assertion that her interest in charity work was relatively new.

Many things he'd told me weren't adding up.

Evans hadn't given me a personal picture of Sunny; he'd chosen one that anyone could've clipped out of the newspaper.

Sunny didn't sport a wedding ring, which made sense if she were meeting a secret lover.

But what if she and Evans weren't married? There hadn't been time to verify their marriage record before I'd been thrust into this "urgent" situation. Had that been his intent?

In being so eager to earn his approval, I'd neglected to follow the first three rules of the detection business: check, double-check, and triple-check sources.

My only source was the wronged man himself.

Another thought struck me.

What if Evans had employed misdirection because *he* was the spurned lover looking for revenge?

What if what I relayed to Evans was putting Sunny in danger? Is that another reason he didn't want me talking to her? Because

I might warn her?

Now I didn't know what to do. As I considered my options, Sunny slipped out a side door.

That made my decision easier; I followed her.

The breeze caught the door as I stepped outside, banging against the brick hard enough that it bounced back and slammed itself shut. So much for a covert entry.

Down the alleyway a flame flared, highlighting the angles of Sunny's face as she lit a cigarette.

At least I had an excuse to approach her.

I sauntered over, smile in place. "Oh hey. Can I bum a smoke? I just realized I left my pack at home."

"Sure." She flipped open a mother-of-pearl-adorned cigarette case. I plucked one out, leaning forward as she flicked the lighter.

The first puff seared my lungs and I coughed.

Cool, Vivi, real cool.

Sunny exhaled a slow stream of smoke in a manner as sultry as Marlene Dietrich. Then she said, "You're really bad at this, sweetheart."

"At smoking?" I choked out after another drag.

"That too." She eyed me coolly. "But mostly I meant you're bad at skulking around. Did you really think I wouldn't notice you following me all night?"

The cigarette froze halfway to my mouth. "But I—"

"Don't bother to deny it." Another sexy inhale and exhale. "Are you another one of Evan's floozies?"

Before I could process *floozies*, she jabbed me in the chest, the cigarette between her fingers close enough to set my hair on fire. "I don't know what promises that bastard made to you, but they're all lies. He won't get a dime from me after the divorce. Not one red cent."

I held up my hands. "Whoa. Hold on, sister. I'm *not* involved with him."

Sunny relaxed against the wall, but her face remained tight. "Then what do you want?"

I didn't waver in my response. "Proof that you're stepping out on him."

"He still believes if he can prove my infidelity that I'll pay him to keep that off the legal paperwork as the cause for our divorce?" An indelicate snort escaped her. "Dream on. I don't give a damn who the paperwork blames; I just want rid of him." She eyed me distrustfully. "How'd you get roped into spying for him if you're not his latest conquest?"

The perfect half-truth popped into my head. "I'm a secretary for James Wentz. Evans came in and spilled his troubles while he waited for Jimbo to get out of a meeting. I didn't ask for his confidence, but I didn't discourage it either. I felt sorry for him, okay? When he asked if I could help him out 'just this one time,' I felt guilty saying no. So here I am."

"At least you're not here to kill me." Her gaze dropped to my purse then moved back up to meet my eyes. "Or are you? You carrying a little pearl-handled Derringer to pop me with?"

"God, no. I'm a secretary. And if I'd known the divorce was a done deal, I never would've come."

"Too bad you *aren't* a killer. I'd pay you to take him out. I'd get more sympathy as a widow than I'll get as a divorcee."

"What happened between you two? He made it sound like you were happily married until his accident."

"Accident," she scoffed. "Of course that's what he told you; that's what he tells everyone. In the meantime, he's made me out to be a superficial shrew who's embarrassed by his disability. Even my father thinks I've lost my marbles demanding a divorce, claiming love conquers all." She shrugged. "But it'd never been love between us. He liked my money, and I liked his...fat wad."

I choked on an inhale and she laughed.

"Evan is my second husband. Before Evan I'd been married off to my father's business rival, a necessary union to keep an equitable merger between our warring companies. Henry was considerably older than me and his libido reflected that. But I did my duty and bore him an heir, whom he sent off to boarding school as soon as the lad was old enough. Then Henry did me the ultimate favor and died while I was still young." Her gaze landed on my wedding ring and returned to my face. "Your marriage…was it a love match?"

I shook my head. "I married him for stability and security."

"Smart. Anyway, after a sufficient mourning period for Henry, I'd begun to wonder what I'd been missing. That's when I met Evan. He worked for Washburn Industries—directly with my father—as company spokesman. Everyone adored him. With that handsome mug of his and delightful charm…well, it didn't take long for him to become the public face of our company. That face had been enough to lure me in; and the way he filled out his suit sealed the deal. He wanted a rich wife, and a permanent tie to the company. I wanted a young husband with a fully loaded libido. It worked out." She tossed her cigarette to the ground. "Until I figured out what kind of man was attached to that spectacular fat wad and I wanted no part of him."

"That truth came about after the accident?"

Sunny afforded me another assessing gaze. Then she said, "To heck with it. If you're working for a lawyer, you're used to keeping your mouth shut."

I nodded.

"I never kept tabs on Evan's solo social activities during our marriage. He did his thing, I did mine. Still, it struck me as odd that he'd agreed to spend a weekend in the wilderness with a 'friend' I'd never heard of. Evan is not a nature lover, especially not winter. So when I received the phone call that Evan had been shot, I was beside myself with worry. Mostly because no one told me *what* body part had been shot off."

A snicker escaped me.

"It was an ugly injury and a scary time. I pulled strings to get him topnotch medical care. During his recovery he received an outpouring of sympathy and support from everyone we associated with, from the employees to our competition. Yet part of me remained skeptical about how the accident happened. Evan refused to talk about it, claiming trauma whenever I brought it up. My suspicions were confirmed when one of the doctors privately told me the injury had been self-inflicted. This doctor had seen a few 'accidents' from men around Evan's age, accidents that happened after Pearl Harbor, accidents that would exclude them from having to go to war."

My mouth dropped open. "For real?"

She held up her hand. "Scout's honor. Anyway, I let that idea fester during Evan's recovery until I couldn't stand not knowing. I discreetly paid a fortune to a shady private dick to track down Beebo, who had disappeared."

No. It couldn't be. There were other P.I.s in the Twin Cities besides Dennis. Before I could stop myself, I blurted out, "Which P.I.? We work with a couple of different ones and they're all shady."

"Mayhew? Marshall? No. It was Marlow." She waved her hand. "I don't remember his first name, but I remember exactly what dirty secret he discovered."

I held my breath.

"Evidently Beebo and Evan *hadn't* been friends before they'd met at a skeevy gentleman's club. While sucking back highballs and ogling blondes, they'd railed against the unfairness of the draft. Evan had suggested helping each other out, planning an 'accident' to earn the 4-F designation. Beebo hadn't taken him seriously until Evan showed up at his cabin a week later.

"Beebo chickened out. So Evan shot himself in the foot with Beebo's gun. He warned Beebo to stick to the original plan and keep his mouth shut."

Anger seethed inside me that Dennis had been so deeply involved in this and hadn't bothered to tell me.

Sunny kept talking. "This investigator tracked Beebo to a military training facility in Kansas. He'd suffered such guilt over the incident that he'd enlisted in the Army." She shook her head. "In the length of a conversation I went from liking my husband to loathing him. How dare he consider himself to be above serving his country? I have three cousins over there. My father survived the Great War and is a decorated veteran. It'd kill him to hear of Evan's betrayal because he enfolded him into the family business. Not to mention how our investors would react if the company spokesman—a member of the Washburn family—went to jail for fraud. We'd lose the faith of our customers. The government could slap Washburn Industries with fines. They could yank our exemption certificate for agriculture workers. Not to mention the slant the newspapers could put on the company. We'd be lucky to be in business at year's end. That snake"—she spat—"is a disgrace, a liar, a faker, and a cheat. I will *not* have my family's sterling reputation for patriotism questioned or our century-old business destroyed because of *his* cowardice."

"What did you do after you received the information from the investigator?"

"Confronted Evan with proof that I knew what he'd done. I asked why he couldn't have gone the conscientious objector route rather than permanently maiming himself. He said if the war drags on, that status would eventually be revoked. Then he got this smug look. He said I wouldn't risk going to the draft board and he acted as if he'd have zero consequences for his cowardly act. Wrong. I had his things removed from my home and served him with divorce papers. I'm keeping his ugly secret as long as he doesn't contest the divorce." She frowned. "So I don't understand why he'd search for infidelity proof now, because even if you told him I had been stepping out, it wouldn't matter."

Rather than confessing I'd been suckered by that face and his sob story, I steered the conversation away from my part in it tonight. "You mentioned he wouldn't receive any money from you. Maybe he's looking for a way to change your mind?"

She barked out a harsh laugh. "Good luck to him with that. *I'm* the one with the ability to blackmail him. One phone call to the draft board and he's in jail."

"If he places one phone call to the newspaper, your business could be ruined."

"I'm living in a Mexican standoff, fearful of who'll take the first shot." Angrily, she pushed off the wall. "Now I need a damn drink."

"I'm sorry that he charmed me into helping him."

Sunny pulled the door open, shooting me a look over her shoulder. "It's that magnetic face of his. It makes ladies stupid. Just be glad he didn't charm you out of your panties too."

The door slammed behind her, and I stared at the gray metal for a long time.

What to do now? Go home? Find a bar to drown my sorrows?

Scratch the last option. If I started drinking I'd never stop.

Dennis had picked a helluva time to disappear. But at least I'd learned where the money he'd hidden had come from.

Through the window I could hear the band launch into "A String of Pearls." Maybe filling my head with music would chase my dark thoughts away. I headed back inside.

I stayed in the building until the place emptied out.

During the past two hours, I'd reached a decision on how to handle Evans. I'd tell him the truth; Sunny hadn't been involved in any clandestine meetings.

Except for the one with me.

But he didn't need to know that.

I slipped out the side door, shivering when the chilly night air flowed over my skin.

Raucous laughter drifted from up the street. The occasional clang of a trolley bell and *beep beep* of car horns echoed against the buildings. The alleyway wasn't completely dark, but it spooked me nonetheless, and I hustled to get out of there.

Halfway to the street I heard, "Vivian?" behind me.

I whirled and found myself facing Evans. "What are you doing here?"

He shifted his body forward, balancing both hands on his

cane like a vaudeville dancer about to do a kick-step. "I couldn't wait until tomorrow to hear what happened tonight."

"But how did you know I'd still be here?"

"I didn't. I took a chance."

The toothy grin he aimed at me fell flat. "I'm afraid you wasted your time and fifty bucks, Mr. Evans. Sunny worked alone all night and left alone. The end."

He bent forward, locking his gaze to mine and whispered, "Liar."

The fine hairs on the nape of my neck stood up at the menace in that one soft word. "I'm telling the truth. Your wife wasn't here to meet a man."

"Oh, I know that."

"How?" I demanded. "Were you spying on her too?"

"No, I was spying on *you*."

"Me? Why?"

"To see if you'd keep your promise to a client or were a liar like your old man."

I eased back a step. So did he. Blithely, I said, "You know my dad?"

He released a mean chuckle. "Too late to play dumb, Vivi. After meeting you today, I knew Dennis's depiction of you as a tart with big breasts and a small brain who can barely answer the phone was another attempt to deceive me."

Wait. What? "How do you know Dennis?"

"He's the snitch who ruined my life."

"You've seen him? Where is he?"

He whispered, "Take a guess."

Cold terror filled me. Dennis was dead. By this man's hand. In sharing this information, I knew Evans considered me as good as dead too.

"I didn't know what shady business Dennis had been up to until tonight," I protested. "You can't hold me responsible for what he's done."

"Looking out for yourself and letting old Denny flap in the

wind? Good for you, Vivi. He didn't deserve your loyalty. But that's a lesson you learned too late." He shoved me deeper into the shadows.

Lightning fast he swung his cane and it connected with my stomach.

The forceful blow sent me stumbling backward until my spine met the building's brick exterior. Before I doubled over to try and catch my breath, he jammed the cane's tip deeply into my sternum, keeping me upright. "Hands flat behind you."

I complied, hating him, hating myself for not seeing the monster beneath his handsome visage.

"I heard your smoke and joke session with Sunny tonight." He tsk-tsked. "I warned you not to talk to her. Several times. And you ignored it."

"I won't tell anyone what we talked about," I wheezed.

"That's what Dennis promised Sunny. But he tracked me down a few days after she paid him off. He tried to blackmail me into getting a piece of my alimony."

I blinked. "But Sunny isn't paying you any alimony."

"Which Dennis didn't know. Made it easy setting up a meeting with that greedy bastard for the first 'payment' so I could give him what he really had coming to him."

Dennis, you poor old fool.

"Before I...*ended* our discussion, Dennis swore you knew nothing about Sunny or why she'd hired him. I couldn't take the word of a blubbering idiot, so I had to confirm that myself there wasn't a paper trail."

"*You* broke into the office."

"Yes. I didn't find anything, which boded well for you at the time...but not so much now. You know things you shouldn't. If it's any consolation, I won't enjoy killing you. Not like I did your husband."

Bile crawled up my throat and I choked it back with rage. "You sadistic bastard. Dennis—"

"Was a two-bit hustler and a drunk who treated you like

garbage," Evans snapped. "So spare me the grieving widow routine. If you'd really been so concerned about him, why hadn't you reported him missing two weeks ago when he first disappeared?"

I glared at him because I hated that he was right.

"Admit it, Vivi. I did you a *favor* by getting rid of him. Too bad you won't be around to enjoy it."

Enraged, I threw myself forward, knocking his cane to the ground. My forehead connected with his nose, but I hadn't hit him hard enough to hear the satisfying crunch of cartilage breaking.

Evans reacted quickly, seizing my flailing arms. He spun me, pressing me face first into the wall. Grabbing a fistful of my hair, he slammed my head against the bricks.

Twice.

A burst of pain exploded through my brain.

Maybe that had rattled a few screws loose because I laughed. "Does it make you feel tough, beating up a woman?"

Another crack vibrated in my skull as he introduced my cheekbone to the bricks.

More pain caused more laughter to erupt. "But you're not tough enough to go to war, are you?"

"Or I'm not dumb enough to be blinded by patriotism."

I hated that smug tone. "You're a coward."

"I'd rather live as a coward than die a hero. But I'm more an opportunist. See, all of Sunny's nephews are off being war heroes." His hand tightened on my hair with such force tears sprang into my eyes. "If all the Washburn heirs die, the company won't have a leader when the old man kicks it. That grumpy bastard would never trust his daughter to run the place. He's fond of saying 'business ain't no place for a dame' which leaves *me* as the best option to take control of all that money and power. But not if Uncle Sam ships me off. Not if I declare myself a conscientious objector—that's an anathema to a veteran like him. So I made the smart choice. A little pain for a lot of gain." He bent his head close again. "You're a lot tougher than your old man. I barely touched him and he sang like a canary," he whispered silkily as he roughly dragged my other cheek across the gritty surface, grinding away skin. "I've killed you all. Except Sunny. But she's next."

"Beebo—"

"Signed his own death certificate when he enlisted."

I blinked away the blood running into my eye.

"And now I'm signing yours."

The scarf around my throat tightened as he used it to yank me away from the wall.

My air supply vanished as Evans fashioned the fabric into a noose.

I thrashed against him, struggling to breathe.

Grunting with effort, he added more pressure.

My body launched into survival mode, my hands flew to my neck, my fingers desperately delving beneath the cloth to try and loosen it.

Evans held fast, squeezing the life out of me one agonizing second at a time.

I fought until my eyeballs bugged out and my vision went hazy.

The *whoosh whoosh whoosh* of my pulse slowing filled my ears. Before I let silence completely take over, words breached my fading consciousness: *Fight it, by* not *fighting it.*

Who said that?

Dennis? my soul shouted into the approaching darkness.

Silence.

I didn't want to die this way, but I felt myself slipping further and further down into the black void.

My sorrowful sob of regret sounded like a death rattle.

Evans paused to listen, his hold on the fabric loosened slightly, allowing me one tiny sip of air. Then another.

It was enough oxygen to push the darkness back so I had one clear thought.

Fight it, by not *fighting it.*

I gradually allowed my body to go limp. Arms first. Then

shoulders. Torso.

At my lack of movement, Evans leaned forward to check if I was still breathing. His grip on the scarf slipped and I greedily filled my lungs.

Then with all the force I could muster, I stiffened my body and stomped the heel of my right shoe onto his right foot, directly on the stump where his toe used to be.

He squealed like a stuck pig and we hit the ground. Him on his side; me on my knees.

I moved first, crawling away, looking over my shoulder in fear that he'd be in pursuit. In my mad scramble to escape I almost ignored the hard object my palm grazed. I chanced a glance down and saw Evans's cane. I had it clasped in my hand before I looked up again.

Evans pushed to his knees, murder in his eyes. "Give me that."

I shook my head.

Letting loose a growl, he lunged for it.

But not fast enough because I'd already risen to my feet.

He lunged again and I swung for the fences.

Shock distorted his face as the cane connected with the side of his head.

He went down. But he came back up, blood pouring from his ear. He lurched more than lunged the next time, but I was ready, landing another hard crack on the same spot on his skull.

He went down, but not all the way down.

So I struck again.

And again.

And again.

And again.

At some point he'd stopped getting up.

Had I even noticed?

When the fugue state I'd fallen into evaporated, his form solidified below me. Blood and bits of matter stained the concrete. His face...not an attractive thing about it now.

The cane tumbled from my hands, and I had to look away.

Please be dead. I don't have the stomach or strength to keep swinging.

But I knew I'd do it if I had to. I couldn't let him live. Not after what he'd done to Dennis. Not after what he'd done to me. Not for what he planned to do to Sunny and her family.

I crouched beside him. My fingers pressed the skin below the spot where his ear used to be. No pulse. I watched his back, looking for the rise and fall that accompanied inhalations and exhalations, but he remained still.

Truly dead.

I wanted to flop on the ground, pull my knees to my chest and sob with relief and grief.

There'd be time for that breakdown later.

My heart continued to race as I set this scene as another robbery gone wrong. If the cops showed up right now, I'd have a case for self-defense with my various wounds. As soon as they discovered I was Dennis Marlow's wife, I'd be under harder scrutiny. The police didn't like private detectives, and they especially didn't like Dennis. And if they hauled me off to the station, how long would they park me in a cell, expecting my husband to show up and bail me out? Things would get more complicated if I confessed that Dennis had been missing for two weeks and I hadn't reported it.

Panicked with those possible scenarios, I patted down Evans's backside, thankful to find his wallet in his back pants pocket. I removed three hundred dollars and left his ID. Then I tossed the wallet a few feet away, placed the scrap of paper he'd given me beneath it, and kept the cane where I'd dropped it.

Time to go.

I brushed dirt off my dress and wiped my face with my scarf before I retied it around my tender neck. My feet were bare. No idea how or where I'd ditched my shoes. I scanned the ground. There. By the wall. But it was my purse. Despite being dizzy, I spun a slow circle. A black shape lay to the left of Evan's body. I picked it up. Left shoe. Before I started another visual sweep of the area, I saw my missing right shoe.

My stomach clenched at the sight. I'd stomped down with such force that it looked like I'd imbedded the heel into the top of his foot. He hadn't worn the fancy loafers; he'd opted for a soft-soled slipper-like shoe—probably to stalk me more quietly, the bastard. An extra burst of anger gave me the strength to pull the shoe free, but it separated, leaving the heel stuck.

I heard a noise outside the mouth of the alley and froze. A couple walked past, hiccupping and laughing in their drunkenness.

That spurred me to dig inside Evans's shoe. A wet substance coated my fingers, making it hard to get a good grip on the pointy heel, which had wedged itself into the hard foam padding on the sole. Another yank and the blood-coated heel came free. I shoved it in my purse and stood.

Guess I'd pull a Shoeless Joe and return home barefoot.

I emerged from the alleyway onto the sidewalk, shuffling along, hoping I didn't look as if I'd just survived the biggest fight of my life.

Stay calm, Vivi.

Late night revelers strode past me, not sparing me a glance.

I'd nearly reached the trolley stop when a male voice behind me said, "Ma'am? I think you dropped something."

I tossed a breezy, "No I didn't," over my shoulder and kept walking.

Two sharp whistle blasts brought me to an abrupt halt.

The beat cop's hard-soled shoes clacked against the cement as he neared me. "You hard of hearing?"

Facing him, I said, "Is there a problem, Officer?" but the hoarse words were barely audible.

He gave me a shrewd once over. "Jaysus, Mary, and Joseph, what happened to you?"

I touched my hair as if to smooth it. "I was on Washington Street looking for my husband. I shouldn't have worn these stupid heels because I fell down once, skidding across the concrete face first. The next time I fell into the mud, snapping my heel." I held up the offending shoe. "Now I get to walk barefoot through these disgusting streets. And I'm so infuriated with that idiot I married..." The sob I held back wasn't entirely faked. "I should've stayed home."

His demeanor softened. "Aye, lass, you should have. Washington Street ain't no place for a lady like you."

Lady? That startled me. Not dame? Well, I suppose the term *lady* suited me better since I'd become a murderess like Lady MacBeth. The urge to cackle nearly undid me.

"Off with ya," the cop said. "Straight home."

He didn't have to tell me twice. I shambled to the trolley station and didn't look back.

The distance to the office was shorter so I headed there.

Inside the familiar rooms, I stripped off my dress and washed up. After slipping into Dennis's old trench coat—the only item of clothing in the office—I raided his stash of booze and uncapped a bottle of whiskey, not bothering with a glass. After I chugged two shots, I lowered into his chair and did a slow spin.

Where did I even begin to sort through all that had happened tonight? Maybe it was shock, maybe it was denial, maybe it was weariness, but I didn't want to deal with it, when a more important question gnawed at me: what's next?

Did I report my husband as a missing person...even when I knew he was dead?

I certainly couldn't report his murder; knowing too few details about it would be as bad as knowing too many.

What if I did nothing? Would anyone besides me even notice the man didn't come around?

Probably not. I'd been running the business the past seven years. Setting up steadier income delivering warrants for the county and securing corporate work. Dennis preferred digging into the sordid cases that had always been his bread and butter. If I could manage to keep a balance of tedious and seedy cases, it'd appear as business as usual.

Dennis was the "face" of the Marlow Detective Agency despite the fact that *my* face was the first anyone saw upon entering the office. But if news got out Dennis was missing? No one would walk through the door, no matter that my competency surpassed Dennis's by a mile. Big swinging private dicks only; this business was no place for a dame.

I snorted. I'd always known I didn't need Dennis to be successful; I just needed clients to believe Dennis was alive and well behind the scenes. That'd be easy peasy lemon squeezy. I'd been covering his ass for years.

Snatching Dennis's old fedora off the coatrack, I plopped it on my head. Then I stretched my legs out on the desk and took a long pull of whiskey.

The detective was in.

A JELLY OF INTRIGUE
O'Neil De Noux

A woman trying not to look beautiful stepped into my office a little after nine a.m. I stood up from the captain's chair behind my oversized mahogany desk and watched her cross my wide office. She had her blonde hair pulled back and wore a loose-fitting blue dress and black mules, a large black purse dangling from her left shoulder. She got close and—*yep*—trying not to look beautiful and failing. She wore only a hint of makeup on that pretty face, no eye shadow above bright blue eyes and only a brush of lipstick on her heart-shaped lips.

"Mr. Caye? The private investigator?" Her voice came in a soft, lilting Mississippi accent.

"Yes."

That's what it says on the smoky glass door. I waved to the chairs in front of my desk.

"Take a seat. Coffee?"

I'd just made a fresh pot of coffee-and-chicory, its scent filing the cavernous office—an upholstery shop before the landlord tore down the walls—with a full bathroom next to a full kitchen on one side, on the other side a wall of windows overlooking Barracks Street, Cabrini Park, and the rest of the French Quarter.

"A mutual friend sent me." She sat and withdrew a cream-colored envelope from the purse. "Tennessee sent me."

Not the state, of course, but my friend Tennessee Williams, whose *A Streetcar Named Desire* had been awarded a Pulitzer

Prize last year.

"He said you were the most discreet person he knows, and this needs the ultimate discretion."

I sat, took out my Moleskine notebook and pen, jotted the date—Monday, September 6, 1948, Labor Day. I asked her name.

"Oh, yes. I am Samantha Holloway. Thomas and I go back a long way." Tennessee's real name was Thomas. "I'm from Columbus as well."

Columbus, Mississippi.

She leaned forward and slid the envelope to me. I leaned forward and scooped it, pulled nine four-by-five, sharp-focused, black-and-white photos, went through them slowly. *Damn.*

She said, "That's James Laurence, of course, and..." She took in a deep breath, "And me."

How many Academy Awards had Laurence won? At least two. *Hollow Point* and *The Ruins of Chandrapur.*

I went through the photos again, the couple climbing out of a swimming pool, both nude, Samantha wringing out her long blonde hair. Larry coming up behind to cup her breasts. She turned her head and they kissed before she took his hand and led him away from the photographer's location. I set my face into expressionless mode before looking up at the naked lady from the pictures.

"He's married," Samantha said.

"I hope this isn't a divorce case."

"Worse. Blackmail."

Samantha slid a white envelope across the desk. The typed note inside read:

I need $2,000
I will send instructions
The Man in Aspic

"Aspic?"

"I looked up the word. Aspic is jelly set in a mold."

A man in jelly?

"The hell does that mean?"

She shrugged, said, "Tennessee sees poetry in it. A man trapped in a jelly of intrigue. The envelope with the pictures and note were slid through the mail slot in the front door of my house. The pictures were taken on the patio behind my house, 907 Royal Street. Between Dumaine and Saint Philip. From the angle of the pictures, they were taken from the unoccupied slave quarters at the back of my property. Two apartments I use for out-of-town guests, when they come."

"You keep the apartments locked?"

She shook her head. "The gate on the fence locks automatically when closed. Need a key to get into the property but the two apartments were unlocked."

"No idea who took the pictures?"

Gotta ask the obvious.

She shrugged, pushed a loose hair from her face.

"No police, right?"

She nodded. "No police. You heard the story of Spencer Tracy and Katherine Hepburn."

"No."

Wait. I mighta heard something.

"They have been an item for a while, but no proof until some enterprising photographer got the goods on them. Howard Hughes paid off the photographer and got the pictures and the negatives. Talking big time money."

"Howard Hughes?"

"Hughes and Hepburn were once an item but Tracy's a married man. Catholic. No divorce. You know."

I nodded to the pictures. "When were these taken?"

"Couple weeks ago. Sunday before James left to start his new movie. Sunday, August twenty-first. It's the only time I went skinny dipping without a bathing cap."

She pulled out another cream-colored envelope, tried to slide it across the desk.

"Five hundred dollars cash retainer and a card with my phone number. Will that be enough?"

I nodded. She looked at her hands.

"James is married to the daughter of the head of the movie studio. If this gets out, the studio will drop him and he'll be blacklisted." Her voice broke. "The studio heads are the ultimate old boys club. I need you to find out who took these photos before he..." Her voice broke and she looked down.

Funny how I didn't notice the clock ticking on the wall behind me before she came in, but now, in this silence, the ticking of the clock counted the seconds until she looked up and took a deep breath.

I said, "Odd he didn't give instructions on how to give him the two thousand dollars. He hasn't figured out the hardest part of blackmail."

She tilted her head a little.

"How to pick up the money without getting caught," I said.

She nodded. "Guess he hasn't figured it out yet."

"That's good."

"Why?"

"He's not good at this."

She stood, closed her purse, and I told her I needed to check out her place.

"I can follow you over."

"I walked."

A minute later, I led her out of the office.

"What's in the little box?" she asked.

"Fingerprint kit."

We walked the uneven sidewalks we call banquettes from my building at Barracks and Dauphine Street to her place six blocks away. I learned she was thirty-five, five years older than me. In those mules, she stood about four inches shorter than my six feet. Another war widow, her husband had been killed at Corregidor. *Damn.*

"You're a vet?"

"Army. Ranger. I was in the sideshow. The Italian Campaign."

"Some sideshow," she said. "Field Marshal Kesselring.

Panzergrenadiers. I looked up that word when I read about it. I've been obsessed with the war a long time. Did you get out unscathed?"

I shook my head. "Wounded in the arm."

"My husband was blown in half. Only one man in his unit survived. Looked me up after." She stumbled on the banquette, and I grabbed her elbow.

"He committed suicide a year ago."

"Do you have a work telephone number? In case I need to call you there."

She shook her head. "My husband was a Charbonnet. A lesser cousin, but still a Charbonnet. I try not to use 'Mrs. Charbonnet' for obvious reasons."

Old money. Big time old money like the Louvier family and Raveneaux, LeRoux, Monlezun.

"Anybody around here know about you and Laurence?"

"We've been discreet. We don't go out. He comes in the middle of the night and leaves in the middle of the night. We stay home. I'm an excellent cook."

She opened the side gate for me before she went into her two-story Creole townhouse, the only building on the block with fresh paint and a second-story wrought-iron balcony with no missing rungs. Typical old French Quarter townhouse with small pieces of masonry peeled away to show its brick-between-cypress log construction. I moved down the alley between the wooden fence and the townhouse to the rear patio dominated by the swimming pool shaded by a line of crepe myrtles along the fence on the other side of the property. No one over there could see the pool. The pool took up most of the patio—an uncommon sight in the Quarter, a thirty-foot-by-hundred-foot pool, edge raised two feet to keep it from flooding during the torrential rains that flooded backyards throughout the city in spring, summer, sometimes in autumn.

The wooden slave quarters at the rear of the property sported the same pale blue paint as the townhouse, its second-story balcony also black wrought iron. From the angle of the photos, the pictures were taken from the apartment on the left. I put the fingerprint kit on one of the two wrought-iron tables behind the pool, opened it and pulled on a pair of latex gloves before dusting the doorknob. Only found a smudged palm print. I lifted it anyway. I went inside, noted the layout—small living room, kitchen on the left, metal spiral stairway to the second floor. A blue sofa dominated the living room, along with a dark green stuffed chair, a fireplace which hadn't been used in a century or more, two ceiling fans I flipped on after I dusted the light switch. No fingerprints. If he'd turned it on, he probably flipped it on as I did with the side of my finger.

Bright morning sunlight filtered through the Venetian blinds of the two windows facing the pool, sunlight revealing a light coat of dust on the hardwood floor. I stood just inside the door and spotted clean spots where the man had walked. Not enough dust to leave a footprint yet enough to show he moved from the door to the first window and then to the sofa. The rest of the floor had no smudges.

I eased to the first window and examined the metal blinds. As suspected, he'd used his fingers to open the thin slats to press his lens through. I lifted a good fingerprint from the Venetian blinds. I find a suspect, I'd be able to put him in the apartment. I looked around the window, the floor, the sofa. He didn't go up the stairs but I went up, found a bedroom and bathroom, French doors opening to the balcony. I checked the other apartment, dusting the doorknob, just in case. No fingerprints. The sunlight showed a hardwood floor with an undisturbed faint coat of dust.

Glad I put on my new gray suit that morning. Canvassing in new duds kept the straights from thinking I'm one of those seedy, boozy private eyes who gets knocked out at least once per case. I've never been knocked out in my life.

An elderly woman, gray hair up in a hairnet and wearing a pink robe, answered the unpainted front door of the one-story

Creole cottage on the downtown side of the townhouse, the house with the view of the pool blocked by the crepe myrtles. I reached out a business card for her to take.

"Hello, I'm a private detective working for the lady next door." I nodded my head to Samantha Holloway's townhouse. "Have you seen anyone out of place around her house lately?"

"I'm a yellow dog Democrat." She tried to hand my card back to me. "I don't vote anymore."

"Have you seen any strange men around the house next door?"

"I used to vote until that damn Hoover got elected." She took a step back and closed the door.

I moved to the next house, remembering my father called himself a yellow dog Democrat—"I'd vote for a yellow dog before I vote for a Republican."

I had better luck at the house on the uptown side of the Samantha's townhouse as a lady with an apron around her yellow dress and holding a broom answered the door of a faded green two-story American-style townhouse with a covered front gallery with plenty of gingerbread trim. I introduced myself, passed her my card and this thin, pretty woman looked at my card for a few seconds before blowing strands of her brown hair from her eyes.

"So, you're a snoop."

"Yes, ma'am. Lucien Caye. What's your name, ma'am?"

She narrowed her left eye a moment, said, "Alice Tunney."

I pointed my thumb toward next door. "Have you seen anyone over there who doesn't belong? Maybe someone who climbed the gate."

"My son said he saw a naked woman in the pool. I can't tell if he's telling the truth. His father hopes he is and keeps looking out the second-story windows, but…" She shrugged. "No naked lady."

"How old is your son?"

"Thirteen."

"May I speak with him?"

"He's at my sister's house up by City Park. He'll be back for school tomorrow."

I nodded toward my card in her right hand. "You think of anything or see anyone suspicious looking around the property next door, call me."

"This isn't a cheating wife or cheating husband case, is it?"

"It's something else entirely."

"My husband runs around on me, but I'll be damned if I'd go to the trouble of having him followed or divorcing him. He takes his business somewhere else, that's a relief." She slipped my card into her apron pocket. "Blonde next door is too pretty for him. She's a knockout."

Directly across Royal Street from Samantha's townhouse stood La Fete Used Books with houses running to the end of the block in both directions until McKinley's Bakery at the St. Philip Street corner. I went straight across to the bookstore and stepped into a dusty place of books stacked on shelves at least ten feet high, the place smelling of peppermint and a hint of mildew. The peppermint scent came from a jar of cellophane-wrapped candy canes in a mug at the counter next to a chipped and scratched replica of the Maltese Falcon. The bespectacled girl behind the counter looked up from the book she was reading and showed her braces with a smile. Cute kid, long brown hair, big brown eyes, small chin.

"May I help you?"

"What are you reading?"

She held up the book. "*Waltz into Darkness* by Cornell Woolrich. It's set in New Orleans."

A blonde on the cover gave a seductive look as she pulled down the strap of her white slip. The blurb read, *He knew she was evil but he couldn't live without her!*

"Cornell? It says William Irish on the cover."

"That's his pseudonym. Cornell Woolrich writes hardboiled mysteries. Just finished reading *Night Has a Thousand Eyes.*

You ever read him?"

"No."

"I love hardboiled fiction."

I handed her a business card. She glanced at it, did a double-take before looking at me.

"Is this real?"

"Yes. It's a card."

She put a hand over her mouth a second, blinked twice before—"You're a private eye?"

"Yep. It's my turn. We take turns. I used to be a cop." I pointed over my shoulder. "The blue townhouse across the street. Have you seen anything suspicious go on over there? Any man climb the side gate? Any man acting strangely?"

She shook her head and leaned forward to see more of me.

"You're too good-looking to be a private eye."

I laughed.

"You stand out, draw the eye of women, even a teenager like me. I'm almost twenty. How tall are you?"

"Six feet. Have you seen anything suspicious over there?"

"Nope, but you need to speak with Conner. Conner Shaw. He comes in at two. Monday, Wednesday, Friday, and Saturday. He's a little obsessed with the blonde woman across the street."

She glanced at my card again. "Lucien Caye. Seems I've seen your name in the newspapers."

I took out my Moleskine notebook and ballpoint, asked her name.

"Catalina Jones. Sacred Heart girl."

"I went to Holy Cross."

She looked at my notebook and said, "I work Monday, Thursday, and Saturday. I'm going to secretarial school. Conner's not a clown exactly but he's close to being one. Warren Easton boy."

Public school boy. In New Orleans, you're connected to your high school forever. I asked for the phone number of the place and put it in my notes. I thanked Catalina and backed away.

"I never met a real private eye."

"Well, I'm the best. The others are clowns." I smiled and she smiled back and the potential was there. In a few years, she could doll up, stroll into the Blue Room, and turn the heads of most any man between sixteen and sixty. I think like that. Comes from being half-French and half-Spanish. I canvassed the rest of the street, including the bakery. Got nothing useful.

The phone rang at 9:10 a.m. Wednesday as I read the morning paper about the Yankees splitting a double-header with the Athletics on Monday. My Yanks were two and a half games behind the damn Red Sox and played them that day.

"A second note came overnight." Samantha sounded breathless. "In the mail slot."

"I'll be right over."

She wore a pale peach sundress and white heels, her hair pinned up on the sides with white barrettes. Her eyes sparkled that morning and her lips were a deep scarlet. She led me back to her kitchen and we sat at a white porcelain-top table with chairs covered in thick red cushions. I'd never seen a red refrigerator or a red coffee pot before. She filled two cups and brought them to the table along with a red sugar bowl and a can of Pet evaporated milk. We mixed our coffee and she pulled out another white envelope. I opened it, saw the typing appeared to be from the same typewriter as the first note:

At 5 p.m. Friday put $2,000 in twenties in envelope under the black cat in La Fete across the street

The Man in Aspic

La Fete. Damn.

I told Samantha about the Maltese Falcon at the front counter. "I'll go see where the black cat is located."

I had noticed the sign in the La Fete window the day before. *Open 10-6 Mon through Fri and 10-8 Sat.* I took a sip of the weak coffee.

"You're gonna pay?"

"What do you think?"

"I think you should ignore the notes. Don't respond. Don't do anything. He won't be sure you got the notes. Have you told Laurence about this?"

She shook her head.

"I'm going to handle this." She gave me a sharp-eyed look. "I mean—you're going to handle this for me."

That's a load off my mind.

"Yes, ma'am."

"I'll get the money ready."

I had planned to interview Conner Shaw who came to work at two p.m., but what had Catalina said about Shaw. He worked Monday, Wednesday, Friday, and Saturday. Today was Wednesday. He worked again Friday. The day the blackmailer wanted the money delivered. I went to La Fete before Conner came to work.

A jowly man with gray hair rang up a sale for a thin woman as I stepped in. He glanced at me as I passed the counter. I browsed the books in the first room, all fiction, nonfiction filled the second room, books stacked floor to ceiling, third room filled with magazines and comic books and a small table across from a rear door. A chipped porcelain black cat sat atop the table. The cat's left eye was closed. No. Missing, and even I knew this was the black cat from Edgar Allan Poe's story.

I unlocked the back door and looked out at an unkempt rear patio of overgrown bushes and weeds. If Samantha puts the money under the cat and I stake out the place, the blackmailer can just come in the back way. Hell, he could come in the middle of the night and I'd never know. Conner could walk out with the money when he closed up. I stepped outside the back door and almost closed it and realized I could see the black cat with the door cracked.

Son-of-a-gun. Thank God criminals are not bright.

Decided not to talk with Conner, yet.

I walked across to Alice Tunney's house. A teenager in a gray khaki school uniform answered the door.

"I'm Ben. You're the private eye. I made my mother describe you. She called you 'Cary Grant without the accent.'"

I didn't tell the kid he favored Howdy Doody with his red hair freckles and overbite. At least he didn't have the big ears.

"What school you go to?"

"Cathedral."

Saint Louis Cathedral Catholic School, not three blocks away.

"I went there."

"Were the nuns mean back then?"

"Of course. Is your mother home?"

"She's at her friend's around the corner. She said to keep you on the porch if you came by because you're a snoop."

I laughed and leaned against the gallery railing. He sat on the top step.

"So, you saw a naked lady out by the pool." I nodded to Samantha's house.

"You're not a cop, right?"

"That's right."

"'Cause I can't get in trouble if she's naked *outside* only if I peek through her window. Right?"

"Yep."

"I seen her twice." He slapped the porch. "Told my friends but she won't come out when they come by."

"Y'all climb in a tree or what?"

"Nope. Just looked out my bedroom window." He pointed to the second story.

I asked him to tell me about the two times.

"She was alone the first time. Came out in a white robe, dropped the robe and I almost fell through the window. She went swimming, floated in the water on her back, Oh, man. She got out and went inside. The second time she had a man with her and he grabbed her…"

Ben cupped his hands in front of his chest. "Really. I seen it."

"Did you see anyone else around the place that time? Anyone looking? Anyone with a camera?"

"Camera? Wish I had one. You seen the lady next door?"

"Have you seen anyone suspicious around the lady's house at any time?"

Ben shook his head, said, "No. Wait a minute. You're not gonna tell her I was peekin'. She won't ever do it again."

I gave the kid my card.

"Who else did you tell about this besides your friends?"

"My mom because I made so much noise, goin' 'Woo. Woo. Woooo.' She told my dad. Oh, and I told the pretty girl in the bookstore across the street. The one who wears the tight skirts. Catalina."

"Did you recognize the man who was with her, the one who...?" I cupped my hands in front of my chest.

He shook his head. "I wasn't looking at him."

I tossed him a quarter. "If you see anyone suspicious, give me a call."

The one who wears the tight skirts. Puberty was working overtime with this kid.

I beat the rain home, dropping by Jeanfreau's Grocery on Esplanade to grab a roast-beef po-boy and thick French Fries, brought it back to the office and ate at my desk with an icy Barq's root beer, the high-caffeine root beer with bite. Fat rain slapped the windows and I thought about the case. This blackmailer was no pro. His solution to the drop was amateurish. Or maybe he wanted to look amateurish.

Called Samantha who answered after the second ring as thunder rolled through the Quarter.

"Some rainstorm," she said. "I have the money."

"I'll be over early to write down the serial numbers and tell you my plan for Friday."

Thursday morning, as I settled in my captain's chair with my coffee and morning paper—my Yankees lost to the Red Sox Wednesday and faced the Beantowners again today, my phone rang.

"I got another note." Samantha said. "This one's different."

"I'll be right over."

The envelope was tan and the typing came from a different typewriter.

I want $1,000 for negatives and prints.

I will be in touch.

Don't screw around with me and no cops.

Mister Big

It came with one of the pictures of Samantha and Laurence standing by the pool, their faces sharp and clear.

"We have two blackmailers?" Samantha asked.

I pulled out my Moleskine and logged the serial numbers of the one hundred twenty-dollar bills Samantha got from her bank.

She asked, "We catch the first blackmailer. What about this second one?"

"We'll wait for him to tell us where to drop off *his* money."

I finished logging and finished our coffee, and I told her my plan.

Samantha said, "I hope your plan works."

That afternoon I went back to La Fete and heard typing as I stepped in. Sacred Heart girl Catalina Jones pounded on an old Underwood typewriter located on the small desk behind the counter. She had her back to me so I waited until she finished a page, pulled it out, and glanced over her shoulder, spotted me, her mouth turning into a big O.

"I didn't hear you come in."

"What are you typing?"

"A short story. I'm trying to be a writer."

"Good."

"It's a murder mystery. Would you read it after I finish it?"

"Sure. Is there a private eye in it?"

"No. It's about an all-girls Catholic high school in New

Orleans where a janitor is found murdered."

Catalina showed off her braces with another smile.

"Boy across the street. Ben. He told you about seeing the naked lady in the pool?"

She let out a sigh. "Oh, yes. He's got a crush on me as well."

"So do I but you're way too young for me."

"I won't always be too young."

Lord, why did I open my mouth?

"Did you tell anyone about the naked lady?"

She stood and stretched. "Yes. Big mistake. I told Conner and he flipped out. He's nineteen, but a young nineteen. I told him to go ask Ben about it, but he said he's too mad at Ben for seeing the woman when he didn't. Why are boys and men so obsessed with naked women?"

"Ask the big guy upstairs. He gave us the sex drive."

She put her hand on her hips. "But we don't fit. Men and woman. I mean we do physically but not mentally and emotionally."

"Like cats and dogs," I said.

"Yep. Like cats and dogs. Will you really read my story?"

"Of course I will. Did you tell anyone else besides Conner?"

"What? Oh, the naked lady. No."

I reminded her she had my card.

"Call me when you finish your story."

"I will." The big brown eyes grew wide and so did her smile. Cute kid.

Heavy rain blew in from Lake Pontchartrain on Friday, tall black clouds darkening the sky. When it cleared, I watched the streets slowly drain. At four thirty p.m., I slipped down the alley next to La Fete, stepping around puddles, and flinched when a gray-and-white cat jumped off a windowsill.

A couple of minutes before five, the back door opened and Samantha nodded at me, turned, and put the envelope with the twenties under the black cat. She went back through the store, and I kept the door cracked open, one eye watching the black cat, occasionally glancing at my wristwatch. Just before six, a young man with his blond hair cut in a flattop boogie—flat on the top, longish on the sides—came into the back room from up front and headed straight for the black cat. He wore a gray shirt and black dungarees. He grabbed the envelope and hurried back through the bookstore. I counted three seconds and went in, found him up by the front counter stuffing the envelope into a canvas briefcase.

"Just put the envelope up on the counter," I said and he jumped.

"Where'd you come from?"

"Back room."

I towered over him, nice looking kid standing about five-six. I took the envelope out of the briefcase and told him to give me the keys to the place. He dug them out of his pocket, so I locked the door and turned the sign around to read CLOSED.

He looked around, head snapping, and I went back, pulled my handcuffs tucked into my belt behind my back, and grabbed his arm, led him to the radiator heater—not on in summertime.

"You right-handed or left?"

"Huh?"

I squeezed his arm but not too hard.

"Right."

I cuffed his left hand to the radiator and patted him down. No gun or knife.

"You can turn over the negatives and prints, Mister Aspic, or you can lose a few teeth, get your arm broken, then give me the negatives and prints."

He looked around again.

"I'm not a police detective. I'm a private detective, which means I don't have to play by the rules—not that rules prevent cops from beating up losers like you. I'm a hired hand. Essentially a thug."

He looked at his shoes.

I reached around him and pulled out his wallet from his rear pocket.

Driver's license read Conner P. Shaw with a North Galvez address. Just off Canal Street. Born July 23, 1929. Nineteen, just as Catalina said. I pulled my zap gloves from my coat pocket, put them on. I stepped close and showed him a fist.

"See the swollen knuckles. Those are lead filings sewn into the knuckles so I won't hurt my hand when I knock your teeth out."

I punched the stack of books atop the counter, sent them flying.

"Tyler has the negatives."

"Who's Tyler?"

"He took the pictures. I just wanted pictures of the naked lady. Tyler recognized the man who was with her. It was all his idea."

Tears formed in the kid's eyes, and I didn't have the heart to tell him there was no way I'd knock out a kid's teeth.

I took out my Moleskine and pen. "Tyler who?"

He gave me the name Tyler Coe and an address on North Tonti, two blocks from North Galvez.

"He there now?"

"He's at work."

"Where?"

"Photo lab at *The Eagle*." Newspaper photo lab.

The Eagle. Stupid bastard.

I stepped over to the telephone next to the counter and got the number to *The New Orleans Eagle* from the operator. I called the number and asked for the photo department.

"Is Lenny Overton in?"

"He just walked in but you're interrupting his meal."

Lenny came on the line. Another ex-police buddy.

"Lenny. It's Lucien. You know a Tyler Coe, works in your lab?"

"Lucien who? I got pizza pie here, Slick."

"Funny." I waited a second. *Is he chewing?*

"Yeah. I know him."

"He there now?"

"I can check."

"Call me back at this number." I read him the number on the phone. "There's a twenty in it for you. Oh, don't tell him anything."

Mister Aspic dropped his chin and cried softly.

"Lighten up. We get the negatives and all the prints, this may just go away."

Lenny called right back. "He's in the developing room."

"Don't let him go anywhere. I'll be right over."

I hung up.

"Hey, Aspic. How do you know Tyler?"

"We went to Warren Easton together."

"Is he nineteen, too?"

"Yeah."

Two idiot teenagers. I stepped over to the Underwood type-writer, rolled in a sheet of paper and typed—*The Man in Aspic.*

He didn't use the Underwood. Neither did Mr. Big.

"Sit on the floor. I'll be back." I took off my gloves.

"You gonna leave me chained like this?"

"I'll be back soon."

"What if the building catches fire?"

"It's been around over a hundred years and hasn't burned down yet. You better be telling me the truth about this Tyler Coe."

It was called newspaper row back at the turn of the century, a line of red-brick buildings on Camp Street. The only paper left on the block was *The New Orleans Eagle,* founded by newspaper-men covering the Battle of New Orleans, so said the plaque next to the front door. Lenny Overton met me just inside the front door. He'd lost more hair but still had a linebacker's build with a square jaw and a beguiling scar on his chin. Got it in a shootout on Canal Street. Fell and cut his face and still caught the armed robber. I'm the one who drove him to Charity Hospital.

Lenny led me though the building.

"What's this about?"

"Fool trying to blackmail a Charbonnet who doesn't want the department involved."

"A Charbonnet? What an idiot." He led me to a small meeting room, told me to wait there.

Lenny brought Tyler Coe in a minute later, the youngster with a confused look on his pretty-boy face. He ran his hands through his curly black hair and looked at me.

"What's up?"

I looked at Lenny. "You searched him?"

"Of course."

I turned to Tyler. "Hello, Mister Big. I want the negatives and all the photos or we go to the Third Precinct." His eyes went wide then narrowed and he took in a deep breath.

"I'm a private eye and your accomplice Conner gave you up. Said all he wanted was pictures of the naked lady. Blackmail was your idea."

Tyler looked at Lenny who told him, "Come on, son. Don't be stupid. Right now the cops aren't involved. Blackmail is serious shit."

Tyler sat in the nearest chair, put his head between his knees and took a couple of breaths.

"The negatives and prints are in the photo lab."

"Where?" Lenny asked.

"Behind the second film dryer. The old blue one."

Lenny went out and I pulled out my Moleskine.

"What does your father do?"

"Accountant."

"Your mother?"

He looked at me, tears in his eyes now.

"Works for the city."

"Where?"

"Mayor's office. She's one of the mayor's secretaries."

"Won't she be proud of you."

Lenny came in with a nine-by-eleven brown envelope. A man wearing horn-rimmed glasses and a black rubber apron followed him in. He introduced the man as Ace Franks, Tyler's supervisor. Lenny passed me the envelope where I found the negatives and another set of the prints. I made sure I had all the negatives as Ace Franks explained to Tyler he was fired.

"Is he going to jail?"

"Not at the moment. Depends on what the victim decides."

Franks said he'd be back with the termination paperwork. I waited for Tyler to look at me.

"This better be all the prints."

"It is."

I stood and pointed at his nose.

"Stay away from the lady. Understand? Don't go around there. Don't send notes. Disappear from her life."

Lenny added, "Nineteen years old and you are an inch away from ruining your life. Stupid kid."

When I got back to La Fete, I told Conner "Mister Aspic" Shaw the same thing about ruining his life when I took off my handcuffs.

"What you two did is not called blackmail in Louisiana. It's extortion. You might be teenagers but you're not juveniles. We're talking twenty years hard labor at Angola State Penitentiary."

I pointed to the floor. "Right now, your punishment is picking up the books I knocked down." I pointed at his nose. "The lady across the street."

I made sure he was looking me in the eyes.

"You ever mess with her again and I'll come down on you like the cavalry in a bad western movie."

My parting shot before I stepped out was a deep-voiced, "There better not be any other prints."

I crossed the street and knocked on Samantha's door and took a step back. She opened the door, and I held up the envelopes, the one she'd put under the black cat and the one with the negatives and prints.

"May I come in?"

Over two icy Falstaffs at her kitchen table, I told her about Mister Aspic and Mister Big.

"Couple of teenagers. Heard about you skinny dipping. Wanted to get pictures of the pretty naked lady. One recognized James. Thank God they weren't real criminals. Just idiots. They won't bother you again. You and James need to be more discreet."

Her hand shook when she raised her beer to take a sip.

"It's okay. It's over now."

She wiped her eyes. "Thomas said you were solid. A good guy."

Good guy. Yeah, that's me.

"How'd he put it? About Mister Aspic?"

"Trapped in a jelly of intrigue. Thomas is a bit of a poet."

She pushed the envelope with the money toward me.

"Keep it. A bonus for the happy ending." I hesitated but she was a Charbonnet.

I finished my beer quickly; she took another sip of hers, those blue eyes locked on mine. I stood and picked up the envelope with the money, a lotta bread in 1948.

"You ever need me. You know where to find me."

A shaky smile came to her pretty lips, and I got out of there before the Frenchman in me tried something stupid.

THE DEAD SNITCH
Doug Allyn

I hate hospitals. I've never had a good time in one, never met anyone who did. When my Jeep tripped a Nazi mine outside Salerno, September of '43, I woke up in a base hospital in Catania, Sicily. Spent six *very* long weeks there, getting stitched, plastered, and bandaged back together. It felt like six years. And after the medics finished patching me up, I spent two more weeks camped out in a transient tent, waiting for my best friend to die. He finally did, and considering how many pieces of him the docs cut away, I suspect death was a blessing when it finally punched his ticket.

Back stateside with a medical discharge, I landed a job with my hometown cop shop, Valhalla, Michigan PD, as a detective. And my first assigned call was, naturally...to a freakin' hospital.

Of a sort. A hospice, actually.

I expected it to be a grim and gloomy place, because the patients aren't there to heal, only to wait out their time, the months or weeks they have left. Or days. But Milady of Grace wasn't so bad. The nurses wore whites, the corridor walls were decorated with colorful murals, even a few Kilroy cartoons. It was the brightest, cheeriest facility I've ever seen.

I still hated it.

I found my guy sitting alone in a sunroom, in a wheelchair equipped with an oxygen tank. He was listening to a Detroit Tigers game on the Zenith console radio, gaunt as a skeleton.

He had a clear plastic cannula in his nose to aid his breathing, and his outfit hung loosely on his bony frame like death camp pajamas. I guessed the dying man was two or three sizes smaller than he used to be. His wispy hair was gunmetal gray, half hidden under a black baseball cap with a star on the bill. Valhalla PD.

"Sergeant Dugan?" I asked.

He glanced up. Slowly. "I'm Doo to my friends, which you ain't. Who are you?"

"I'm Detective Dolph LaCrosse, North Shore Major Crimes."

"Ah. You're the F.N.G. who's takin' over my job? Where you from, son?"

"I'm a local actually, a north Michigan backwoods boy, but I've been away. Enlisted the day after Pearl Harbor, straight out of high school. Army. North Africa, Sicily, then Italy."

"Doing what?"

"I was an MP, bustin' AWOLs, bustin' dopers, bustin' heads. Then criminal investigations. Smuggling mostly. Not so different from here, I expect."

"True dat," he nodded, and I smiled involuntarily.

"What?"

"Haven't heard 'true dat' in a while, Sarge. Where I've been, they don't speak much *patois*."

"No Frenchies where you was?"

"True dat ain't French, it's north country redneck."

"So are we," he shrugged.

"True dat," I said, and we both smiled. But his quickly morphed into a wince.

"You okay, Sarge?"

"I will be," he said, squeezing the plunger on his pain medication drip. "Soon as my buzz kicks in. But if you got anything important to ask me, you'd best get to it. In three minutes I won't remember my damn name."

I quickly ran down my list of the open cases I'd be taking over, picking up a few details on each. Dugan was visibly tiring, though, so I wrapped it up without pushing him.

"Is that it?" he asked.

"Most of it," I said. "Once I get up to speed on these, I'll probably be back."

"Best call ahead," he said dryly, "make sure I ain't out for a jog. Do me a favor?"

"Sure. If I can."

"Can you get me some weed, son? Painkillers here are either aspirins or Mickey Finns. Had a kid who'd slip me a few sticks of homegrown but he ain't been around recent. Help a brother out?"

"I'll see what I can do," I said. Which was a flat lie. I was the friggin' new guy, didn't have the vaguest idea of who to hit up for weed without risking a bust for it. He might be right about the hospital painkillers, but as drifty as he was? With luck, he'd forget he asked.

We sat awhile in silence, listening to the game, waiting for his meds to kick in. And after a few minutes, he sighed softly, and closed his eyes. I thought he'd zoned out. Or maybe died. I rose to go.

"Are you working that reefer deal, sonny?" he asked, his eyes still closed, speech a little slurred. "The shootout at that dive? The Dry Dock?"

"I—saw some paperwork on it, but the drugs make it federal. It's still an open case but all they got is a body, a gunsel out of Detroit, not much more. Why?"

"I was talkin' to a snitch last night. He said the gun is still at the scene. Under the dumpster in the alley behind the bar."

"Under it?" I echoed.

"So he said. Said the shooter dropped his piece on his way out, in case he got patted down, kicked the gun away. Might figure to come back for it, but he hasn't, at least not yet."

"I expect the feds searched that alley pretty good."

"And they probably looked *in* the damn dumpster," Doo agreed, "but maybe not under it. Sometimes things are so obvious, we miss 'em."

"True dat," I agreed. "Who should I pass the tip—to...?" I broke off. Dugan's mouth had dropped open and he began to snore, phlegm rattling in his throat. Out of gas. Down for the count.

I stopped at the nurse's station on my way out, told her he'd nodded off. She said she'd see to him, and I left her to it. She caught me staring at her hands as I turned away. I couldn't help it. It seemed strange to me, seeing nurses without bloody aprons, bloody hands, even their faces were often streaked with red from wiping away sweat. War-paint, they called it, joking as they carted away baskets of severed limbs, or taped-up eyeless sockets.

I hate hospitals, but nurses? They're special people. You don't have to explain much to a nurse. They've seen worse. I promised myself I'd get to know Dugan's nurse better. She was tall, spare. And really pretty.

But first I'd have to get clear of the mess Dugan had dumped in my lap.

Being an F.N.G., a friggin' new guy, is the same grind every-where. Army, Navy, and probably the Boy Scouts. You're expected to walk soft, shut up, and take as much guff as the older guys feel like dishing out. But the greatest sin for an F.N.G. is showing off. Being too good at your job gets you branded as a brown-noser, a suck-up, or worse.

New to the job, I only knew a few cops on the Valhalla force, didn't know any of the feds who were dealing with the Dry Dock shooting, and I definitely didn't want to start my first week by passing along a bum tip. I decided to check out the bar myself.

Like most North Shore towns, Valhalla is centered around a natural harbor, where an inland river meets a Great Lake. The oldest buildings encircled the heart of the harbor, built during the lumber baron days when the loggers ruled the shores. The rest of the town came later, expanding out to the surrounding hills. Cozy, and Christmassy now, its shops were decorated for the holidays, with sleighs and reindeer and carolers, Christmas lights aglow in every shop window. Very festive, not counting the Dry Dock, which was still taped up as a crime scene.

The building was locked and barred, but nobody was guarding the alley. I ducked under the police tape, found the dumpster, checked beneath it, and bingo! Came up with the weapon. A blunt little Browning .25 auto. Twenty-fives are usually considered hooker's guns, because they're small, but they can punch a half dozen dime-sized holes in you from across a room. And this one...was recently fired, from the smell of the muzzle.

I checked the magazine. Mixed rounds, Remingtons and Federals. A street piece, then, not store bought. I bagged it, tagged it, then stopped by the station and handed it off to the desk sergeant on duty, with a brief note on where I'd found it. Then I headed home to my rented room, crashed out on the sofa, and promptly dreamed my way back to Salerno, driving that Jeep again, joking with Billy Foster, knowing the Nazi mine would tear his legs off in a few minutes. But somehow I couldn't warn him, no matter how I tried. And as the dream replayed, over and again, I forgot about the gun, and the old cop dying slow and hard in that cheery hospice sunroom. I almost forgot I hated hospitals. Until the next day.

When I arrived at work, Valhalla PD Chief Marge Kazmarek was at the front desk, waiting for me. Marge is a queen-size woman, nearly six feet tall and wide as a semi, gray hair tightly permed as a Brillo pad. She was in her long-sleeved, winter uniform, no badge, no name tag, none necessary. Everybody in Valhalla knows Chief Kaz.

"Agent Tanaka from Narcotics and Dangerous Drugs was waiting in my office when I came in this morning," she said, as we fell into step. "He's all bent out of shape because you messed with his crime scene. What the hell were you doing there?"

"Recovering a weapon. I got a tip."

"*You* got a tip? From who? You've been overseas for—no, wait, don't tell me," Marge sighed, as I held the office door open for us. "I love surprises."

Tanaka was waiting. Nearly as wide as he was tall, with a shaved head and a Fu Manchu, the agent looked like he'd soldiered with Genghis Khan, and with the same attitude. He didn't bother to get up, maybe because he was carrying an extra hundred pounds of blubber around his waist. A fat cop? I couldn't remember the last time I'd seen one. In the Army, everybody's lean, mean, and hungry. Especially MPs. Tanaka's seedy Sears off-the-rack sport coat was probably chosen to camouflage the flab at his waist. If so, it didn't.

"Is this the F.N.G. that messed up my crime scene?" Tanaka asked, swiveling his chair to face me, but talking only to Marge.

"Dolph LaCrosse," I said, offering my hand. He ignored it. Maybe didn't see it. I let it drop. "I didn't mess with squat, Agent," I went on. "The scene was unguarded, I just waltzed in."

"A green rook, your first week on the job, and you just happened to turn up a murder weapon a half dozen officers missed?"

"I'm the new guy, but I'm not a rook. I've been doing police work in places you couldn't find on a map. I got a tip, I checked on it, and when it panned out, I turned it in, and signed for it. What part of procedure did I miss?"

But as soon as I said it, I knew.

"Ah hell," I said, shaking my head. "You found the piece, but left it in place, hoping the shooter would come back for it. Sorry about that."

"Sorry doesn't cover it, rook. The Dry Dock shooting was a dope deal that blew up. The dead guy was a bodyguard from Detroit with mob connections. His boss was probably here to make a buy."

"Reefer," I said. It wasn't a question.

"Michigan green," he nodded. "High-grade product, grows wild up here, a cash crop for local rednecks. Friends of yours, maybe?"

"I probably grew up with guys in the weed trade, Agent, but Valhalla's a small town. If I know them, they know me, and they know I've been an overseas MP the past three years, even if you don't. Agent."

"Who told you about the gun?"

"A confidential informant."

"I want a name."

"You don't get one. That's what confidential means."

"Then you'd better come up with one, and quick. This thing isn't over, rookie. The buyer had a briefcase full of cash. The shooter ripped him off."

"How? What happened, exactly?"

"We aren't entirely clear on that," Chief Kaz put in. "They were talking, the buyer left the table to hit the restroom. While he was gone, his bodyguard pulled a piece, but the local kid had a .25 up his sleeve. He capped the bodyguard, but was probably wounded himself. There was blood."

"The gunfire triggered a stampede out of the bar," Tanaka went on. "In the confusion, everybody got lost."

"Along with the drugs, and the money," Chief Kaz sighed. "It's a total cluster."

"You called the shooter a kid?"

"That's what the bodyguard called him, before he died, but that's all we've got, that's why we left the gun. When he comes back for it—"

"He won't," I said. "It was a throwaway."

"How do you know that?" Tanaka demanded.

"The clip had two brands of ammunition," I explained. "If you buy a gun in a shop, you get a box of ammo with it. One brand. Buy it on the street, you get whatever rounds the guy's got in his pocket. If your kid wants a gun, he'll just buy another one."

"He'd better buy it quick," Tanaka snorted. "That Motown thug lost his cash stash *and* the weed. If he goes home broke, he'll get capped himself. He's gotta find that kid. And the money."

"And so do we," Chief Kaz finished, "which brings us to you, Detective. Gloves off. Who tipped you about the weapon?"

"Someone who's not involved."

"He must be involved, if he knew about the gun."

"He got a tip and passed it on to me. I'm telling you he's not involved."

"I'll decide who's involved, rook," Tanaka snapped. "He had to be connected to this somehow; it's the only way he could know about the weapon. Maybe he was a lookout or even a driver. Witnesses heard a car peeling out. So either your witness is dirty, or should we be looking a lot harder at how you *really* heard about it?"

He reached up to brush an invisible bit of lint off my lapel, giving me a smug smile as he did so. And it occurred to me that he'd never been in a street fight, or even a playground scuffle, because he had no idea how close he was to getting his lights punched out.

Chief Kaz picked up on it though.

"Look, he gave us the gun, LaCrosse, maybe he has more. Can't hurt to ask him, right?"

"What's the problem?" Tanaka pressed. "Is he some shell-shocked GI buddy? If you don't want to deal with it, pass him along to me. I guarantee he'll give up everything in short order."

"No need for that," I said evenly, "he's cooperating. I'll check into it and get back to you."

But as I turned away, Tanaka grabbed my arm. "Just remember, this is a federal case now, rookie, we have jurisdiction—"

"And we'll cooperate a hundred percent," Chief Kaz said hastily, waving me to silence. "Detective LaCrosse will work his guy, you work your leads, and at the end of the day, we'll all share. Deal?"

Deal.

And so, on my second day on the job, I went back to my un-favorite place on the planet, the hospice. Fortunately, the same nurse was on duty, the tall one with dark hair, dark eyes, and immaculate hands. Not a blood stain in sight, which still seemed strange to me, after my time in the medical tents in Catania, where even the walls were sprayed bloody. I wondered if I'd ever make it all the way home to civvy street.

The duty nurse's name tag read Marie, like the Tommy Dorsey tune, and if she was pleased to see me, she concealed it well. She was more concerned about a second visit so soon.

"You need to go easy on him, Detective. He's more fragile than he seems. You were lucky yesterday; he was having a good day."

And today he clearly wasn't. I found Dugan in the sunroom again, alone in his wheelchair, sucking oxygen, as he'd been the day before, but in a very different frame of mind. He was in obvious pain today, his face was drawn taut in a grimace, and from his vague responses, I wasn't sure he remembered who I was. He kept drifting in and out of focus, coherent most of the time, but other times...not so much. When I asked about the shooting at the Dry Dock, he just stared at me blankly, clearly baffled.

"Not my case, sonny, why ask me? Hell, I've been stashed in this place for a month. All I know about that mess is what I read in the papers."

Which brought me up short. Because it was a lie. The tip he'd given me had been rock solid. I'd found the damned gun exactly where he said it would be, and he could only have known it was there if someone told him, someone who was involved.

But I couldn't push it. Dugan was trying hard to maintain a game face, but he was very weak today, kept fading in and out. He should have been resting, husbanding what little strength he had left, which was clearly fading fast. He finally nodded off in mid-sentence.

The tall nurse was watching us from her duty station.

I gave her a Gallic shrug. She rose and walked over, took his pulse without waking him, then shook her head.

"Sorry about this," I said. "I shouldn't have pushed him."

"No, you shouldn't have," she agreed, "but I wouldn't be too concerned. You're the first visitor he's had in some time. I think he was happy to talk shop with someone, however briefly."

"He mentioned talking with somebody a few days ago. Who would that be?"

"I—wouldn't know. He's had no visitors who registered. In fact, he's had very few visitors since he transferred in."

"How long has he been here?"

"He was reassigned from Samaritan six weeks ago. Chief Kazmarek stopped by once or twice, but she didn't stay long."

"What about phone calls?"

"There are no phones in the rooms. The only outside line is in the lobby, and he hasn't registered to use it."

"But—look. *Some*one he talked to gave him a tip that turned out to be really important. Who would that be?"

"No visitors have signed in to visit Sergeant Dugan's room, Detective. He does prefer the sun room, though, which is open to all patients."

"So he could have been talking with another patient?"

She hesitated, just for a moment. The way people do when they're about to lie, trying to think their way through it—but then she shook her head. And decided to go with the truth. Maybe.

"As you've probably noted, we have very few ambulatory patients here, Sergeant," she said carefully. "I've never seen Sergeant Dugan with another patient. You're his first visitor in days. He's usually alone."

He was definitely alone now. Lost in the mist of his fading strength.

"He should rest now," Marie said. "I'll take him back to his room." I offered to handle his chair and she didn't object. We wheeled him down the corridor together in an uneasy silence. I had a feeling that she was holding something back, but I couldn't think of a way to get past her guard.

Then, as we approached his door, Dugan shifted around to

look back.

"Hey, you made it," he said, clearly delighted to see whoever was catching up with us. I glanced over my shoulder, then stopped dead in my tracks. There was no one there.

But Dugan obviously thought there was, carrying on a friendly banter with...empty air. It was like watching someone on a phone, hearing their half of the conversation. I glanced at the nurse. She'd paused to take Dugan's pulse, but if she was listening to him, she gave no sign.

"What's going on, miss? Is he okay?"

"Hardly, Detective," she said quietly, turning to face me, keeping her voice low. "He's fading rapidly. Renal failure, respiratory failure, advanced lung cancer. It's not a matter of *if* with him, only which one will take him first. I doubt he'll see the weekend."

"But he's...talking. To someone."

"Not to us."

"So he's what? Babbling? It doesn't sound like that to me."

"No, I—you're right, he is talking, but not—Look, it's a situation that arises, sometimes, but we're advised not to discuss it, even with family."

"I'm not family, miss. I'm a police officer and Sergeant Dugan gave me valuable information yesterday about an active homicide case. I'm not looking to give anyone a hard time, but I need to know whether he's credible or not. You've gotta help me out here."

She looked away a moment, clearly mulling her options.

"For what it's worth, I've spent the past couple of years in and out of combat, miss," I added. "I've seen pretty much every kind of death there is, up close and personal, and I've lost friends in ways you can't even imagine. I wouldn't push you on this if it weren't important, but I need to know what's happening here. Is Dugan mentally stable? Or is he breaking down, hallucinating, maybe?"

"That's a possibility, though he's not heavily medicated.

239

But...sometimes, as patients approach terminus? They begin having conversations with..." She swallowed. "With...entities, who...are not physically present."

"You're kidding. So...he's what? Seeing ghosts? Or something like it? Hallucinating?"

"Possibly," she admitted. "But often...their conversations seem quite coherent, and even informative. Misplaced insurance papers, car keys—"

"You can't be serious."

"And your reaction is the exact reason we don't discuss it outside the profession," she said briskly, carefully replacing Dugan's wrist on his lap. "It's easy to dismiss it as a whim or a fantasy, Detective, but it happens often enough that it's covered in our manuals, and anyone who deals with terminal patients has seen it more than once, though *what* we're seeing, exactly, is...well. A matter for conjecture, as I'm sure you can imagine."

"What I'm seeing just makes me curious, lady. How much weed is he toking?"

Her lips narrowed. "What?"

"C'mon, miss, I know he's been doing some reefer for the pain. Don't worry, I'm not a narc and I don't give a damn how he gets through the day. Medics used local dope in Sicily when they were short of painkillers. But he's on something, right? How much, and how does it affect him?"

She eyed me for a *very* long moment, then shrugged.

"Reefer, the local cannabis, grows wild in the state forest. It's an ancient first nation remedy, especially effective as an antiemetic, and countering nausea. Given the demand from casualties overseas, clinical painkillers are in short supply here, especially for patients not expected to recover."

"Like Doo."

"I—yes. Like Sergeant Dugan," she nodded, reluctantly, I thought.

"Okay," I nodded, "so your drug supply is short, and you substitute a local product. Or someone does. Where does it come from?"

"Through the back door," she said simply. "Local kids culti-vate guerilla patches in the deer woods. Patients make their own arrangements."

"So Doo has a connection? With whom?"

Again that hesitation, the liar's tell. But so brief that I couldn't be sure which way she decided—

"With my nephew," she said, taking a deep breath. "Kenny Corbeau. He pops in now and again, to say hello."

"And doesn't bother to sign in, since he's not here to see a patient, he's here to see you. But he does see patients, doesn't he? Patients like Doo?"

"I wouldn't know," she said flatly. "We chat, and catch up, then I leave to make my rounds and Kenny...sees himself out."

"And visits Doo on his way?"

"Again, I wouldn't know." But her shrug told me all I needed.

"And this nephew of yours, will you see him soon? Like today?"

"I really couldn't say. He's a bit of a free spirit."

"When did you see him last?"

"It's—been a few days."

"Is there a chance he's been doing business somewhere else? Maybe at a local pub? Like the Dry Dock, for instance?"

She froze at that, but before she could reply—

"He's coming," Dugan said quietly, without looking up, startling us both. I shifted his chair around to face him, but there was no recognition. His eyes were barely slits.

"What's wrong, Doo? What are you trying to say?"

His face clouded over, shaken by a wave of pain.

"He's not coming for you. He's got a picture. Of Marie. He'll kill her!"

I straightened slowly, shaking my head. He was clearly out of it now. Babbling.

"What is it?" Marie asked.

"Nothing," I said. "He's lost it."

"No!" Dugan gasped, seizing my wrist. "He's coming! He'll kill her! He's on the stairs!" His grip on my wrist felt like a damned vise. I couldn't imagine what it was costing him to hold it.

"What is he saying?" Marie asked.

"He's not making sense!" I said, struggling to jerk my wrist free. "Something about a stairway, and someone coming! To harm you!" I managed to twist free of his grip. "Damn!" I breathed. "Do you have any idea what he's raving about?"

"That someone wants to harm me? Hell no!"

"What's this about a stairway?"

"There's only one, the fire escape at the end of the corridor—wait! Where are you going?"

But I was already on the move, limping down the hallway toward the doorway marked Fire Stairs. But I was too late, too slow with my banged-up knees. I'd only covered half the distance when the fire door burst open and a gunman lunged out, bearded, in a black leather jacket, jeans, and boots, an Army .45 clutched in his fist.

"Police!" I shouted. "Halt! Drop your weapon!" He didn't. He had his chance, in those final seconds. His gun was already drawn; he could have opened fire. Probably should have.

But that was the problem. He'd come here looking for a nurse to knock around. Instead he met a cop, who'd been waist deep in war for three long, bloody years.

Dropping into a combat crouch, I opened fire, nailed him three times, center mass, a triangle around his heart that stopped him like he'd run into a wall. He pitched forward, face down on the tiled floor, made no attempt to break his fall. Twitched and jerked a moment. Then stopped.

I knelt by his body, felt for a pulse, but didn't find one. Or expect to. A senseless death. No need for it. He should have tossed his gun. Maybe he would have if I'd given him a few more seconds. But maybe not. And I wasn't the only one at risk in that corridor. He had his chance, and made a lousy choice. In most theaters of the war, you don't get that much.

I frisked him. His driver's license had a Detroit address. Found a photo in his vest, a picture of Marie, the nurse, taken in front of the hospital in her white uniform, standing with a young guy who bore a strong family resemblance. Nephew Kenny, I guessed.

"Nurse?" I called. No answer. "Marie?" I rose, looking around. No one else in sight. Well...not counting Mr. Dead Detroit.

I trotted back down the corridor, checking each room I passed. Found Marie in a room at the end of the hall, helping Dugan from his chair into bed. I lent a hand and she needed one. Doo was barely functional now. He conked out the second his head hit the pillow.

It was just as well he did. I needed answers he didn't have.

When I showed Marie the photo I took off the gunman, she recognized it. It came from her nephew Kenny's apartment. Desperate to find the kid, the dealer must have burglarized his place, found the picture, and figured she'd know where to find him.

But he was wrong. She didn't know. Said she hadn't seen him in days.

Was it true? I nodded politely, as though I believed her, while looking her over. She met my glance without backing off an inch. A tall, slim, good-looking woman who didn't have to work at it. No obvious makeup, no eye shadow or rouge. Definitely *not* a flake or a head case.

Was she jerking my chain about Dugan's conversations with...whatever? It didn't seem like it. And what the hell would be the point? I couldn't come up with one.

Which meant she actually thought she was letting me in on some weird-ass truth. One she apparently believed, but I didn't buy for a second.

Until the uniforms found Kenny's car.

It was hiding in plain sight in the long-term parking lot at the airport. He was still in it. Doornail dead.

Rigor mortis had come and gone. The coroner guessed he'd bled out within hours of the Dry Dock shooting. He'd been there the whole time.

Which left me...nowhere. With no rational explanation.

I told the chief as much truth as I could, without getting myself committed to a funny farm, and together we fashioned a cover story that wrapped up the major facts of the case.

It didn't get past Tanaka, who recognized a snow job when he heard it. He was fat and lazy, but he was also an old-time cop, and knew that every case has loose ends, questions that go unanswered. This one had a few more than usual, that's all. So the fat man decided to take the win, close the books, and move on. If he had questions, he didn't ask them. Which was lucky for me. Because I had no answers. Especially for the big one.

Dugan was barely conscious, maybe dying, when he warned me that the gunsel was coming. And there's no way he could have known that. Unless...well. There's just no way.

Marie the nurse believes that the dying sometimes converse with the dead. She doesn't address the "why," or "how" of it, or what it means, if anything. But apparently it...happens. Sometimes. A few paragraphs in their training manuals mention it, with no attempt at an explanation.

As for me? After three years of war, I don't believe in much, and the little faith I have left doesn't cover what went down. But I don't need faith for that. Dugan saved us. Sent me to a place he'd never been, to face a thug he couldn't possibly know about.

I have no explanation for that, and the facts in evidence don't line up in any logical order.

Except for...maybe one small incident.

In Salerno, my unit was taking fire from German artillery, and we took cover in an old Roman villa. I hit the dirt in some kind of mausoleum, a room stacked with ancient caskets, most of them shattered by shellfire. Rubble, or close enough.

There was a phrase carved above the door, *Mors solum*

initium. It was Latin, but our medic was Catholic. He said it meant: *Death is only the beginning.*

At the time I thought it was nonsense.

But now?

Maybe not.

Maybe not.

REMEMBRANCE IN DEEP RED
PJ Parrish

The figure in the trench coat wavered as it came down the dock. I instinctively got a firmer grip on the boat hook. I had been using it to pull in a loose line, but with its ten-foot reach and sharp hook, it made for a handy weapon in a pinch.

The figure stopped abruptly, and I could see now it was woman. For a second, I thought she was going to jump into the water, and I sighed. I was a little hungover and the last thing I wanted to do was to jump into Grand Traverse Bay and be a hero.

The woman resumed her unsteady path toward me. It took me a moment to recognize her. "Damn it, Meijer, don't creep up on me like that." I set the boat hook aside. "I thought you were in Ann Arbor with that guy."

She gave me a twisted smile. "It's over, Mavis."

Three weeks ago, my best friend Eunice Meijer met a fudgie—that's what we call tourists—named Dirk something at Sleder's Tavern. She ended up going back to his hotel, and I didn't hear from her for a week. When she finally called it was to announce Dirk had gone back downstate, and that she missed him. The sex was mind-blowing, she told me, which was saying a lot because I knew that Meijer had cut a pretty wide swathe through Michigan's man flesh. She was going to drive down to Ann Arbor. "I'm going to give him the biggest surprise of his life," she said.

That was yesterday. The surprise didn't go well, from the looks of her now. Hunched on the bunk in my cabin, Meijer was pale, and shivering, her red hair plastered to her head. It was cold for mid-September, and I hadn't bothered to refill the *Muñequita's* propane heater yet.

"I really could use a G and T, Mavis old girl," Meijer said.

Her gray eyes were pinballing all over the place, so I poured her plain Schweppes. She took the glass but didn't drink. I was trying to recall what I could about Dirk from the night I met him at Sleder's. All I could remember was him bragging about being some kind of assistant to University of Michigan football coach Bump Elliott. I also remembered thinking that he was too pretty for a man. And he was itchy, laughing too much. I kept thinking of that movie *The Sweet Smell of Success* and how Burt Lancaster described Tony Curtis: "I'd hate to take a bite out of you. You're a cookie full of arsenic."

Dirk was sexy, yeah. But he was dumb. Too dumb for Eunice Meijer, the first woman Rhodes Scholar from Michigan State. When I finally told Meijer this as we were saying good night outside Sleder's, she quoted Dorothy Parker: "I require only three things of a man. He must be handsome, ruthless, and stupid."

Meijer shucked off the Burberry now. I was shocked to see she was wearing a black silk strapless bathing suit, fishnet stockings, and patent leather heels. This must have been the big surprise for old Dirk. It's funny what smart women will do for men with short attention spans.

Meijer closed her eyes and let out shudder. "Oh man, I can't get this to stop," she said.

"Can't get what to stop?"

She collapsed back in the bunk. It was then I noticed the blood. There was a spray of it across her neck and left shoulder.

She jumped when I grabbed her arm. "What did he do to you?" I demanded.

"What?" She jerked away from me.

"What did he do to you?"

She shook her head. "Nothing. He didn't touch me."

"You're bleeding."

"It's not my blood."

Meijer began to shiver again. I grabbed a blanket and draped it over her shoulders. Those awful, bouncing, desperate eyes finally landed on mine.

"I think I killed his wife," she said.

A couple of years back, I had business cards made up. I was low on cash and lower on ambition. In the winter, I had been teaching kids how to ski down at Boyne Mountain and in the summers, I did lifeguard duty at the Grand Hotel on Mackinac Island. I'd never had a real job. The only thing I was good at was puzzles and math. When I was twelve, I could do the crossword in the *Detroit Free Press*, so my dad started getting me puzzle books—acrostics, word search things, cryptograms. That led to chess, and by fifteen I was beating my dad. I don't know why, but I can see patterns in everything.

After I graduated from MSU, there wasn't much work for a woman with a double major in math and French. Be a teacher, Dad said, you'll never starve. Truth is, I don't much like kids. Much to Dad's dismay, I moved up here to Traverse City, bought a rundown houseboat, and became a ski-beach bum. But I missed using my brains. One day, the old guy in the next slip asked me for help on his taxes. He paid me forty bucks. Word got around and that led to other "fixer" jobs—helping a widow through probate, analyzing data for an insurance agent, and lately doing computer programming for a guy at IBM who was too lazy to learn. I thought about going back to MSU to get better at the computer stuff. It was 1968, after all, and the world was changing fast. But I wanted to help people, not get stuck in a room with machines.

So, my business cards read: *Mavis Magritte, Salvage Consultant, Slip C12, Duncan Clinch Marina, Traverse City, Michigan.*

I became a de facto private eye. I helped a woman get her

kids back from her ex-husband. I found a missing grandfather with dementia. I took on the state adoption records system to reunite a man with his birth mother. I tracked down lost dogs. I made just enough to get by. I lived off my need to be needed.

Meijer was asleep now, stretched out on the bunk. As I took the glass from her hand, my eyes lingered on the fishnet stockings. The right one was ripped.

Tomorrow I'd figure out what exactly my friend needed.

By nine the next morning, I was on the road to Ann Arbor. Before I left, Meijer had filled me in on some background about her and Dirk. During his week's stay in Traverse City, she and Dirk had gotten into role playing during sex—he'd ask her to dress up as a maid or a nurse and he would, well, hell, I didn't want to hear that part. Dirk's favorite gig, though, was to tie Meijer to the bed and sing "I've Got You, Babe."

That's why Meijer had decided to dress as a Playboy bunny, to up the ante. She also admitted that she had taken a pill Dirk had left her, something he called a Red Devil. It made sex even better, he claimed. I didn't tell her Red Devil was slang for uppers. I could only imagine what the drug did to Meijer, who never touched anything stronger than a gin and tonic.

Meijer had also finally been able to reconstruct much of what had happened to her in Ann Arbor, including where Dirk lived. I found Dirk's house, an old Victorian in the shadow of the stadium. Meijer told me she had gotten in through an unlocked kitchen door and hid in the front closet to wait. For three hours, she waited in the bunny costume, crouched in the dark, surrounded by the stink of dirty tennis shoes and Ben-Gay. She felt humiliated, she said. I imagined the Devil made her really jumpy.

Finally, Meijer heard the front door open. She opened the closet, ready to tear into Dirk. A blonde woman was standing there, holding a bag of groceries.

"Who the hell are you?" the woman demanded.

At this point in her retelling to me, Meijer had stopped and pushed her palms into her eyes. "It was out of control," she said. "I couldn't stop the feeling that it—that I—was out of control."

Meijer remembered the woman screaming, something about not putting up with one more of her husband's bimbo bitches, and running to the kitchen. Meijer grabbed her raincoat to make a run for it. She remembered stumbling over a gym bag near the door. She remembered getting hit hard on the head, seeing a frying pan clatter to the floor, and then turning to see the blonde coming at her with a kitchen knife. She could remember nothing after that. She said everything was just a "big raging red blank" until she walked up the dock to my houseboat.

I sat in my car outside Dirk's house, trying to figure out what to do. Finally, I made my way to the back door. It was still unlocked, and I went in. There was a grocery bag on the linoleum. I waited to hear something. Not a sound. I went into the living room and stopped cold.

A woman lay face down on the wood floor. She was blonde, wearing a pale blue coat. There was a large red stain under her left shoulder. I pulled in a deep breath, crouched down, and picked up the woman's wrist. No pulse. I pressed my trembling fingers against her neck. Nothing.

I looked around for the kitchen knife but didn't see anything. Except...a fuzz of something white under the woman's sleeve. It was fake bunny ears, covered in blood, part of Meijer's bunny costume.

I knew I had to call the cops, but something stopped me. Maybe it was Meijer's eyes when she had stared up at me and said, "I think I killed his wife."

I think...

I've never taken any drug stronger than aspirin, but I've seen people who have. I had one case where a distraught mom asked me to find her missing teenage daughter. I tracked the girl down to a hippie flop house in Detroit and the girl was so crazy-zonked on LSD, I had no choice but to call an ambulance. Meijer said she had taken only the one upper. But I kept remembering what Meijer's eyes looked like last night, like a cat was inside her scratching to get out. An upper didn't last that long. An upper didn't make you feel like you were out of control. I was guessing Dirk had given her LSD.

I carefully extracted the bunny ears from under the blonde's sleeve and slipped them into my coat pocket. I scanned the room, looking for any other sign that Meijer had been here, like an overnight bag, but she was positive she had left her suitcase in her car. I was also looking for that kitchen knife. It should have been there, but it wasn't.

I had to get back to Meijer and somehow make her remember exactly what had happened. Then we'd go to the cops and make the case for self-defense. I made my way back to the kitchen door. I was careful to wipe the knob as I closed the door behind me.

It was late afternoon when I made it back to Traverse City. Inside the houseboat, Meijer was curled up on the bunk dressed in a pair of my sweats. The TV was on, tuned to a football game, but I knew Meijer wasn't watching it. She looked up at me hopefully.

I guess my expression told her. Her eyes filled, and she looked away quickly. "She's dead, Eunice," I said.

Meijer flinched. She hates her old romance-novel first name, just like I hate mine. Freshman year, we vowed to call each other only by our surnames. It was modern, more warrior-woman. But sometimes we slip. And at that moment, I felt like I didn't have a very good grip on anything.

"I found these, right next to her body," I said, holding out the bunny ears.

Meijer started to reached for them then pulled back. She was frowning hard. "I was watching the news," she said softly. "To see if there was any mention of Dirk's wife. But there was nothing about it."

"Try to remember," I prodded. "She had the knife. You had to defend yourself…"

She was silent, staring at the ears. I sighed and glanced at the TV. It was the Michigan-Michigan State game, and it was just ending. I got up to turn it off and that's when I heard the commentator say his name.

"Defensive Coordinator Dirk Kaiser had a big day today…"

And there he was, on the sidelines getting a big bear hug from Bump Elliott. I quickly did a time calculation in my head.

Yesterday, Friday around two p.m., Meijer arrived at Dirk's house in Ann Arbor. Football teams routinely went to their away games the day before, so Dirk most likely had bused to Lansing with the team before Meijer got to his house. Right now, he was still in Lansing. Which meant he didn't even know yet that his wife was lying there dead on the living room floor. Which was why it hadn't made the Saturday news yet.

I looked back at Meijer. She was holding the bunny ears, shaking her head. "I just remembered something," she said softly. "You said you found these next to the body. That's not possible."

"Why not?"

"I took them off when I was in the closet. They were giving me a headache." She looked up at me. "I know I left them in the front closet."

My brain began to whir. Meijer said she had tripped over a gym bag as she fled the house. I was positive there was no gym bag in that living room when I searched it. Which meant only one thing—Dirk returned to get it before he left for Lansing.

"You didn't kill her, Meijer," I said.

I laid out my theory for her. Meijer had blood on her when she got to my place last night, so there had to have been fight. The wife had maybe gotten wounded, but it was my guess she was still alive when Dirk returned to get his bag.

"But I never wore a bunny costume before," Meijer said. "How would he know it was me there?"

"His wife told him. She was able to describe you as a short redhead and that was all Dirk needed to know. He killed his wife and put the ears by her body."

But there was one thing I couldn't figure out. Meijer gave voice to it.

"But why would he kill his wife?"

Every murder has a motive. Who knew what dark currents ran beneath Dirk Kaiser's marriage?

"I don't know," I said. "All I know is you didn't kill her."

Meijer began to cry.

The murder made the eleven o'clock news. Even up here, the murder of a U of M football coach's wife would make the news. Meijer and I watched in silence—the film footage of cop cars outside Dirk's house, with a reporter standing outside, breathlessly giving the details.

"The body of Elaine Rogers Kaiser was found about nine tonight by her husband Dirk Kaiser when he returned from Lansing with the team. Police suspect Mrs. Kaiser might have interrupted a burglary in process and was killed. The neighborhood has been plagued with break-ins lately..."

The camera lights then caught Dirk, being led to a squad car by two cops. He threw up a hand to shield his face, but not before there was a good shot of his expression—shocked and grieving. It was a great acting job, I had to admit.

"Elaine Kaiser was the only daughter of Jerome Rogers, founder of the Ann Arbor-based Pyro-Tech company," the reporter went on. "Mr. Rogers is ranked number eighty-four on the Forbes list for 1968. The family is known for its philanthropy, most recently donating four million for the new U of M fieldhouse and stadium upgrading..."

"There's your why," I said. "Dirk wants her money."

Meijer looked back at the TV. Dirk stared back at us, tears in his eyes now. A cookie filled with arsenic.

* * *

I thought about taking Meijer to the police right after that. But she was exhausted, and it was nearly midnight. We'd go first thing in the morning. She hadn't eaten anything, she confessed, and I didn't have much in the larder. I headed out into the night. It was cold and moonlit, and Grand Traverse Bay was eerily beautiful, not a ripple breaking the inky expanse. It was a short walk to Sleder's for takeout, and I knew the bartender would throw in a fifth of gin.

I was just coming back, passing the dockmaster's house, when I sensed something was off. The marina lot was pretty empty this time of year and I recognized the only two cars—my old Mercedes and a rusted truck. There was a third one, though, that hadn't been there when I left. I went up to the blue Mustang and put a hand on the hood. It was warm and still ticking. I went around back to check out the Michigan plate.

That was when I noticed the big decal on the bumper. A blue and gold *M* with a ferocious wolverine head. I headed quickly toward my houseboat's slip. It was at the end of the dock and I stopped about halfway there.

The houseboat's lights were out. I set the takeout bags down and slowly moved forward. With the bright moonlight, I could make out the water rippling around the houseboat. It was rocking.

I crept up to the houseboat and eased down onto the deck. The companionway door was shut. I heard someone moving around inside, and Meijer saying, "no, no, no…"

And then I heard Dirk.

"Come on, baby…"

He wasn't as stupid as I thought. He must have checked Meijer's apartment, and not finding her there, he then tried to track me down. One trip to Sleder's and anyone there would have been able to tell him where I lived.

"No, Dirk," Meijer said. "Get away from me."

"It's okay, babe. Everything's great. Don't you see?"

"I know what you did, Dirk. You killed her."

He laughed softly. "No one will believe that. They believe me. I've got the perfect alibi. I wasn't there." He laughed again. "I've been wanting to get away from Elaine for years, but the money...yeah, I wasn't going to give that up. You fixed it for me, babe. Now I want you to do something else for me."

"What?"

"I want you to be a good girl and come with me. We're so fine together, and I'm gonna have a lot of insurance money soon, babe. I want you to come away with me."

"Forget it, Dirk. I'm going to the cops."

"Nope, nope." The sugar was suddenly gone from Dirk's voice. "You're coming with me. You either come with me easy or you come with me hard. And if it's hard, they're never find your body in the woods."

The boat began to rock hard, and I could hear them struggling. The door latch jangled. I ducked around the side into the shadows. Dirk had Meijer up on the deck now and she was fighting hard and screaming. But the dockmaster was gone for the night and I was the only one there.

I frantically scanned the deck for something I could use as a weapon. The boat hook was propped up against the cabin where I had left it last night. I grabbed it.

Dirk had Meijer in a neck lock, dragging her up the ladder. I had one chance. I swung and the boat hook came down hard on his head. Stunned, he dropped his grip on Meijer, and she fell back to the deck in a heap. He turned toward me.

He stared, like he was looking at a ghost. Then blood began to drip into his eyes. He blinked, once, twice. Then he lunged at me.

I backpedaled fast. I had just enough time to raise the boat hook again. This time it hit him square in the jaw. He staggered, screaming, and grabbed his head. And then, suddenly, he was gone.

A splash.

I ran to the side. Dirk was in the water, flailing and still screaming. I felt Meijer at my side, clutching my sleeve. Dirk disappeared beneath the inky water.

"Jesus! You killed him!" Meijer yelled.

Dirk bobbed back to the surface, moaning and sputtering.

"He's still alive," I said.

We watched Dirk sink and resurface again, this time face down, but still moving. He wasn't going to make it a third time.

"Ah what the hell," I said.

I tossed the boat hook down and jumped into water. I grabbed him, did the classic lifeguard vise grip, turn, and trawl. Meijer helped me drag him back onto the deck. It was like trying to haul up a dead whale. Dirk was out cold, bleeding badly, but still breathing. Meijer and I sat there, staring at him, trying to catch our breath. Finally, I got some mooring line, and we tied him up, securing him to a couple of cleats.

"What now?" Meijer asked, panting.

"We call the cops."

Meijer nodded grimly.

"But one thing first." I went up to the bag I had left on the dock and retrieved the bottle of gin. I took it below and mixed two stiff G and T's.

Dirk was just coming to when I came back out on the deck. I sat down cross-legged next to Meijer and handed her a glass. Dirk struggled against the ropes and finally gave up and slumped back. He stared at Meijer and then really hard at me.

I stared back and raised my glass. "I got you, babe," I said.

THE CASE OF THE ILLUSTRIOUS BANKER
John McAleer

From the Desk of
Professor John W. Dilpate
Berkeley Square, London
4 August 1929

If it weren't for my dear friend Mr. Henry von Stray and I, Inspector Bernard Renyalds would undoubtedly still be gnawing on soda biscuits in his Scotland Yard office while pondering the strange and baffling events behind the Derrycastle murder.

It was a bright and crisp spring morning when I entered the sitting room of the tidy flat I share with von Stray at No. 121B Berkeley Street, London. I was on sabbatical from the University Clifford and had just completed a brisk early walk through the public garden only to find myself stepping into thick aromatic clouds of pipe smoke. The great private detective, Henry von Stray, sat ensconced in his favorite parlour easy chair, his London briar pipe at full steam. He was reading the latest edition of the *London Star*. After removing my khaki blazer and flat cap, I slid into my easy chair opposite him near a set of windows overlooking the morning throng of industrious Londoners.

Von Stray greeted me without lifting his eyes from the newspaper. "And how is my dearest friend and able colleague, Professor John W. Dilpate, on this refreshing April morning?"

I patted the sides of my stomach and said to my companion,

"I seem to recall something about a hearty breakfast?"

"Breakfast?"

"Indeed, von Stray. Let me refresh your memory: pots of hot coffee, boiled eggs, sausage, hot cakes, crumpets, strawberry-rhubarb jam, and cheese. Oh, and some of that delicious honey you manage to procure from that retired chap you consult at irregular intervals. We're growing boys, you know?"

"My dear Dilpate, you'll lose that slight frame of yours if you continue to partake in such feasts," said von Stray, in his jovial voice.

I looked at von Stray over the tops of my gold-rimmed spectacles. I paused for a moment as I was still getting used to my companion's clean-shaven face. Exigent circumstances necessitated his moustache's removal during the singularly strange case of the Murder at Lord Beachy's. "Codswallop!" I protested. "I don't carry a half-stone more than I did during my boxing days with the Royal Navy—and I dare say any addition is the result of muscle tone. My brisk walks and regular Indian club exercise regimens see to that."

I began a short lecture on the fascinating modern science behind Indian club physical fitness training methods, such as the poise-and-drop, inward sweeps, and shoulder braces, but it was no use trying to engage the great criminologist von Stray on this exciting subject. Whatever held his attention in the *Star* had put an abrupt end to our breakfast plans. It wouldn't be the first time.

He folded the newspaper neatly and said to me, "Did you see this item in the *Star* about the bewildering death of D. P. Derrycastle of the London Trust Company?"

I waved my hand through a thick fog of Prince Albert tobacco smoke, and adjusted my seating position to avoid the exhaust bursting from von Stray's pipe. "Not the same D. P. Derrycastle accused of swindling A. F. Scott back in 1915?"

Von Stray lightly rubbed the small scar located on the upper left side of his forehead. A small "memento" as he calls it from his service in the trenches during the war. "Precisely. I've always had a feeling that Scott really was swindled. But as you may recall, Dilpate, his case was thrown out of court. He died in less than six months, leaving a wife and child. His wife evidently could not bear the humiliation and disgrace, for she disappeared shortly afterwards and has not been heard of since."

"Yes," I said, "a nasty affair."

"No doubt a black eye to the justice system," said von Stray, knocking out his pipe into the ruffled clam-shell ashtray he kept on top of an end table he constructed from Massaranduba wood imported from Brazil. "But now let's get back to the present Derrycastle matter. I suppose you will be interested to know how he met his unfortunate death?"

I nodded and von Stray read the following item from the *Star*:

Noted Banker Dead! Police Suspect Foul Play!

London—As Mr D. P. Derrycastle, President of the London Trust Company, entered his office yesterday morning, he stopped in his outer office to tell his secretary, Miss Ethel Kirby, to come into his private office at 9.15 a.m. to take a letter he would dictate to her. It was then 9.0 a.m.

At 9.05 a.m., Mr Samuel Gogan entered Derrycastle's office to talk over some business with him. He left a few minutes later. When Miss Kirby entered Derrycastle's office to take the letter at 9.15 a.m., she did not see him in the office. She thought he had gone into the vice president's office by the private door connecting the two rooms, so she sat down to wait for him to return.

After she had been waiting a few minutes, she became impatient and decided to investigate. As she started to rise from her chair, she noticed a foot protruding from behind Derrycastle's large desk. Upon investigating, she found—much to her horror and dismay!—Derrycastle's body lying on the floor behind the desk. She summoned the clerks located in the bank's outer office, and they quickly sent for a doctor.

A local doctor, Nigel Kenyard, arrived on the scene and determined that Derrycastle had been electrocuted. He said the police had better be summoned, as it looked as if Derrycastle had been murdered.

The police have detained Gogan as a suspicious party, but, as of yet, have not arrested him for killing Derrycastle. The guilty party appears to have left no clues.

Inspector Bernard Renyalds of Scotland Yard admits frankly that this is the most baffling case since the affair of the Westminster Miser. Inspector Renyalds added that it was a mystery as to how Derrycastle was electrocuted as his office had not been updated with electricity.

Miss Kirby was held for questioning, but later released. She is now resting in her home at 2½ Denton Street, suffering from nervous strain due to the strenuous ordeal she has undergone in the last 24 hours. Miss Kirby came to London from Blackpool five years ago and has been Derrycastle's secretary for two years.

Von Stray laid down the paper, "I am quite confident that our very dear friend, Inspector Renyalds, will ask my help in solving this curious affair, as he has done in many of his former cases."

"Ah, yes," I said, rubbing my moustache and noting that it was in desperate need of a trim and waxing. "It seems to me he rarely solves a case without our help. Take the case of the Westminster Miser, for example. I am willing to wager five pounds he'll be here within an hour."

Scarcely had my words been spoken when we heard the sharp ringing of the doorbell.

I swung my head in the direction of the front entrance. "Who the deuce could that be calling at this hour of the morning?"

Von Stray moved to the edge of his seat, his pipe canted in his left hand. "Pray answer the door, Dilpate, my good fellow. I believe that is the inspector now."

I opened the door and in stepped a tall, dark-complexioned man approximately forty years old sporting a thick, red moustache—Inspector Renyalds himself. He was rather plump, but with a muscular build through the shoulders and his barrel chest.

"Good morning, Professor," rumbled the inspector in his stentorian voice. "Is Mr von Stray available?"

"Indeed I am, Inspector," said von Stray, rising with enthusiasm. "I was expecting you. No doubt you are here to obtain my assistance in the Derrycastle case."

"How did you know?" said Renyalds, removing his derby hat.

"You have asked for my help with all other important cases you have been connected with for the past several years," said von Stray.

"I am quite sure you do not know all the facts of the Derrycastle case," said the inspector, lifting his blocky chin a notch. "We have been fortunate enough to keep our latest discoveries out of the paper."

"Perhaps," said von Stray, waving his hand over my easy chair inviting Renyalds to sit, "even greater fortune will shine upon you by acquainting us with all the known facts to date."

Inspector Renyalds found his way to my easy chair and began to fill us in on the remarkable events. Before he started, my companion stepped away from his chair and paced the room. His hands were clasped behind his back and his pipe clenched between his teeth. As he paced, I glanced at the portrait of his great-grandfather Captain Frederick von Stray that hangs above the sitting room fireplace. He served as a distinguished Danish infantry officer in the previous century. I often think the dearly departed Captain—his keen grey eyes on constant lookout—takes as much interest in von Stray's adventures as I do. I then cleared myself from the decks and glided into von Stray's vacated seat

"Very well then," began the inspector, rubbing his square jaw with a hand the size of a ham. "Upon questioning Miss Kirby, we found that Derrycastle and Gogan were engaged in a bitter argument during their conversation a short time before Derrycastle's mysterious death. Since we discovered this interesting fact, we have questioned Gogan. At first he denied the charges, but after putting him under considerable pressure, we finally got him to admit that he had a heated discussion with Derrycastle during his meeting with him. But he still insists that it was a mere disagreement over a business matter and has no bearing on the case whatever. He's gone through quite a grilling and still won't break down and confess to the crime. Tough as auntie's mutton he is. Now I am not quite sure that he is guilty."

"Why, Inspector?" I enquired. "It seems plain as a pikestaff. No one else was present to commit the ghastly deed. Unless of course the bank's vice president is responsible?"

The inspector shook his head. "The vice president's door adjoining Derrycastle's office was deadbolted from Derrycastle's side. Besides, he was out on business. Anyway, the vice president couldn't have entered without Derrycastle himself opening the door and then locking it again from his side. The only other passage is through Miss Kirby's outer office and she insisted none of the clerks or vice president entered through her office. No one gets in or out without passing her."

Von Stray said, "And you credit Miss Kirby's statement on this point as well as the vice president's alibi, Inspector?"

"I regret to say that I do. I say 'regret' because their statements only add to the puzzle. We haven't found any motive other than

Gogan's argument with the victim."

Von Stray asked, refilling his pipe with deliberate care, "Are there any windows in Derrycastle's office?"

Renyalds shook his head. "None. This fact only adds to my worries, so I've come here to ask for your help, von Stray. Will you be kind enough to contribute your invaluable time and assistance to this case by doing a little investigation on the side? Lest, I'm ashamed to admit, we might possibly be on the wrong trail—though I don't see how."

"I surely will," said von Stray, lightly massaging his scar. "Always have time for others and others will have time for you. Besides, you don't know how this case interests me."

In his excitement, Renyalds nearly crushed his derby with his huge hands. "Sterling, von Stray! Sterling! You may question any of the people connected with the murder, and you can visit the crime scene as often as you like. I only hope that you and Professor Dilpate will find some clues."

Von Stray plucked a match from his Royal Doulton "Old Salty" mug, struck it against the brick fireplace, and lit his pipe. The burning tobacco filled the room with subtle notes of cocoa and molasses. He said, through puffs of tobacco smoke, "If my usual luck keeps up, as it has since my crime-solving career started, I think we will."

"Well," said the inspector, "I will have to make my visit brief as there are several smaller details to attend to." Renyalds pulled a wrinkled envelope out of his hat and handed it to me. "Speaking of details, here's a small letter of introduction I pre-pared in case you need it during the course of your investigation—Yard stationery and all."

I accepted the envelope and nodded. "Indeed! Thank you, Inspector. Quite official."

Von Stray removed his pipe long enough to ask, "Oh, by the way, Inspector, have you found out for certain if Derrycastle did in fact die by means of electrocution?"

"Most certain," confirmed the inspector. "The police surgeon's postmortem has reached the same conclusion as Dr Kenyard. Derrycastle's hands were terribly burned from what appears to be some kind of strong electric current. A nippy bit of work indeed."

I put my spectacles up. "Impossible. According to the *Star* you said Derrycastle's office had no electricity!"

Von Stray whisked his pipe stem from his mouth. "Careful, Professor. According to the *Star* report the inspector merely stated that the office had not been *updated* with electricity."

"That's true, von Stray," Renyalds said, pulling on his reddish moustache. "But I agree with the professor. I don't see the difference."

I turned an inquiring gaze on my companion. "Yes, neither do I?"

"Perhaps it's a small matter," von Stray conceded. "Just one more question, Inspector. Did Gogan say what his disagreement with Derrycastle concerned?"

The inspector showed the palm of his right hand. "Turns out Gogan is one of those crack-pot inventor types. Claims the bank refused to underwrite his latest contraption—a radio with pictures." The inspector snickered, "Tommy-rot."

Here I observed the familiar bright twinkle fill my companion's left eye. He then walked over to Renyalds and gave him a firm handshake. "Thank you and good day, Inspector. I hope to have some *sterling* news for you when I see you next!"

With a further exchange of compliments Inspector Renyalds parted.

After the inspector left we breakfasted quickly. During breakfast von Stray skimmed through one of his scrapbooks from his voluminous collection of newspaper articles and other odds and ends. I was just about to excuse myself to groom my moustache when he said, "Dilpate, my good fellow, I think our friend the inspector is on the wrong trail, so hurry now and put on your coat and fetch your umbrella. We are going to do some real investigating."

My companion fetched his ivory-handled walking stick presented to him by the great American stage actor Barney McNulty who found himself peripherally entangled in "The Case of Sir Moreland's Lost Pearls."

"Where to?" I asked.

"To where the trail first leads us, my dear professor. Where else!" von Stray said, flipping on his ancient, wool-tweed cap.

"Always in riddles," I said, wrestling my way into my coat, "always in riddles. Umbrella! There's not a cloud in the sky. And what about my moustache?"

Von Stray, already halfway out the front door, shouted, "By all means take it with you if you must."

Von Stray hailed a cab after we left the apartment and instructed the driver to take us to the residence of Miss Kirby at No. 2½ Denton Street. This proved to be a large apartment house under the name of Denton Chambers. We had little trouble locating Miss Kirby's apartment, and five minutes later we were comfortably seated on a large Victorian divan in her parlour.

Miss Kirby was a comely and dignified woman of about three-and-twenty. Upon questioning Miss Kirby, von Stray found that her story was the same as the one she had told the police.

At the conclusion of her account, von Stray pointed to a nearby table. I noted the familiar bright twinkle in his left eye as the great detective said to Miss Kirby, "I couldn't help noticing the photograph of the beautiful woman beside you, Miss Kirby."

The photograph my colleague referred to was encased in a small, ornate, gold-tone frame and resting on the walnut end table convenient to Miss Kirby. Next to the photograph sat a porcelain vase holding a fresh, single white lily.

Miss Kirby became of a crimson colour just before picking

up the photograph. "Well...er...this was my dear cousin." She then casually returned the photograph to the table facing it away from our view. A hint of sadness filled her blue eyes. No doubt this poor, innocent young lady still suffered from shock.

"My apologies, Miss Kirby. I thought I noted a family resemblance, but I didn't mean to intrude into your personal matters."

"Oh, think nothing of it, Mr von Stray," said Miss Kirby as a shy smile played about her lips. "I will be only too glad to assist you in any way I can, so that this ghastly affair can be solved and the guilty party brought to justice."

Von Stray nodded politely and rose from the divan. "We must be going and I assure you, Miss Kirby, you will soon realize what a help you have been to us."

After bidding Miss Kirby a cordial good day, we departed.

As we made our way through the crowded streets of London, a drizzly bit of rain greeted the city. I opened my umbrella (which I had the good sense and foresight to bring) and then we continued on our way, each of us no doubt analysing what we had learned from Miss Kirby. There could be no question about it in my mind. With Miss Kirby confirming her account of the events and the vice president's unshakable alibi confirmed by Scotland Yard, the only possible culprit left was Gogan.

I was about to share my conclusions with von Stray when he stopped before a telegraph office on Regent Street and said, "Dilpate, wait here a minute." He disappeared into the telegraph agency while I took some additional cover under the awning of an ancient Piccadilly peanut vendor.

Big Ben was chiming the quarter after one when the vendor cast an eye at me cornerwise and said despondently, "Sorry for your troubles, guv."

"Er...troubles?" I enquired, while selecting a bag of roasted peanuts.

He appeared even further crestfallen now. "Pardon me, guv,

but your moustache is in a frightful flap with the rest'a your face. She must 'a broke your poor wee 'eart I bet that ol' she devil did."

"See here, old man—" I began, ready to lay the old bloke out in lavender, but my verbal walloping was cut short when von Stray popped out of the telegraph office. I paid for my peanuts and left the vendor abruptly.

My companion and I walked back to our digs, where we settled into our respective easy chairs to ponder the baffling problems before us. At first opportunity, however, I excused myself and put order to my untidy moustache. I always think better when properly groomed.

When I returned, a bag of peanuts had found their way into my possession. I also found von Stray in deep contemplation, absently massaging his memento. I knew better than to disturb my friend's solitude, so I refrained from asking him questions about his strange visit to the telegraph office. I had just cracked the last peanut shell when von Stray announced, after what seemed like an eternal silence, "Dilpate, I've despatched a telegram to Blackpool and expect an answer at any time. While waiting, what would you say to dinner at the Barrymore Club?"

I quickly crumpled up my empty peanut bag and lobbed it into the fireplace. "Excellent suggestion. I always think better on a bit of English fare. If memory serves me correctly Miss Alcorn's famous pigeon pie and pickled salmon headline the menu this evening."

After partaking of a light, but nourishing meal at the Barrymore Club with our good friend from the Fraternal Order of Benevolent Walnuts, Sir Percy Stonyhurst Berrycloth, we returned to our humble retreat. My companion rummaged through his files and scrapbooks for the remainder of the evening. I spent the time classifying some rare beetle specimens, which the noted Professor Ambrose Leanaou of Harvard University had sent me from South America. Little did I realize, as I pondered my prized collection of insects, that von Stray was making some most interesting discoveries in the brief time we had been on the Derrycastle case. At 11.30 p.m. we deemed it advisable to retire.

I am an early bird. At 8.0 a.m. next morning, after conducting my Indian club exercise regimen in the public garden, I found von Stray seated at the dining table with a delightful spread consisting of deviled sole, homemade raisin scones, boiled eggs, butter, quince jam, honey, and piping hot coffee. Von Stray became an excellent cook after the war.

On the breakfast table, a small envelope from the telegraph agency sat beneath a walrus tusk honed into a letter opener. My companion was massaging his scar as he usually does when engaging in deep analytical thought. From this I deduced he'd received some important reply from the previous day's telegraph inquiry. A morning edition of the *London Star* was also on the table. I adjusted my spectacles and could make out from the headlines that the *Star* was openly accusing Scotland Yard of being baffled with the Derrycastle murder.

I cleared my throat and sat down. "Not that it is any of my business, von Stray, but I would like to know what this telegram business is all about. I thought you would soon tell me, but as you have still advanced no explanation, I'll take it upon myself to ask."

"You know curiosity killed the cat, my dear Dilpate." Von Stray poured me a cup of piping hot coffee. "I am going to keep you in suspense a little while longer. Then it will surprise you all the more. However, I will venture so far as to say that the crime will be solved within twenty-four hours."

"By Jehoshaphat, von Stray," said I, reaching for one of his warm scones, "your ability to make bricks without straw never ceases to amaze me."

Von Stray smiled as he reached for his jar of honey. "Correction, my learned friend. It's the honey, not the straw that forms my bricks. Remember, 'He who eats honey, thinks honey.' Furthermore," he continued, after helping himself to a generous spoonful of honey, "poor Gogan is an innocent man and will be completely exonerated from any connection with this crime."

I lathered a scone with butter and quince jam. "You're talking in riddles as far as I'm concerned. But lead on, von Stray."

"If I am able to obtain the direct evidence I need, my supposition will be watertight," he said, rising to clear his dishes. "And I hope to find that direct evidence this morning."

I sprang up from the table, nearly spilling my coffee. "When do we start! If we've cleared Gogan, the trail can only lead to this Dr Kenyard. I'd bet my last shilling he deliberately bungled the facts of the case in order to draw the authorities off the scent. Claiming that Derrycastle's death was caused by electric shock—fiddle-faddle! I bet that old parsimonious blighter Derrycastle was poisoned somehow."

"You're getting ahead of yourself, old man," said von Stray, now snatching up a battered leather bag he carries for search purposes. "But the inspector is right that this is a nippy bit of work indeed. Every second we waste, an innocent man rots behind bars. Let's not make the same obvious mistakes the authorities have. As I have said many times, 'Cases resting solely on circumstantial evidence tend to invite false inferences.'"

Von Stray and I visited the London Trust situated at the corner of Pell Street and Firling Avenue to examine the scene of the murder. As we approached the bank, a brisk, ruddy-faced police constable ordered us to an abrupt halt. We recognized him at once as our good friend, Constable Vincent Hastings. Since I have been recording the exploits of von Stray and his unique analytic methods of crime detection, I have taken particular note of how von Stray's war memento (and I might add my own service in the Royal Navy) have given us considerable sway with other civil servants who served in the big scrap. We had also assisted Hastings with a little problem involving a beautiful Italian acrobat a while back, so I knew he would be delighted to see us on the job.

"Ah, Hastings, old chap," von Stray said, presenting our credentials from Inspector Renyalds providing us with authorization to enter the crime scene.

"No need for a bushel of nipperty-tipperty paperwork, Mr von Stray," said Hastings, waving away the document with a gentle wag of his nightstick. "You're one of us blokes." He then pointed his nightstick in my direction. "Who's this chap again...?"

Von Stray responded. "This is my colleague Professor Dilpate as you may recall."

"Oh...right. Okay, 'e can enter as long as 'e's with you, Sir," Hastings said, producing a pass-key to unlock the bank's front door.

I was just about to enter the bank when Hastings lowered his nightstick in front of me like a railroad crossing gate. "'Old your 'orses there, mate, 'ave to turn off the bank alarm system. Complicated bit 'a machinery it is."

Just over the threshold of the London Trust entrance, Hastings switched on the electric lights. He then opened a small alarm box containing a maze of wires and contraptions, pulled out a special key, fit it into the box and turned the key to disengage the alarm system. Needless to say I was fascinated by the complexity of the alarm system and Hastings's skill in disengaging it so efficiently.

"All set, gents." Hastings touched his helmet rim and left us to examine the crime scene.

Von Stray instructed me to look through Miss Kirby's desk and office, while he entered Derrycastle's private office. Her office consisted of a standard secretary's desk, gas lamps, an old No. 10 Remington typewriter, water-cooler, a couple of oak filing cabinets, and, among a few other unimportant items, a wastepaper basket.

Twenty minutes had elapsed when von Stray emerged and enquired if I had found anything of interest. I replied that I found nothing save some crumpled sheets of paper in the wastepaper basket with some bits of wires and old tools underneath.

"It struck me as a rather odd place to dispose of them," I said.

"Ah!" said von Stray with an air of delight. "That is just what I anticipated." He then opened several of the crumpled papers and examined them. "Just what I suspected, Dilpate. These sheets are blank."

"More riddles, von Stray?" I said, rubbing my chin.

"I believe, Dilpate, that our investigation is near complete." Von Stray then swept the wires and tools into his leather bag. "First, come with me. I'd like to check a couple of more items with you present."

I followed von Stray into Derrycastle's office. Von Stray turned up a gas lamp, but the windowless office remained a bit dim. It was an austere setting consisting of a few oak filing cabinets, large mahogany desk, humidor, large ashtray, pen and ink, and, among other unimportant items, a candlestick telephone. My companion removed a small electric torch from his leather bag. After turning it on he held its beam of light against the deadbolt locking mechanism located on the door connecting to the vice president's office.

After examining it for a moment he held out a hand in my direction. "Pray, Dilpate, may I borrow your spectacles?"

I took them off reluctantly and handed them to him. "I don't know why you don't keep a magnifying glass in that bag of tricks you carry. You're always borrowing my spectacles on these occasions."

Von Stray put them on and examined the deadbolt more closely. "Why use one magnifying glass when I can examine the evidence through both eyes belonging to my able collaborator in the detection of crime!"

I showed remarkable restraint. "Well...please don't twist up the frames like you have a tendency to do."

After examining the deadbolt for what seemed an extended period, he pulled off my spectacles as if he were pulling a string of yarn and then handed them back to me. "Here, Dilpate, take a look."

I straightened out the delicate spectacle frames and put them back on. I then stooped down to examine the area in question. "I don't see anything, von Stray. No fresh scuff or scratch marks on the locking mechanism." I twisted the deadbolt back and forth a few times. "It's in perfect working order."

"Precisely. As you can see there are no fresh signs of tampering. This independently corroborates Miss Kirby's statement to Scotland Yard that no one could enter Derrycastle's office from the vice president's office without someone unbolting the lock from Derrycastle's side. With this type of deadbolt it logically follows that it must be re-bolted from Derrycastle's side as Inspector Renyalds found it had been."

"I quite agree," I said to my companion. "Of course, I never doubted Miss Kirby. A fine, respectable, young woman of great intelligence."

Von Stray said without check, "Yes, old chap...A woman of superior intelligence indeed."

He then walked over to Derrycastle's desk and began examining the candlestick telephone. Anticipating his next move I handed him my spectacles. When he was through with his examination, he said, whisking off my spectacles, "By Jove, Dilpate! Just as I suspected. Upon closer examination these are undoubtedly fresh markings around the telephone's wiring connections."

While repairing my frames, I enquired, "Marks and no marks, what does it all mean, von Stray?"

"It means we're off to Scotland Yard to report our findings!"

We hailed a cab and in less time than it takes to tell, we were seated in the comfortable New Scotland Yard office of Inspector Renyalds on Victoria Embankment overlooking the River Thames.

"Inspector," said von Stray, "I believe that I've found a solution to this terrible crime. Direct your men to arrest Derrycastle's secretary, Miss Kirby."

"What!" said the inspector, rising with a start from his chair and nearly sending it swiveling into the Thames.

Von Stray repeated calmly, "Arrest Miss Kirby."

Even I was taken aback by von Stray's words.

"Why, that's impossible," said the inspector.

"Not quite," said von Stray as he filled his briar pipe. "However, to set your mind at ease, I'll tell you what our investigations have disclosed."

"Very well." Renyalds scooped a soda biscuit out from a side pocket of his houndstooth jacket. "Get on with it."

"A baffling affair," explained the great detective. "Professor Dilpate and I decided to pay Miss Kirby a visit and question her concerning the murder. While there, I chanced to see a photograph resting on a nearby table. I immediately noticed that Miss Kirby bore a remarkable resemblance to the woman in the photograph. I simply asked Miss Kirby the identity of the woman, but she replied nervously 'a dear cousin'. Then she picked up the photograph and returned it facing away from my line of vision.

"This aroused my curiosity, for I had a vague memory of seeing that photograph somewhere before. Suddenly, it came to me that the lady in the photograph was the wife of A. F. Scott who, you remember, claimed some fourteen years ago that he was swindled by Derrycastle."

Renyalds bit into his biscuit and chewed rapidly. "Yes, go on."

"As you already know," von Stray continued, "Miss Kirby claims she was born in Blackpool. I had my suspicions, so I despatched a telegram to the registry of births at Blackpool, inquiring if a Miss Eunice Kirby was born there. I received a negative answer this morning. This confirmed my suspicions that Miss Kirby was, in reality, A. F. Scott's daughter. I knew then that she was the one who killed Derrycastle to avenge her father's disgrace and untimely death. I needed more proof, however.

"Therefore, I visited the scene of the crime with my invaluable coadjutor, Professor Dilpate, and while he searched Miss Kirby's outer office, I did a little investigating of my own in Derrycastle's private office. There I found that the wires to his candlestick telephone had been tampered with recently. I further confirmed this with Professor Dilpate as witness."

I nodded. "Yes...completely confirmed—you can bank on it, Inspector."

Von Stray proceeded. "I immediately realized that someone— no doubt Miss Kirby—had created an electronic connection in such a manner that whoever touched the metal receiver and metal stem of the telephone would be electrocuted. While the bank's offices had not been updated with electricity, the main lobby of the bank had. Moreover, the bank was equipped with an intricate electrical alarm system. A system undoubtedly tapped into by Miss Kirby to carry out her cold-blooded plot.

"In Miss Kirby's haste to cover up her deed, she was forced to leave the wires and other implements required in her wastepaper basket. Despite her feeble attempt to conceal the wires under freshly crumpled-up sheets of blank paper, Dilpate found the implements there. So this clinched the case. Miss Scott, alias Miss Kirby, came here from Blackpool to avenge her father's death."

After polishing off his biscuit, Renyalds said, "Sterling analysis, von Stray. That certainly settles the hash."

I joined in. "Yes, brilliant."

"There's more," resumed von Stray. "She obtained a position at the bank, working hard and succeeded in becoming Derrycastle's secretary. This was just the chance she was waiting for. She carefully planned the crime and executed it with precision. After Gogan left, she waited until she heard Derrycastle pick up the receiver. When she heard a dull thud, she went into his office, disconnected the wires she had arranged, and hung the receiver back onto the telephone. She left Derrycastle where he had fallen behind his large desk."

Noting Renyalds's astonishment, I saw the need to bolster von Stray's analysis of the events. "Von Stray's correct, Inspector. This has always been the only logical conclusion. Further, once we ascertained that no one but Miss Kirby could have entered or exited Derrycastle's office without access to the deadbolt, this left only Miss Kirby as the possible culprit. As I have said many times, 'Crimes that...er...resist circumstantial evidence...er...often invite false instances.'"

Renyalds raised his chin and said to me with the utmost sincerity, "That's always been my crime-fighting creed, Professor."

I let von Stray wrap up our analysis of the crime.

"This method of murder was a clever move on Miss Kirby's part," my able colleague resumed, "because it left the police baffled as to how Derrycastle was electrocuted. As you noted, Inspector, his office had not as yet been updated with electricity. Yet the puzzling fact remained that the police surgeon corroborated Dr Kenyard's on-scene cause of death by electrocution. After concealing the implements used, she ran into the outer office screaming to the clerks that Derrycastle was dead. Later, she told the police that during the time she was in Derrycastle's office sitting in the chair in front of his huge desk, she had no idea anything out of the ordinary was wrong."

Renyalds made a square fist and pounded the surface of his desk with excitement. "Amazing! I knew we could untangle the clues if we pulled the right strings! They don't call me the 'Old Foxhound' for nothing."

"If you wish, Inspector," I offered, "we will give you full credit for solving this unspeakable crime."

Von Stray was speechless over my generous suggestion.

"Thank you, old man," said Inspector Renyalds, nearly crushing my hand with both of his. "A little kudos from the super never did a hard-working public servant like myself any harm. But getting back to Miss Kirby, since we haven't incarcerated her yet, she may attempt to escape. We better head down to her flat now and arrest her with all despatch."

The three of us were soon on our way to No. 2½ Denton Street. Von Stray turned on the police car's radio just in time to catch the following announcement: "*Car 12, rush immediately to Denton Chambers. A lady is about to jump from the roof. That is all.*"

Von Stray turned down the radio's volume and said, "Quick, Inspector, or we may be too late!"

When we arrived, we found a huge crowd gathered around Miss Kirby's apartment building. We followed von Stray as he fought his way madly through the crowd and rushed up to the roof of the building. We were just in time to see Miss Kirby throw herself from the roof to inevitable destruction on the street below.

In Miss Kirby's parlour, von Stray found a note penned under her real name, Miss Eunice Scott. The note sat against the porcelain vase holding what was now a wilting lily. He read the note aloud.

> To Whom it may Concern:
> I, Eunice Scott, have avenged the death of my father, A. F. Scott, by killing D. P. Derrycastle, the man who swindled my father and hastened his death. There is nothing more to live for, as my mother passed away two years ago.
> Hoping to see you all in eternity,
> Miss Eunice Scott, alias Miss Kirby.

Later that evening, back in quarters, von Stray and I sat in our respective easy chairs overlooking a quiet Berkeley Square. Snifters containing a delightful French brandy accompanied us.

"Well, Dilpate," said my companion, pinching off a heap of tobacco he kept in the compartment of a miniature banyan-wood elephant, "this unhappy affair did not come out exactly as I wished. Nevertheless, Gogan is cleared of all wrongdoing, so there is some justice after all."

I sniffed my brandy and then nodded at the portrait of Captain von Stray. "Indeed. No doubt Inspector Renyalds and Scotland Yard will be calling on us again considering how quickly we cleaned up this mysterious case."

"Yes, Dilpate," von Stray said, smiling as he raised his snifter to me, "*we* certainly did."

ABOUT THE CONTRIBUTORS

The author of eleven novels and more than 130 short stories, **DOUG ALLYN** has been published internationally in English, German, French and Japanese. His most recent, *Murder in Paradise* (with James Patterson), was on the *New York Times* Best Seller list for seven weeks. More than two dozen of his tales have been optioned for development as feature films and television. Mr. Allyn studied creative writing and criminal psychology at the University of Michigan while moonlighting as a guitarist in the rock group Devil's Triangle and reviewing books for the *Flint Journal*. His background includes Chinese language studies at Indiana University and extended duty with USAF Intelligence in Southeast Asia during the Vietnam War. Career highlights? Sipping champagne with Mickey Spillane and waltzing with Mary Higgins Clark. "Twice an Edgar Allan Poe Award winner, and the record holder in the Ellery Queen Mystery Magazine Readers Award competition, Doug Allyn is one of the best short story writers of his generation—and probably of all time. He is also a novelist with a number of critically-acclaimed books in print."—*Ellery Queen Mystery Magazine*

USA Today and *Wall Street Journal* best-selling author **LORI ARMSTRONG** is also the two-time Shamus Award-winning author of *Snow Blind*, in the Julie Collins mystery series, and *No Mercy*, in the Mercy Gunderson series. She has won the WILLA Cather Literary Award for *Hallowed Ground* and was a finalist for the books *Shallow Grave*, *No Mercy*, and *Merciless*. *Shallow Grave* was nominated for a High Plains Book Award. Lori is also a *New York Times* best-selling author and *USA Today* best-selling author of contemporary, western, and erotic romances under the name Lorelei James. She lives in western South Dakota. For more information and the latest updates, visit Lori's website, LoriArmstrong.com, like Lori's author page on Facebook, follow Lori on Twitter, join Lori's Facebook discussion group, and sign up for Lori's newsletter.

Born in New Orleans, **O'NEIL DE NOUX** writes novels and short stories with forty-three books published, more than four hundred short story sales, and a screenplay produced in 2000. Much of De Noux's writing is character-driven crime fiction, although he has written in many disciplines including historical fiction, children's fiction, mainstream fiction, mystery, science fiction, suspense, fantasy, horror, western, literary, religious, romance, erotica, and humor. Mr. De Noux is a retired police officer, a former homicide detective. His writing has garnered a number of awards including the United Kingdom Short Story Prize, the Shamus Award twice (given annually by the Private Eye Writers of America to recognize outstanding achievement in private eye fiction), the Derringer Award (given annually by the Short Mystery Fiction Society to recognize excellence in short mystery fiction), and Police Book of the Year (awarded by PoliceWriters.com). Two of his stories have been featured in the Best American Mystery Stories annual anthology (2003 and 2013). In 2012, O'Neil De Noux received an Artist Services Career Advancement Award from the Louisiana Division of the Arts for *Battle Kiss*, a 320,000-word epic novel of the Battle of New Orleans. He received the 2015 Literary Artist of the Year President's Award from the St. Tammany Parish Arts Council, St. Tammany Parish, Louisiana. He is a past vice-president of the Private Eye Writers of America. For additional O'Neil De Noux material, go to: ONeilDeNoux.com.

BRENDAN DUBOIS is the *New York Times* best-selling author of twenty-six novels, including *The First Lady* and *The Cornwalls Are Gone* (March 2019), co-authored with James Patterson, along with *The Summer House* (June 2020), and the upcoming *Blowback*, September 2022. He has also published nearly two hundred short stories. His full-length novels include the eleven novels in the Lewis Cole series, as well as the Dark Victory science fiction trilogy. Brendan's short fiction has appeared in *Playboy, The Saturday Evening Post, Ellery Queen Mystery Magazine, Alfred Hitchcock Mystery Magazine, Analog, Asimov's Science Fiction Magazine, The Strand Magazine, The Magazine of Fantasy & Science Fiction,* and numerous anthologies including *The Best American Mystery Stories of the Century* and *The Best American Noir of the Century.* Six times his short fiction has been selected for the Best American Mystery Stories anthologies. His stories have won him two Shamus Awards from the Private Eye Writers of America, two Barry Awards, two Derringer Awards, the Ellery Queen Readers Award, and three Edgar Allan Poe Award nominations from the Mystery Writers of America. In 2021 he received the Edward D. Hoch Memorial Golden Derringer for Lifetime Achievement from the Short Mystery Fiction Society. He is also a *Jeopardy!* game show champion, and lives in New Hampshire.

MARTIN EDWARDS is the author of twenty novels, including *Gallows Court* and *The Girl They All Forgot* as well as a major history of crime fiction, *The Life of Crime.* He has received the CWA Diamond Dagger, British crime writing's highest honour, for the sustained excellence of his work. He has also won the Edgar, Agatha, H.R.F. Keating and Macavity awards, the Short Story Dagger and Dagger in the Library, plus the Poirot Award for his contribution to the genre. He is president of the Detection Club, a former chair of the CWA, and consultant to the British Library Crime Classics.

JOHN M. FLOYD's work has appeared in more than 350 different publications, including *Alfred Hitchcock Mystery Magazine, Ellery Queen Mystery Magazine, Strand Magazine, The Saturday Evening Post,* three editions of the Best American Mystery Stories, and the 2021 edition of the Best Mystery Stories of the Year. A former Air Force captain and IBM systems engineer, John is also an Edgar Award finalist, a Shamus Award winner, a four-time Derringer Award winner, and the author of nine books. In 2018 he was the recipient of the Edward D. Hoch Memorial Golden Derringer for Lifetime Achievement in short mystery fiction.

CAROLINA GARCIA-AGUILERA is the Cuba-born, Miami Beach-based, award-winning author of ten books including the Shamus Award-winning novel, *Havana Heat.* Garcia-Aguilera is also a contributor to numerous anthologies, but is perhaps best known for her Lupe Solano series. Her books have been translated to twelve languages and a film was made from *One Hot Summer,* her seventh book. Garcia-Aguilera became a private investigator—a profession she has practiced for thirty-five years—in order to credibly write novels and short stories featuring a P.I. as a protagonist.

KRISTEN LEPIONKA is the author of the Roxane Weary mystery series. Her debut, *The Last Place You Look,* won the Shamus Award for Best First P.I. novel and was also nominated for Anthony and Macavity awards. *What You Want to See* won Shamus and Goldie awards. She is a cofounder of the feminist podcast Unlikeable Female Characters and she lives in Columbus, Ohio, with her partner.

LIA MATERA is the author of twelve crime novels in two series, one featuring politically conflicted lawyer Willa Jansson and the other, high-profile litigator Laura Di Palma. Matera has also published eleven short stories and a novella. She is a graduate of Hastings College of the Law in San Francisco, where she was editor-in-chief of the *Constitutional Law Quarterly*. She is a member of the California Bar and was a teaching fellow at Stanford Law School before becoming a full-time writer. Two of her novels—*A Radical Departure* and *Prior Convictions*—were nominated for the mystery genre's top prize, the Edgar Allan Poe Award. Three were nominated for the Anthony Award, and two were nominated for the Macavity Award. "Dead Drunk," first printed in Scott Turow's *Guilty as Charged,* won the Private Eye Writers of America Shamus Award for Best Short Story of 1996. It was included in *The Year's Twenty-Five Finest Crime and Mystery Stories*, edited by Joan Hess, 1997, and reprinted in *The World's Finest Mystery and Crime Stories*, edited by Ed Gorman, 2000, *A Century of Noir,* edited by Mickey Spillane and Max Allan Collins, 2002, and *Shamus Winners, Volume II: 1996— 2009,* edited by Robert J. Randisi, 2012. Her story, "Snow Job," published in *Ellery Queen Mystery Magazine* (January/February 2019), was nominated for a 2020 International Thriller Award. A collection of nine of her short stories, *Counsel for the Defense and Other Stories*, was published by Five Star Press. *Lovers and Lawyers*, a more recent ebook collection from Mysterious Press/Open Road Media, includes two additional stories and a novella. She was also the editor of *Irreconcilable Differences*, an anthology of twenty original tales by well-known crime writers.

After serving in World War II in India as a U.S. Army Tech Sergeant, **JOHN MCALEER** would return home to work on John F. Kennedy's first campaign for congress and go on to graduate from Harvard University with a Ph.D. in English Literature. The author of more than a dozen books including the Pulitzer Prize-nominated biography, *Emerson: Days of Encounter*, Dr. McAleer won the Edgar Allan Poe Award for *Rex Stout: A Biography* and published critically acclaimed books on Thoreau, Dreiser, and James M. Cain as well as the definitive and best-selling Korean War novel, *Unit Pride.* The *Washington Post* compared his novel of manners, *Coign of*

Vantage, to the works of Oscar Wilde, Evelyn Waugh, and Lewis Carroll. A Bostonian and a professor of English Literature at Harvard and then Boston College for more than half a century, and a permanent fellow at Durham University, he also co-authored the best-selling *Mystery Writing in a Nutshell* and edited the *Thorndyke File*. A past president of the Thoreau Society, Dr. McAleer also served with Don Henley on the Project to Save Walden Woods. His short story "The Case of the Illustrious Banker," featuring London-based private detective Henry von Stray, was first written during the Golden Age of Mysteryand recently discovered more than eighty years later. The story appears for the first time anywhere in *Edgar & Shamus Go Golden*.

PJ PARRISH is the *New York Times* best-selling author of fourteen Louis Kincaid and Joe Frye thrillers, two stand-alone thrillers, and the novella *Claw Back*. The author is actually two sisters, Kristy Montee and Kelly Nichols. Their books have appeared on both the *New York Times* and *USA Today* best-seller lists. The series has garnered eleven major crime fiction awards, and an Edgar Award nomination. Parrish has won two Shamus Awards, one Anthony Award, and one International Thriller Award. Her books have been published throughout Europe and Asia. Parrish's short stories have also appeared in many anthologies, including two published by the Mystery Writers of America, edited by Harlan Coben and the late Stuart Kaminsky. Their stories have also appeared in Akashic Books' acclaimed *Detroit Noir*, and in *Ellery Queen Mystery Magazine*. They also contributed an essay to a special edition of Edgar Allan Poe's works edited by Michael Connelly and an essay on *Jaws in Thrillers: 100 Must Reads*, edited by David Morrell and Hank Wagner. PJParrish.com.

ART TAYLOR is the author of the story collection *The Boy Detective & The Summer of '74 and Other Tales of Suspense* and of the novel in stories *On the Road with Del & Louise*, winner of the Agatha Award for Best First Novel. Mr. Taylor also won the Edgar Award, the Anthony Award, and several Agatha, Macavity, and Derringer awards for his short fiction. His work has also appeared in Best American Mystery Stories. He is an associate professor of English at George Mason University. ArtTaylorWriter.com.

GAY TOLTL KINMAN has nine award nominations for her writing. She has published several short stories in American and English magazines and numerous anthologies, including *Coast to Coast Private Eyes*, Michael Connelly's *Murder in Vegas;* children's books; a YA gothic novel; adult mysteries, and other collections of short stories. Several of her short plays were produced—now in a collection of twenty plays, *The Play's the Thing*. Ms. Kinman has published many articles in professional journals, newspapers, and books, including the Mystery Writers of America's *How to Write a Mystery*; and has co-edited two nonfiction books. For the Private Eye Writers of America Shamus Awards, Ms. Kinman has served as a judge on all the committees, then chair of each. She also served as the overall chair of the Shamus Awards for several years. For the Mystery Writers of America Edgar Awards, she has served as a judge for the Best Young Adult Mystery committee; then chair of the Best Juvenile Mystery, and the presenter to the winner of that category at the annual Awards Banquet. Ms. Kinman has library and law degrees and had the honor of interviewing literary luminaries such as Sara Paretsky, Marcia Muller, and Joseph Wambaugh.

ANDREW MCALEER is the author of the *101 Habits of Highly Successful Novelists, Mystery Writing in a Nutshell* (co-authored with Edgar winner John McAleer), *Positive Results*, and *Fatal Deeds*. For many years he had the honor of co-editing with Shamus Award-winner Paul D. Marks the *Coast to Coast* crime fiction series (Down & Out Books). Past president of the Boston Authors Club, Mr. McAleer teaches at Boston College and is a winner of the Speckled Band of Boston's Sherlock Holmes Bowl Award. He works full-time as a police officer and served in Afghanistan as a U.S. Army historian. Visit him at: AMcaleer.com.

BOOKS

On the following pages are a few
more great titles from the
Down & Out Books publishing family.

For a complete list of books and to
sign up for our newsletter,
go to DownAndOutBooks.com.

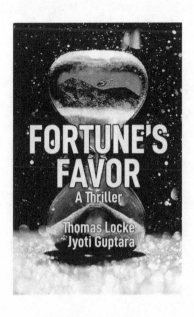

Fortune's Favor
A Thriller
Thomas Locke and Jyoti Guptara

Down & Out Books
November 2022
978-1-64396-286-3

Imagine a world where privilege is stolen and handed down from generation to generation—supernaturally. When a disgraced accountant is hired to shadow a mysterious Indian couple, she partners with them to steal an ancient object that has kept Asia's elites in power for generations.

The first collaboration by bestselling authors Thomas Locke and Jyoti Guptara, the international, intergenerational writing duo.

Getting Dunn
Tom Schreck

Down & Out Books
November 2022
978-1-64396-287-0

Discharged from the army and back in the States and unable to cope, TJ Dunn spirals into an emotional daze, spending her days working at a suicide hotline and her evenings moonlighting as an exotic dancer. Her only outlet for her anger is a punching bag at the local boxing ring where she works out with a handsome trainer, Duffy.

Just when she thinks she's reached her limit, an anonymous phone call shocks her back to life and gives her a new mission, justice for those she loves and she won't stop at anything to do it.

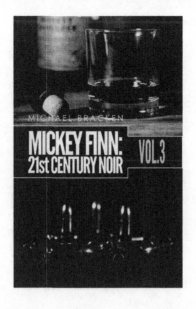

Mickey Finn: 21st Century Noir
Volume 3
Michael Bracken, editor

Down & Out Books
December 2022
978-1-64396-279-5

Mickey Finn: 21st Century Noir, Volume 3, the latest entry of this hard-hitting series, is another crime-fiction cocktail that will knock readers into a literary stupor.

Contributors push hard against the boundaries of crime fiction, driving their work into places short crime fiction doesn't often go, into a world where the mean streets seem gentrified by comparison and happy endings are the exception, not the rule.

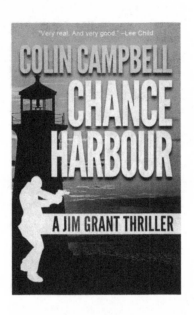

Chance Harbour
A Jim Grant Thriller
Colin Campbell

Down & Out Books
December 2022
978-1-64396-277-1

Dementia is robbing the old man in the ICU of any coherent thoughts until his face finally clears. "Okay. I know what happened. I need you to call my son. He's with the Boston Police at Jamaica Plain."

But Jim Grant isn't at Jamaica Plain; he is getting over being resurrected. Until he gets a call to say his father is seriously ill. But Grant arrives too late. His father has been abducted. A bomb has exploded outside a diner. And the FBI wants to know how his father knows a Russian oligarch who is even older than he is. For father and son it could be the last chance to reconcile their differences. It might also be the last chance for everything.

Made in the USA
Las Vegas, NV
06 November 2023